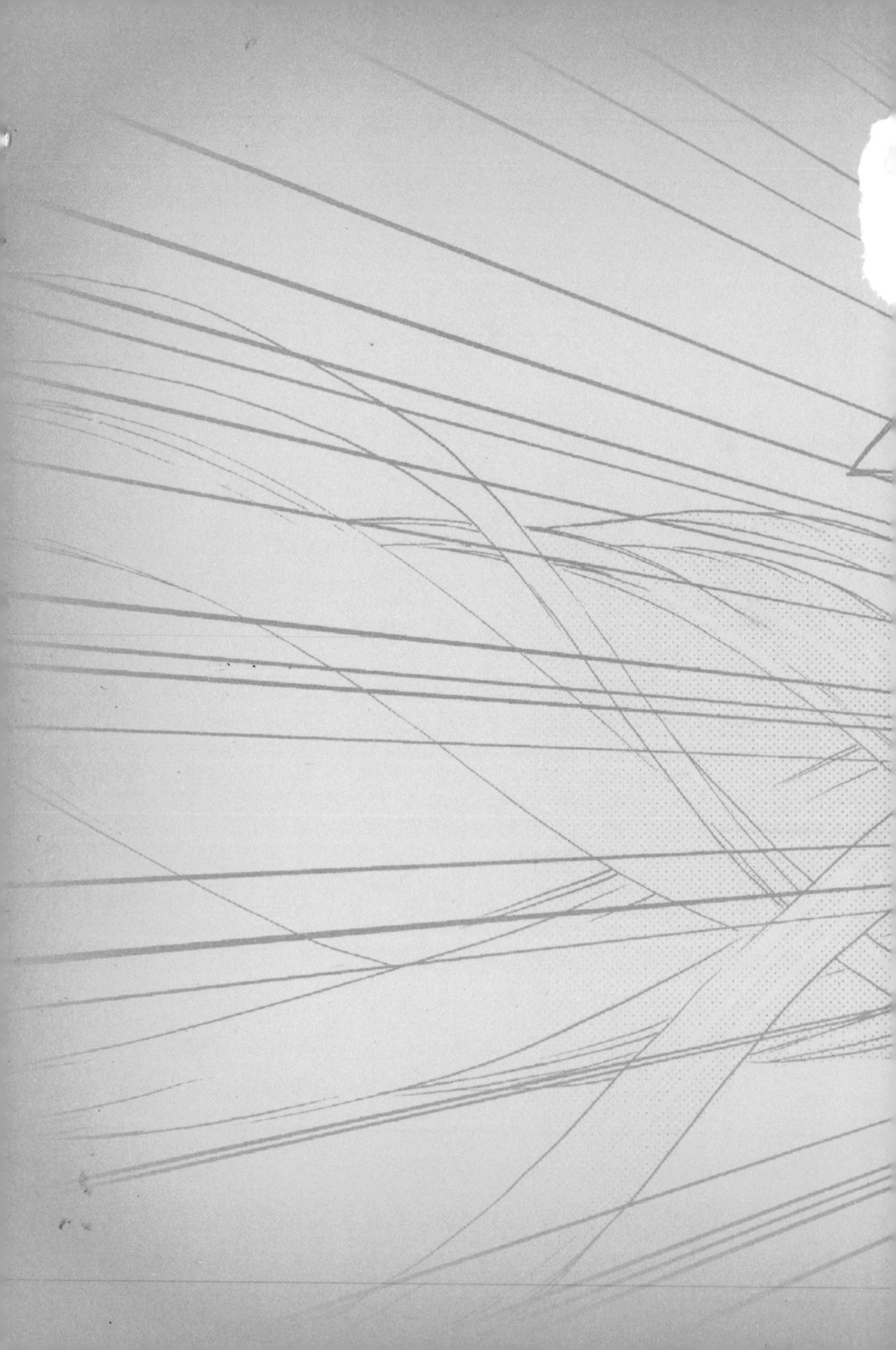

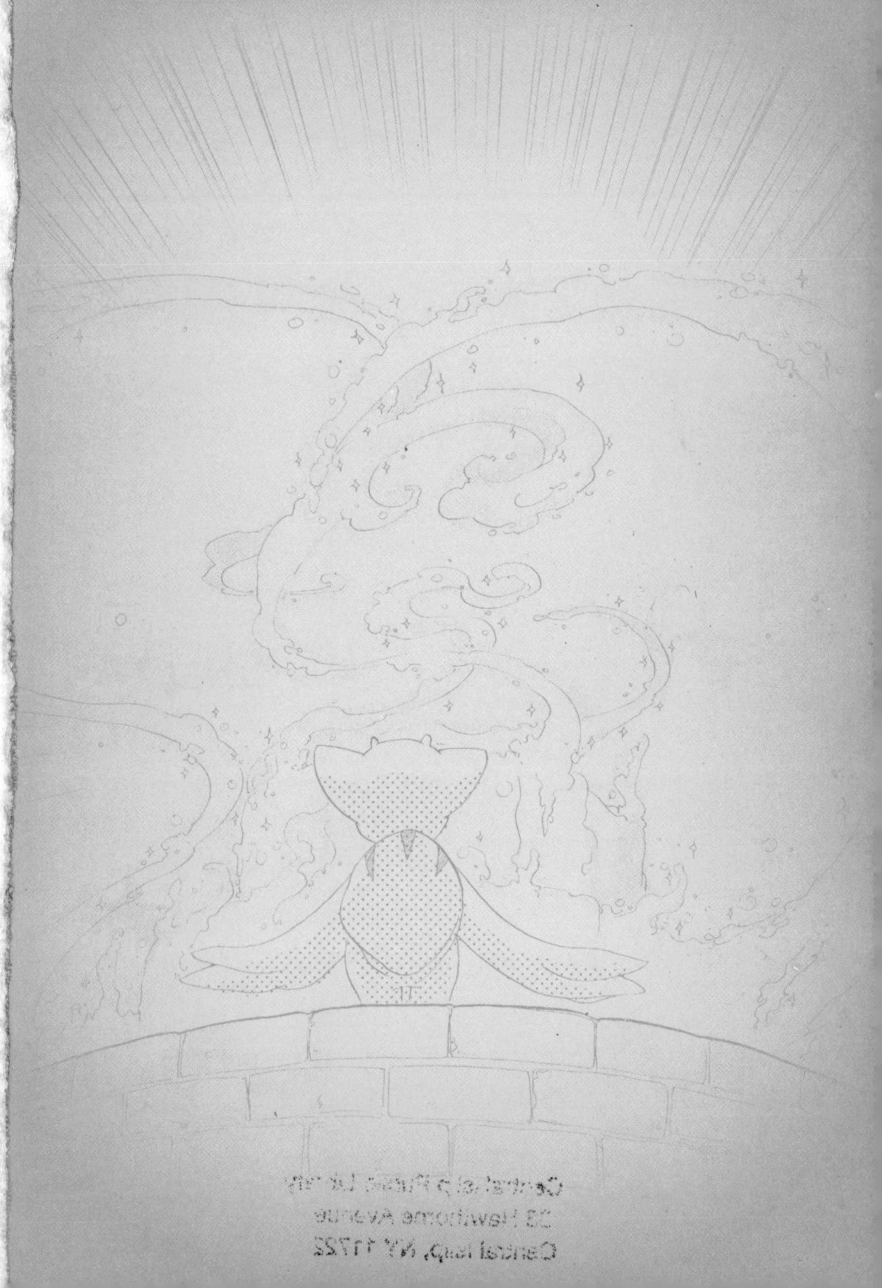

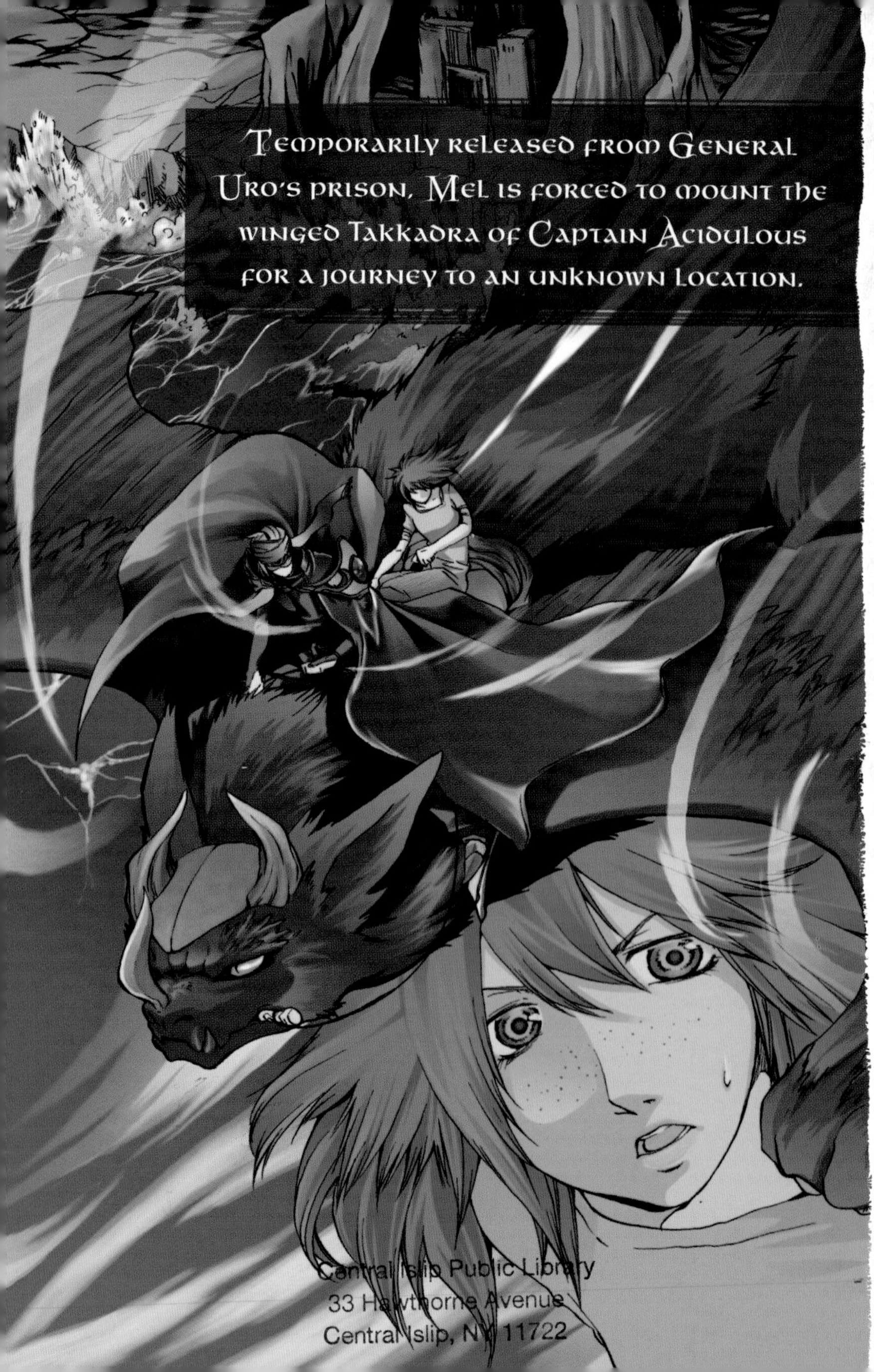
Temporarily released from General Uro's prison, Mel is forced to mount the winged Takkadra of Captain Acidulous for a journey to an unknown location.

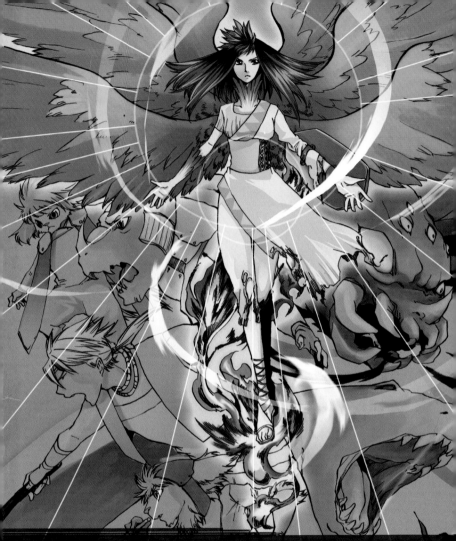

COMPLETING A PATH SET BY QUEEN FRASINELLA,
NAOMI, NOW SEPARATED FROM DOUG, JIM, AND RAINBOW,
HAS SUCCEEDED IN RELEASING HER GUARDIAN, SUZAKU.
BURNING WITH SUZAKU'S FLAME, NAOMI LEADS FLY
AND THE UMLI PEOPLE INTO BATTLE.

COPYRIGHT © 2010 BY RAITETSU MEDIA LLC AND RAY PRODUCTIONS

FIRST U.S. EDITION 2010

LIBRARY OF CONGRESS CATALOGING-IN-PUBLICATION DATA IS AVAILABLE.
LIBRARY OF CONGRESS CATALOG CARD NUMBER PENDING
ISBN 978-0-7636-4950-0

10 11 12 13 14 15 SCP 10 9 8 7 6 5 4 3 2 1

PRINTED IN HUMEN, DONGGUAN, CHINA

THIS BOOK WAS TYPESET IN CCLADRONN ITALIC.

CANDLEWICK PRESS
99 DOVER STREET
SOMERVILLE, MASSACHUSETTS 02144

VISIT US AT WWW.CANDLEWICK.COM

WWW.VERMONIA.COM

VERMONIA

The Rukan Prophecy

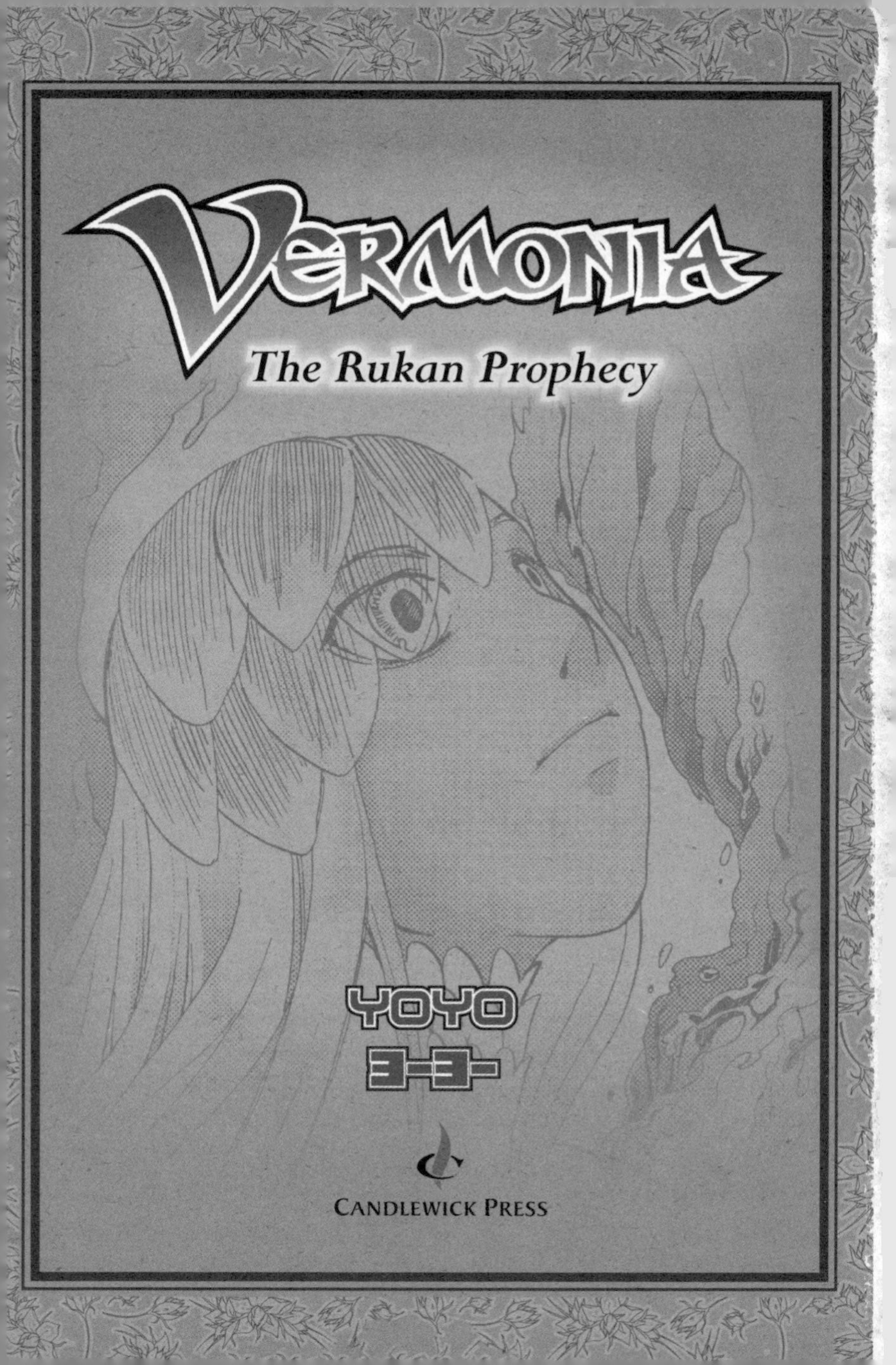

YOYO

ヨーヨー

CANDLEWICK PRESS

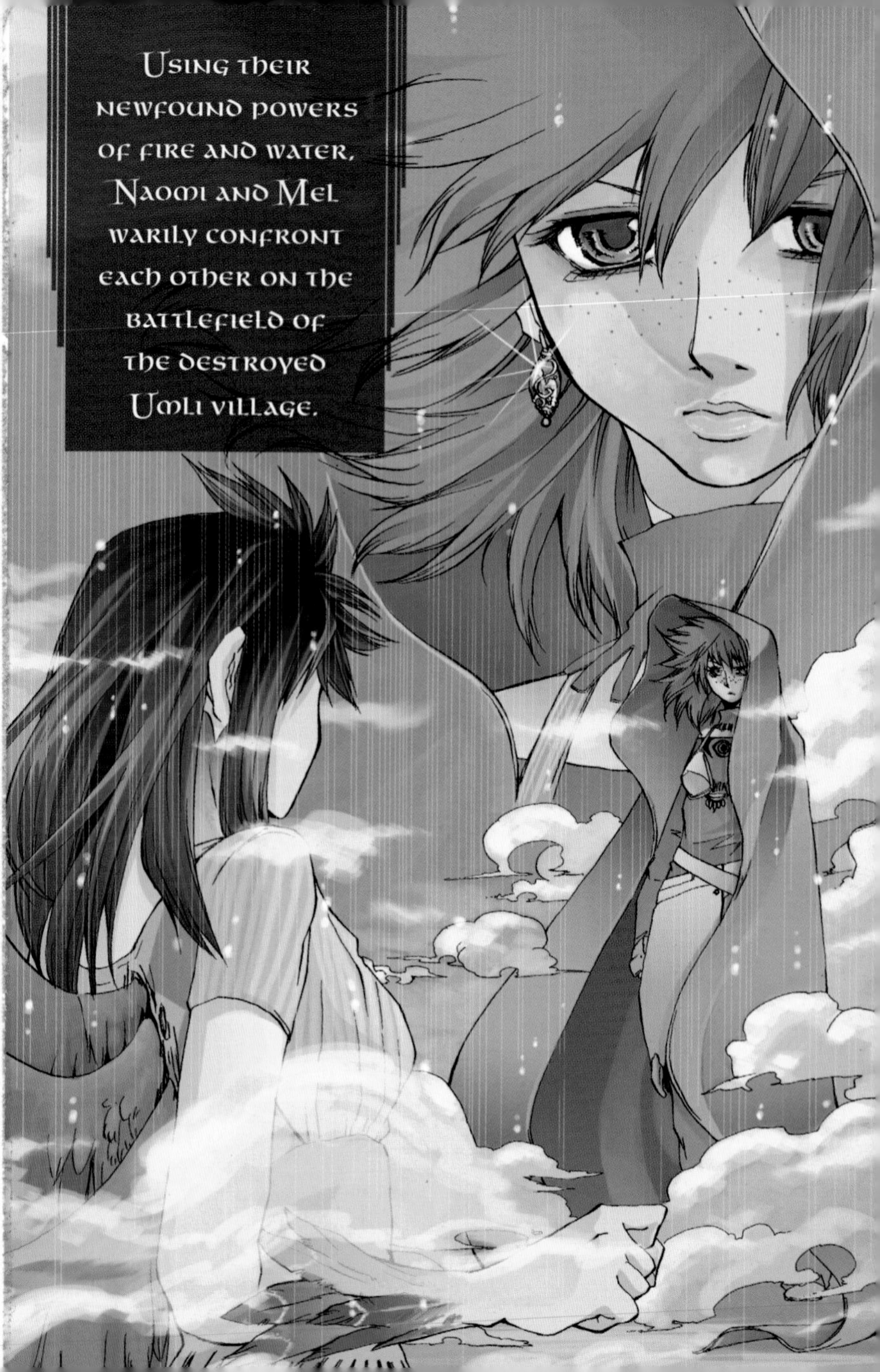
Using their newfound powers of fire and water, Naomi and Mel warily confront each other on the battlefield of the destroyed Umli village.

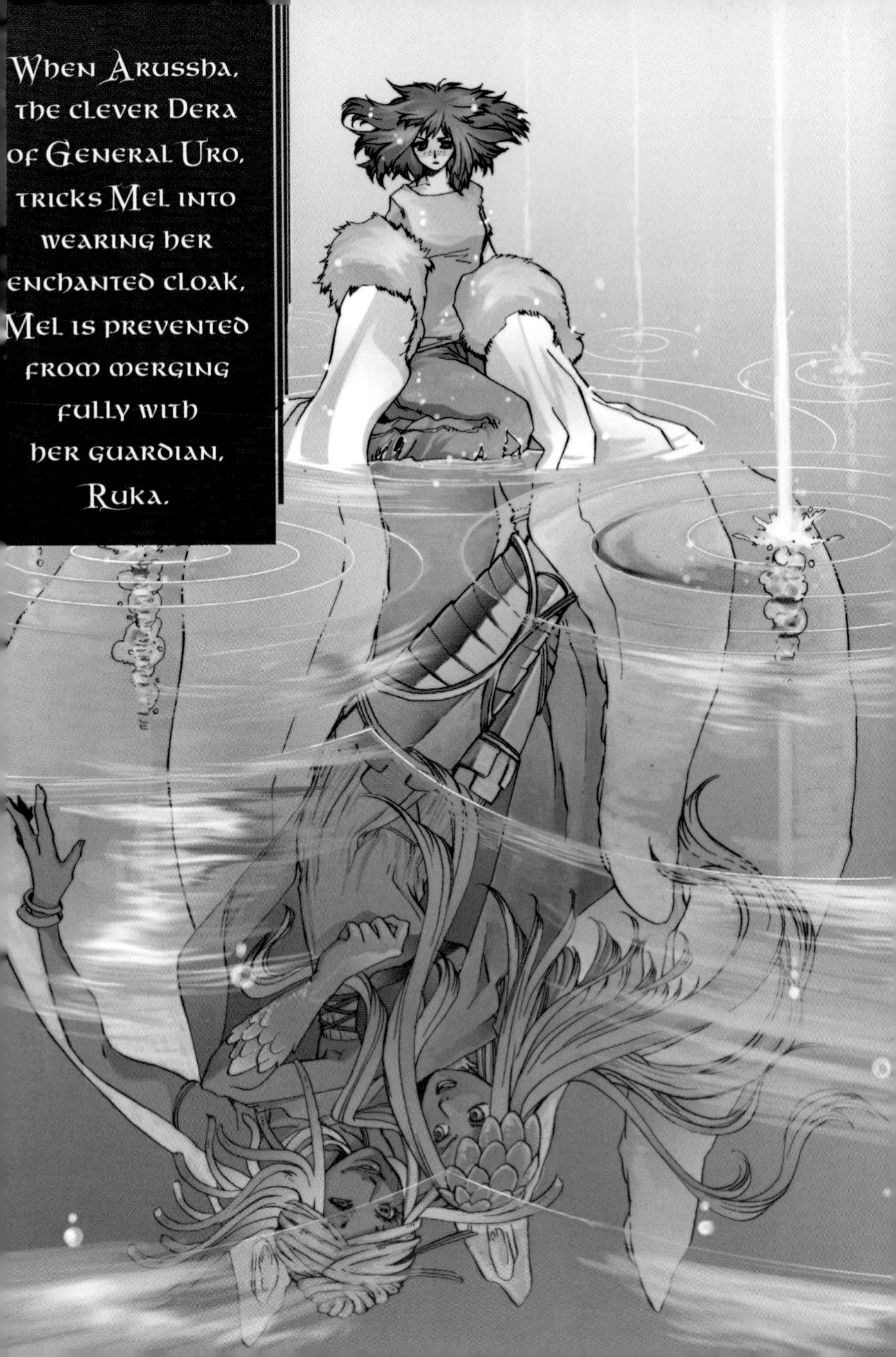
When Arussha, the clever Dera of General Uro, tricks Mel into wearing her enchanted cloak, Mel is prevented from merging fully with her guardian, Ruka.

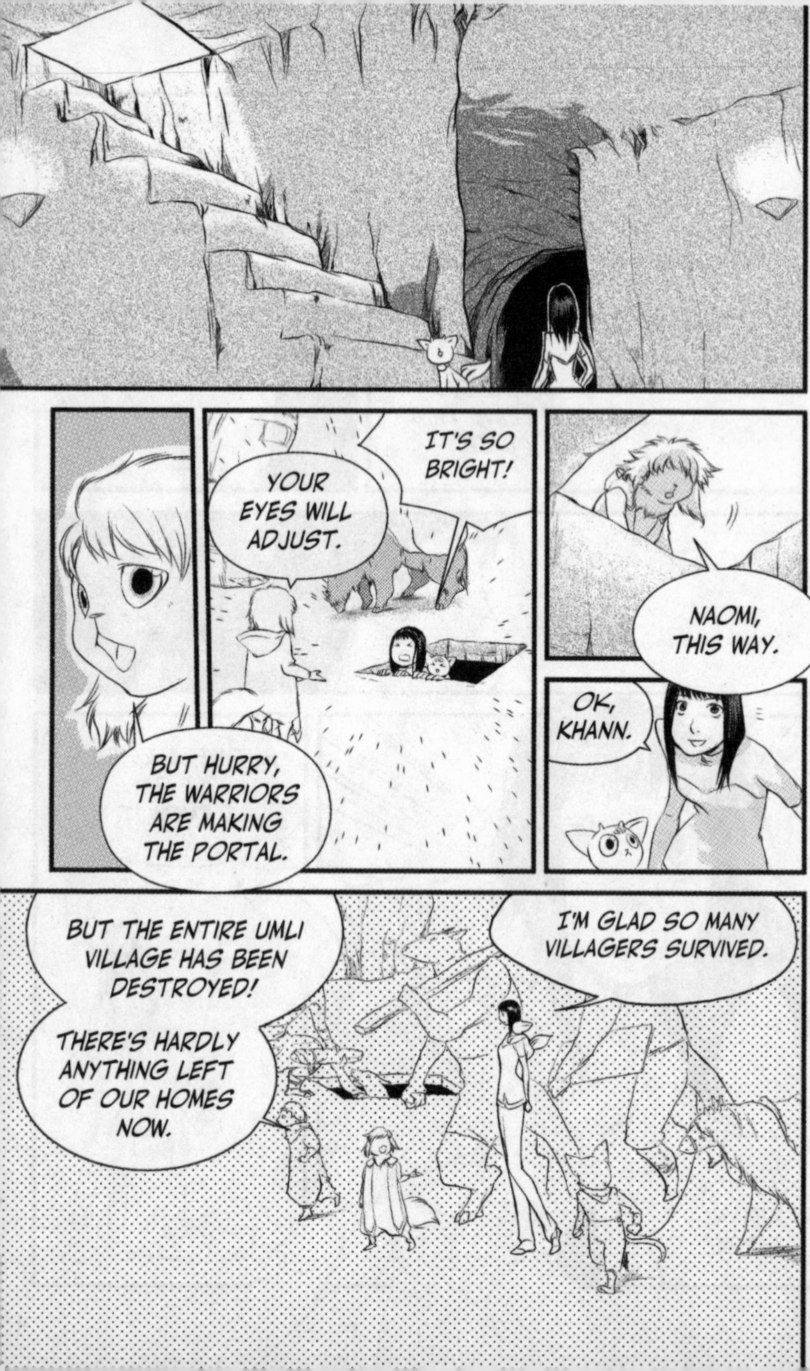
NAOMI, THIS WAY.
OK, KHANN.
IT'S SO BRIGHT!
YOUR EYES WILL ADJUST.
BUT HURRY, THE WARRIORS ARE MAKING THE PORTAL.
I'M GLAD SO MANY VILLAGERS SURVIVED.
BUT THE ENTIRE UMLI VILLAGE HAS BEEN DESTROYED!
THERE'S HARDLY ANYTHING LEFT OF OUR HOMES NOW.

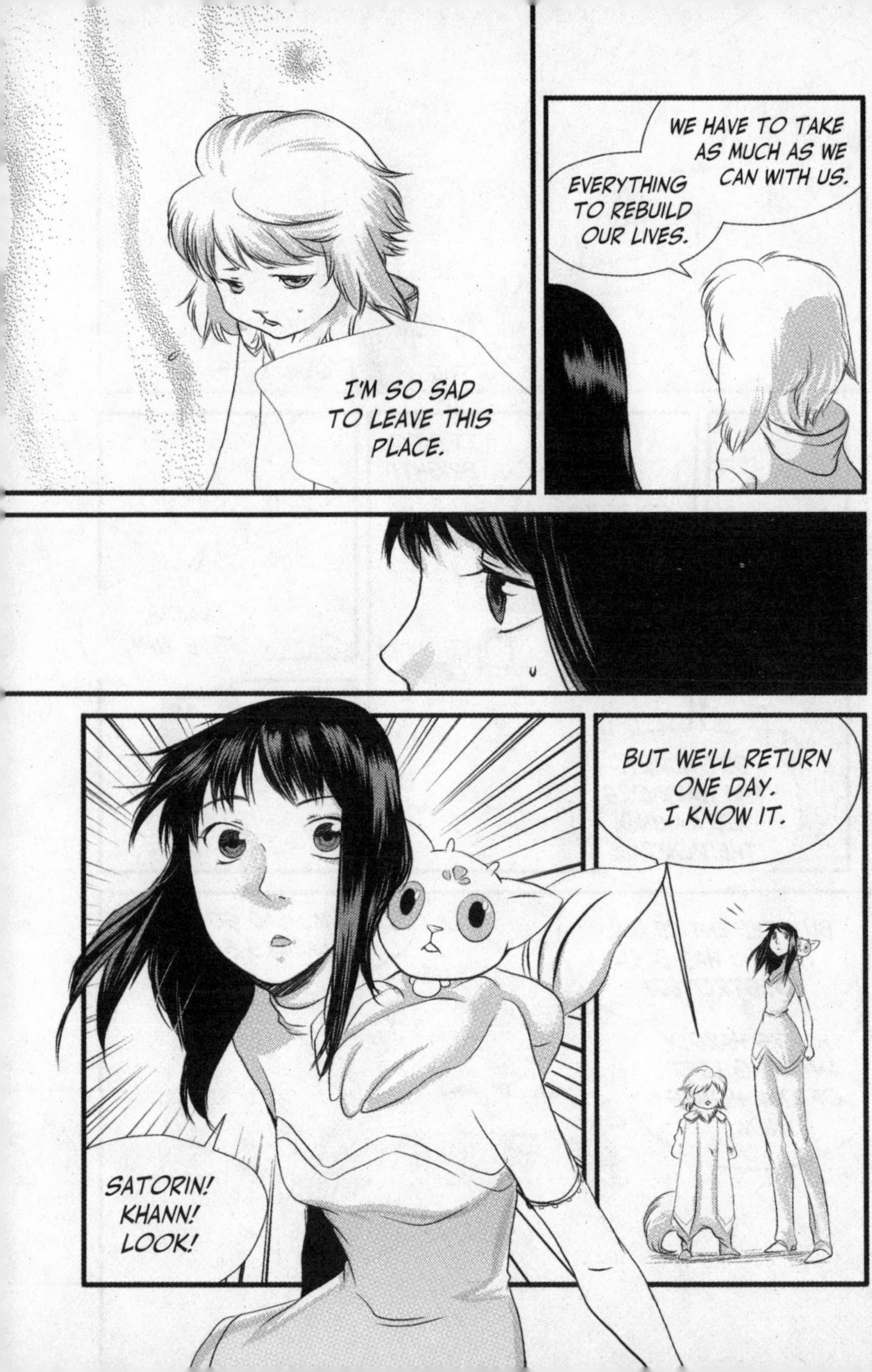
WE HAVE TO TAKE AS MUCH AS WE CAN WITH US.
EVERYTHING TO REBUILD OUR LIVES.
I'M SO SAD TO LEAVE THIS PLACE.
BUT WE'LL RETURN ONE DAY. I KNOW IT.
SATORIN! KHANN! LOOK!

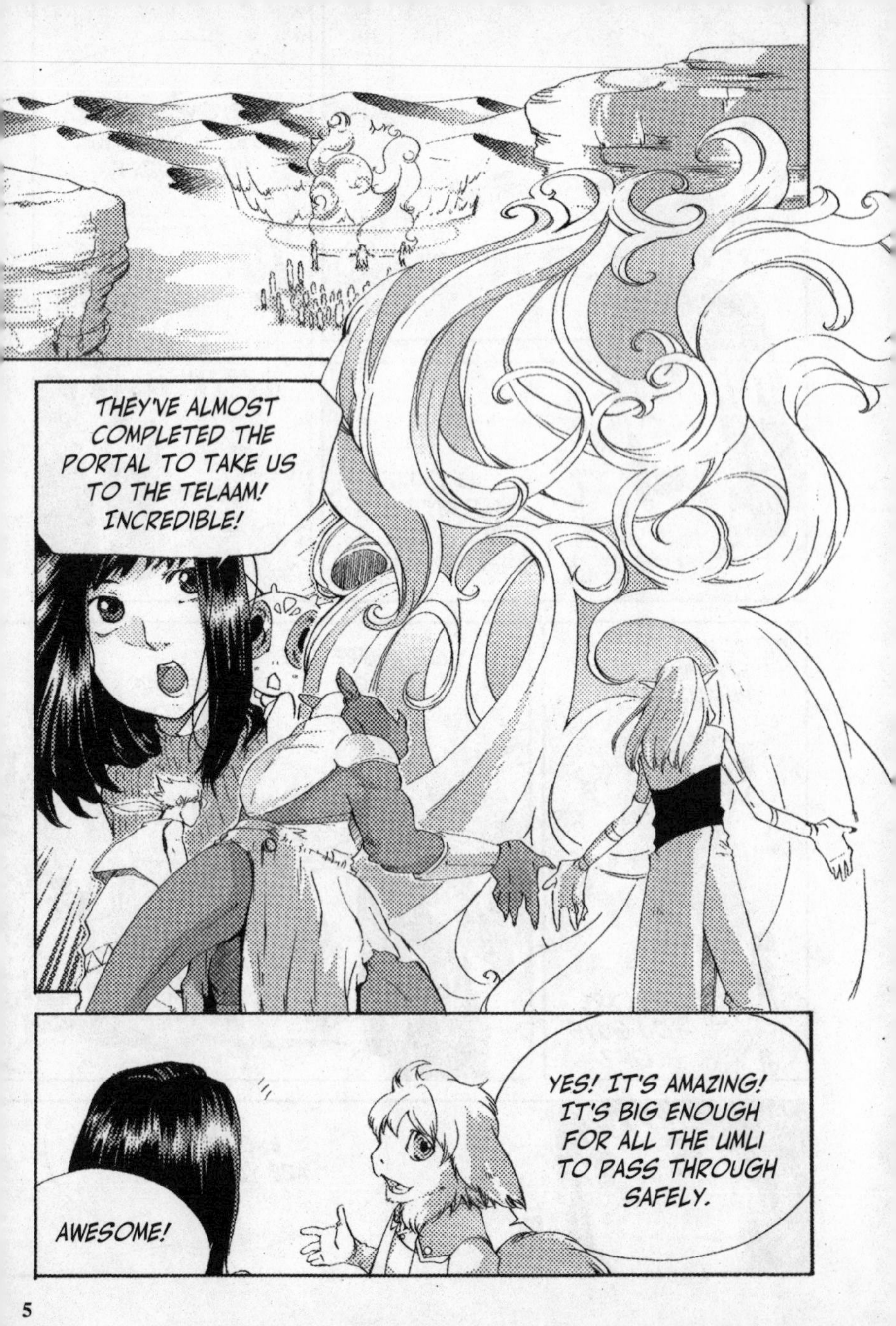
THEY'VE ALMOST COMPLETED THE PORTAL TO TAKE US TO THE TELAAM! INCREDIBLE!
YES! IT'S AMAZING! IT'S BIG ENOUGH FOR ALL THE UMLI TO PASS THROUGH SAFELY.
AWESOME!

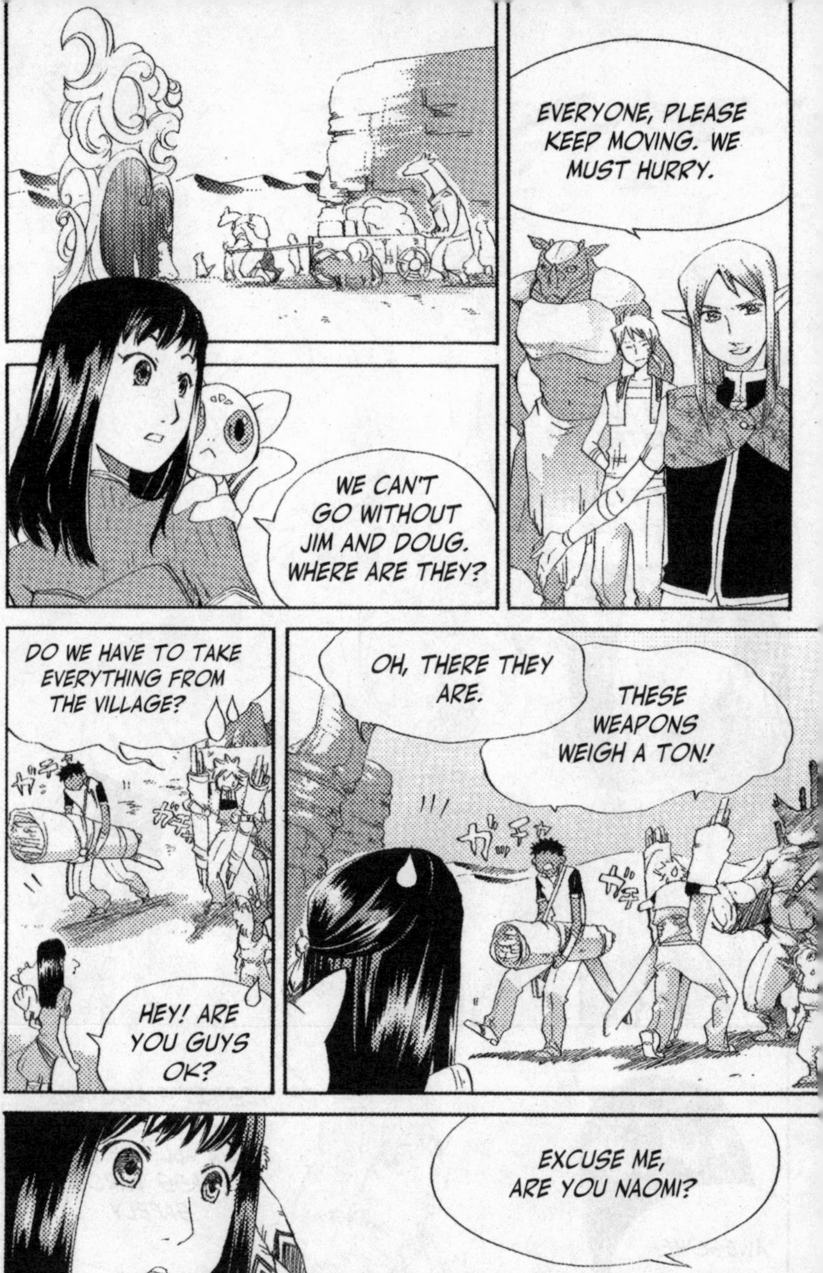

EVERYONE, PLEASE KEEP MOVING. WE MUST HURRY.
WE CAN'T GO WITHOUT JIM AND DOUG. WHERE ARE THEY?
OH, THERE THEY ARE.
THESE WEAPONS WEIGH A TON!
DO WE HAVE TO TAKE EVERYTHING FROM THE VILLAGE?
HEY! ARE YOU GUYS OK?
EXCUSE ME, ARE YOU NAOMI?

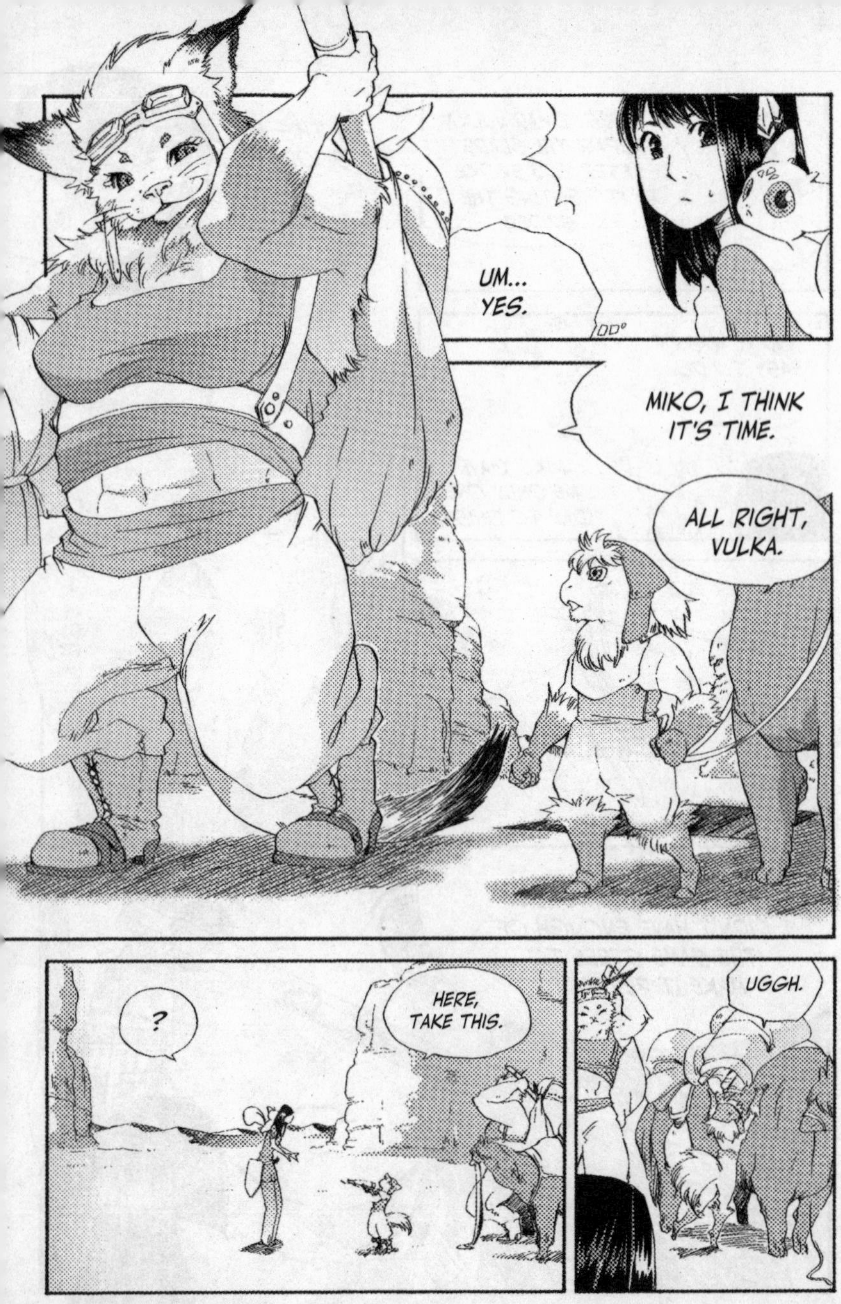
UM...
YES.
MIKO, I THINK
IT'S TIME.
ALL RIGHT,
VULKA.
UGGH.
HERE,
TAKE THIS.
?

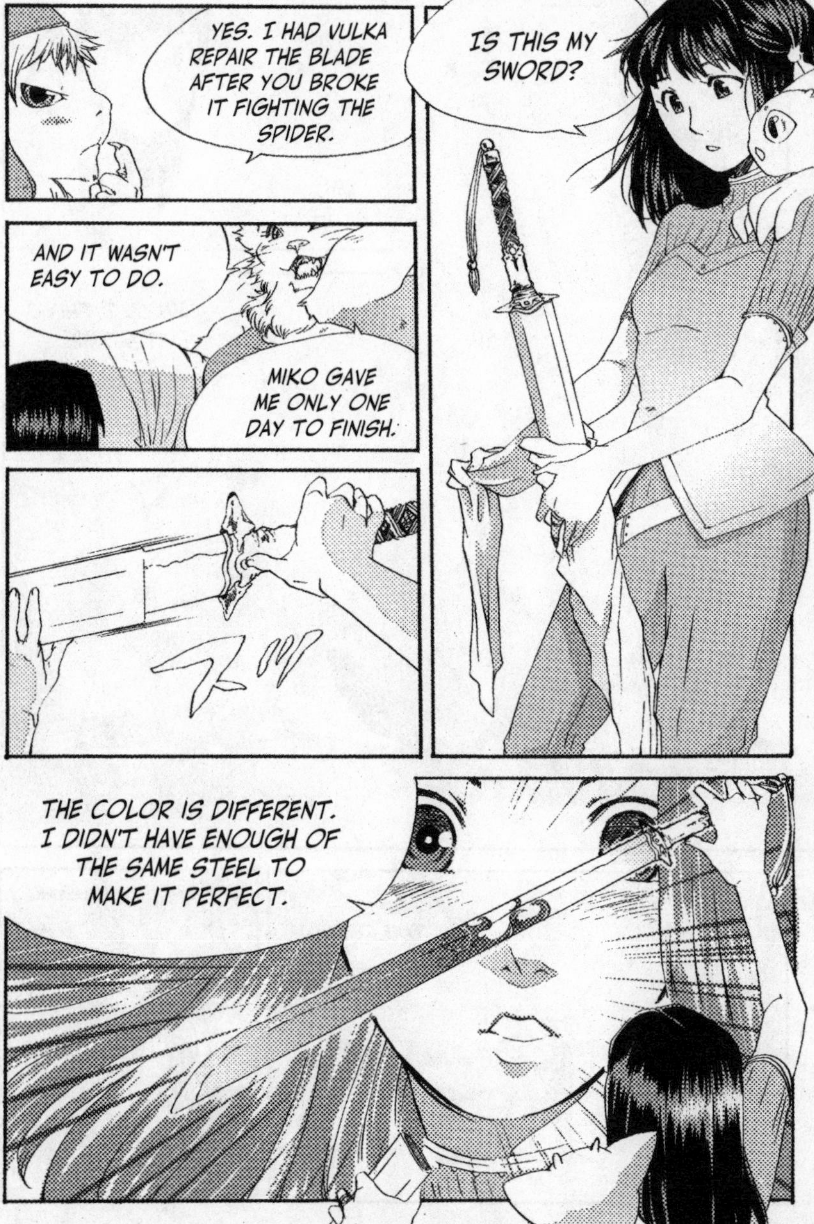
IS THIS MY SWORD?
YES. I HAD VULKA REPAIR THE BLADE AFTER YOU BROKE IT FIGHTING THE SPIDER.
AND IT WASN'T EASY TO DO.
MIKO GAVE ME ONLY ONE DAY TO FINISH.
THE COLOR IS DIFFERENT. I DIDN'T HAVE ENOUGH OF THE SAME STEEL TO MAKE IT PERFECT.

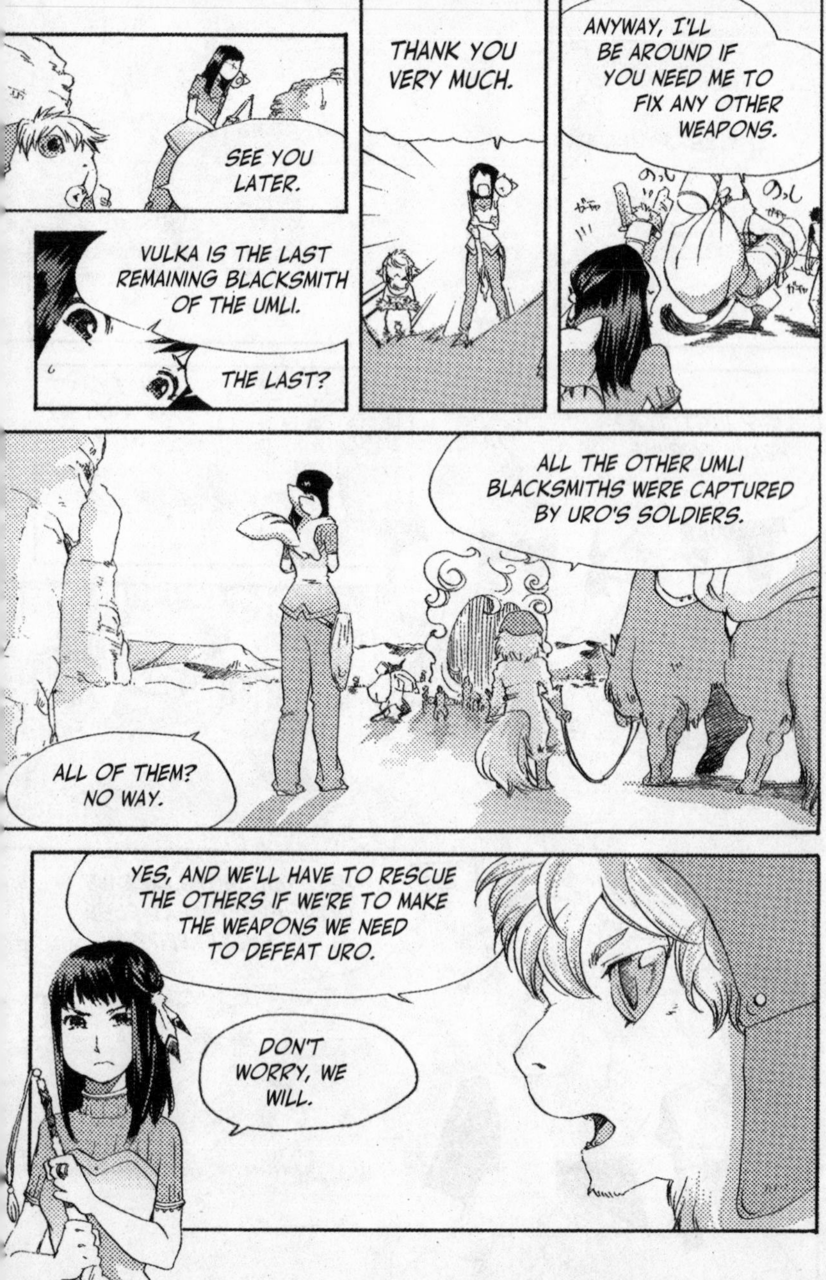
ANYWAY, I'LL BE AROUND IF YOU NEED ME TO FIX ANY OTHER WEAPONS.
THANK YOU VERY MUCH.
SEE YOU LATER.
VULKA IS THE LAST REMAINING BLACKSMITH OF THE UMLI.
THE LAST?
ALL THE OTHER UMLI BLACKSMITHS WERE CAPTURED BY URO'S SOLDIERS.
ALL OF THEM? NO WAY.
YES, AND WE'LL HAVE TO RESCUE THE OTHERS IF WE'RE TO MAKE THE WEAPONS WE NEED TO DEFEAT URO.
DON'T WORRY, WE WILL.

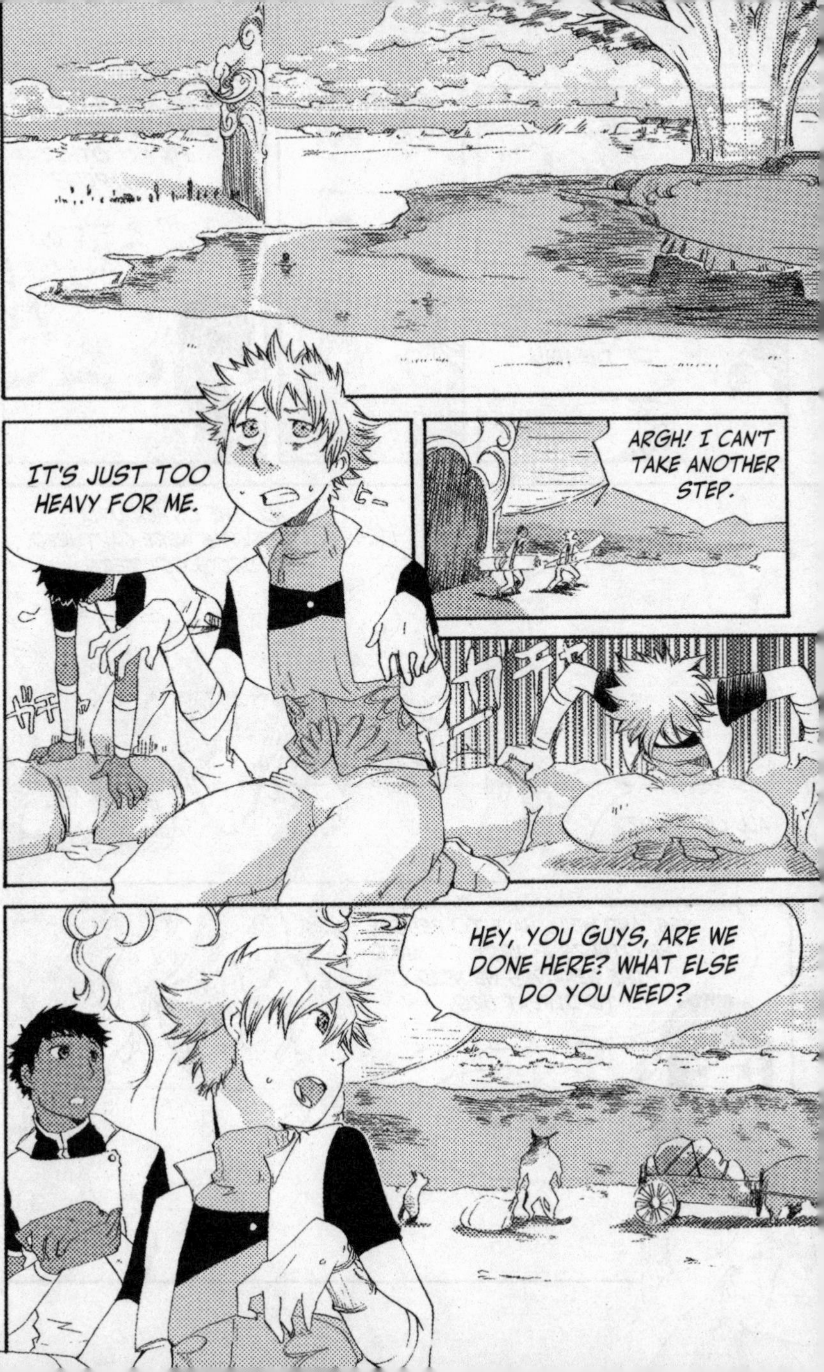
ARGH! I CAN'T TAKE ANOTHER STEP.
IT'S JUST TOO HEAVY FOR ME.
HEY, YOU GUYS, ARE WE DONE HERE? WHAT ELSE DO YOU NEED?

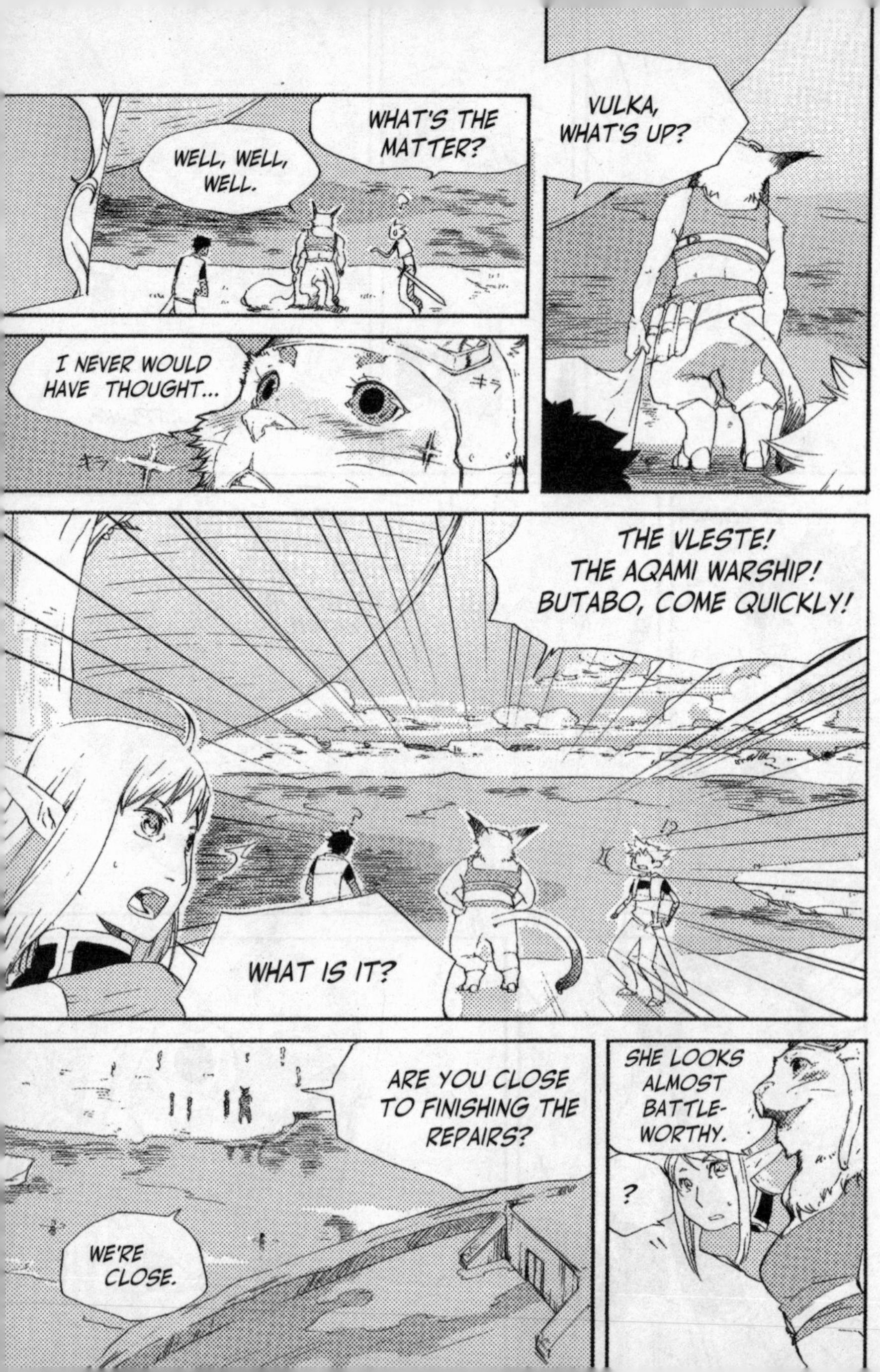
VULKA, WHAT'S UP?
WHAT'S THE MATTER?
WELL, WELL, WELL.
I NEVER WOULD HAVE THOUGHT...
THE VLESTE! THE AQAMI WARSHIP! BUTABO, COME QUICKLY!
WHAT IS IT?
SHE LOOKS ALMOST BATTLE-WORTHY.
?
ARE YOU CLOSE TO FINISHING THE REPAIRS?
WE'RE CLOSE.

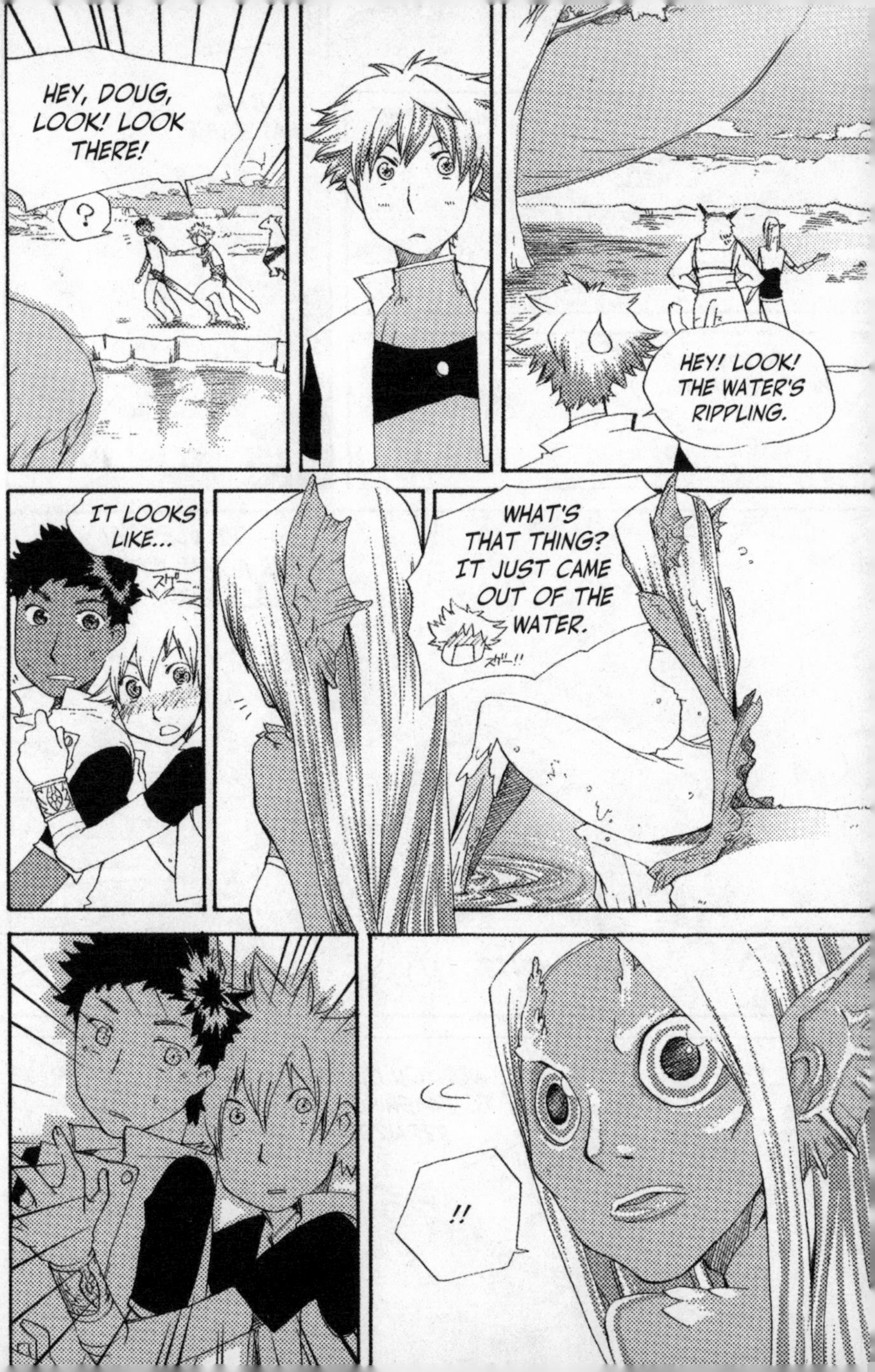
HEY! LOOK! THE WATER'S RIPPLING.
HEY, DOUG, LOOK! LOOK THERE!
?
WHAT'S THAT THING? IT JUST CAME OUT OF THE WATER.
IT LOOKS LIKE...
!!

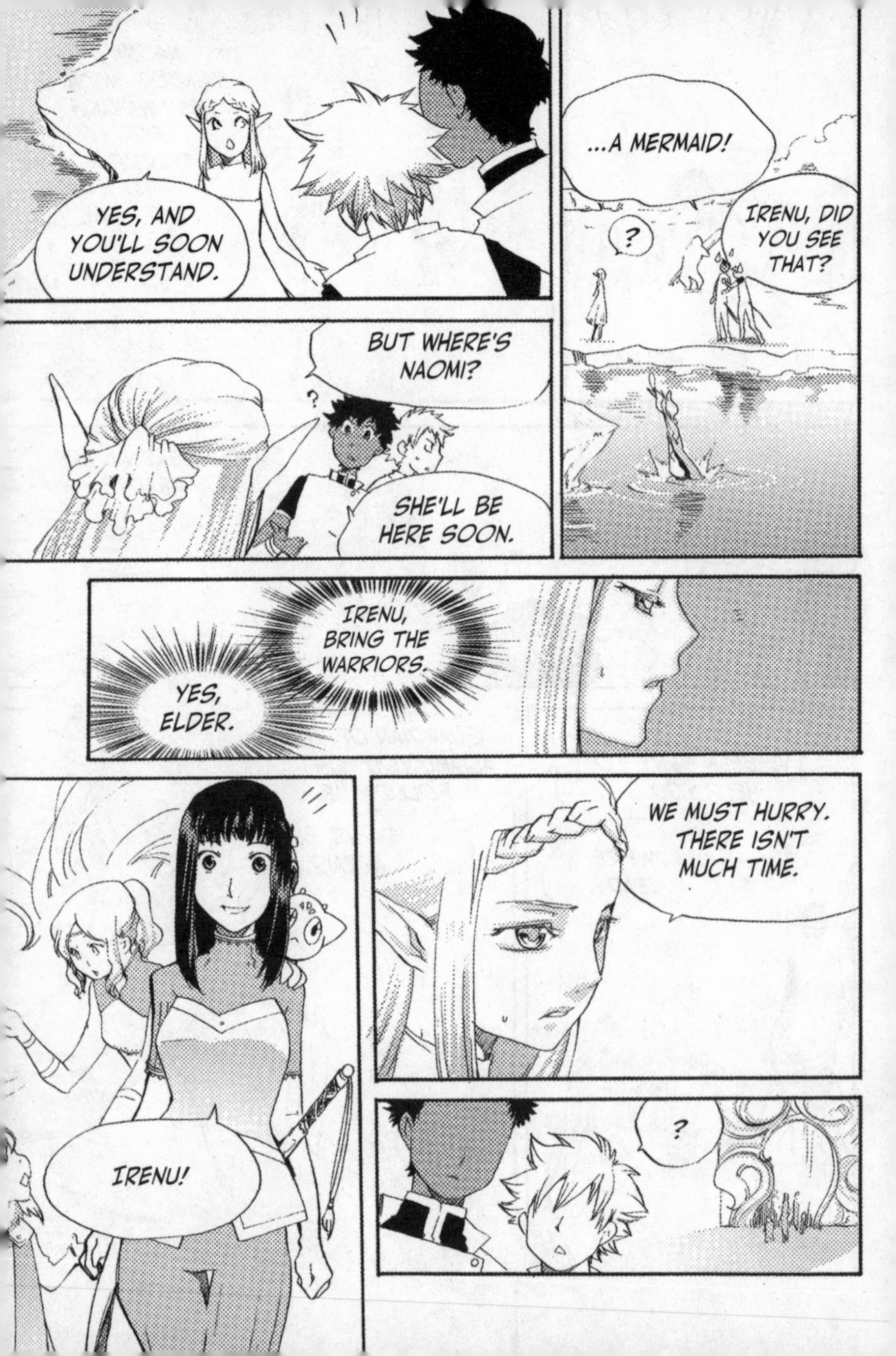

...A MERMAID!
?
IRENU, DID YOU SEE THAT?
YES, AND YOU'LL SOON UNDERSTAND.
BUT WHERE'S NAOMI?
?
SHE'LL BE HERE SOON.
IRENU, BRING THE WARRIORS.
YES, ELDER.
WE MUST HURRY. THERE ISN'T MUCH TIME.
?
IRENU!

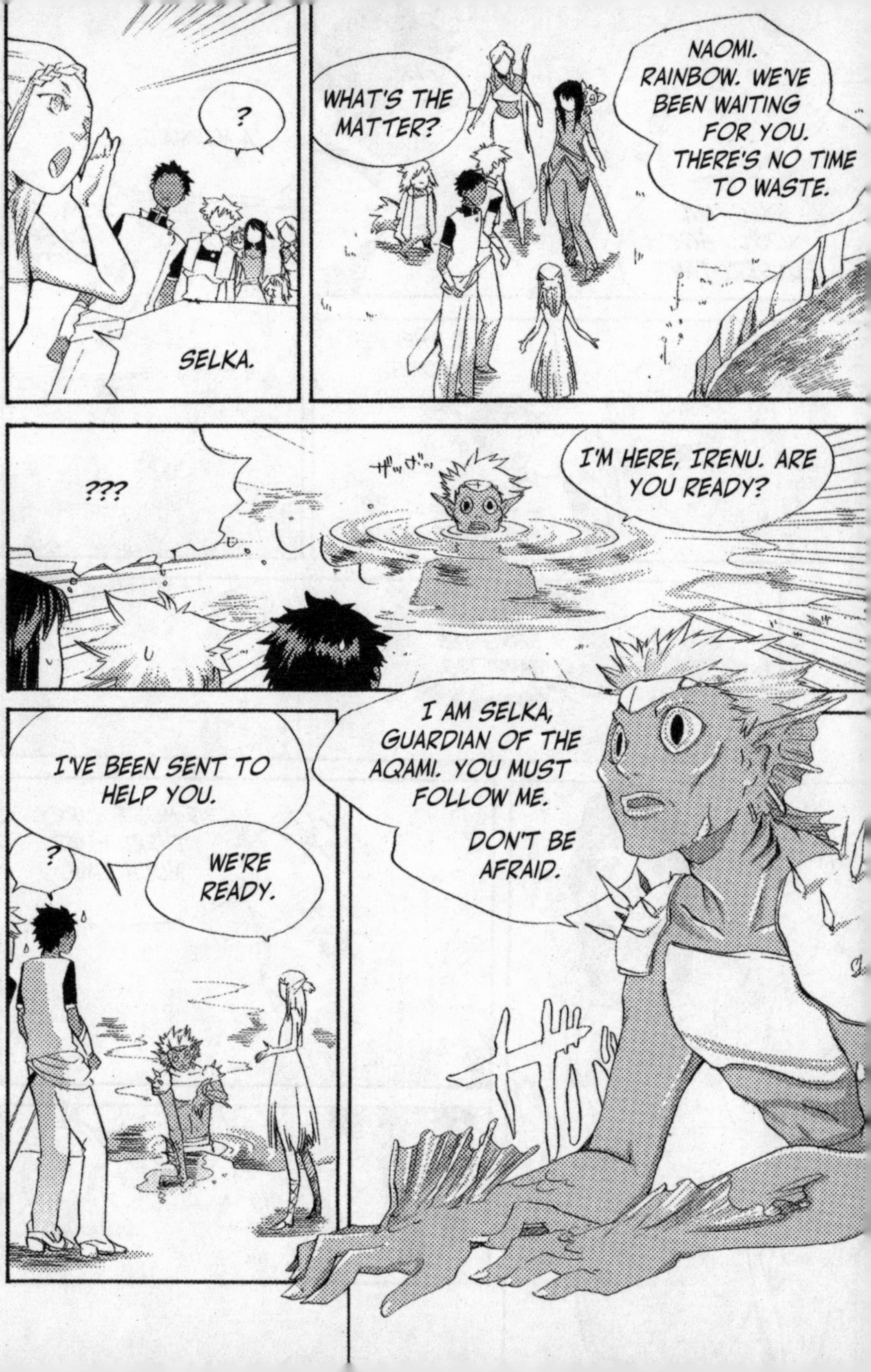
NAOMI. RAINBOW. WE'VE BEEN WAITING FOR YOU. THERE'S NO TIME TO WASTE.
WHAT'S THE MATTER?
?
SELKA.
I'M HERE, IRENU. ARE YOU READY?
???
I AM SELKA, GUARDIAN OF THE AQAMI. YOU MUST FOLLOW ME.
DON'T BE AFRAID.
I'VE BEEN SENT TO HELP YOU.
WE'RE READY.
?

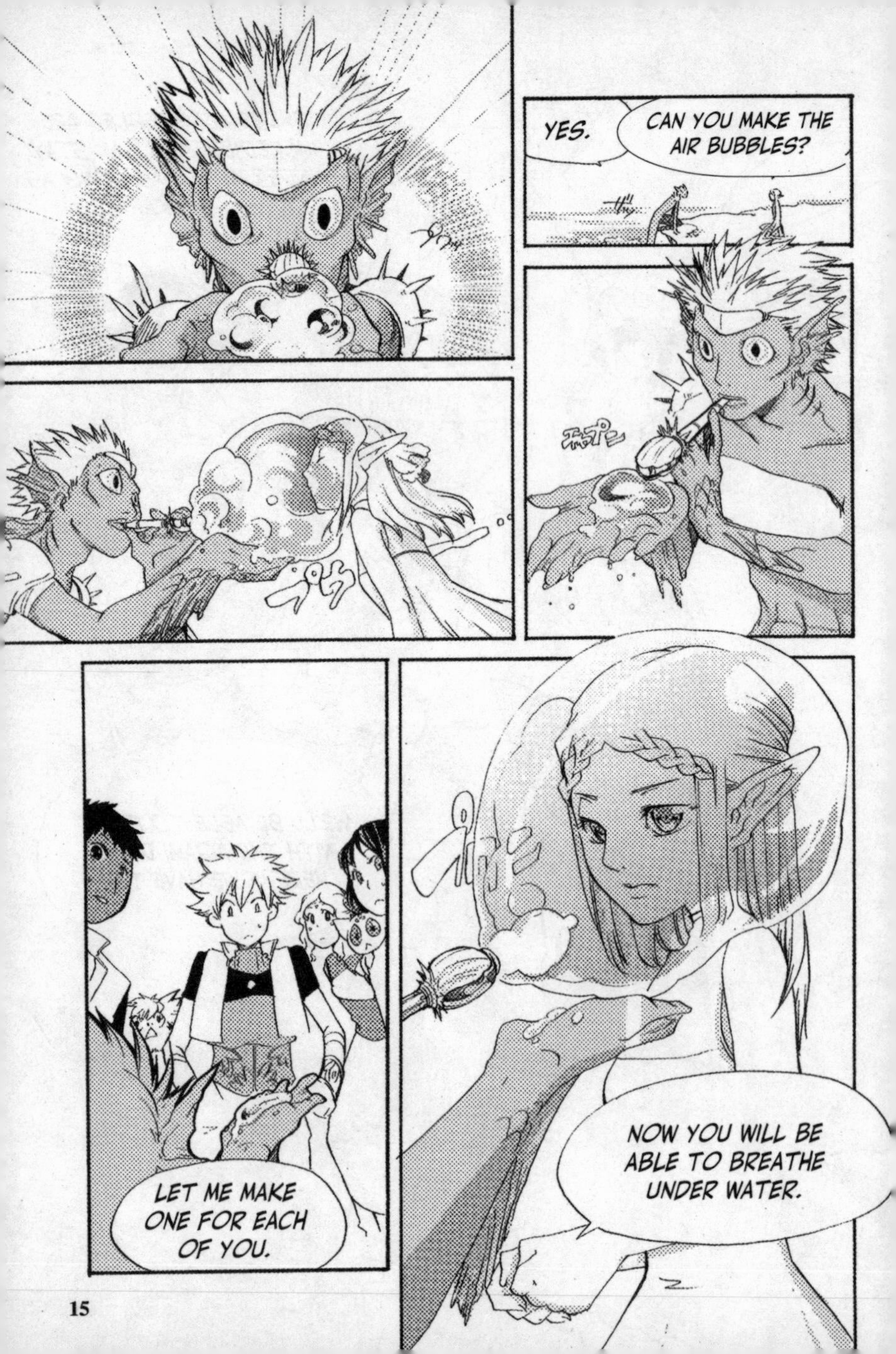
CAN YOU MAKE THE AIR BUBBLES?
YES.
NOW YOU WILL BE ABLE TO BREATHE UNDER WATER.
LET ME MAKE ONE FOR EACH OF YOU.

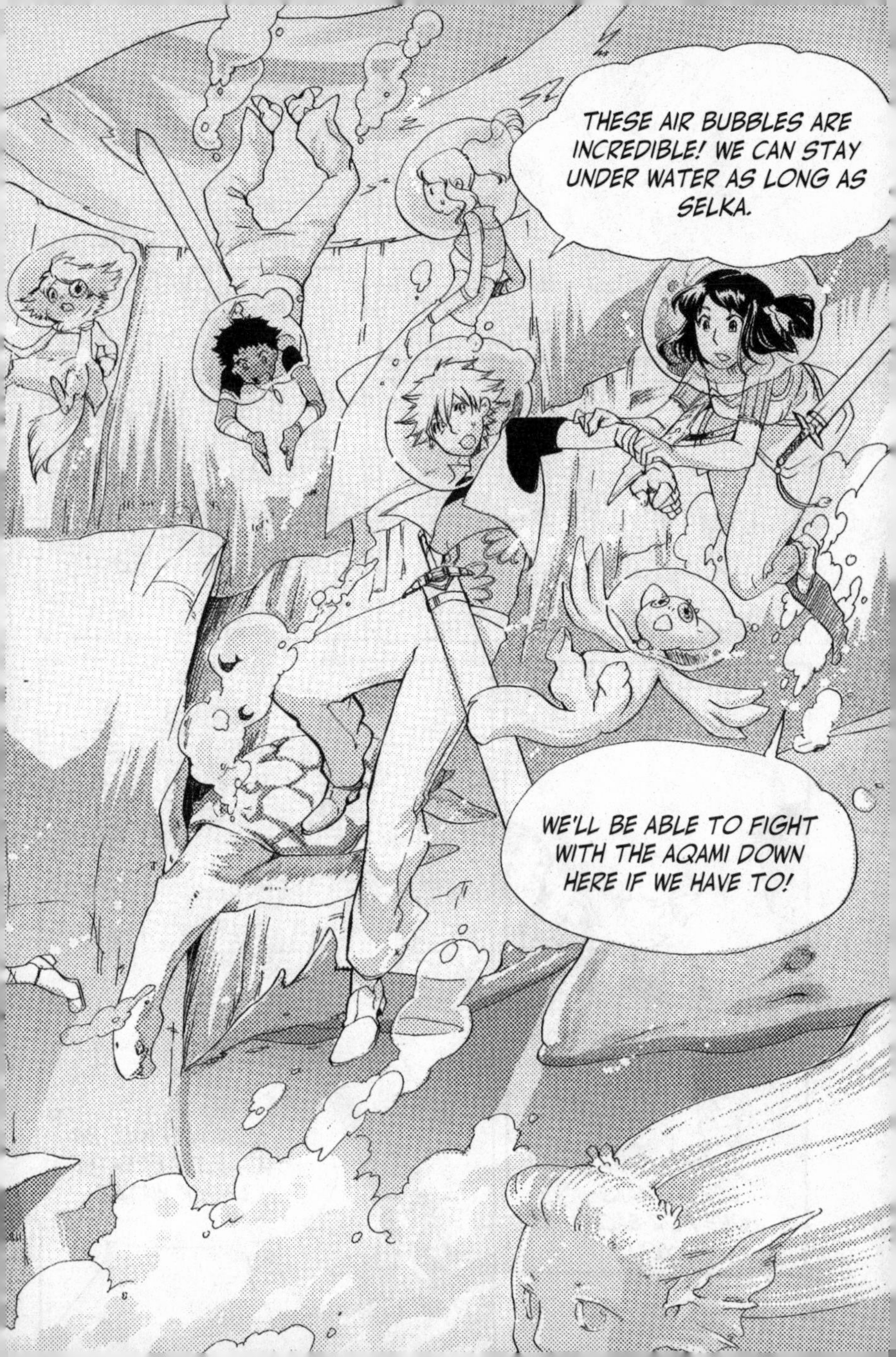
THESE AIR BUBBLES ARE INCREDIBLE! WE CAN STAY UNDER WATER AS LONG AS SELKA.
WE'LL BE ABLE TO FIGHT WITH THE AQAMI DOWN HERE IF WE HAVE TO!

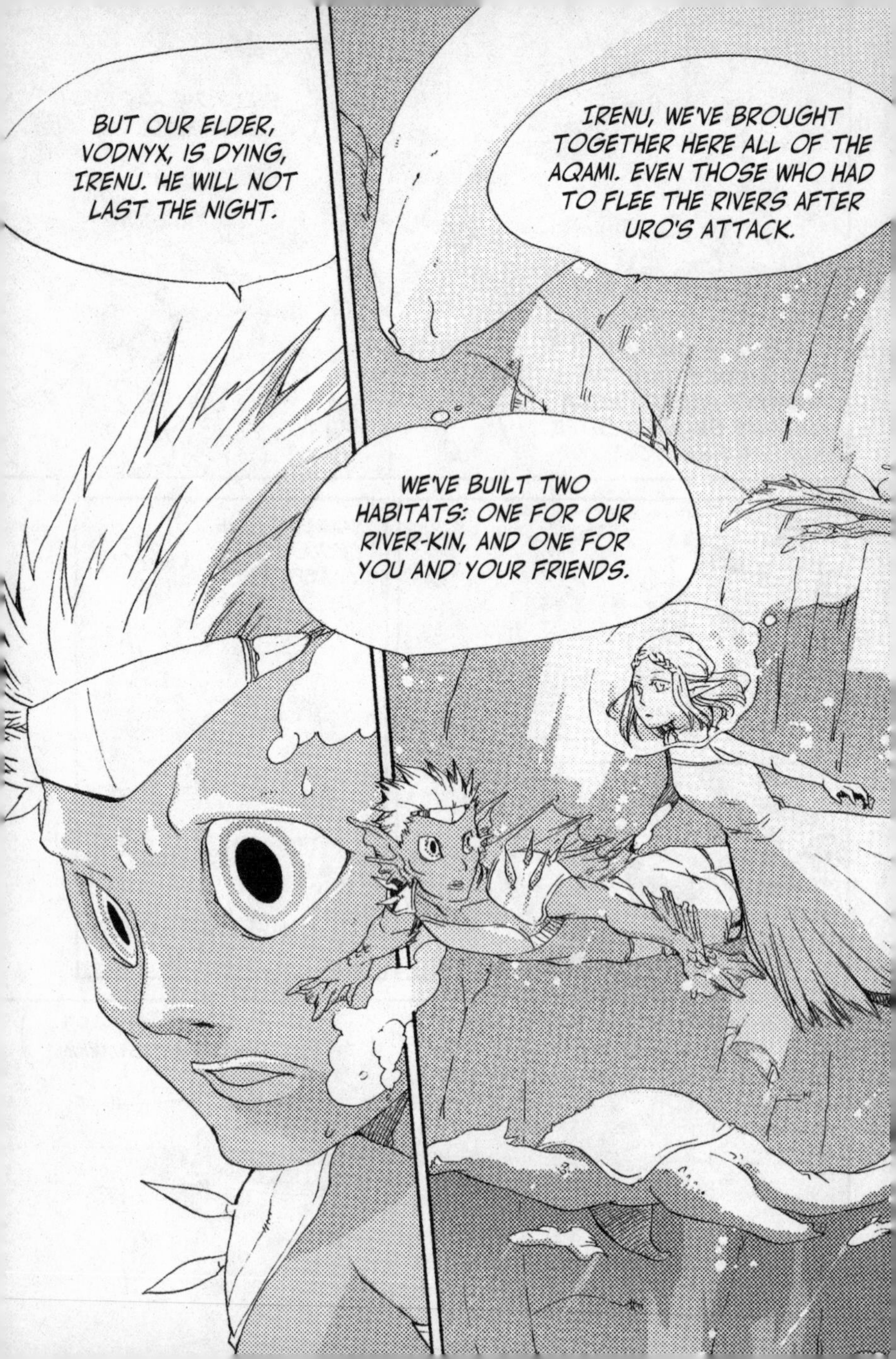
IRENU, WE'VE BROUGHT TOGETHER HERE ALL OF THE AQAMI. EVEN THOSE WHO HAD TO FLEE THE RIVERS AFTER URO'S ATTACK.
WE'VE BUILT TWO HABITATS: ONE FOR OUR RIVER-KIN, AND ONE FOR YOU AND YOUR FRIENDS.
BUT OUR ELDER, VODNYX, IS DYING, IRENU. HE WILL NOT LAST THE NIGHT.

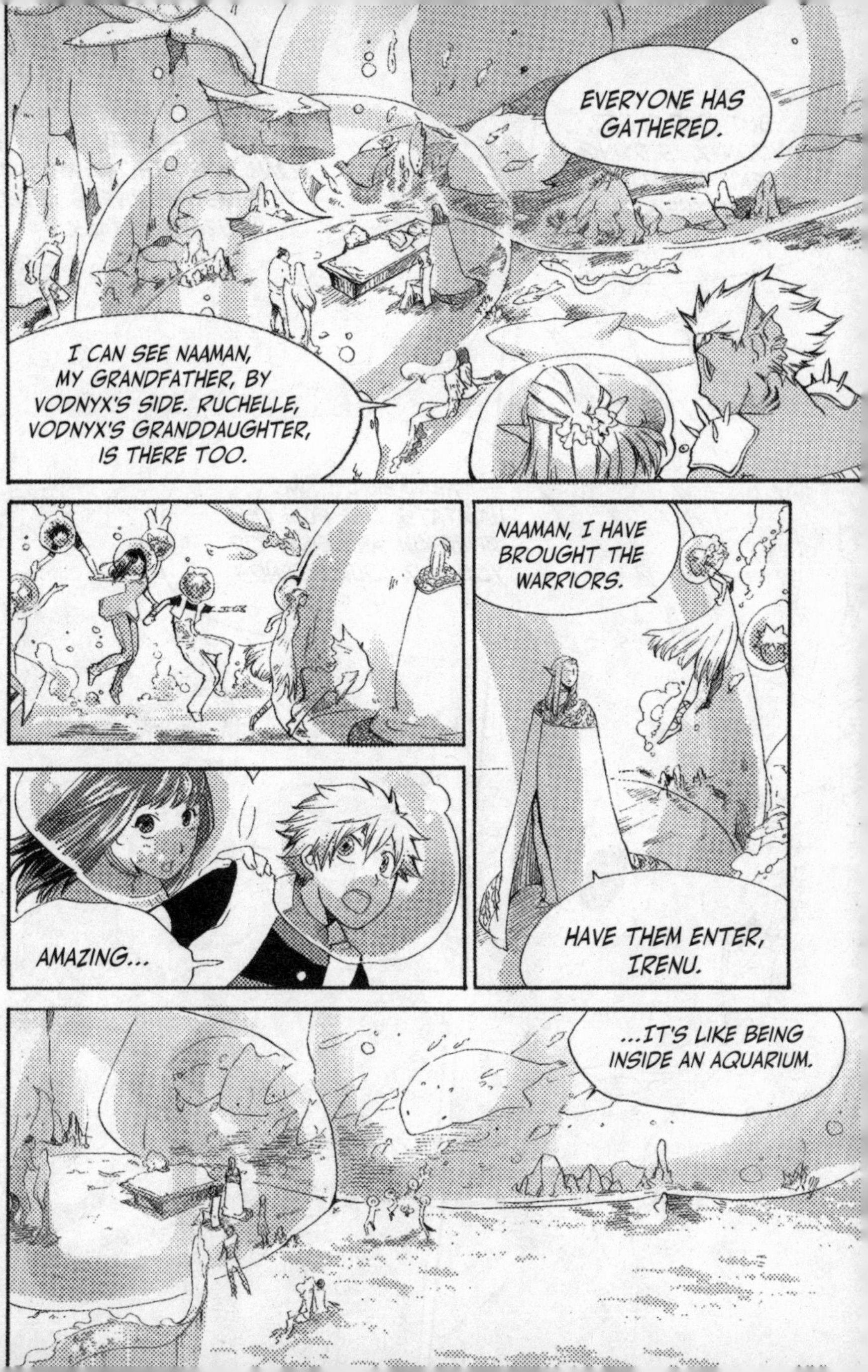
EVERYONE HAS GATHERED.
I CAN SEE NAAMAN, MY GRANDFATHER, BY VODNYX'S SIDE. RUCHELLE, VODNYX'S GRANDDAUGHTER, IS THERE TOO.
NAAMAN, I HAVE BROUGHT THE WARRIORS.
HAVE THEM ENTER, IRENU.
AMAZING...
...IT'S LIKE BEING INSIDE AN AQUARIUM.

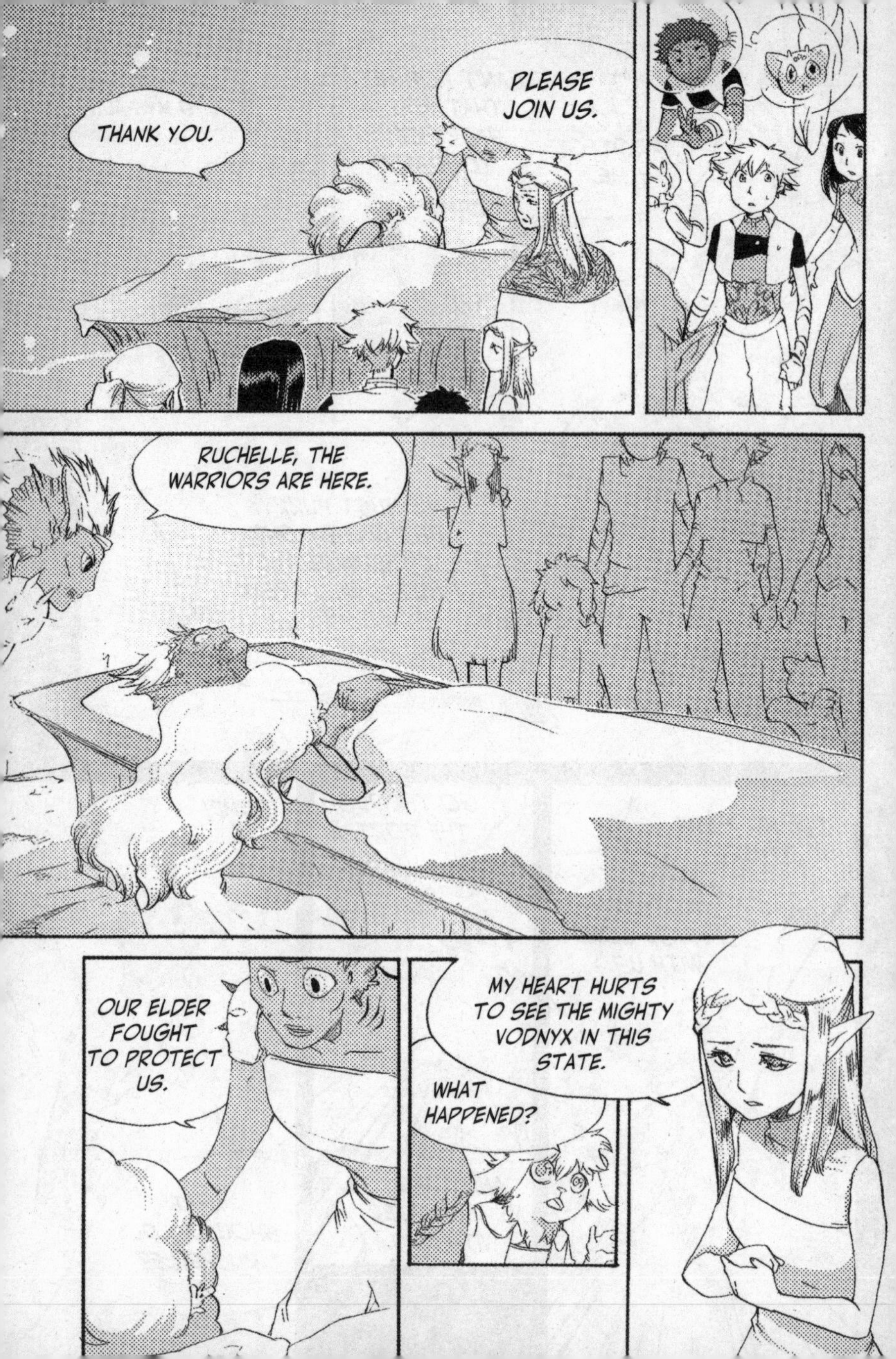
PLEASE JOIN US.
THANK YOU.
RUCHELLE, THE WARRIORS ARE HERE.
MY HEART HURTS TO SEE THE MIGHTY VODNYX IN THIS STATE.
WHAT HAPPENED?
OUR ELDER FOUGHT TO PROTECT US.

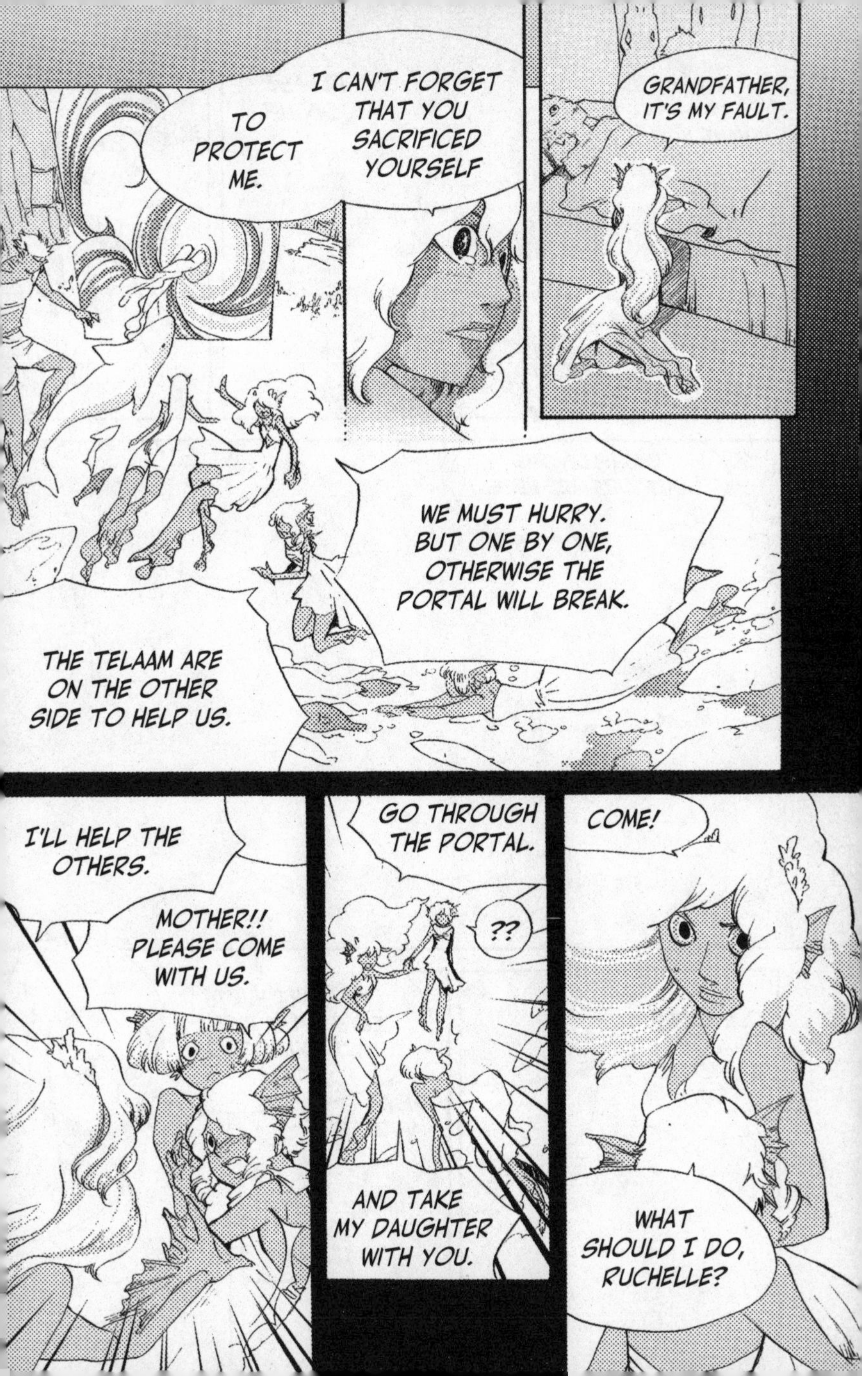
GRANDFATHER, IT'S MY FAULT.
I CAN'T FORGET THAT YOU SACRIFICED YOURSELF
TO PROTECT ME.
WE MUST HURRY. BUT ONE BY ONE, OTHERWISE THE PORTAL WILL BREAK.
THE TELAAM ARE ON THE OTHER SIDE TO HELP US.
COME!
WHAT SHOULD I DO, RUCHELLE?
GO THROUGH THE PORTAL.
??
AND TAKE MY DAUGHTER WITH YOU.
I'LL HELP THE OTHERS.
MOTHER!! PLEASE COME WITH US.

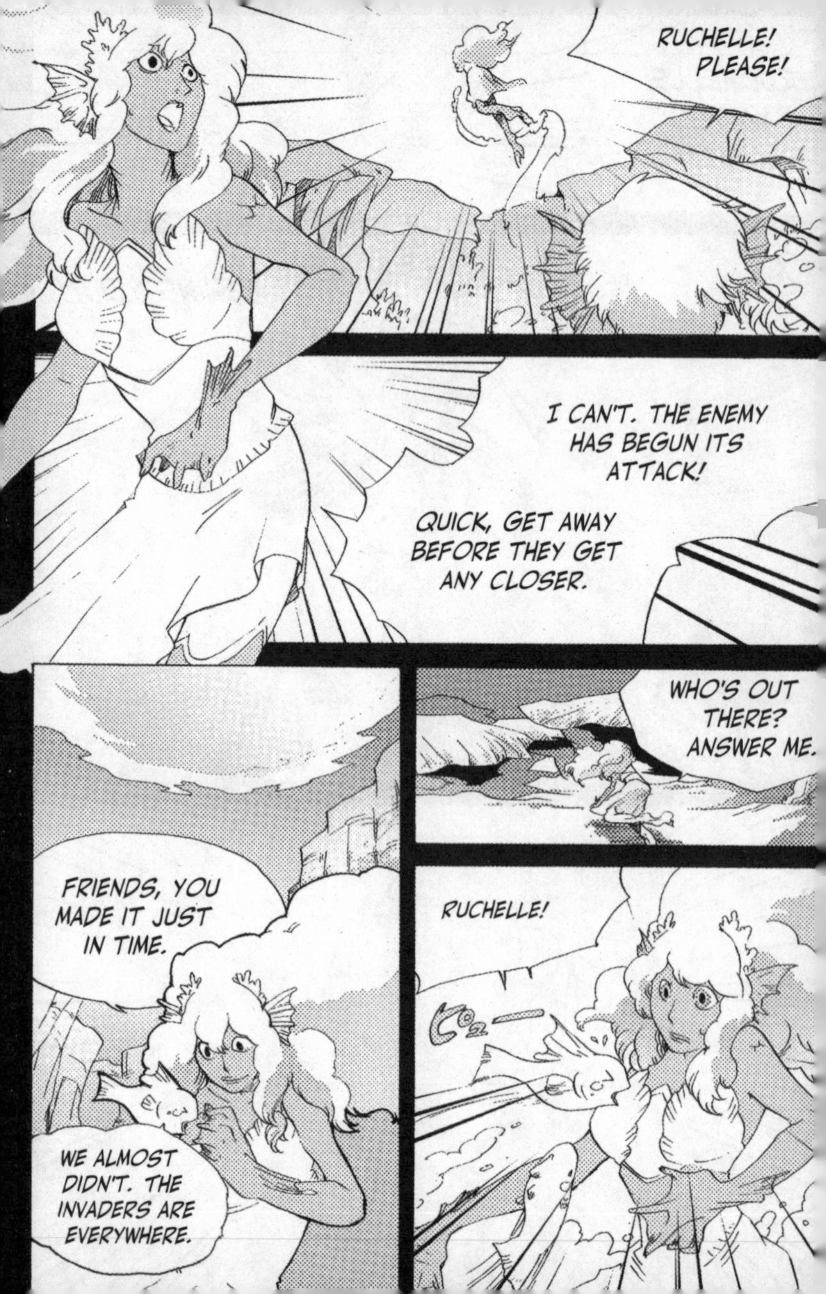
RUCHELLE! PLEASE!
I CAN'T. THE ENEMY HAS BEGUN ITS ATTACK!
QUICK, GET AWAY BEFORE THEY GET ANY CLOSER.
WHO'S OUT THERE? ANSWER ME.
RUCHELLE!
FRIENDS, YOU MADE IT JUST IN TIME.
WE ALMOST DIDN'T. THE INVADERS ARE EVERYWHERE.

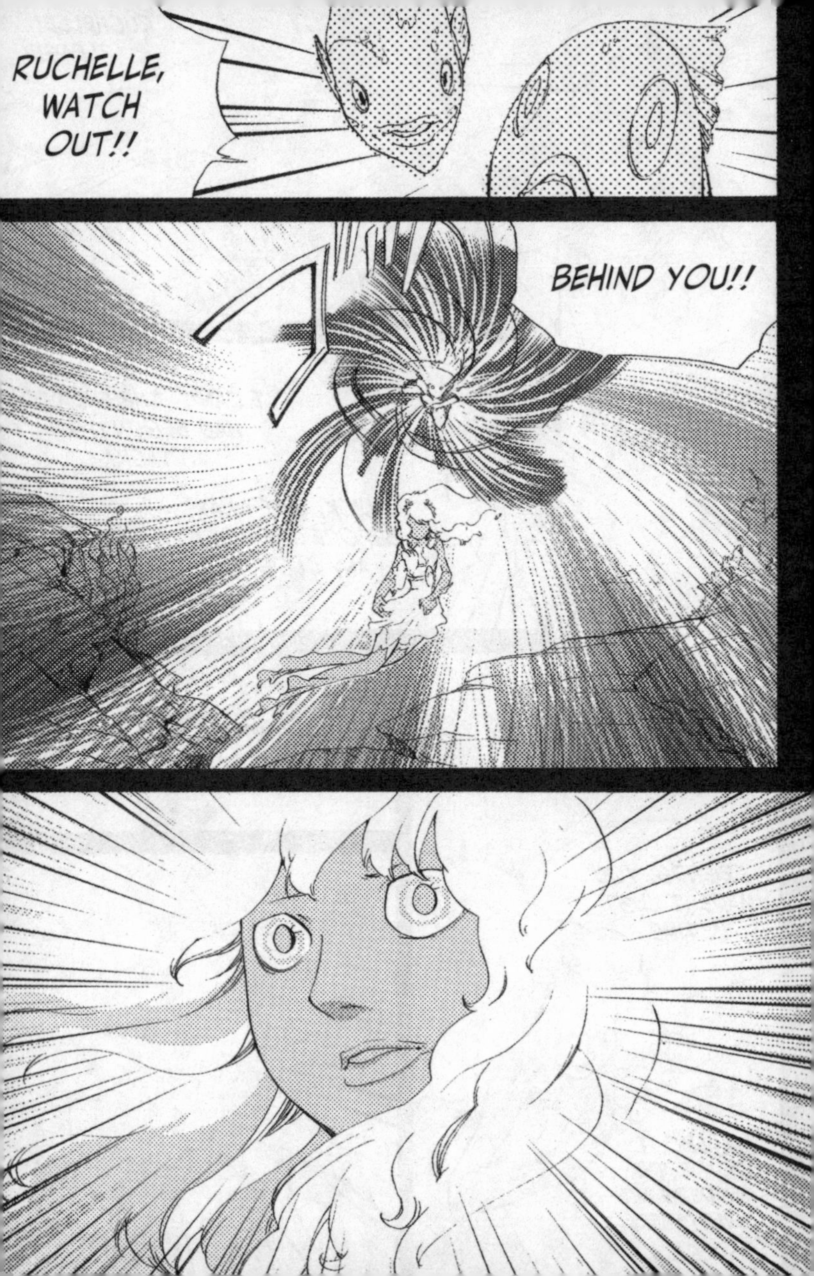
RUCHELLE, WATCH OUT!!
BEHIND YOU!!

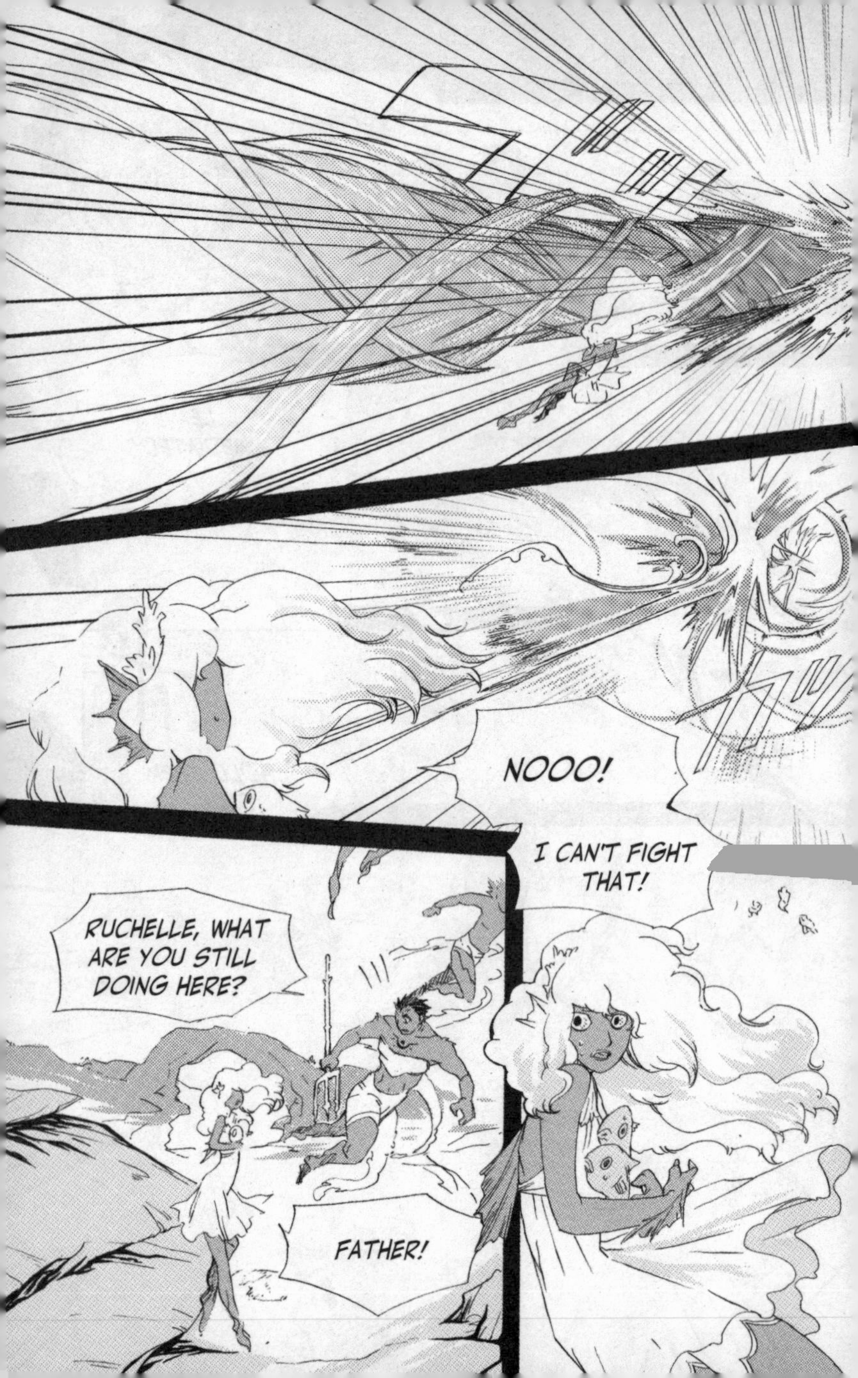
NOOO!
I CAN'T FIGHT THAT!
RUCHELLE, WHAT ARE YOU STILL DOING HERE?
FATHER!

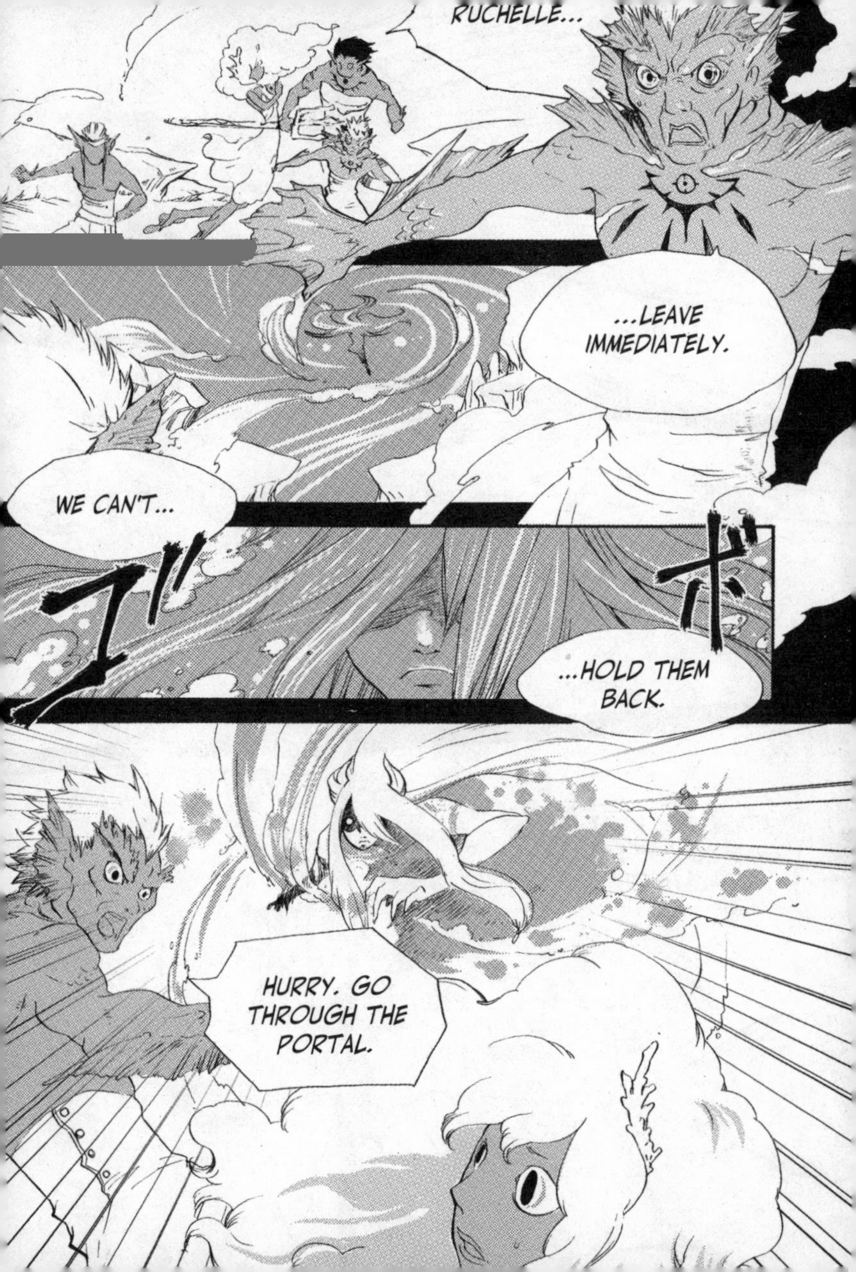
RUCHELLE...
...LEAVE IMMEDIATELY.
WE CAN'T...
ゴボ
...HOLD THEM BACK.
HURRY. GO THROUGH THE PORTAL.

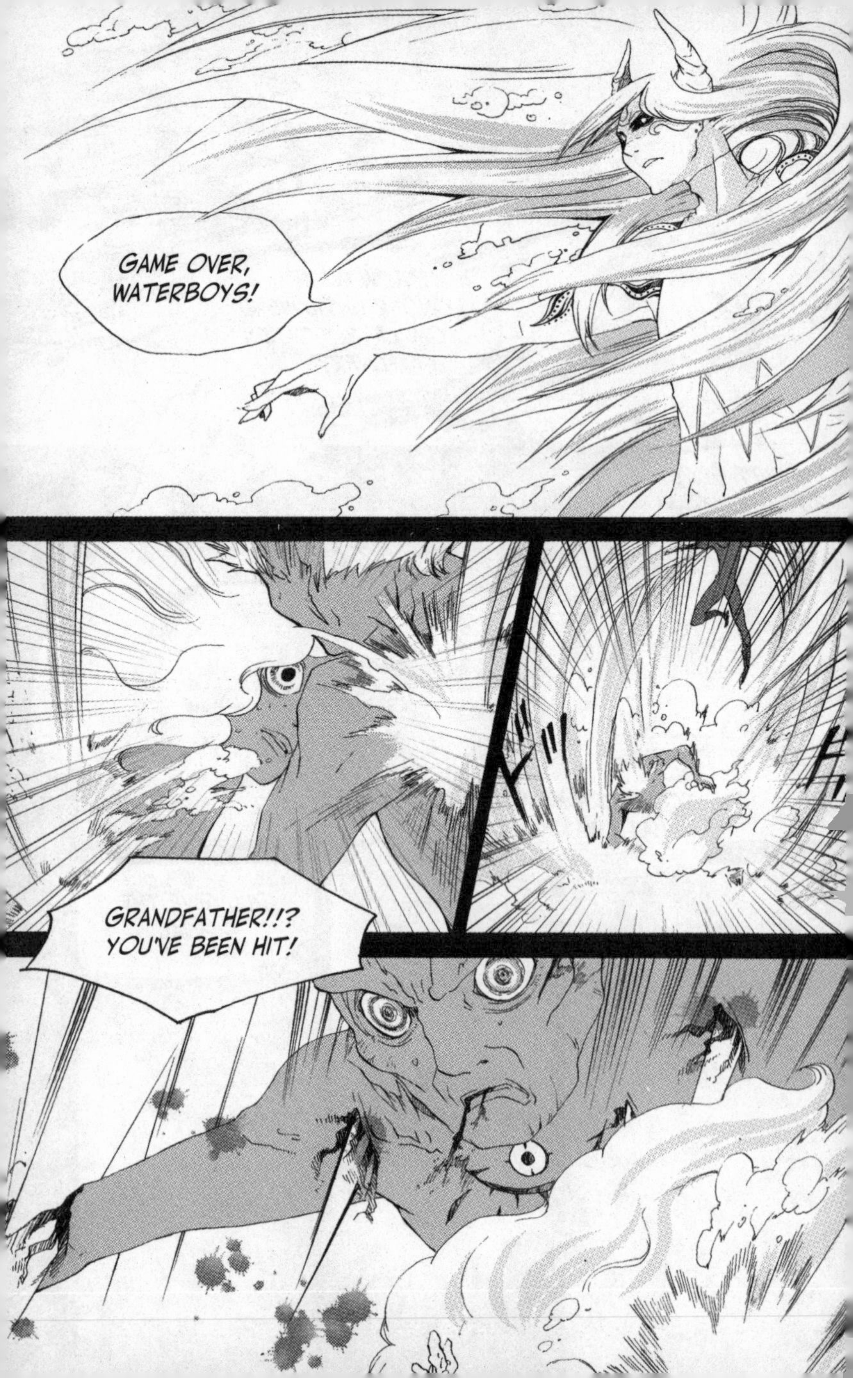
GAME OVER, WATERBOYS!
GRANDFATHER!!? YOU'VE BEEN HIT!

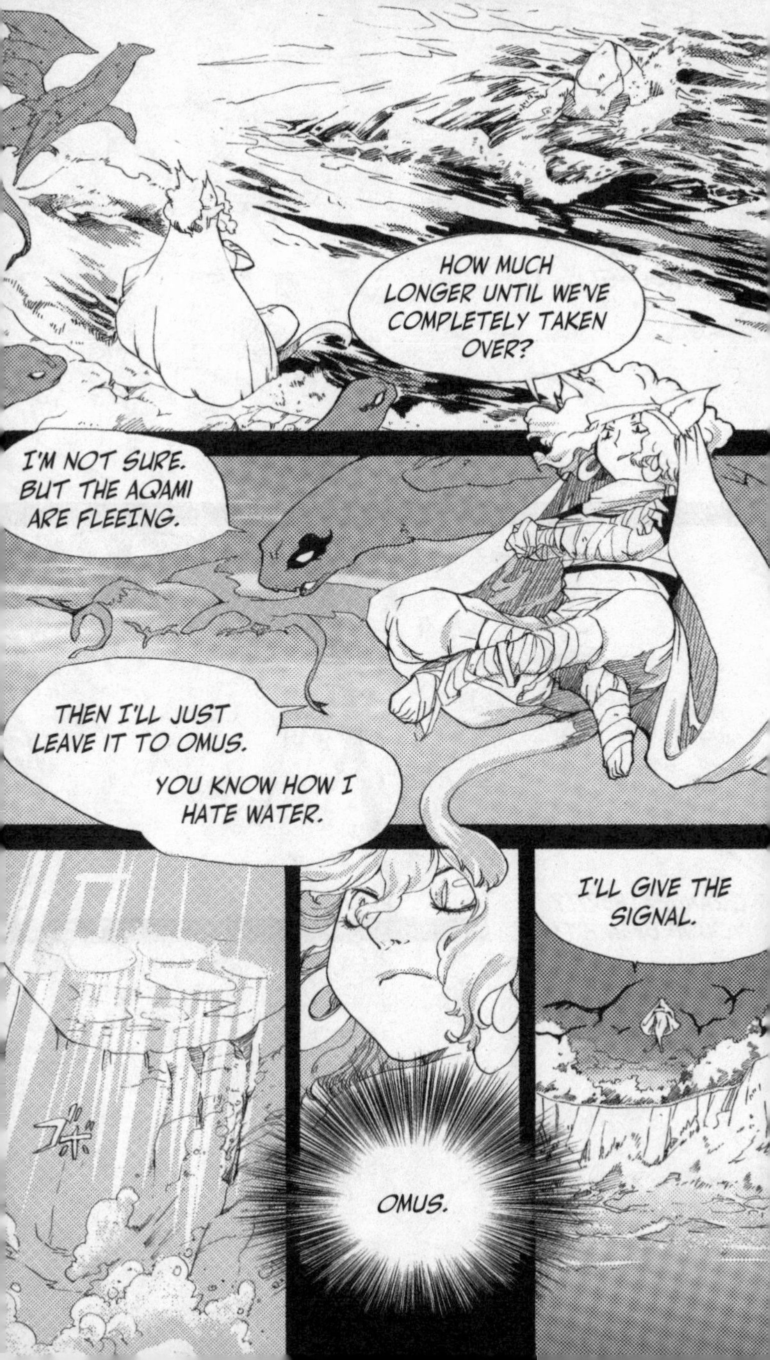
HOW MUCH LONGER UNTIL WE'VE COMPLETELY TAKEN OVER?
I'M NOT SURE. BUT THE AQAMI ARE FLEEING.
THEN I'LL JUST LEAVE IT TO OMUS.
YOU KNOW HOW I HATE WATER.
I'LL GIVE THE SIGNAL.
OMUS.

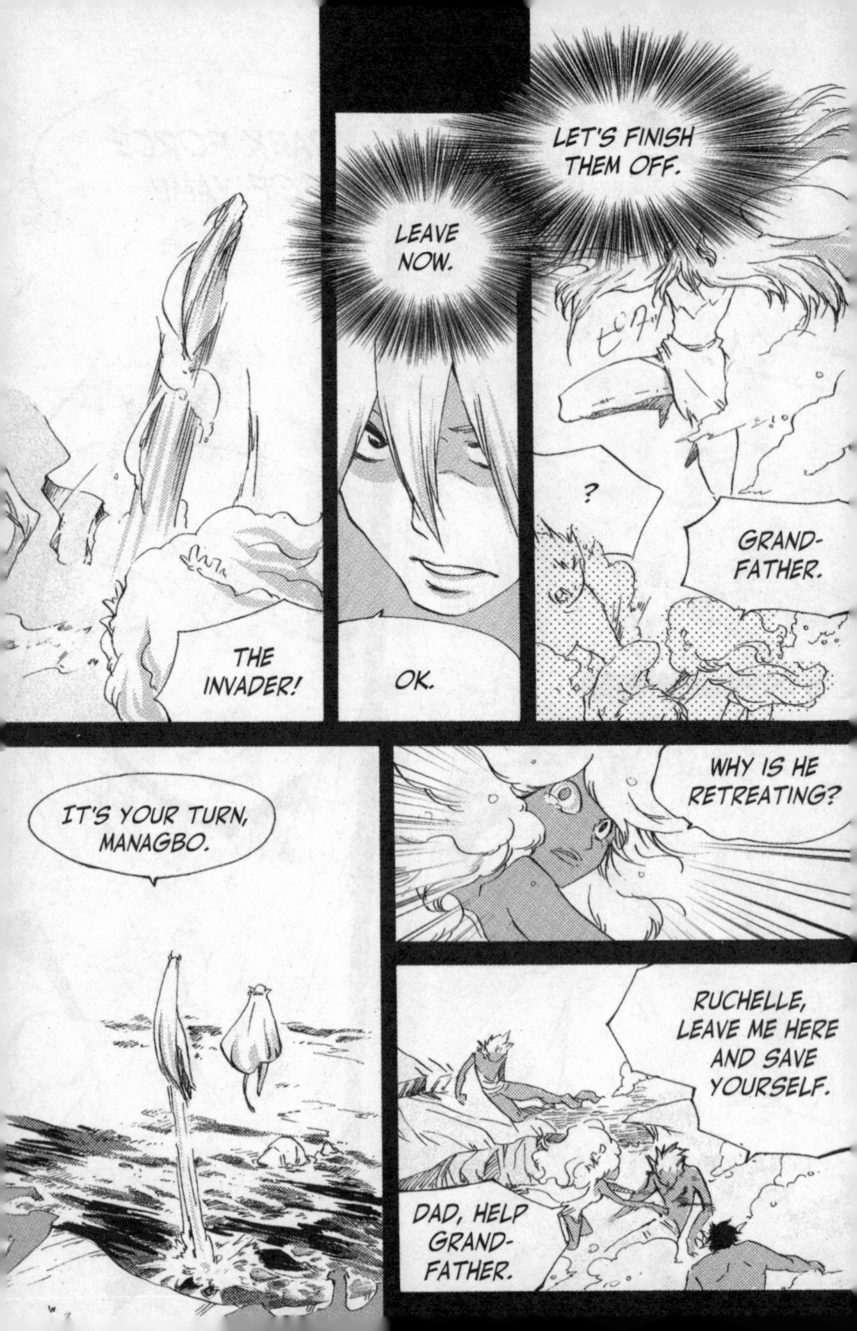
LET'S FINISH THEM OFF.
?
GRAND-FATHER.
LEAVE NOW.
OK.
THE INVADER!
WHY IS HE RETREATING?
RUCHELLE, LEAVE ME HERE AND SAVE YOURSELF.
DAD, HELP GRAND-FATHER.
IT'S YOUR TURN, MANAGBO.

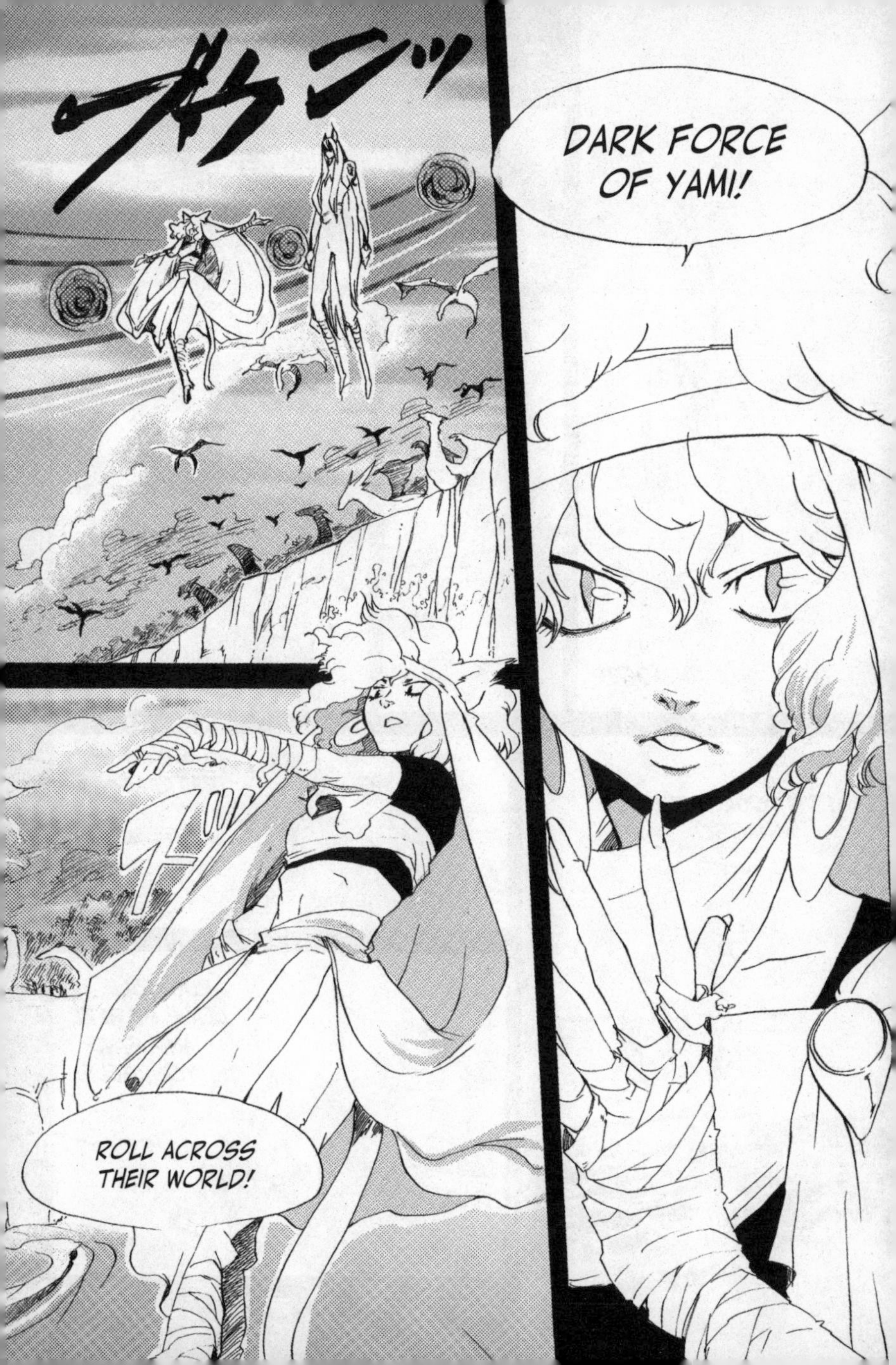
DARK FORCE OF YAMI!
ROLL ACROSS THEIR WORLD!

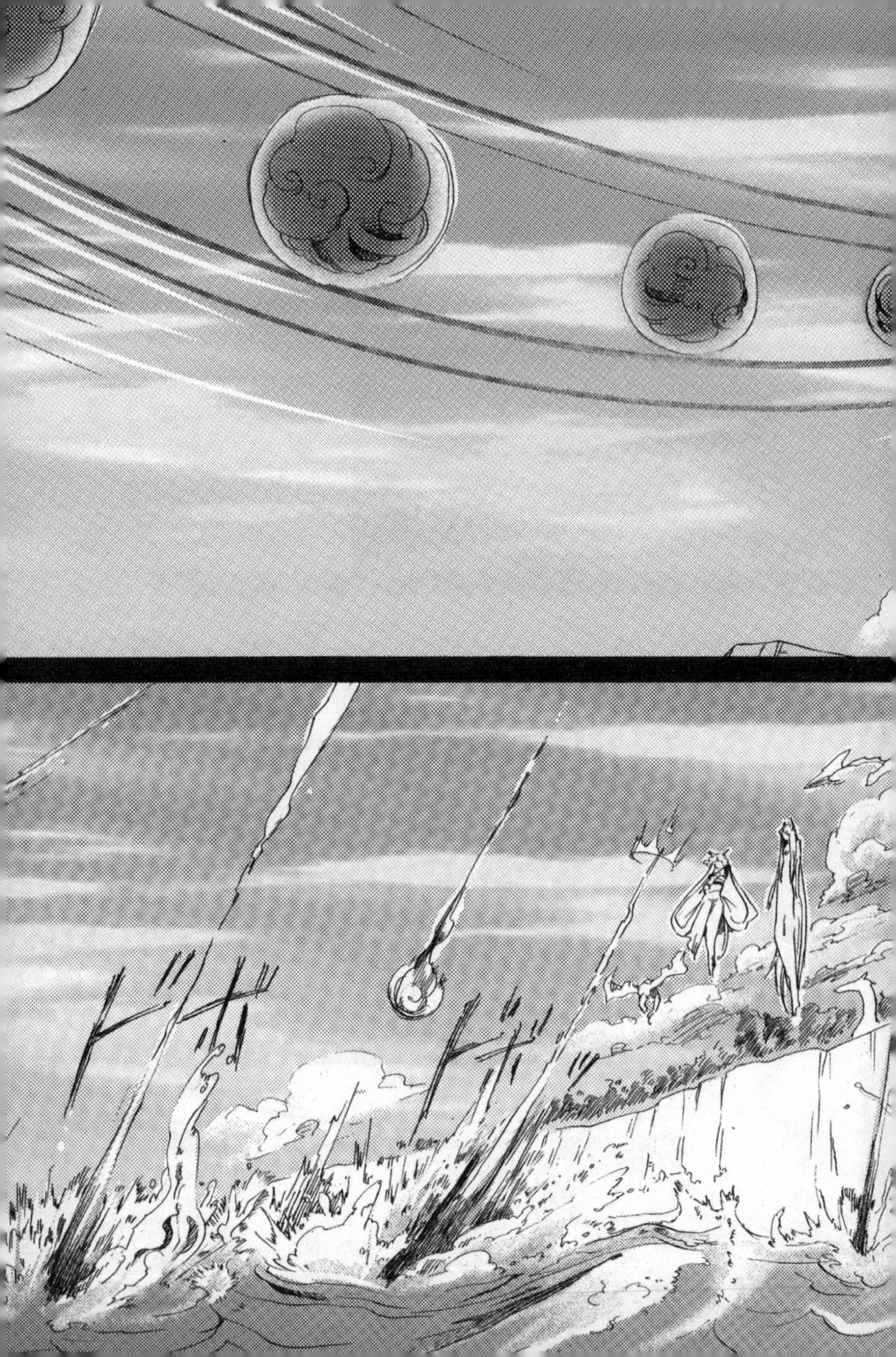
ドガ
ドガ

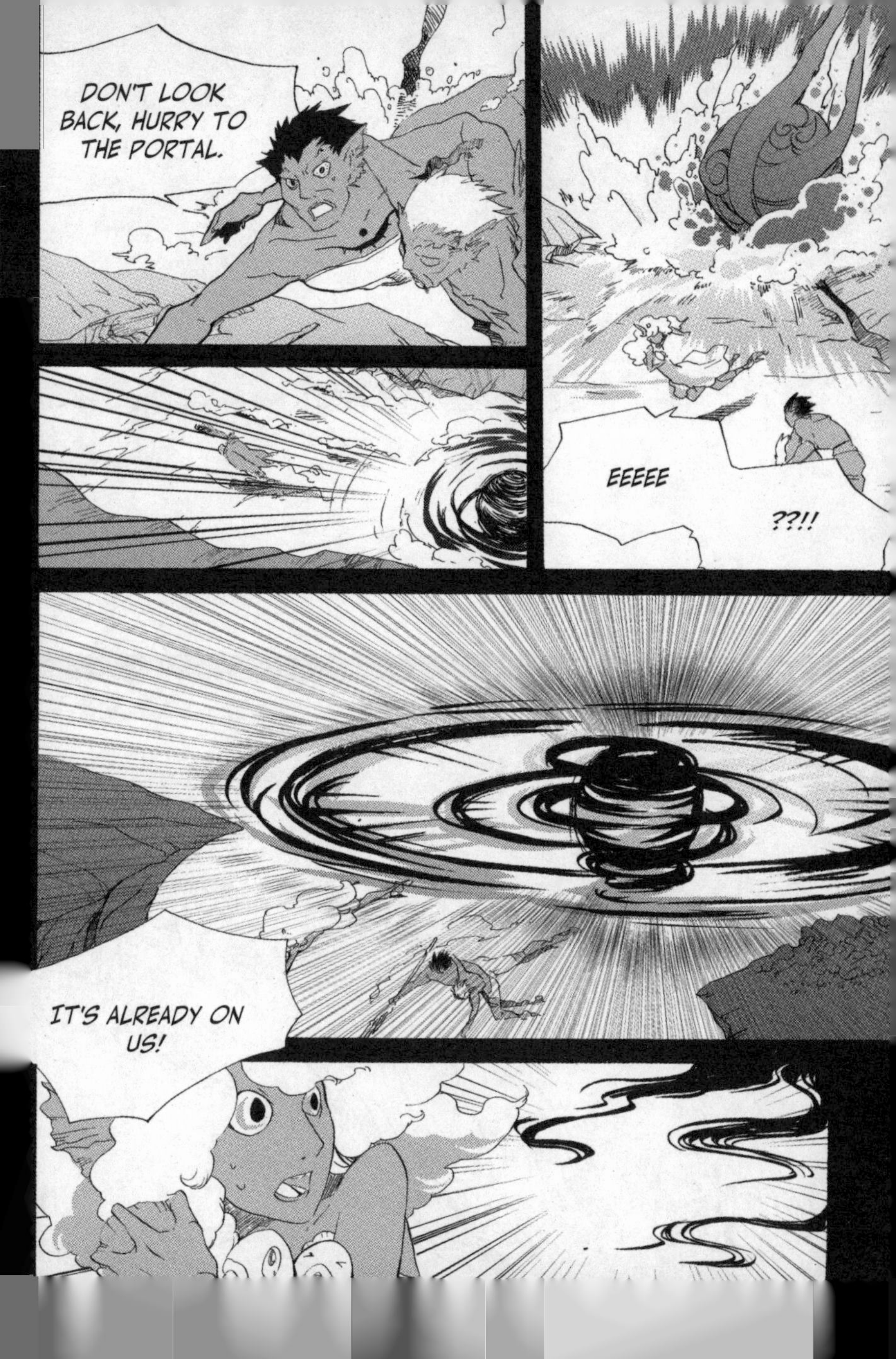
EEEEE
??!!
DON'T LOOK BACK, HURRY TO THE PORTAL.
IT'S ALREADY ON US!

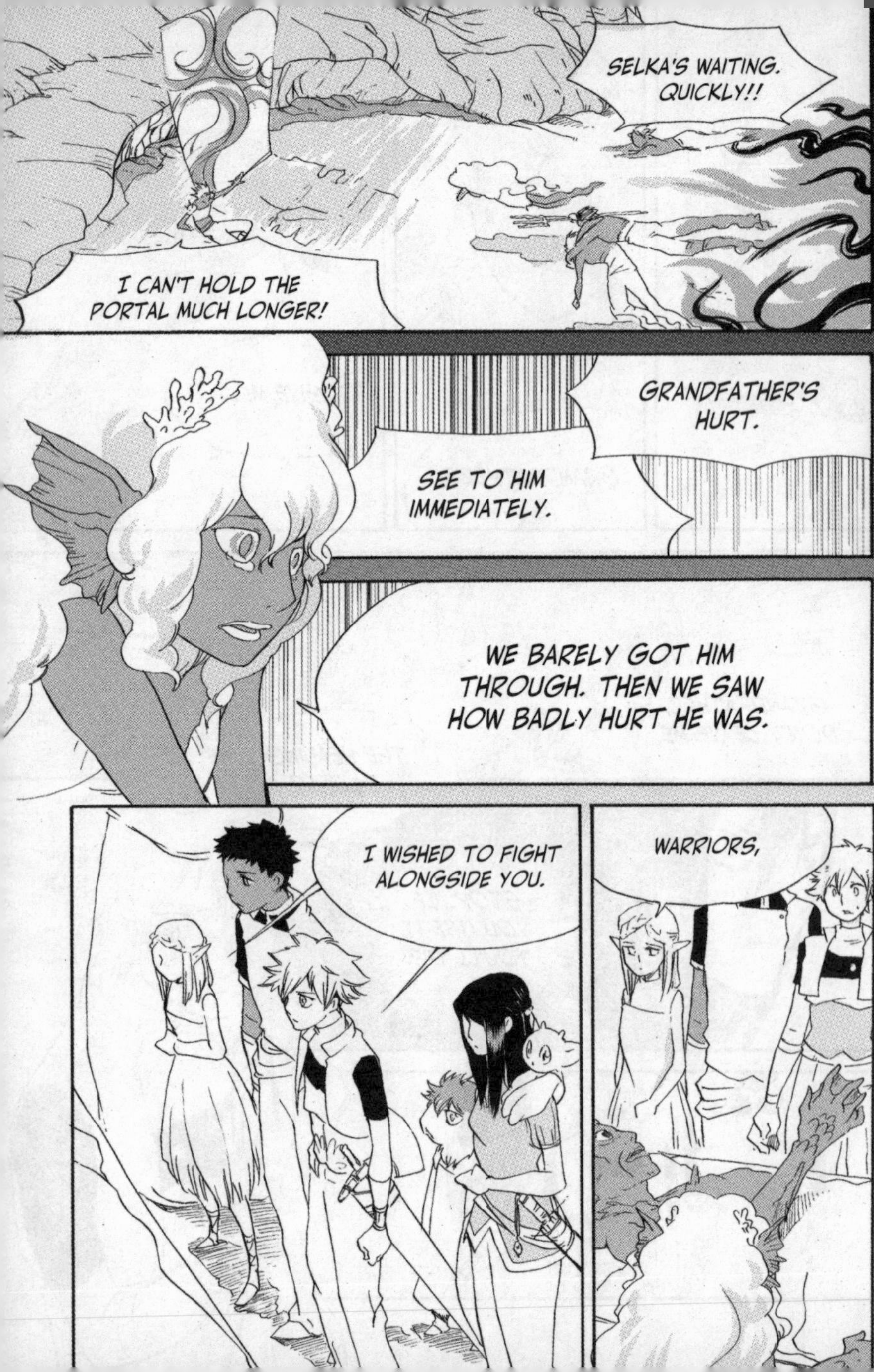
SELKA'S WAITING. QUICKLY!!
I CAN'T HOLD THE PORTAL MUCH LONGER!
GRANDFATHER'S HURT.
SEE TO HIM IMMEDIATELY.
WE BARELY GOT HIM THROUGH. THEN WE SAW HOW BADLY HURT HE WAS.
WARRIORS,
I WISHED TO FIGHT ALONGSIDE YOU.

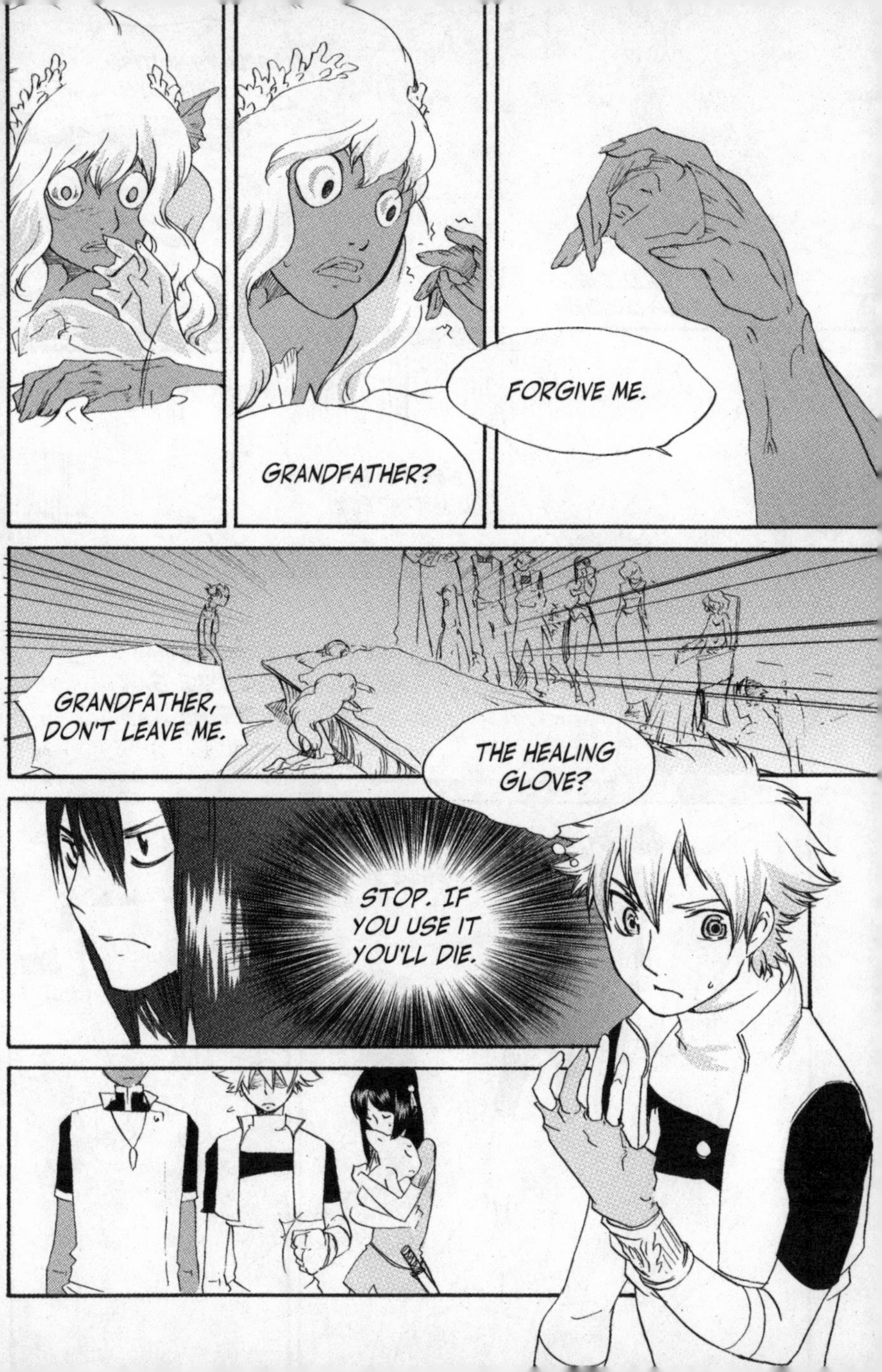
FORGIVE ME.
GRANDFATHER?
GRANDFATHER, DON'T LEAVE ME.
THE HEALING GLOVE?
STOP. IF YOU USE IT YOU'LL DIE.

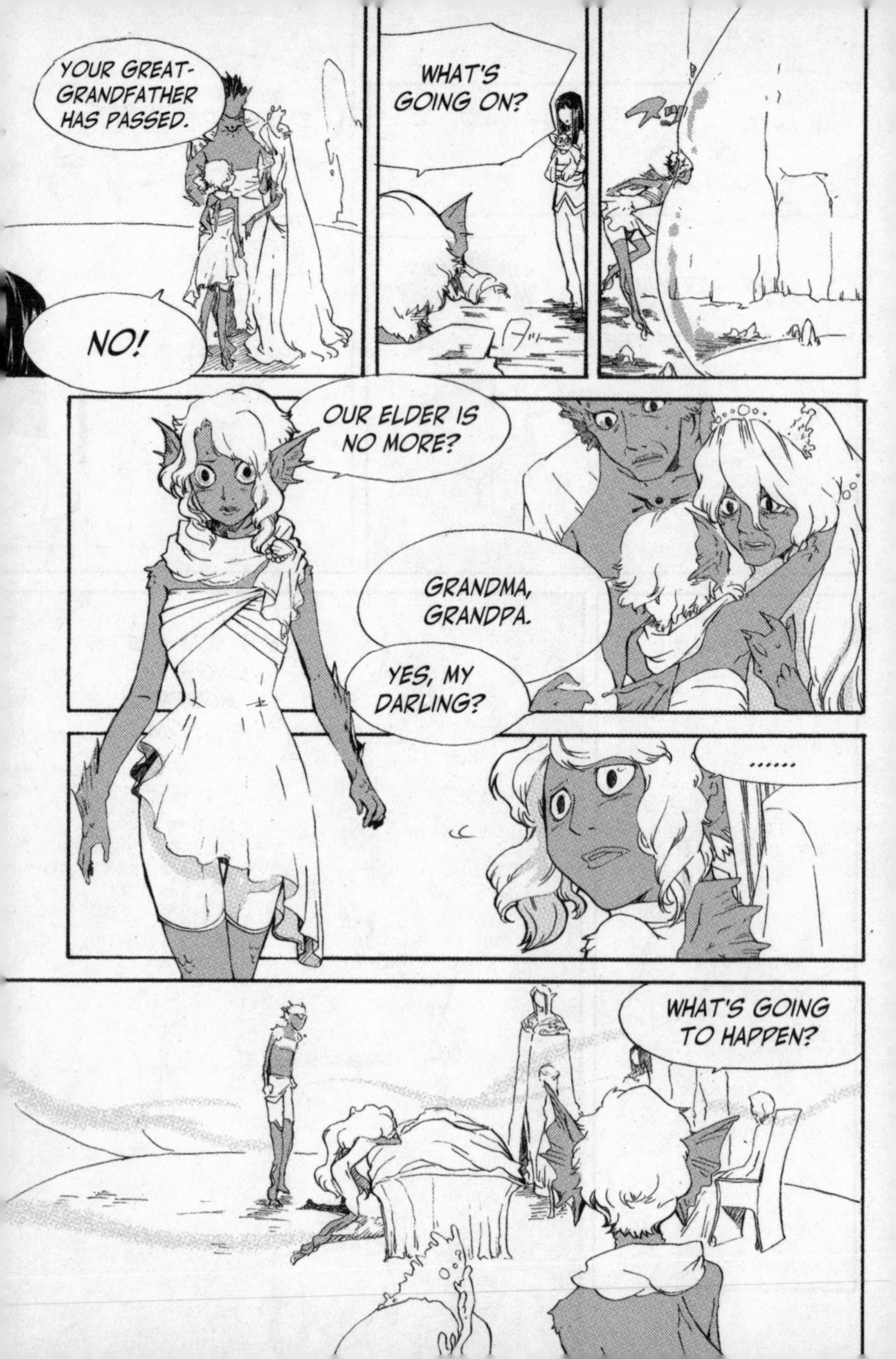
WHAT'S GOING ON?
YOUR GREAT-GRANDFATHER HAS PASSED.
NO!
OUR ELDER IS NO MORE?
GRANDMA, GRANDPA.
YES, MY DARLING?
......
WHAT'S GOING TO HAPPEN?

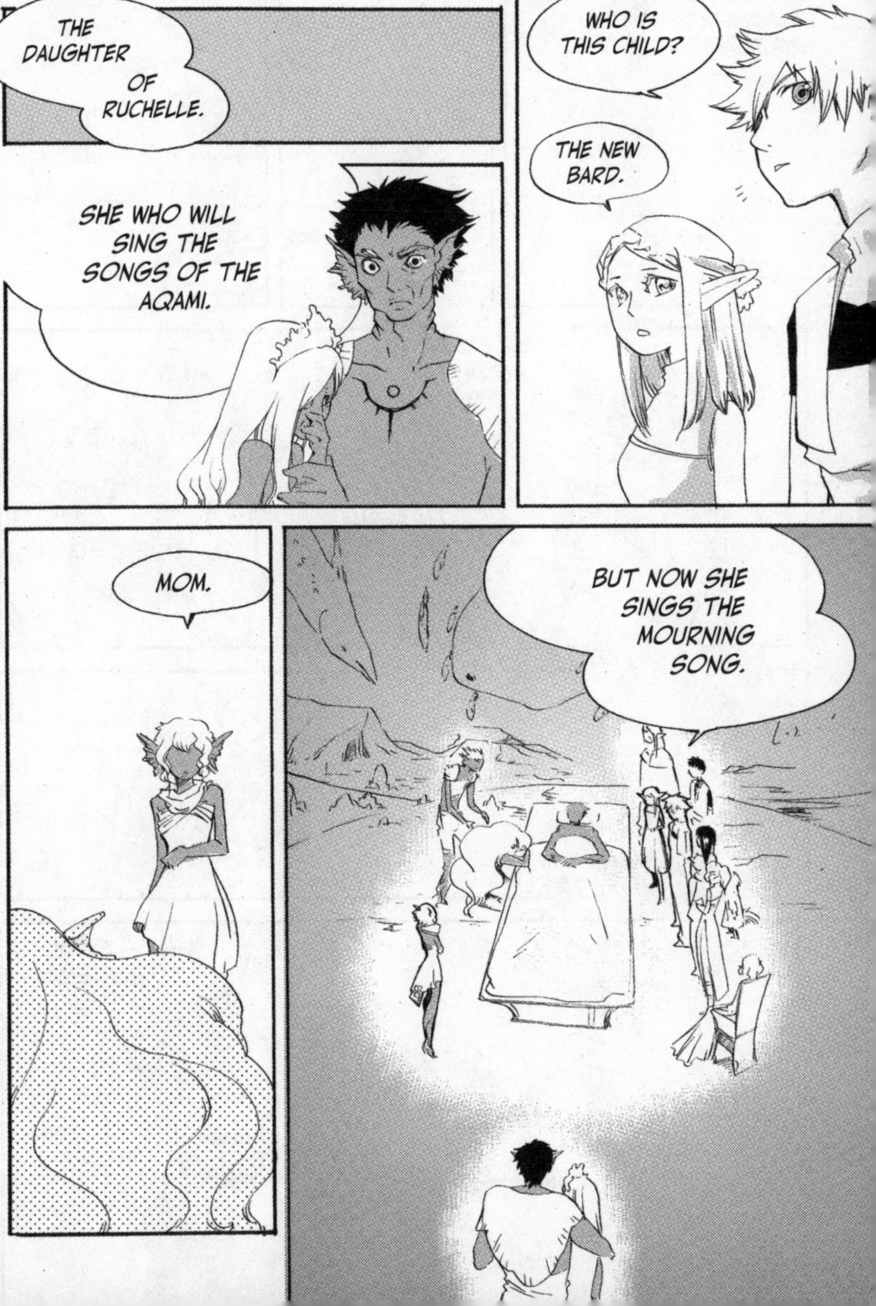
WHO IS THIS CHILD?
THE NEW BARD.
THE DAUGHTER OF RUCHELLE.
SHE WHO WILL SING THE SONGS OF THE AQAMI.
BUT NOW SHE SINGS THE MOURNING SONG.
MOM.

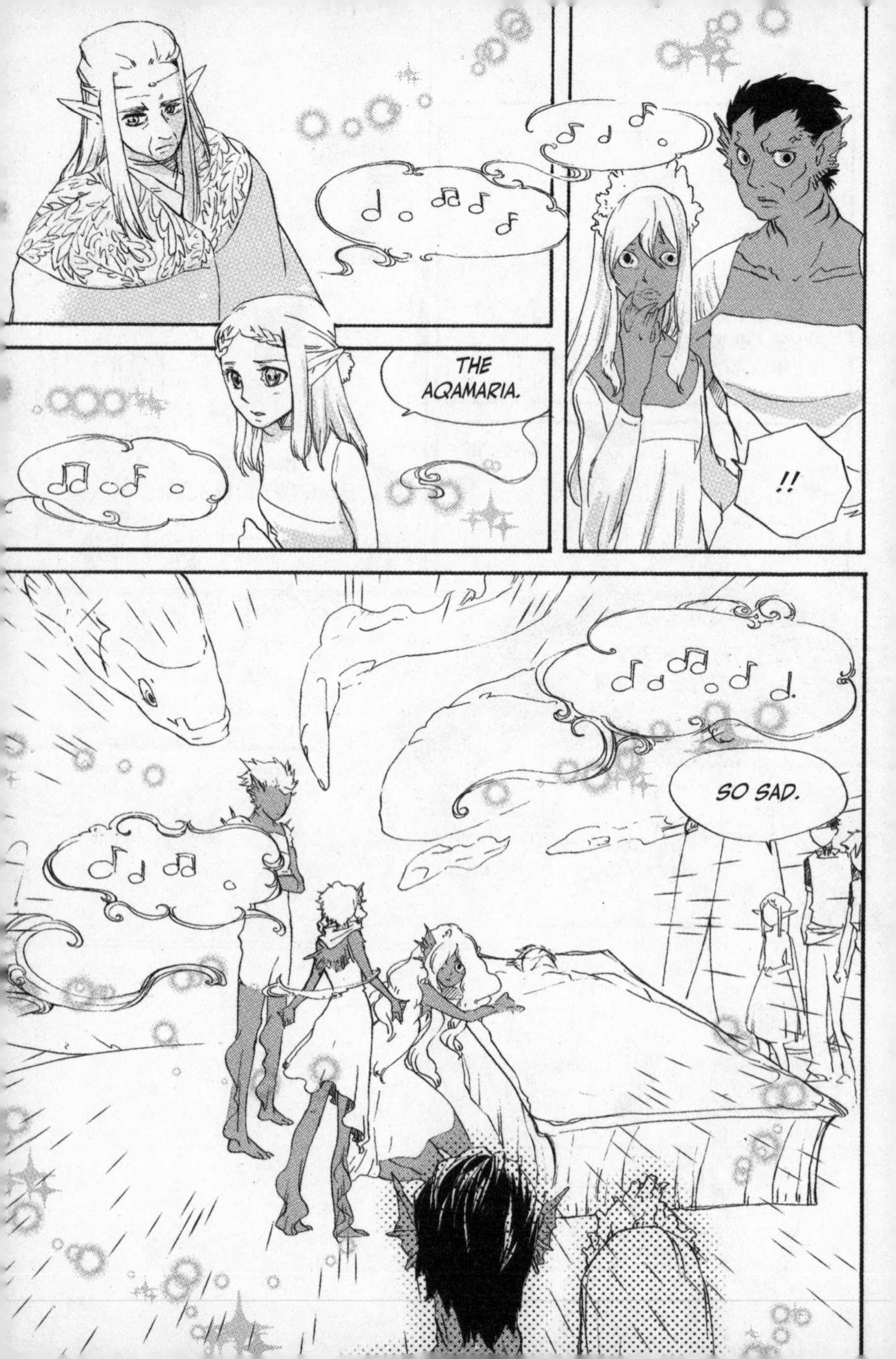
!!
THE AQAMARIA.
SO SAD.

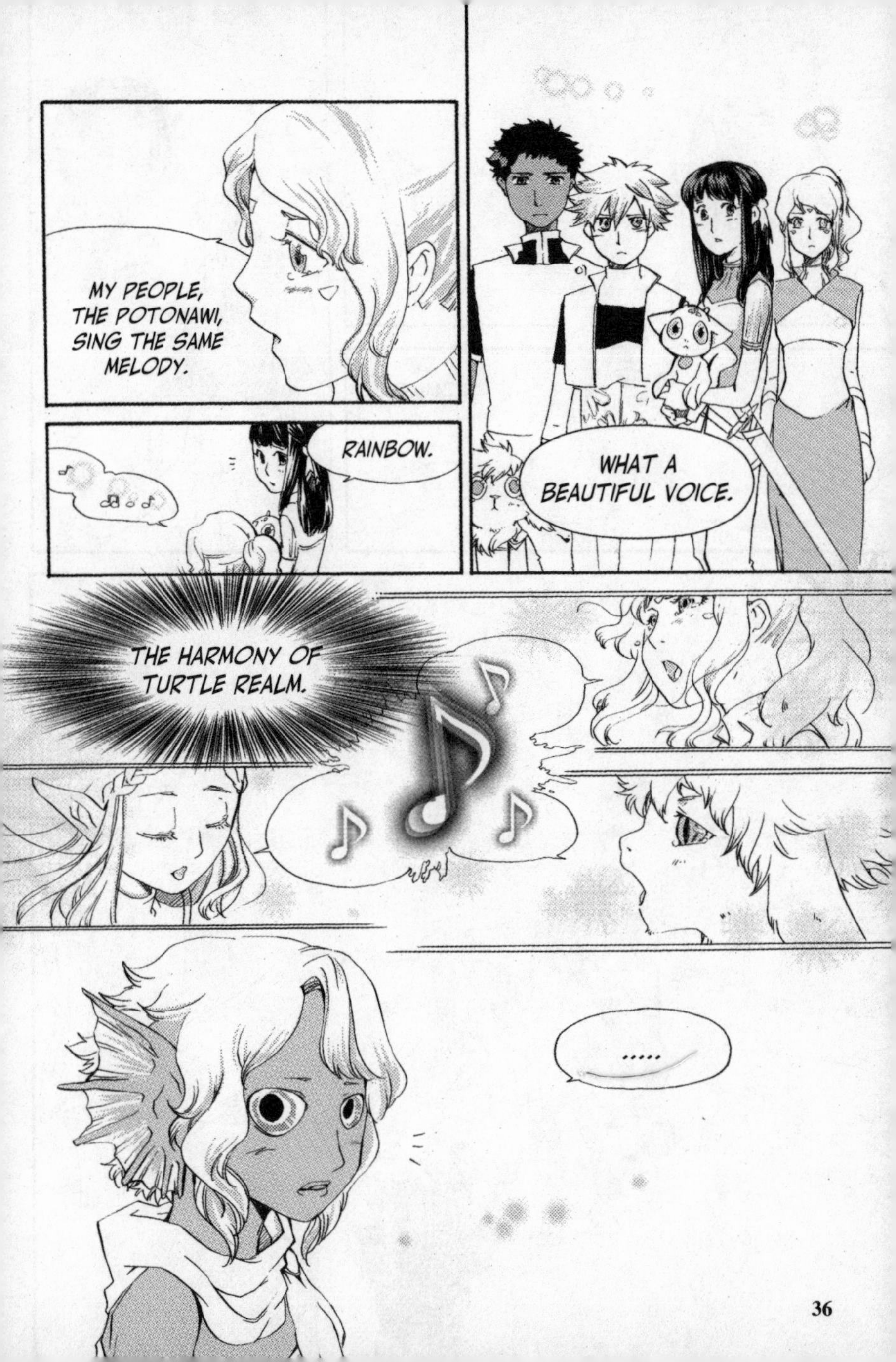
WHAT A BEAUTIFUL VOICE.
MY PEOPLE, THE POTONAWI, SING THE SAME MELODY.
RAINBOW.
THE HARMONY OF TURTLE REALM.
......

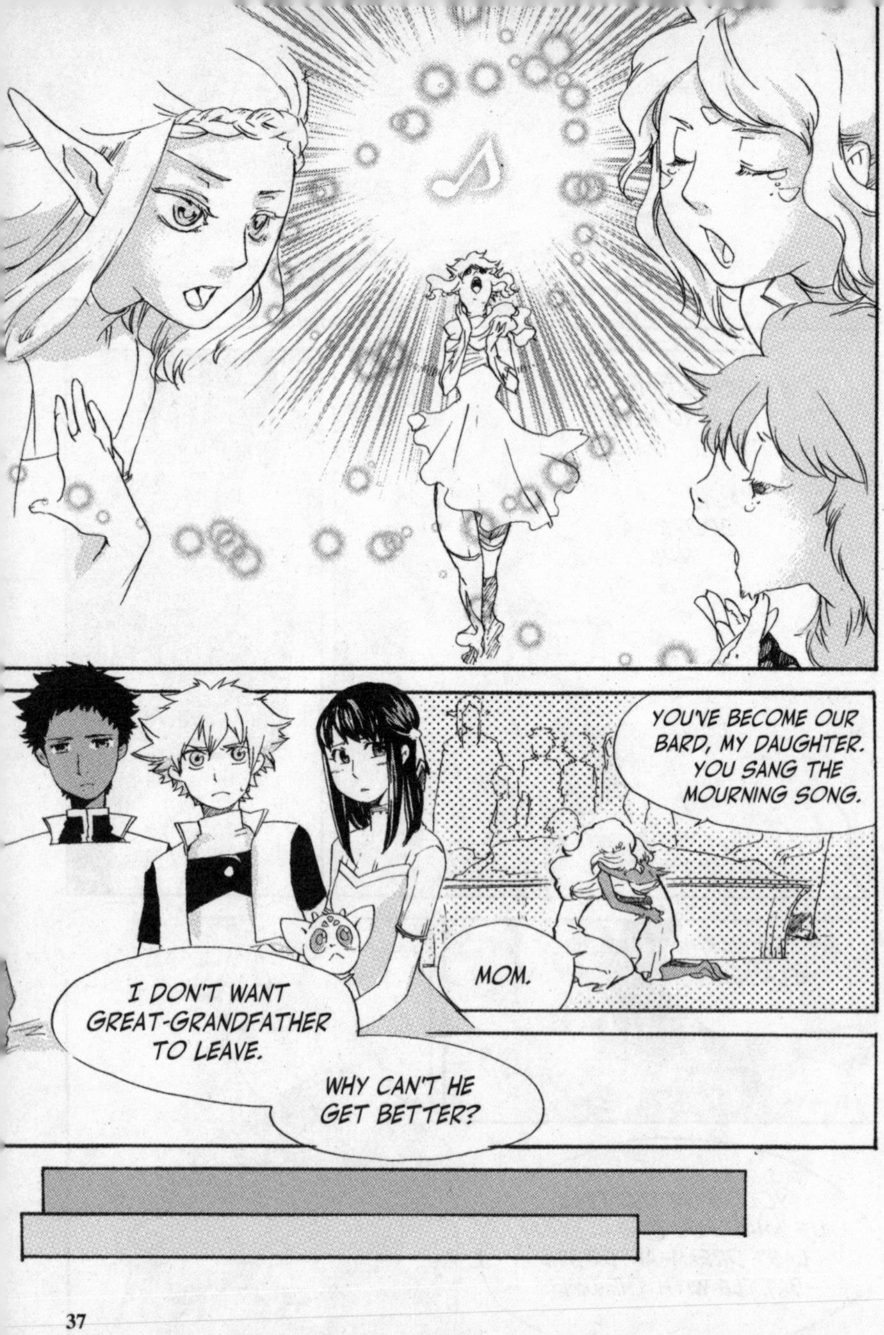
YOU'VE BECOME OUR BARD, MY DAUGHTER. YOU SANG THE MOURNING SONG.
MOM.
I DON'T WANT GREAT-GRANDFATHER TO LEAVE.
WHY CAN'T HE GET BETTER?

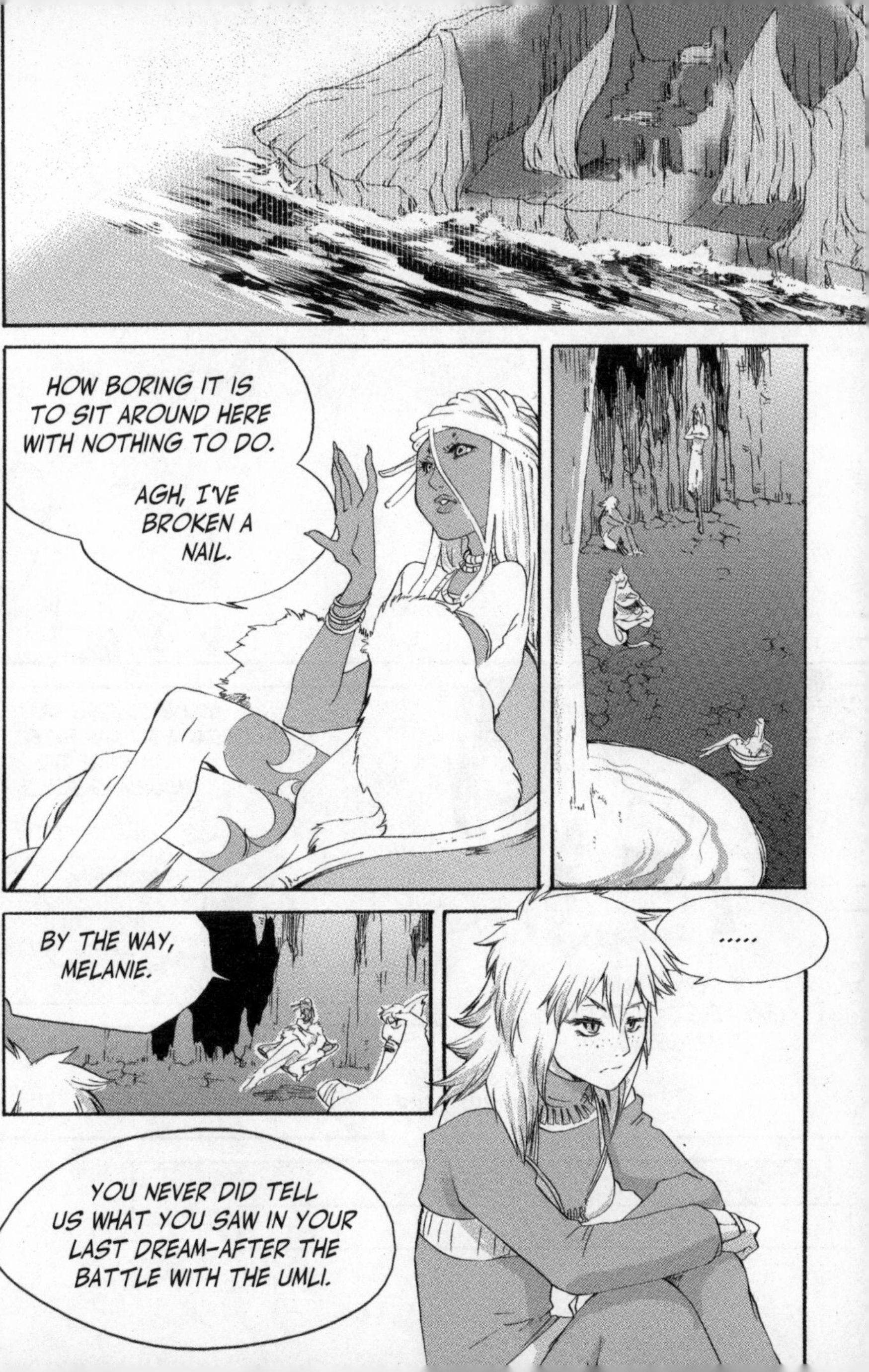
HOW BORING IT IS TO SIT AROUND HERE WITH NOTHING TO DO.
AGH, I'VE BROKEN A NAIL.
.....
BY THE WAY, MELANIE.
YOU NEVER DID TELL US WHAT YOU SAW IN YOUR LAST DREAM–AFTER THE BATTLE WITH THE UMLI.

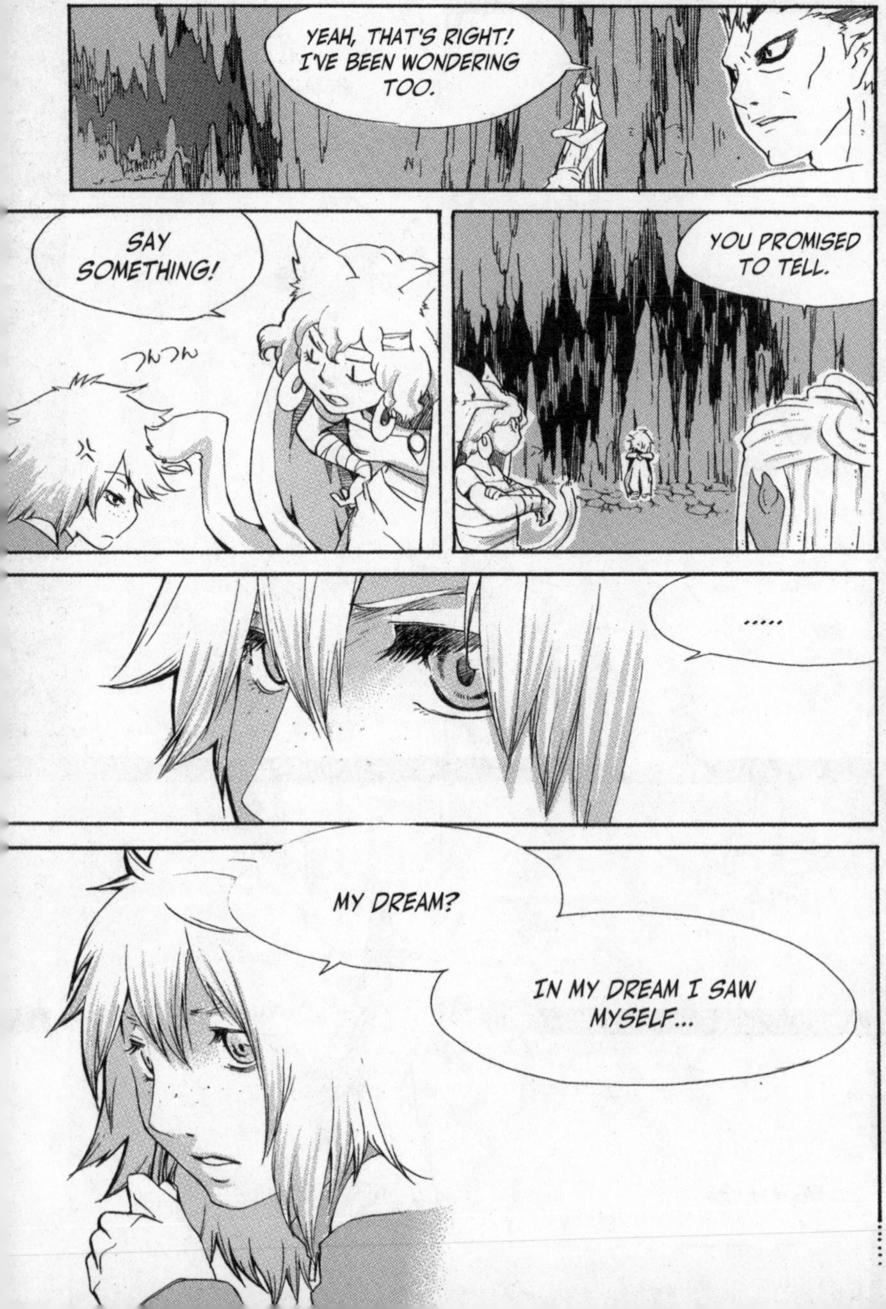
YEAH, THAT'S RIGHT! I'VE BEEN WONDERING TOO.
YOU PROMISED TO TELL.
SAY SOMETHING!
つんつん
.....
MY DREAM?
IN MY DREAM I SAW MYSELF...

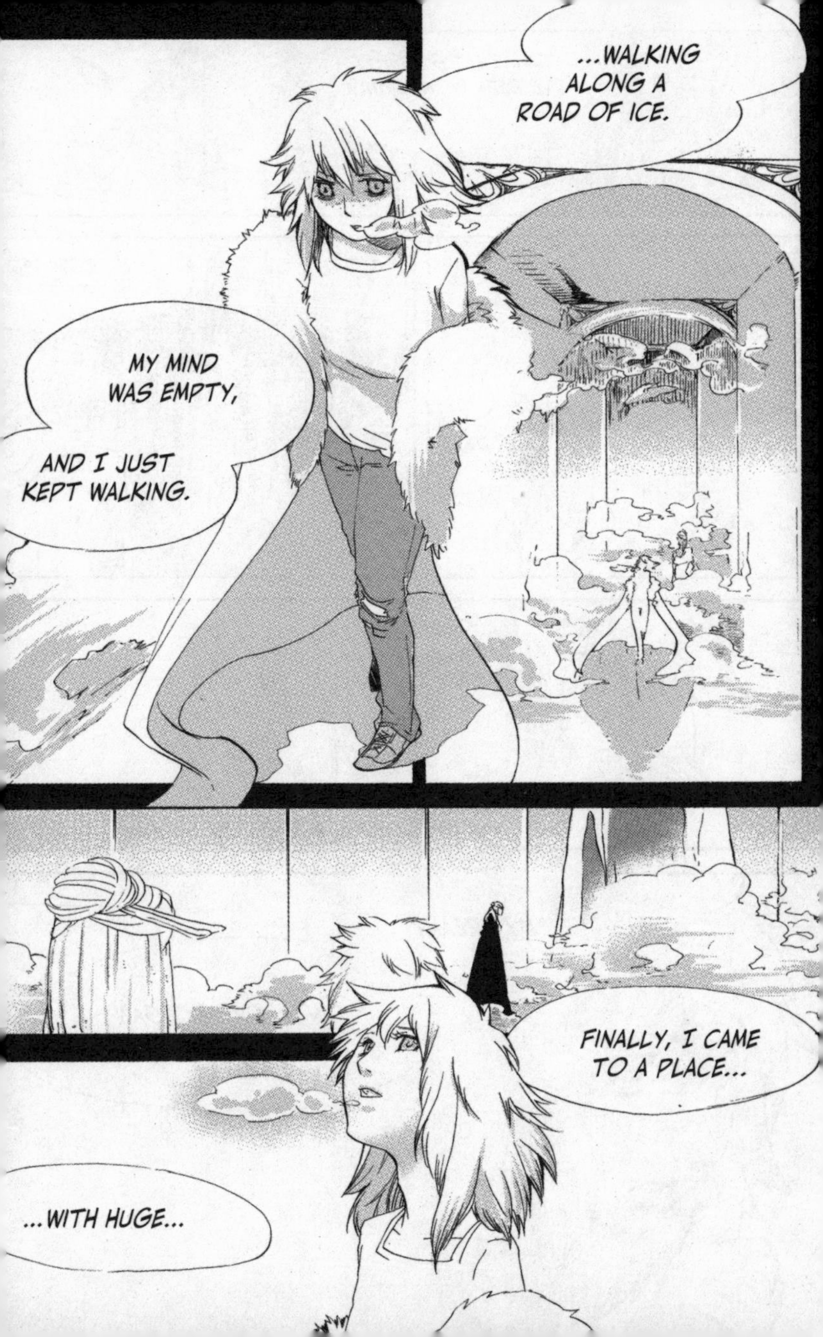
MY MIND WAS EMPTY,
AND I JUST KEPT WALKING.
...WALKING ALONG A ROAD OF ICE.
FINALLY, I CAME TO A PLACE...
...WITH HUGE...

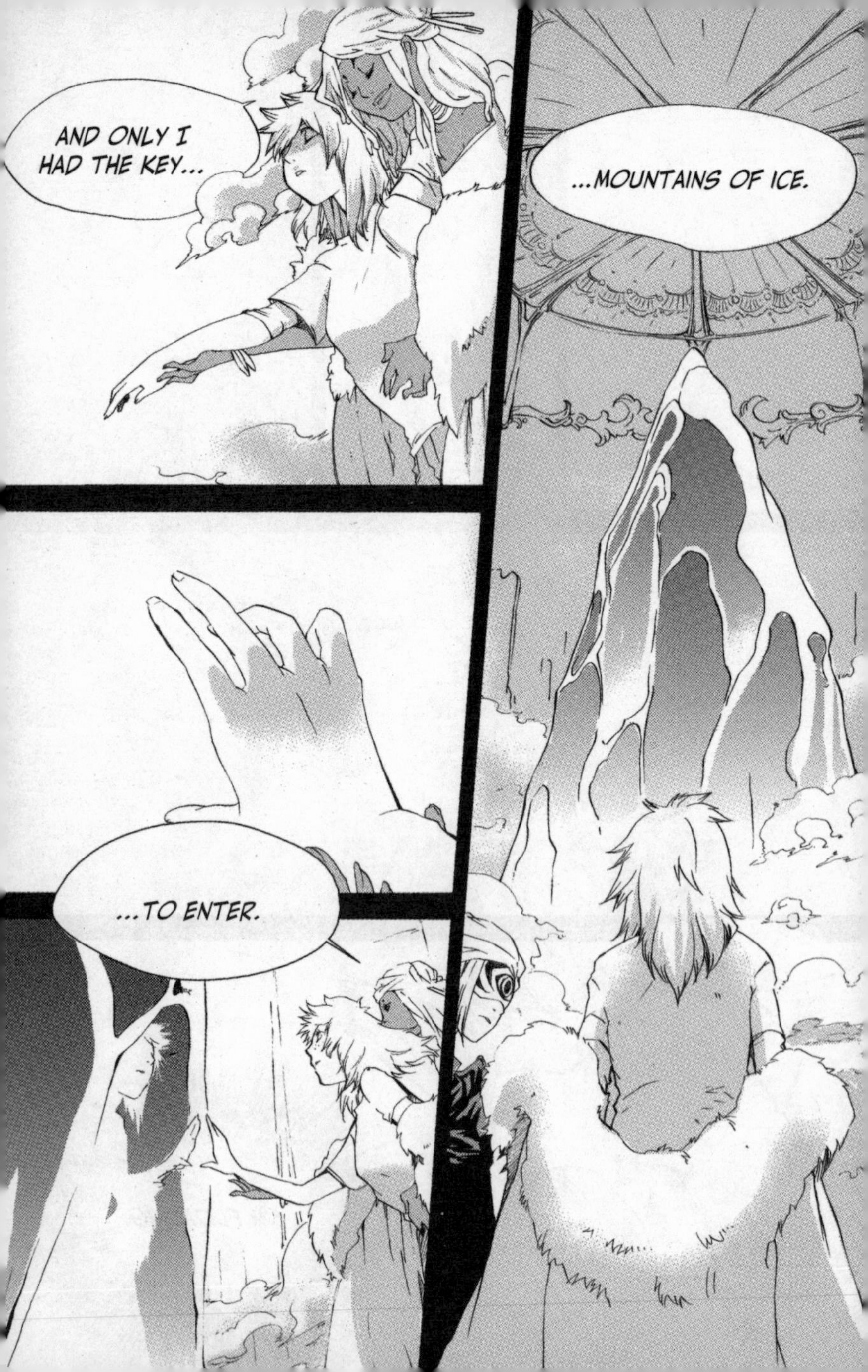
...MOUNTAINS OF ICE.
AND ONLY I HAD THE KEY...
...TO ENTER.

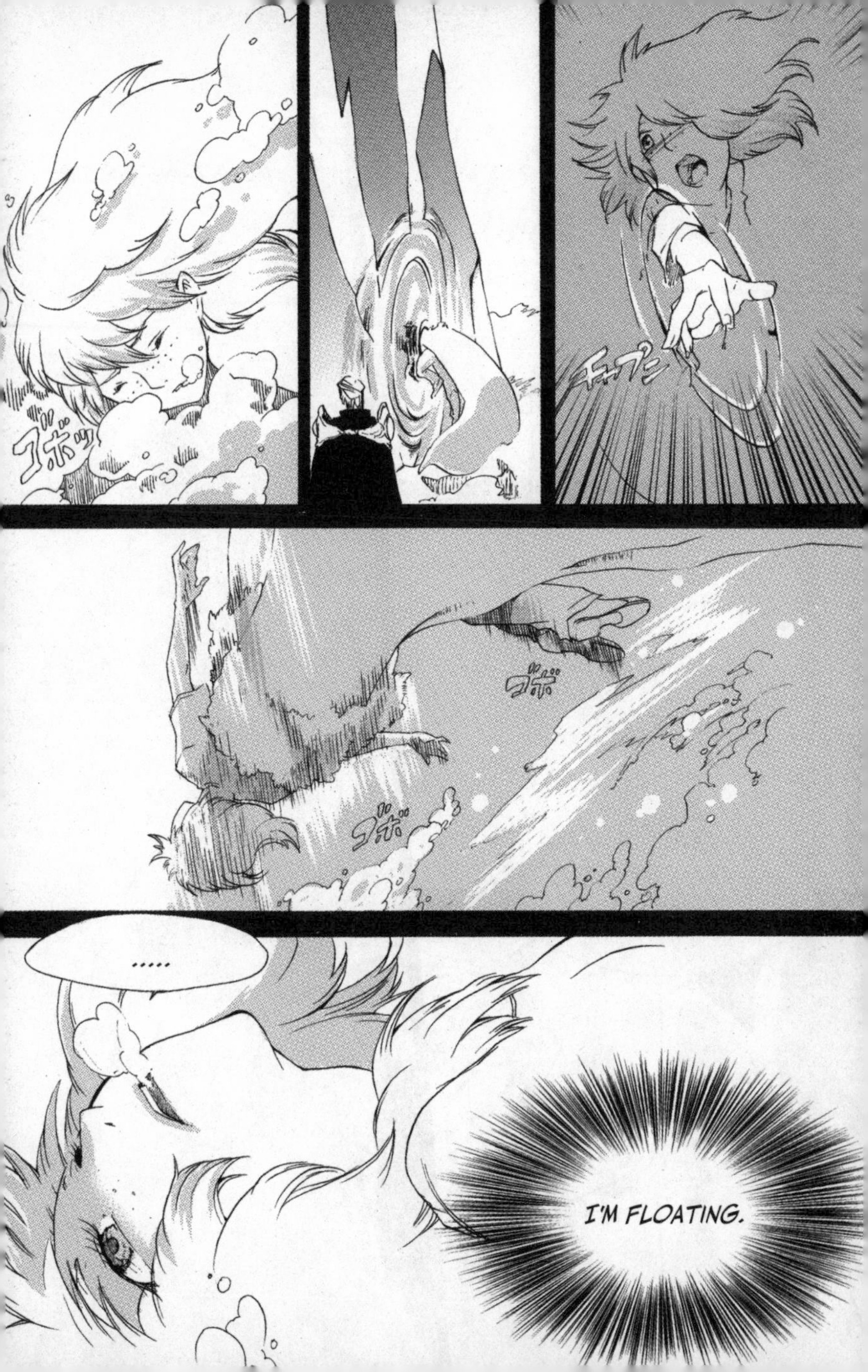
チャプン
ゴボッ
ゴボ
ゴボ
......
I'M FLOATING.

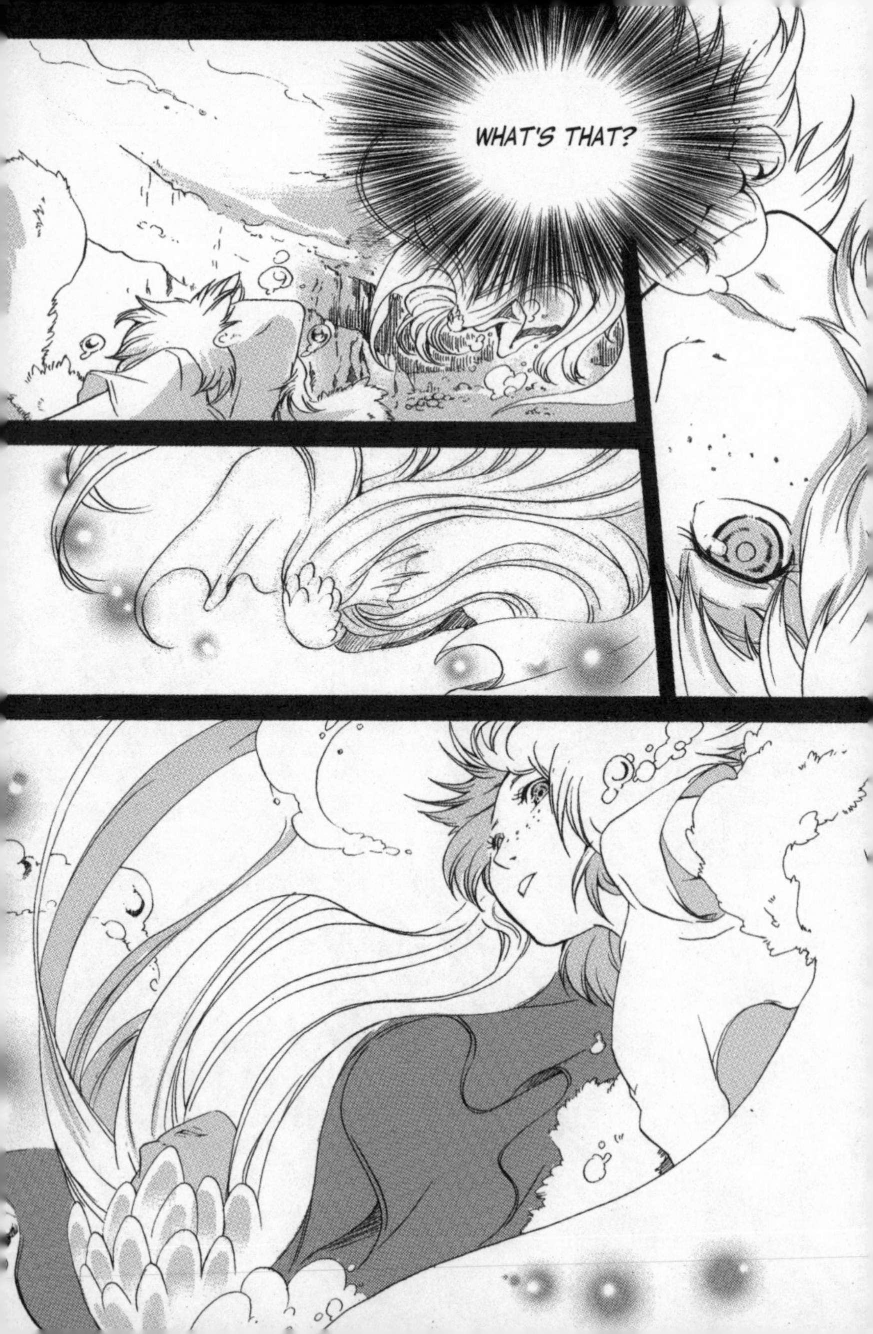
WHAT'S THAT?

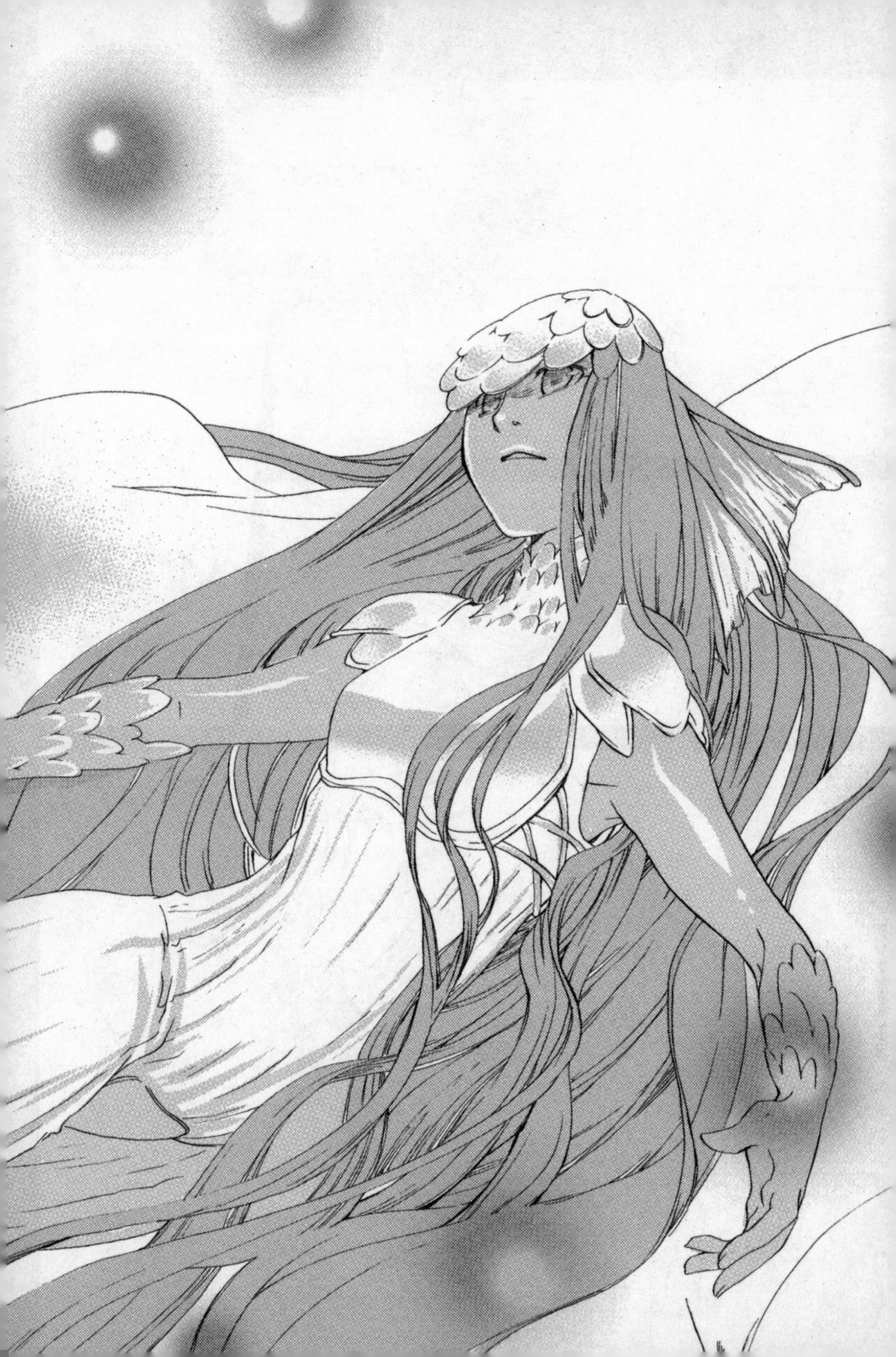

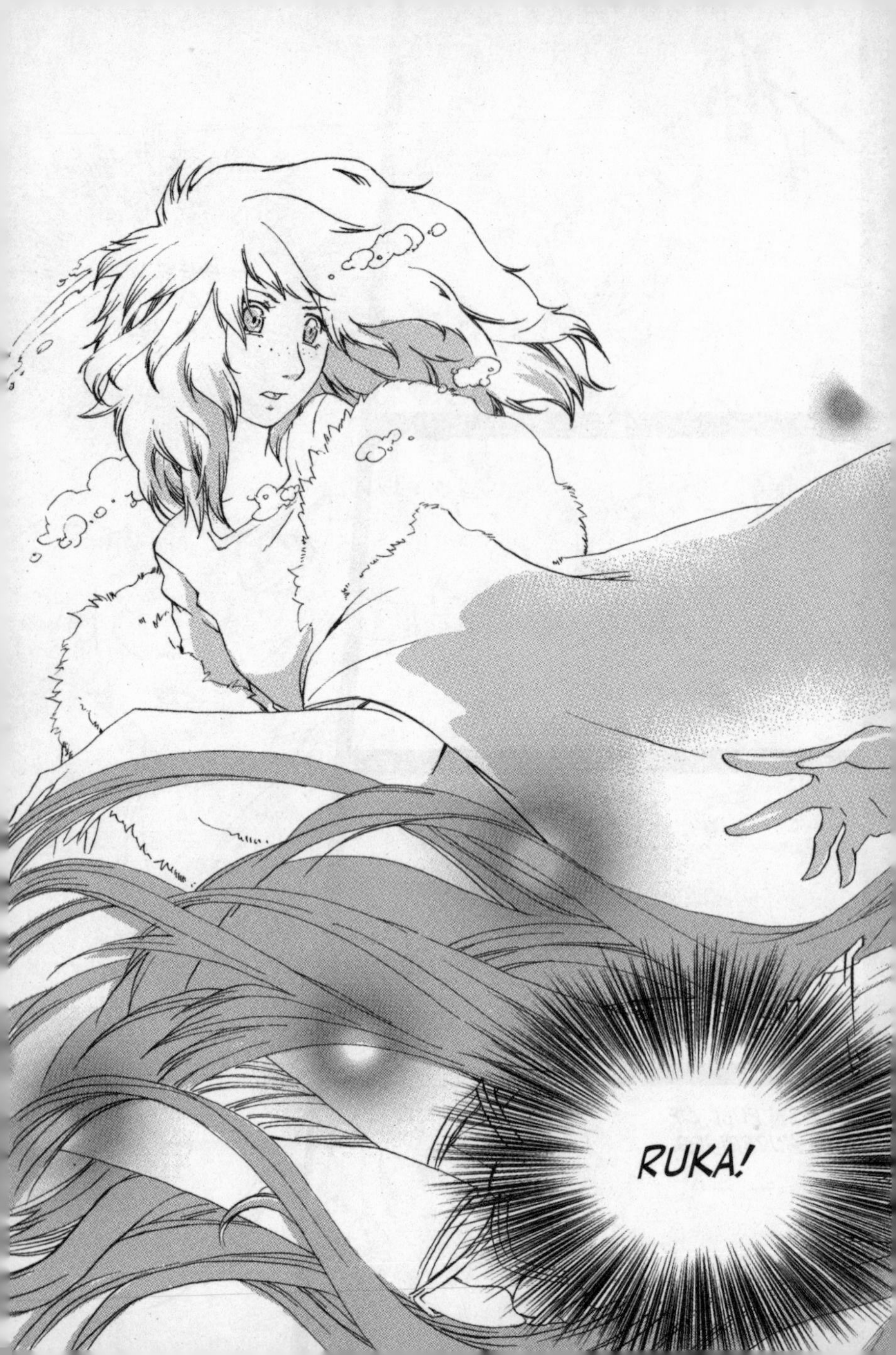
RUKA!

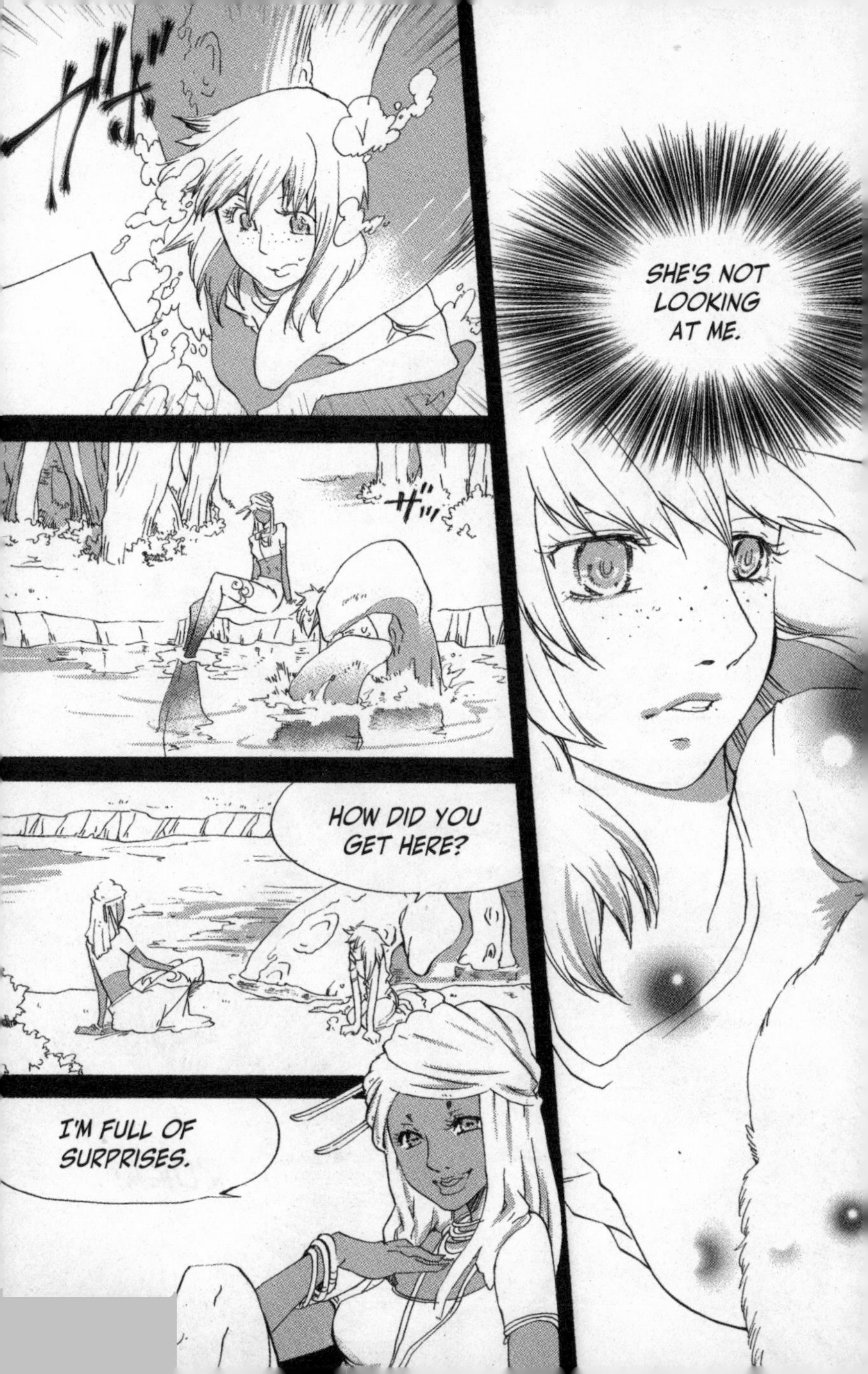
SHE'S NOT LOOKING AT ME.
HOW DID YOU GET HERE?
I'M FULL OF SURPRISES.

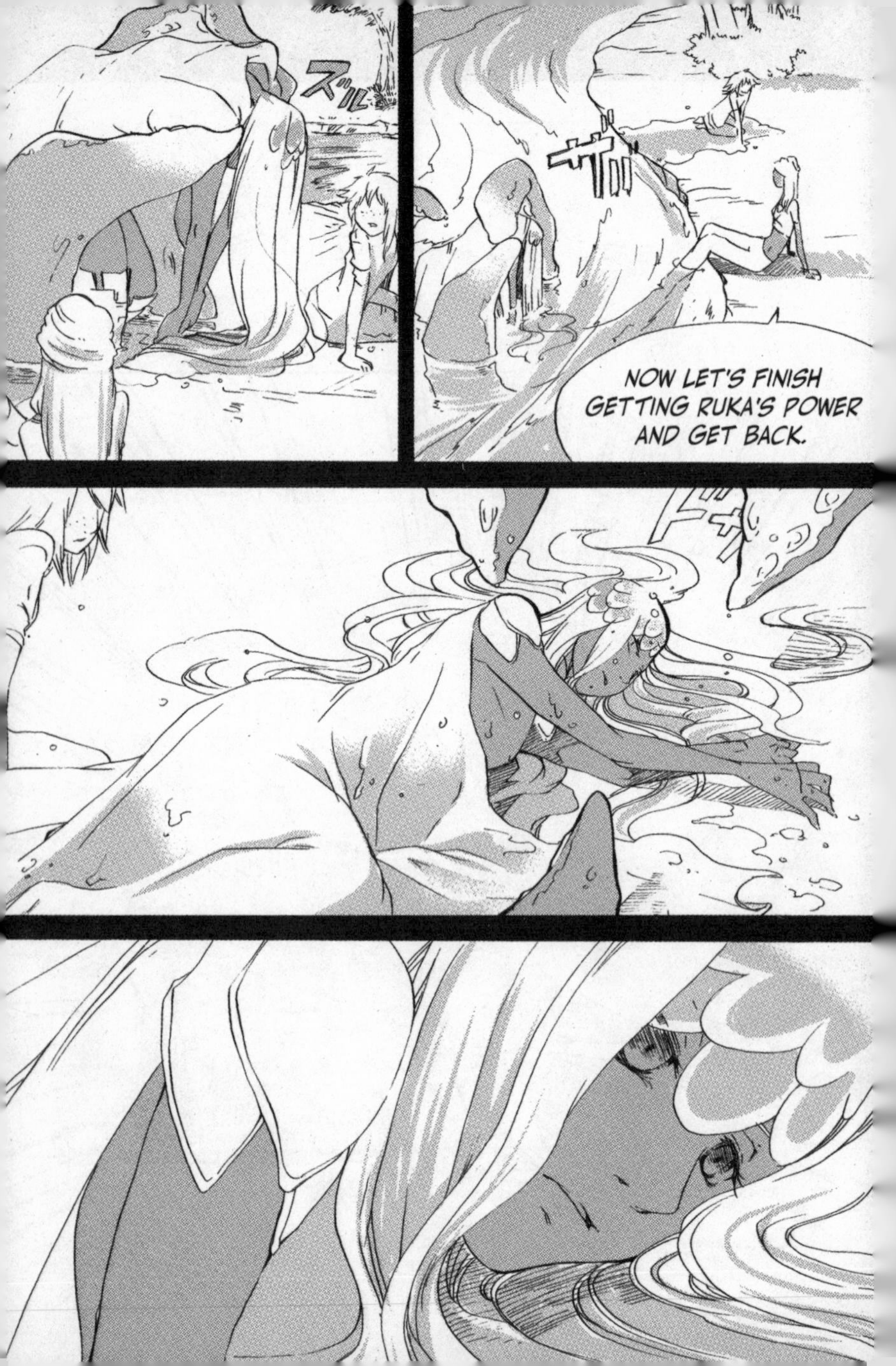
NOW LET'S FINISH GETTING RUKA'S POWER AND GET BACK.

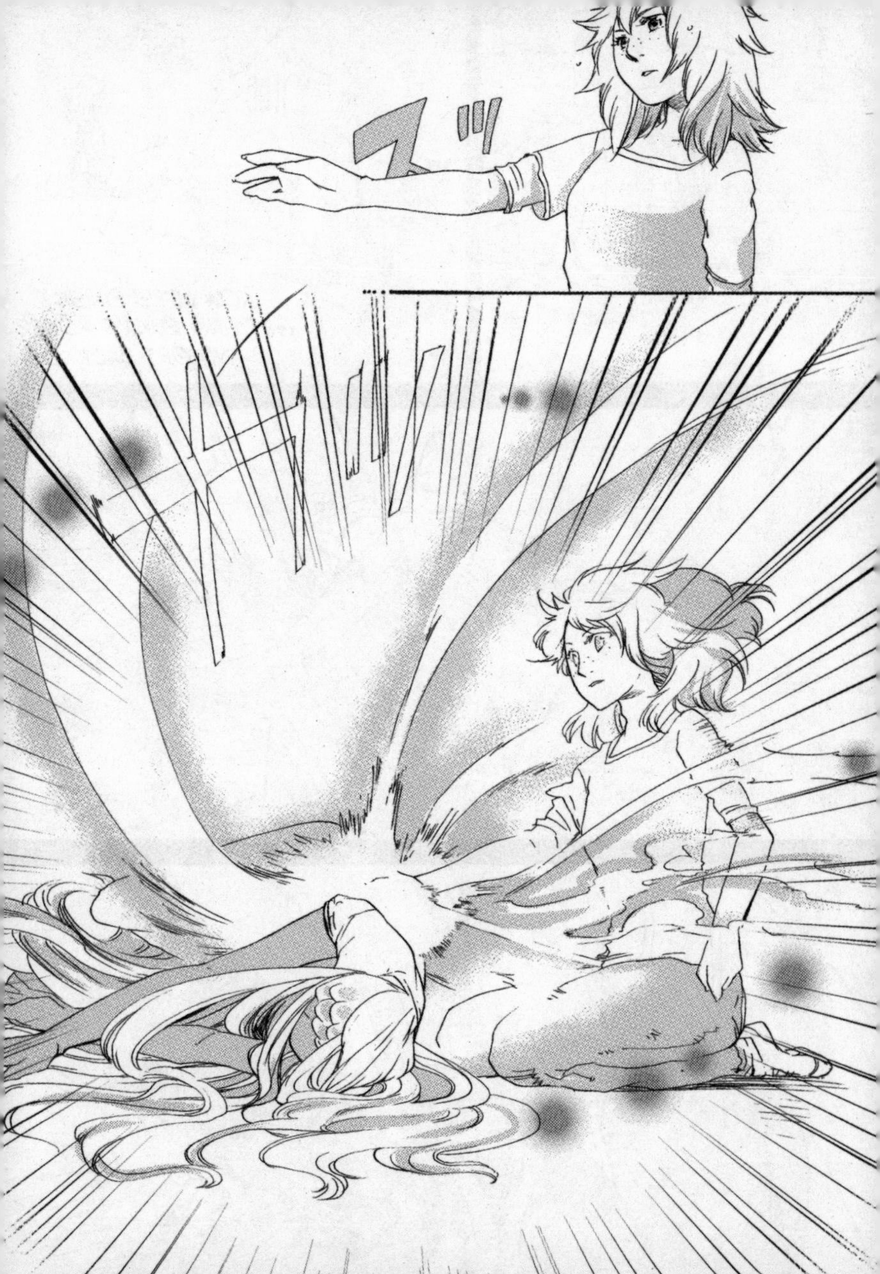
ズッ

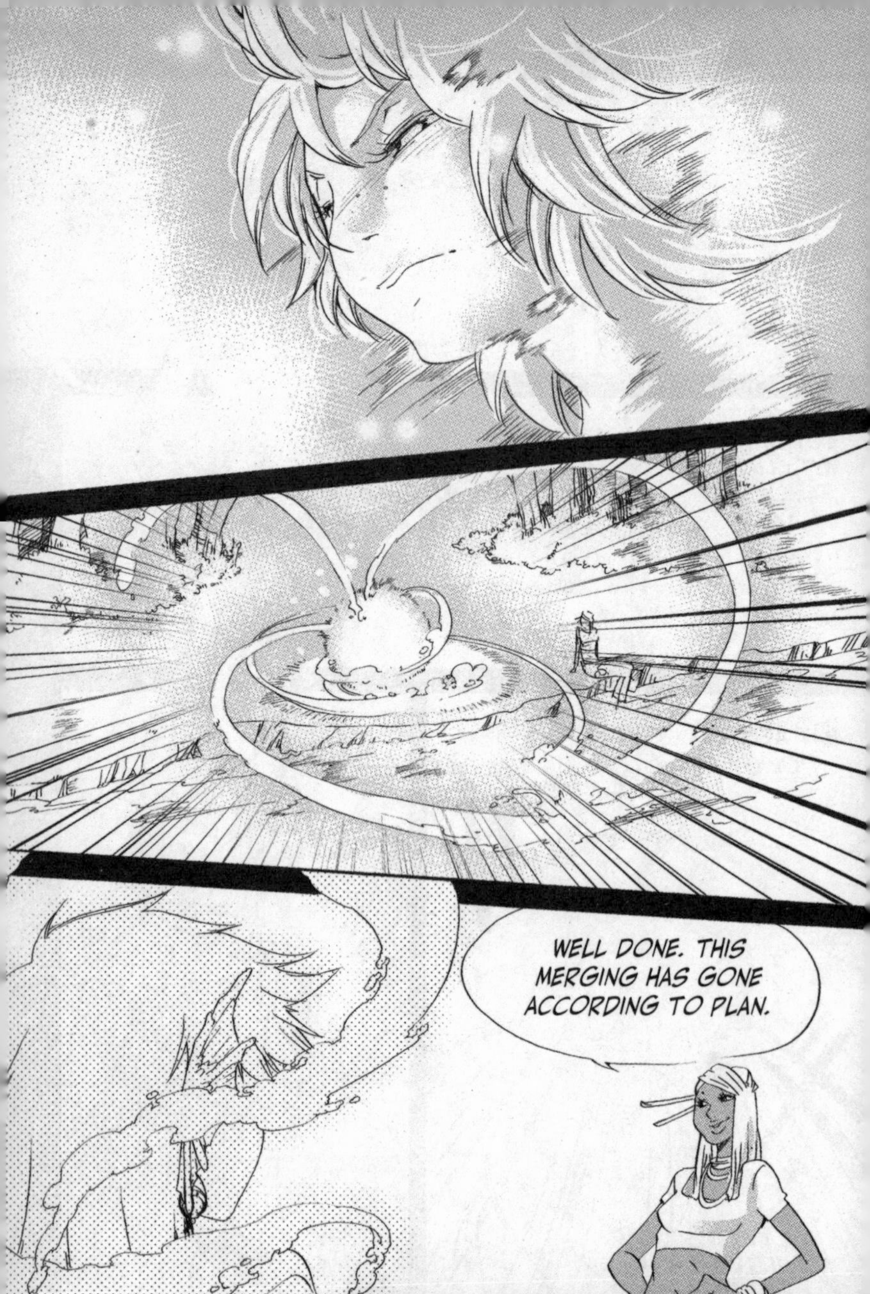
WELL DONE. THIS MERGING HAS GONE ACCORDING TO PLAN.

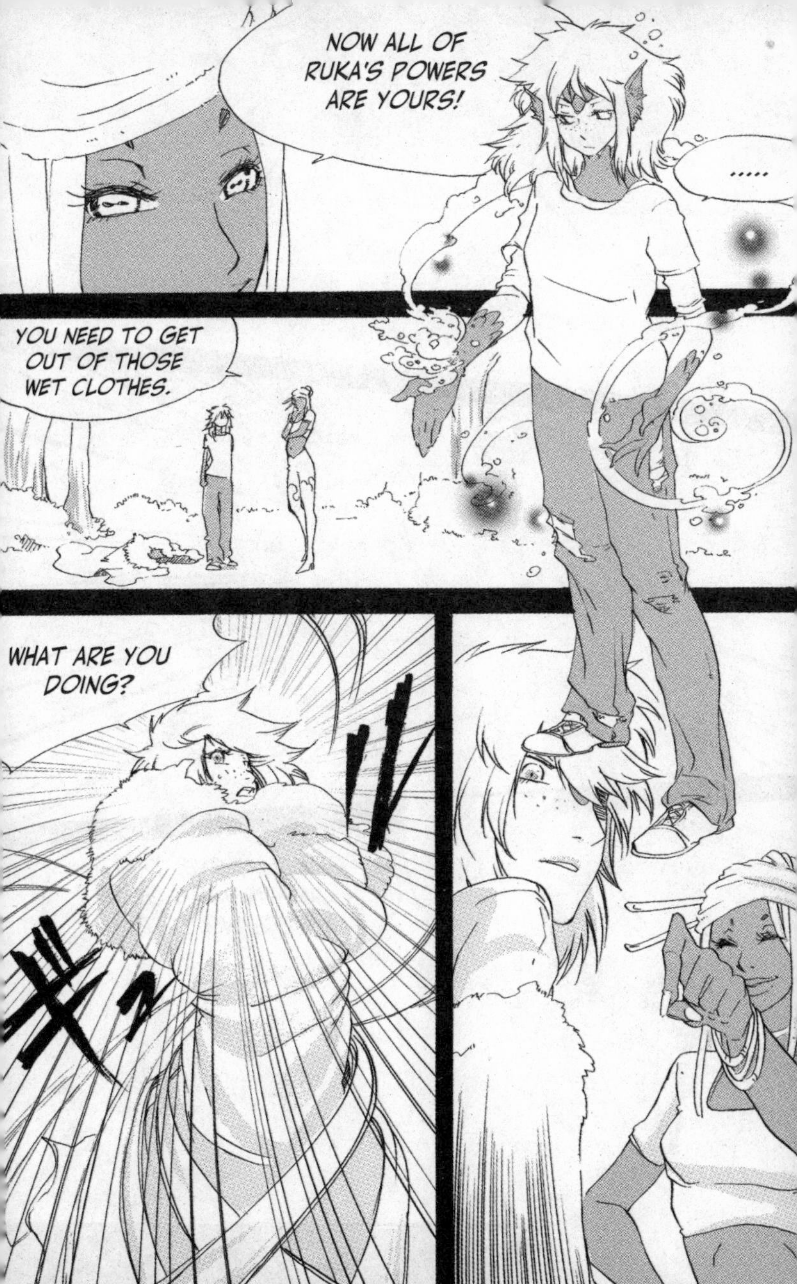
NOW ALL OF RUKA'S POWERS ARE YOURS!
......
YOU NEED TO GET OUT OF THOSE WET CLOTHES.
WHAT ARE YOU DOING?

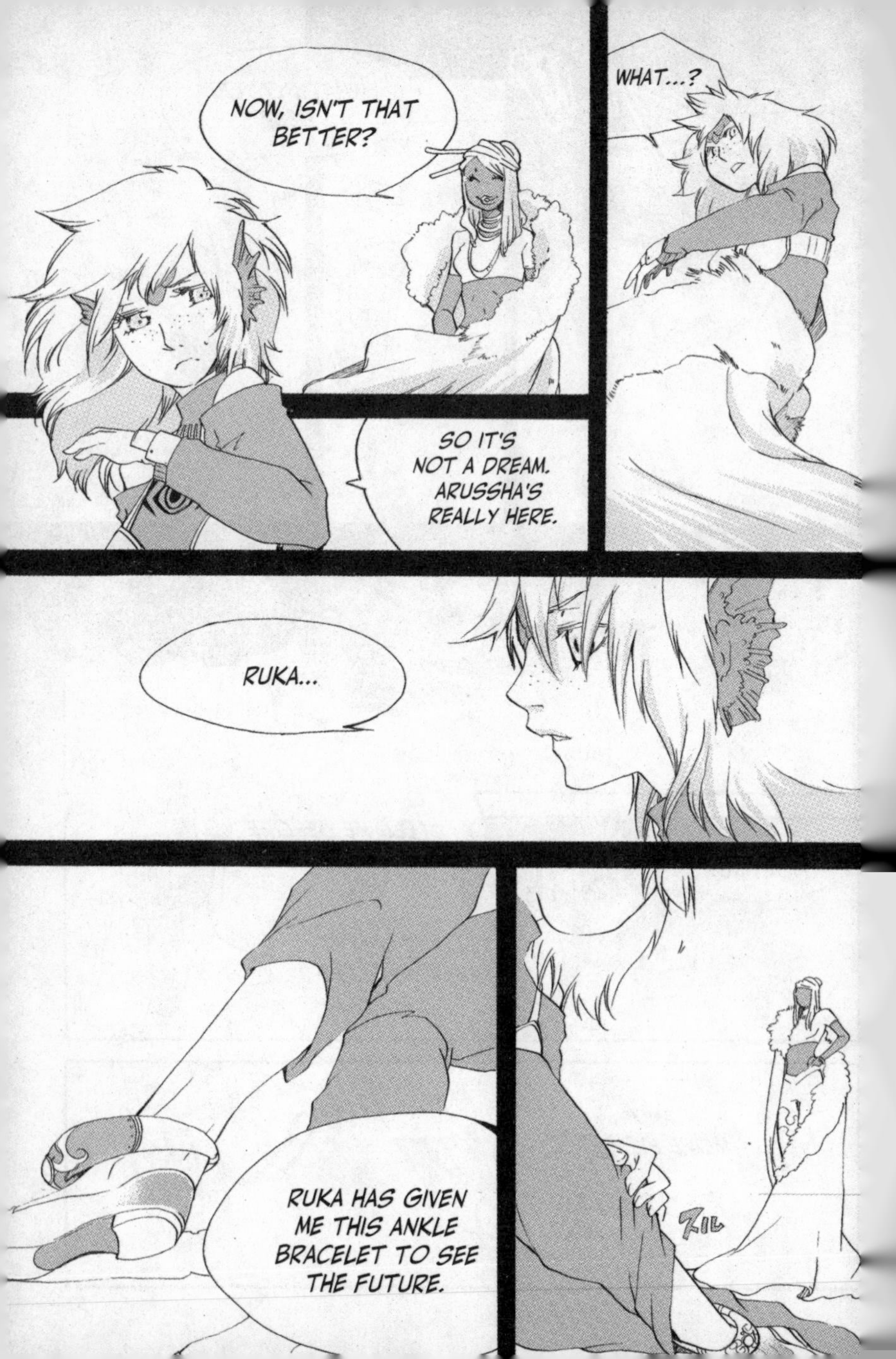
WHAT...?
NOW, ISN'T THAT BETTER?
SO IT'S NOT A DREAM. ARUSSHA'S REALLY HERE.
RUKA...
スル
RUKA HAS GIVEN ME THIS ANKLE BRACELET TO SEE THE FUTURE.

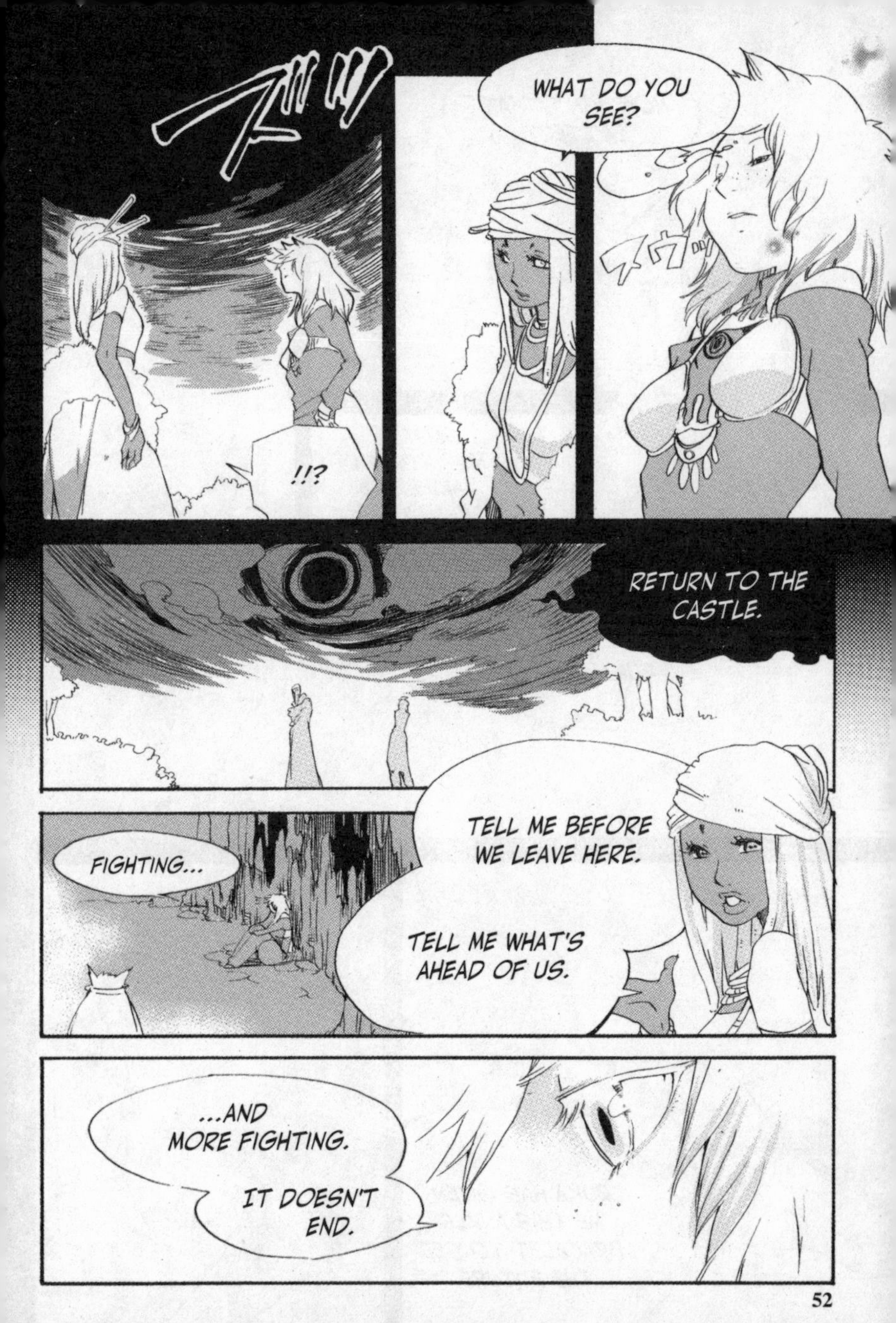
WHAT DO YOU SEE?
!!?
RETURN TO THE CASTLE.
TELL ME BEFORE WE LEAVE HERE.
TELL ME WHAT'S AHEAD OF US.
FIGHTING...
...AND MORE FIGHTING.
IT DOESN'T END.

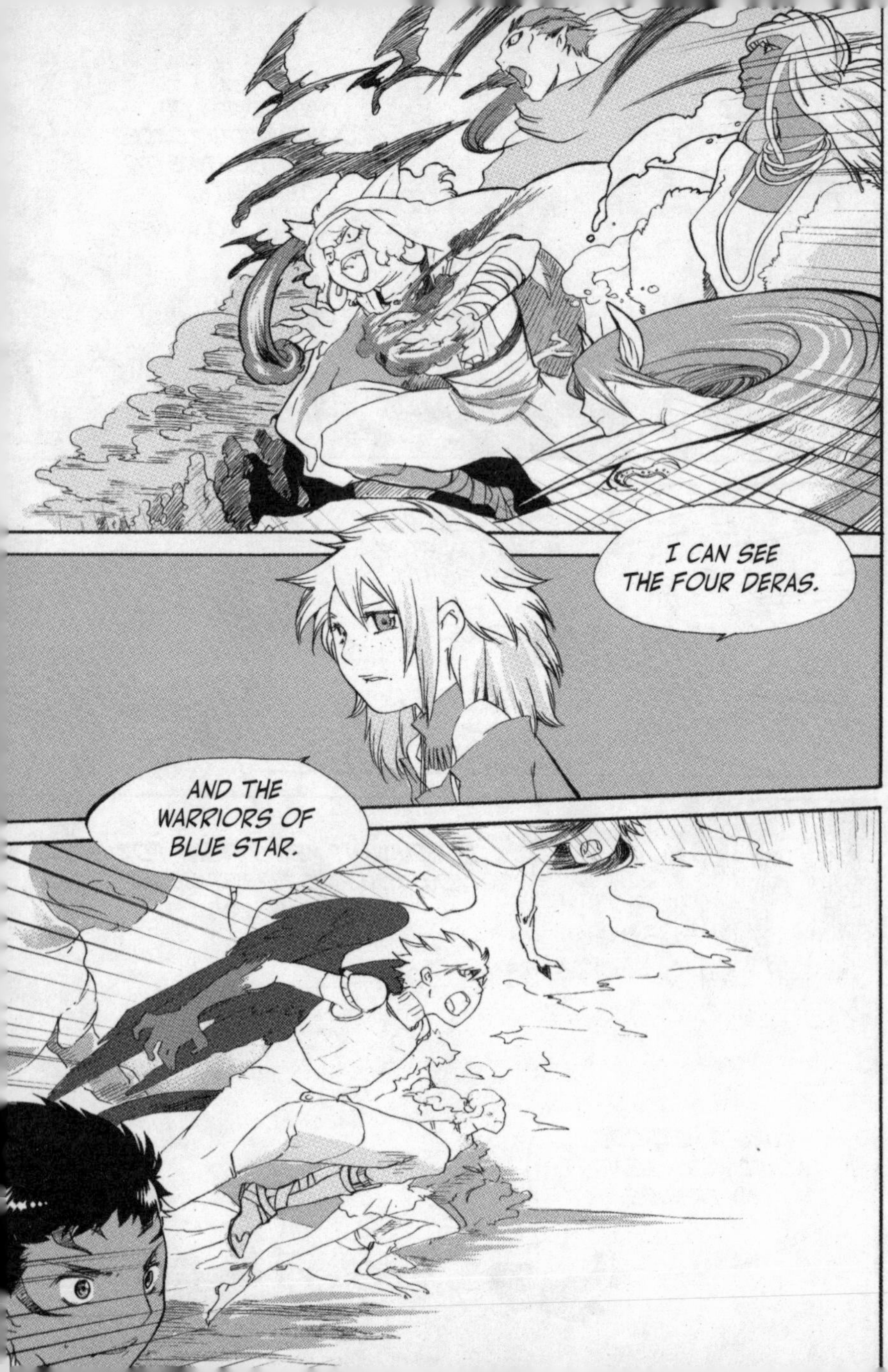
I CAN SEE THE FOUR DERAS.
AND THE WARRIORS OF BLUE STAR.

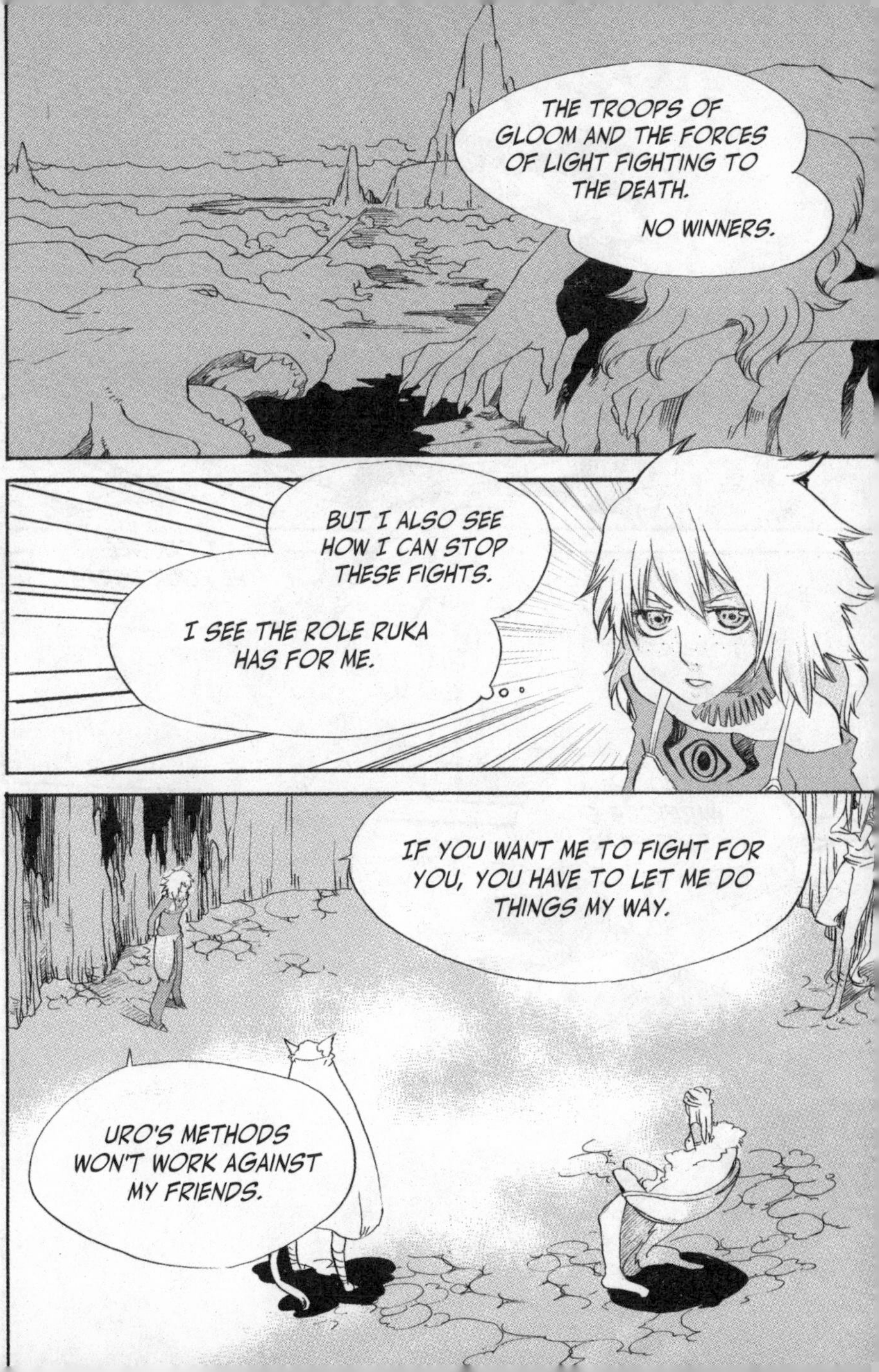
THE TROOPS OF GLOOM AND THE FORCES OF LIGHT FIGHTING TO THE DEATH.
NO WINNERS.
BUT I ALSO SEE HOW I CAN STOP THESE FIGHTS.
I SEE THE ROLE RUKA HAS FOR ME.
IF YOU WANT ME TO FIGHT FOR YOU, YOU HAVE TO LET ME DO THINGS MY WAY.
URO'S METHODS WON'T WORK AGAINST MY FRIENDS.

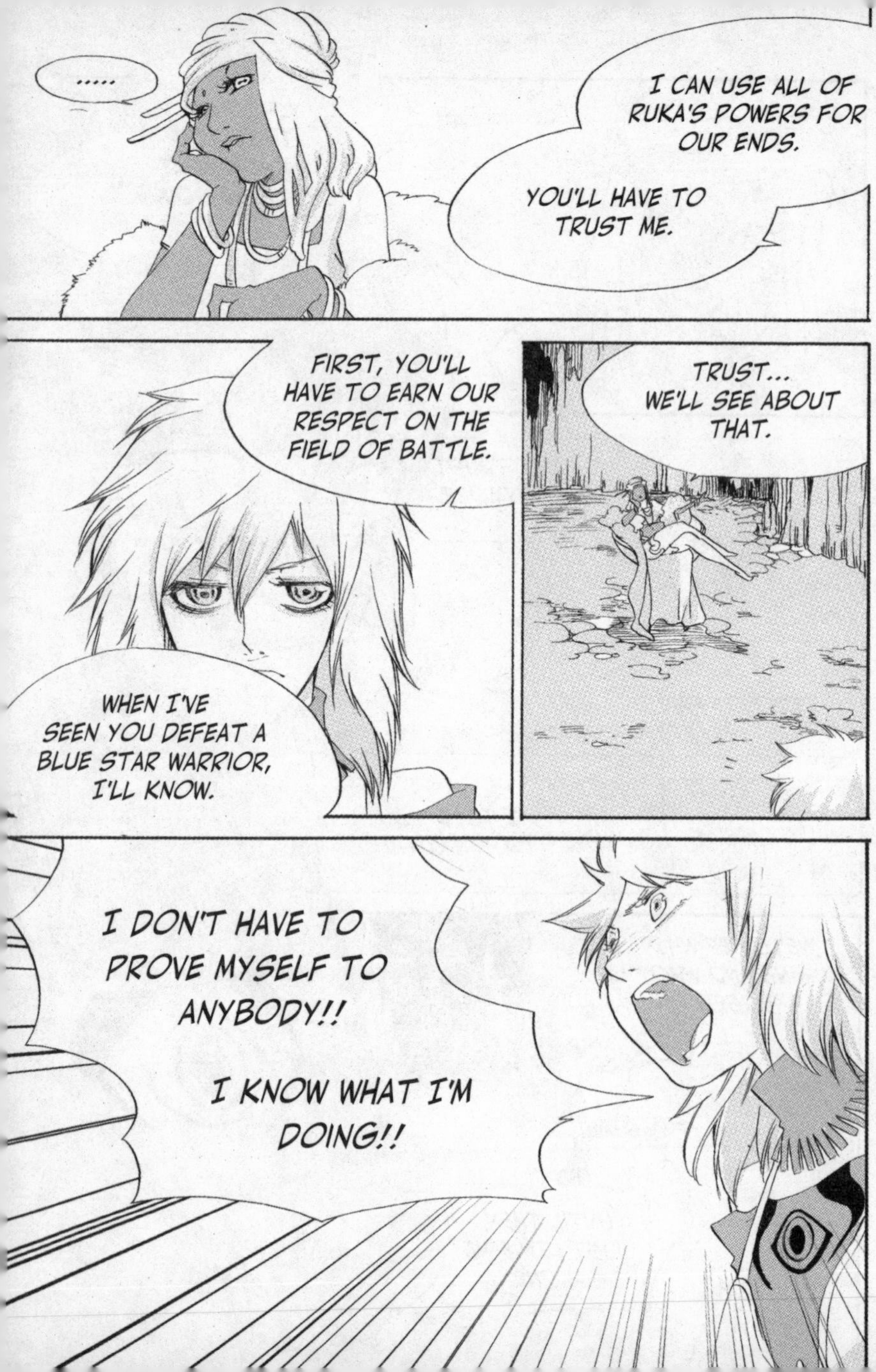
I CAN USE ALL OF RUKA'S POWERS FOR OUR ENDS.
YOU'LL HAVE TO TRUST ME.
.....
TRUST... WE'LL SEE ABOUT THAT.
FIRST, YOU'LL HAVE TO EARN OUR RESPECT ON THE FIELD OF BATTLE.
WHEN I'VE SEEN YOU DEFEAT A BLUE STAR WARRIOR, I'LL KNOW.
I DON'T HAVE TO PROVE MYSELF TO ANYBODY!!
I KNOW WHAT I'M DOING!!

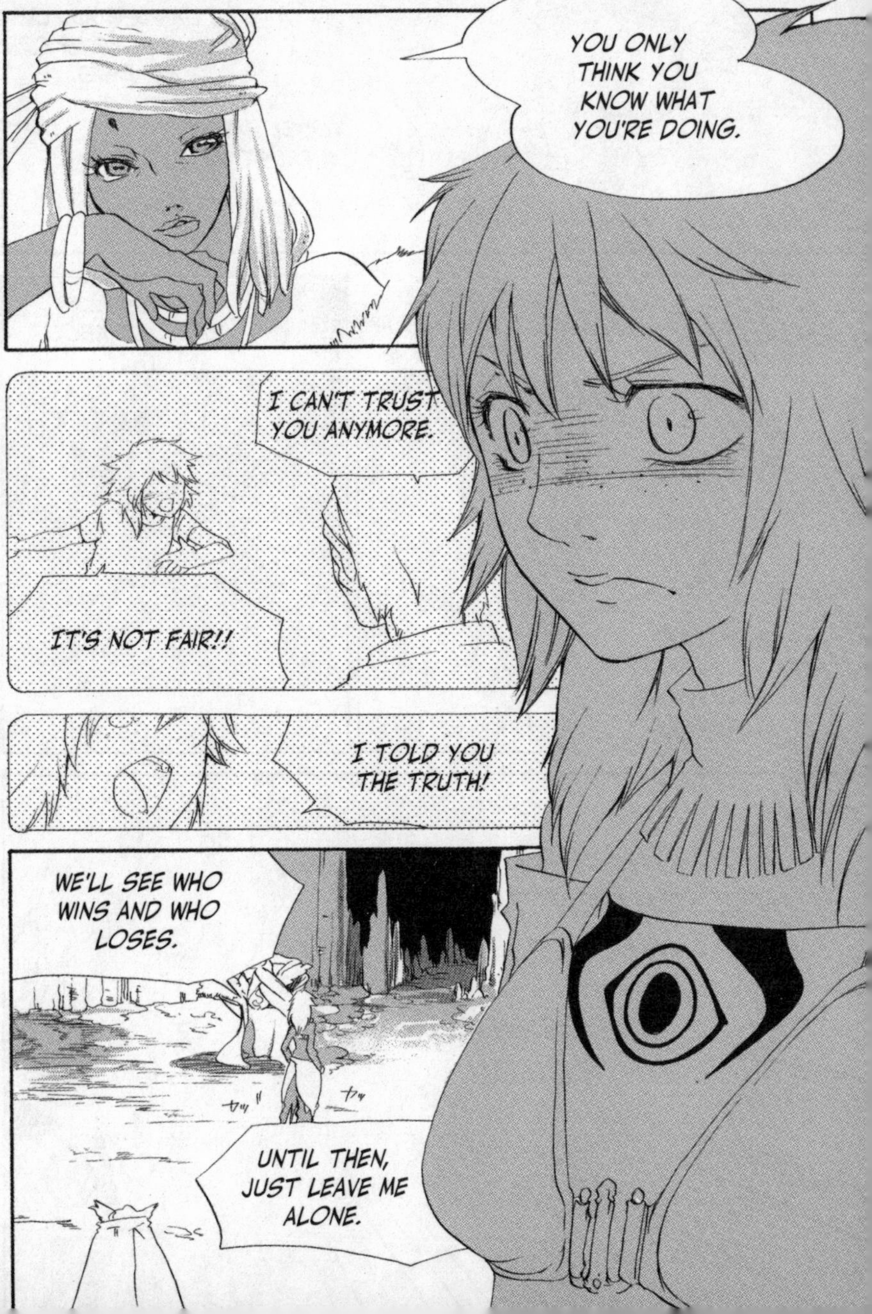
YOU ONLY THINK YOU KNOW WHAT YOU'RE DOING.
I CAN'T TRUST YOU ANYMORE.
IT'S NOT FAIR!!
I TOLD YOU THE TRUTH!
WE'LL SEE WHO WINS AND WHO LOSES.
UNTIL THEN, JUST LEAVE ME ALONE.

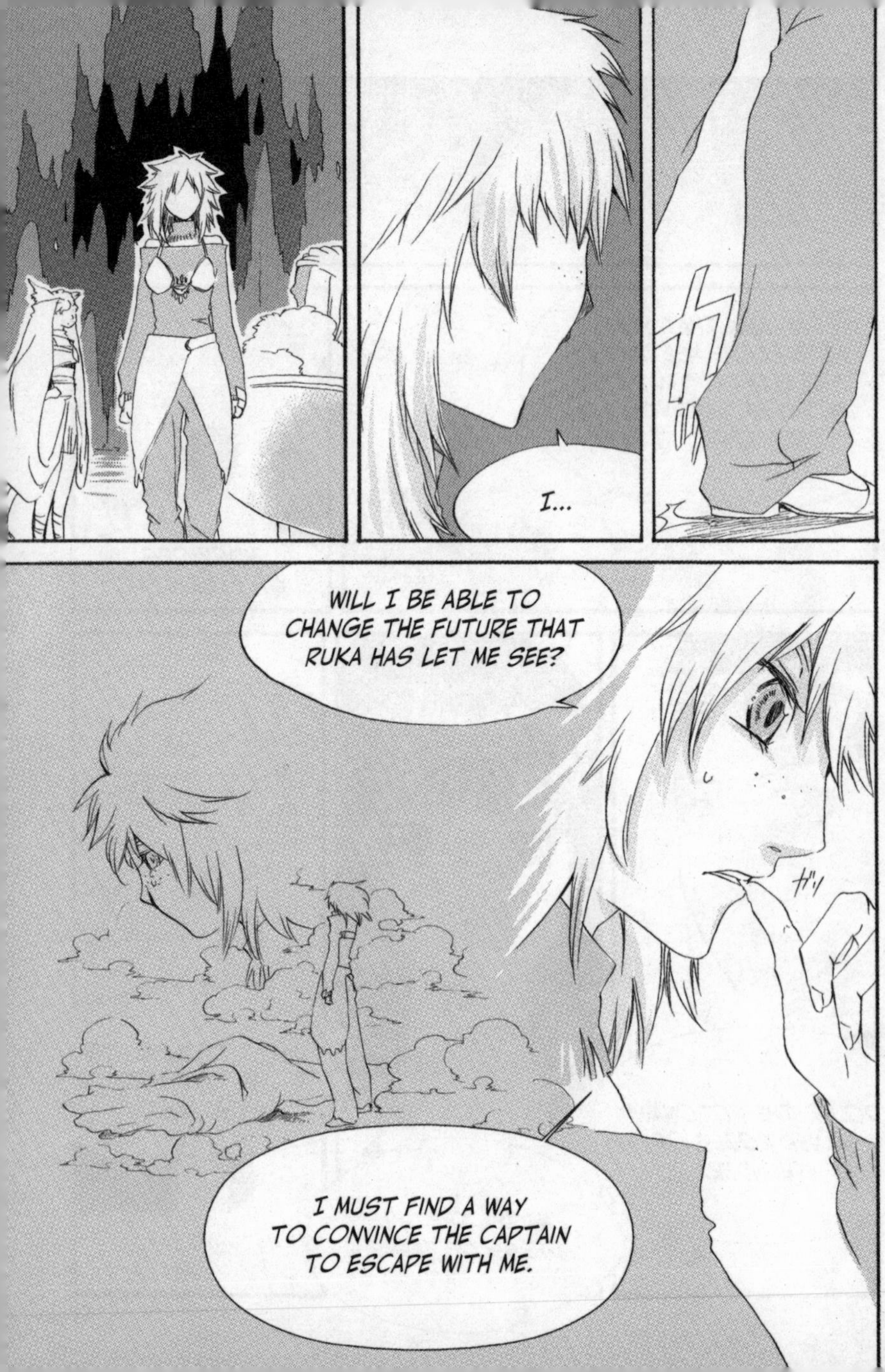
I...
WILL I BE ABLE TO CHANGE THE FUTURE THAT RUKA HAS LET ME SEE?
I MUST FIND A WAY TO CONVINCE THE CAPTAIN TO ESCAPE WITH ME.

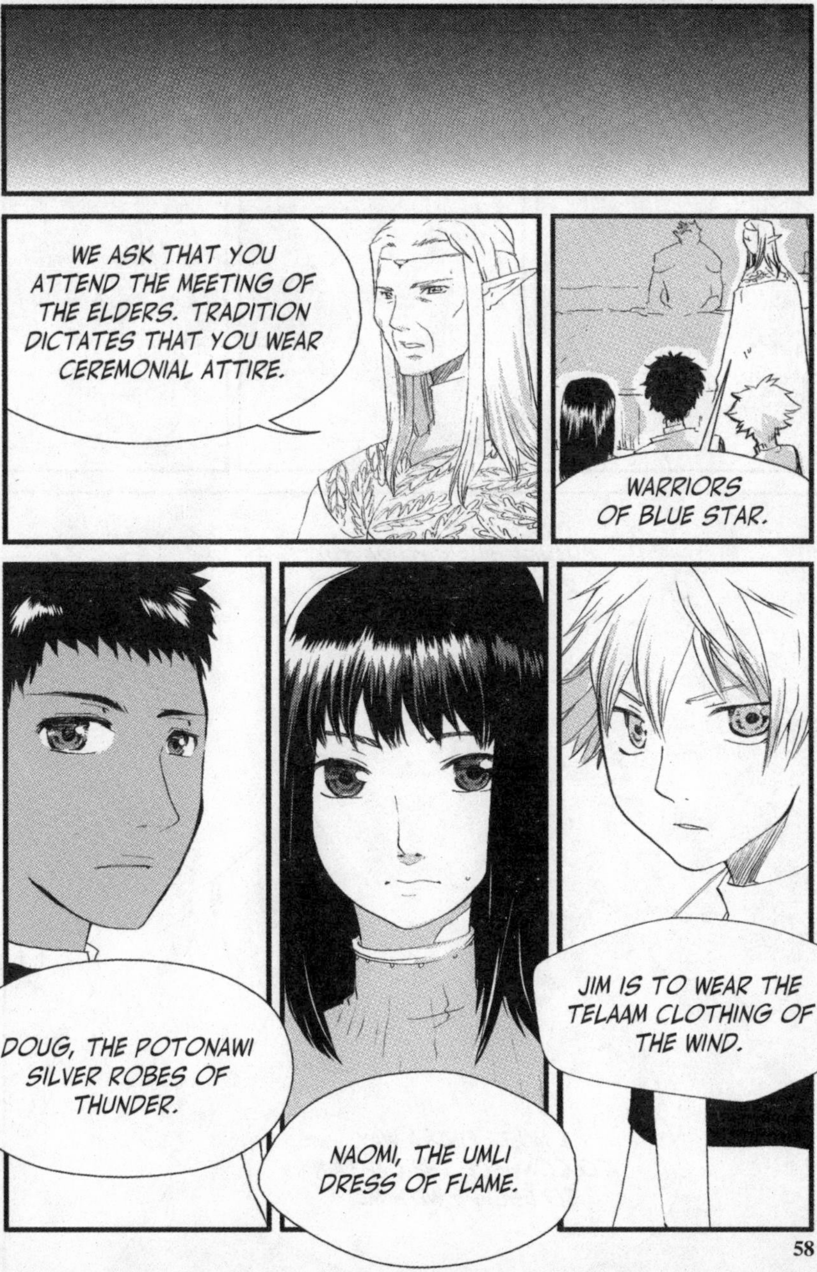
WARRIORS OF BLUE STAR.
WE ASK THAT YOU ATTEND THE MEETING OF THE ELDERS. TRADITION DICTATES THAT YOU WEAR CEREMONIAL ATTIRE.
JIM IS TO WEAR THE TELAAM CLOTHING OF THE WIND.
NAOMI, THE UMLI DRESS OF FLAME.
DOUG, THE POTONAWI SILVER ROBES OF THUNDER.

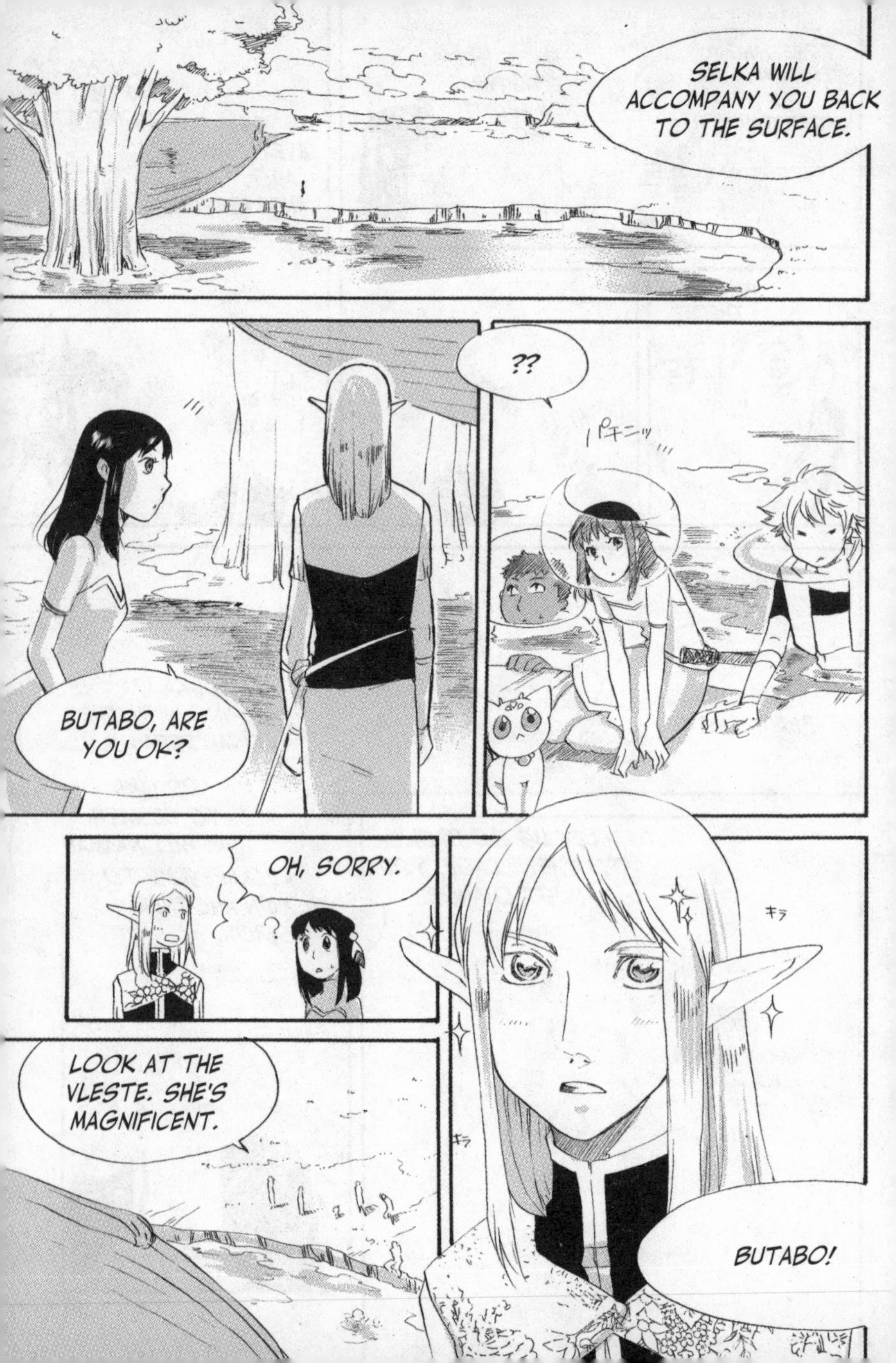
SELKA WILL ACCOMPANY YOU BACK TO THE SURFACE.
??
パキニッ
BUTABO, ARE YOU OK?
キラ
キラ
BUTABO!
OH, SORRY.
?
LOOK AT THE VLESTE. SHE'S MAGNIFICENT.

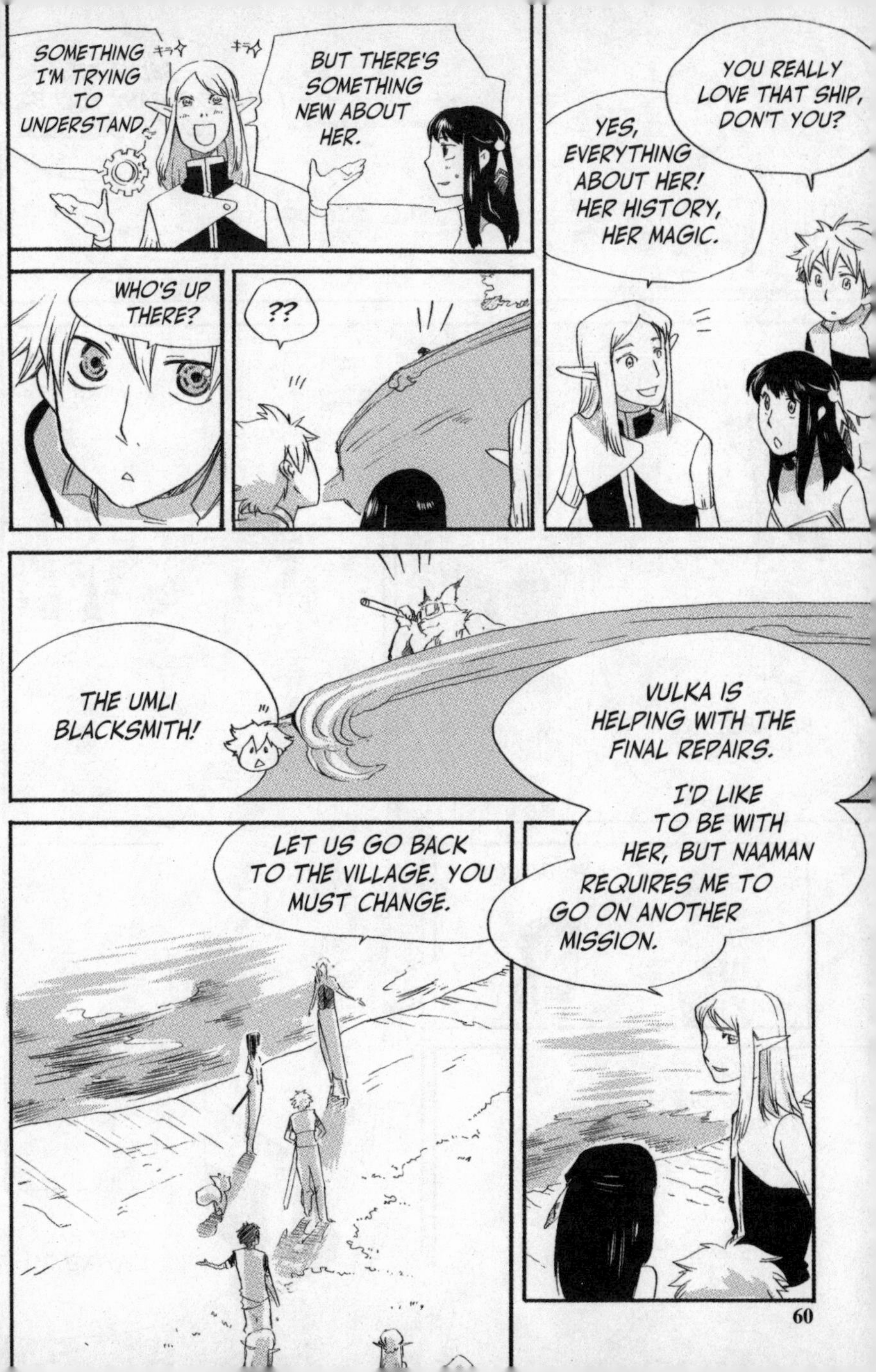
YOU REALLY LOVE THAT SHIP, DON'T YOU?
YES, EVERYTHING ABOUT HER! HER HISTORY, HER MAGIC.
キラ
BUT THERE'S SOMETHING NEW ABOUT HER.
キラ
SOMETHING I'M TRYING TO UNDERSTAND.
??
WHO'S UP THERE?
VULKA IS HELPING WITH THE FINAL REPAIRS.
THE UMLI BLACKSMITH!
I'D LIKE TO BE WITH HER, BUT NAAMAN REQUIRES ME TO GO ON ANOTHER MISSION.
LET US GO BACK TO THE VILLAGE. YOU MUST CHANGE.

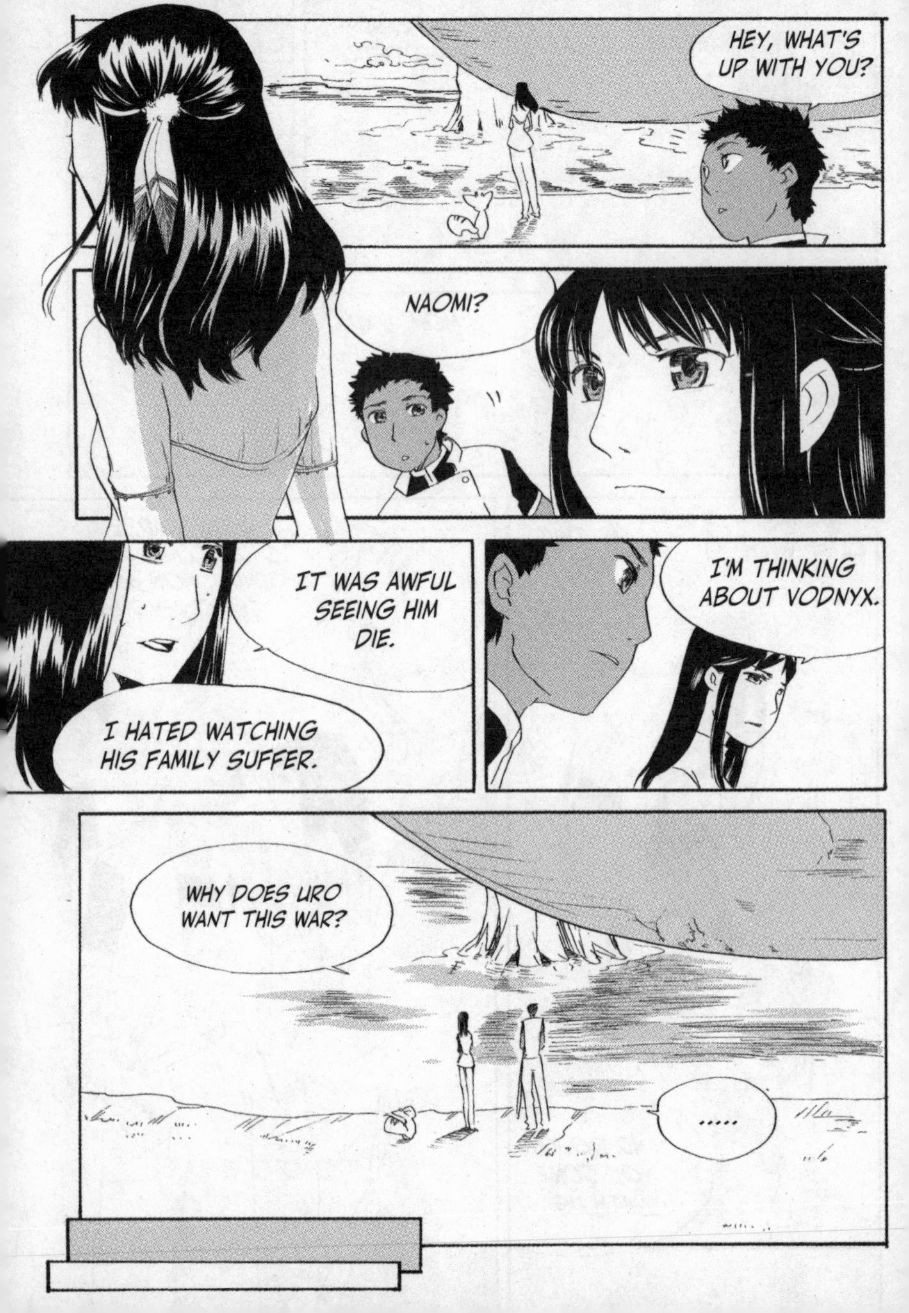
HEY, WHAT'S UP WITH YOU?
NAOMI?
I'M THINKING ABOUT VODNYX.
IT WAS AWFUL SEEING HIM DIE.
I HATED WATCHING HIS FAMILY SUFFER.
WHY DOES URO WANT THIS WAR?
......

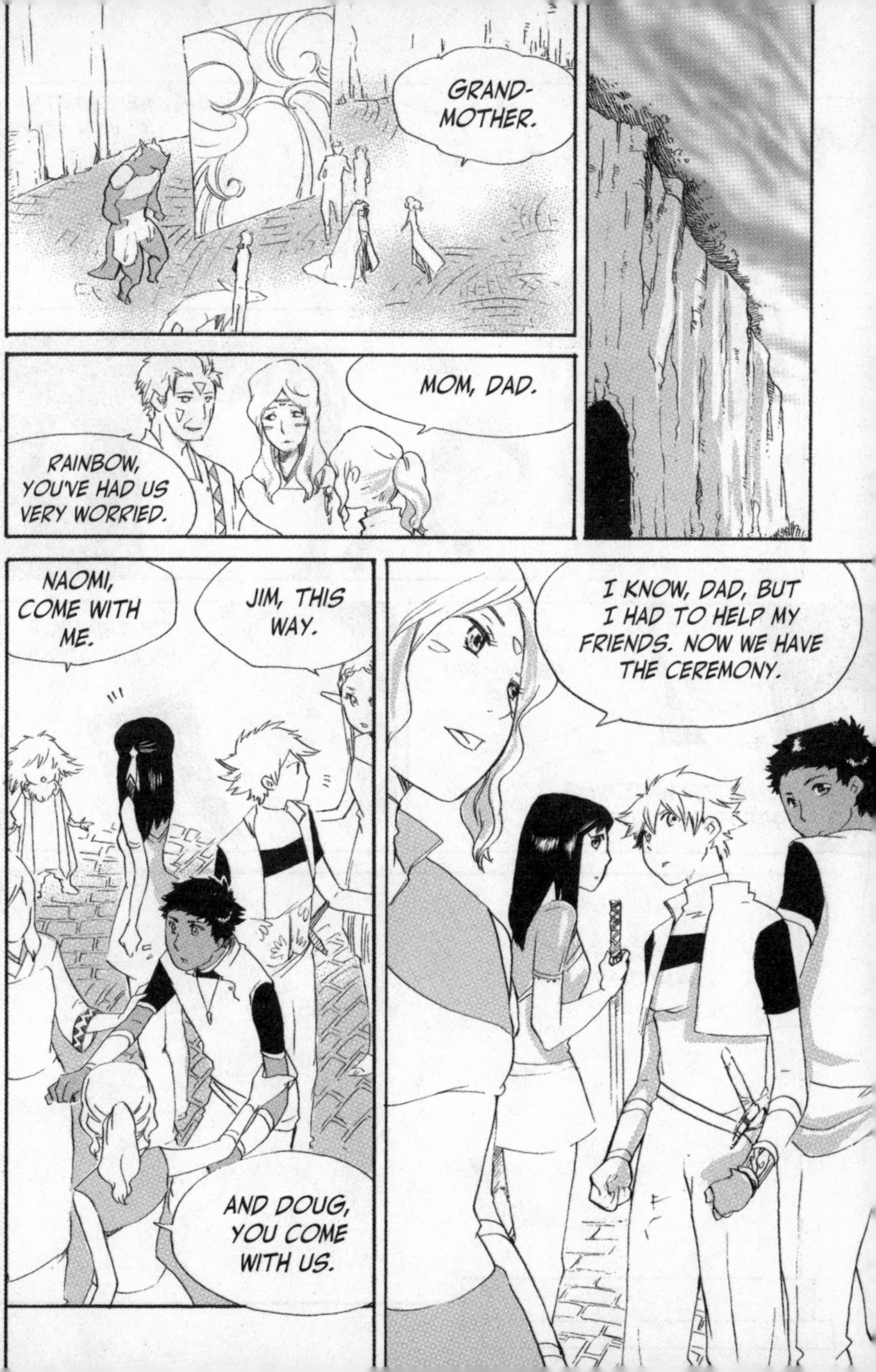
GRAND-MOTHER.
MOM, DAD.
RAINBOW, YOU'VE HAD US VERY WORRIED.
I KNOW, DAD, BUT I HAD TO HELP MY FRIENDS. NOW WE HAVE THE CEREMONY.
JIM, THIS WAY.
NAOMI, COME WITH ME.
AND DOUG, YOU COME WITH US.

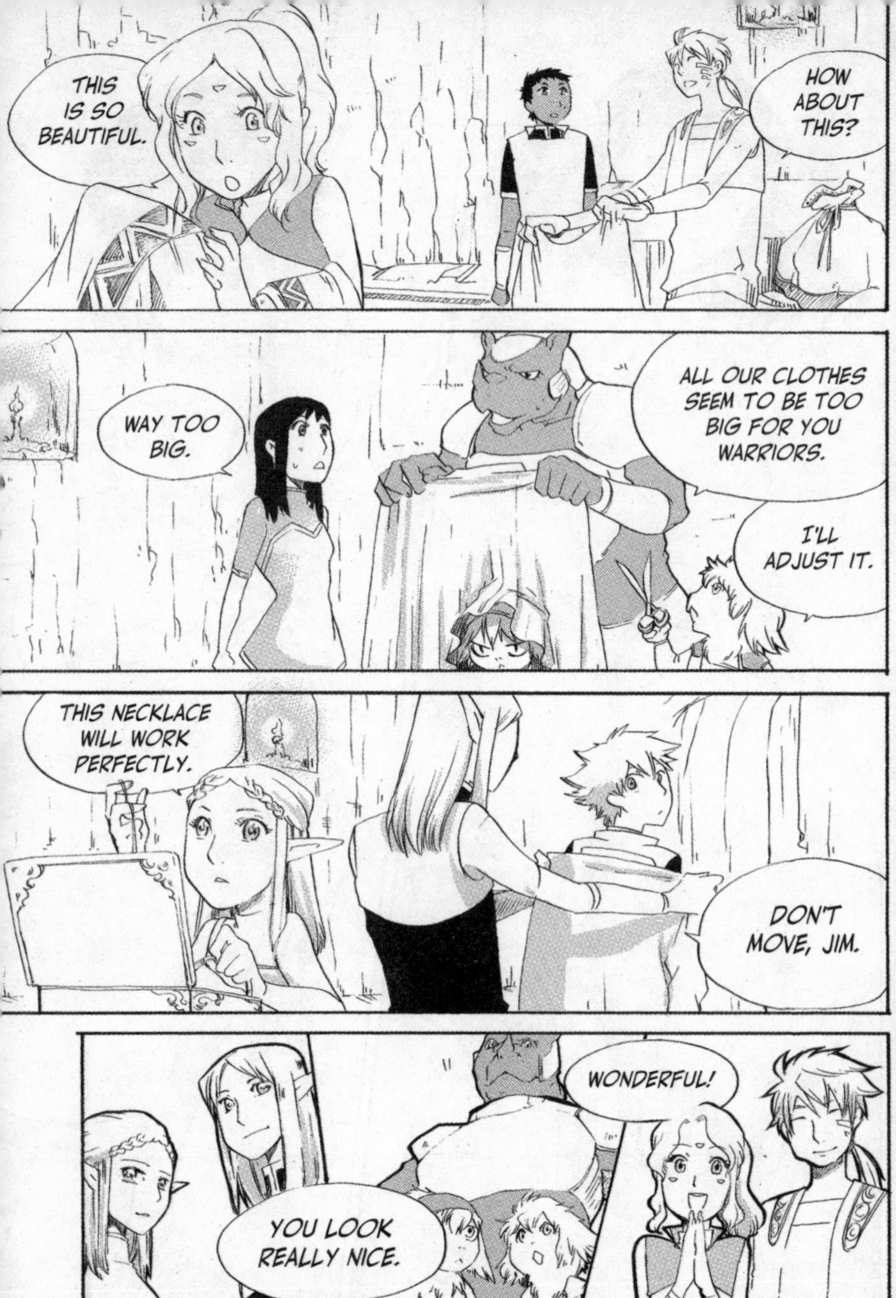
HOW ABOUT THIS?
THIS IS SO BEAUTIFUL.
ALL OUR CLOTHES SEEM TO BE TOO BIG FOR YOU WARRIORS.
WAY TOO BIG.
I'LL ADJUST IT.
DON'T MOVE, JIM.
THIS NECKLACE WILL WORK PERFECTLY.
WONDERFUL!
YOU LOOK REALLY NICE.

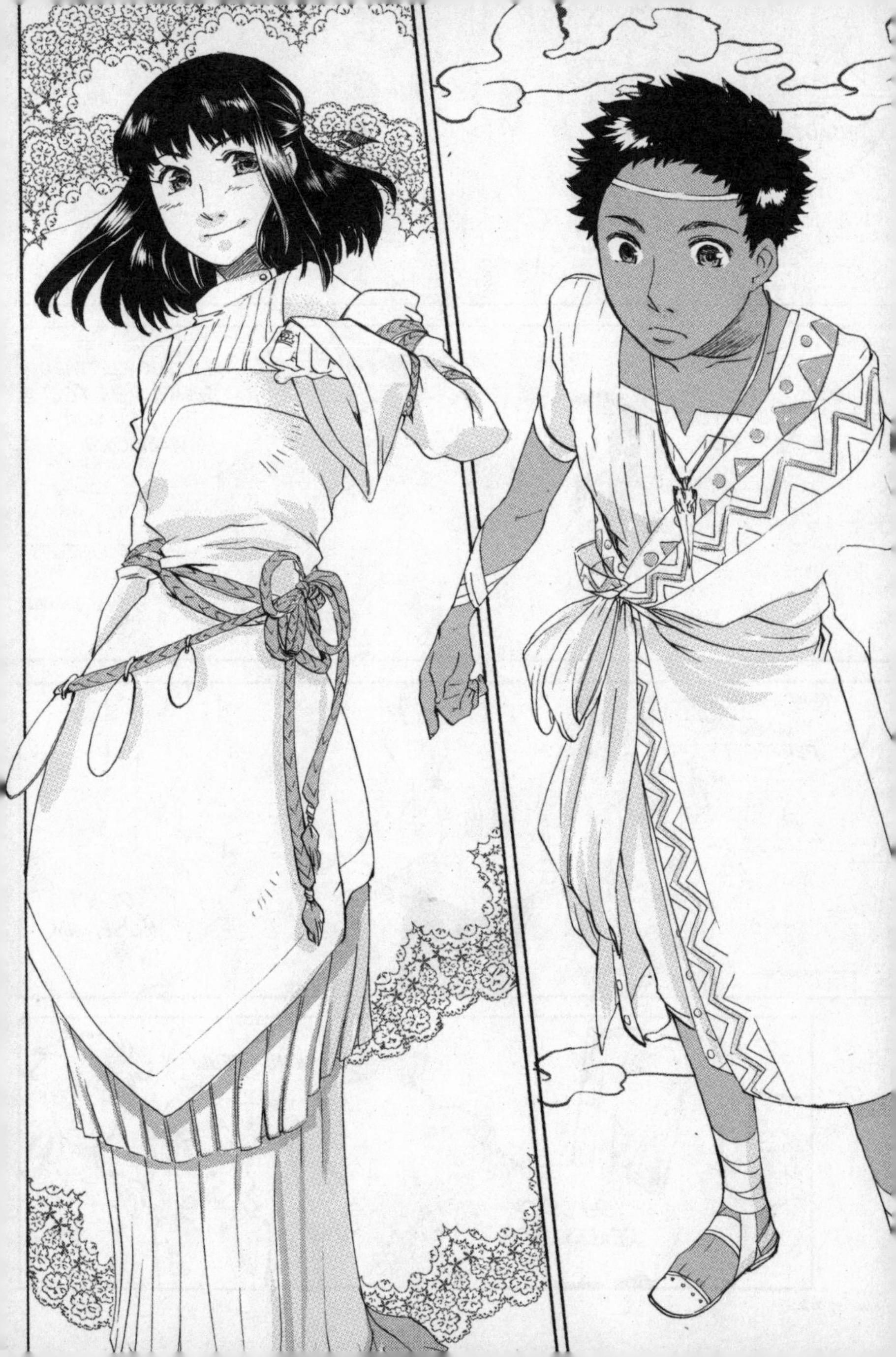

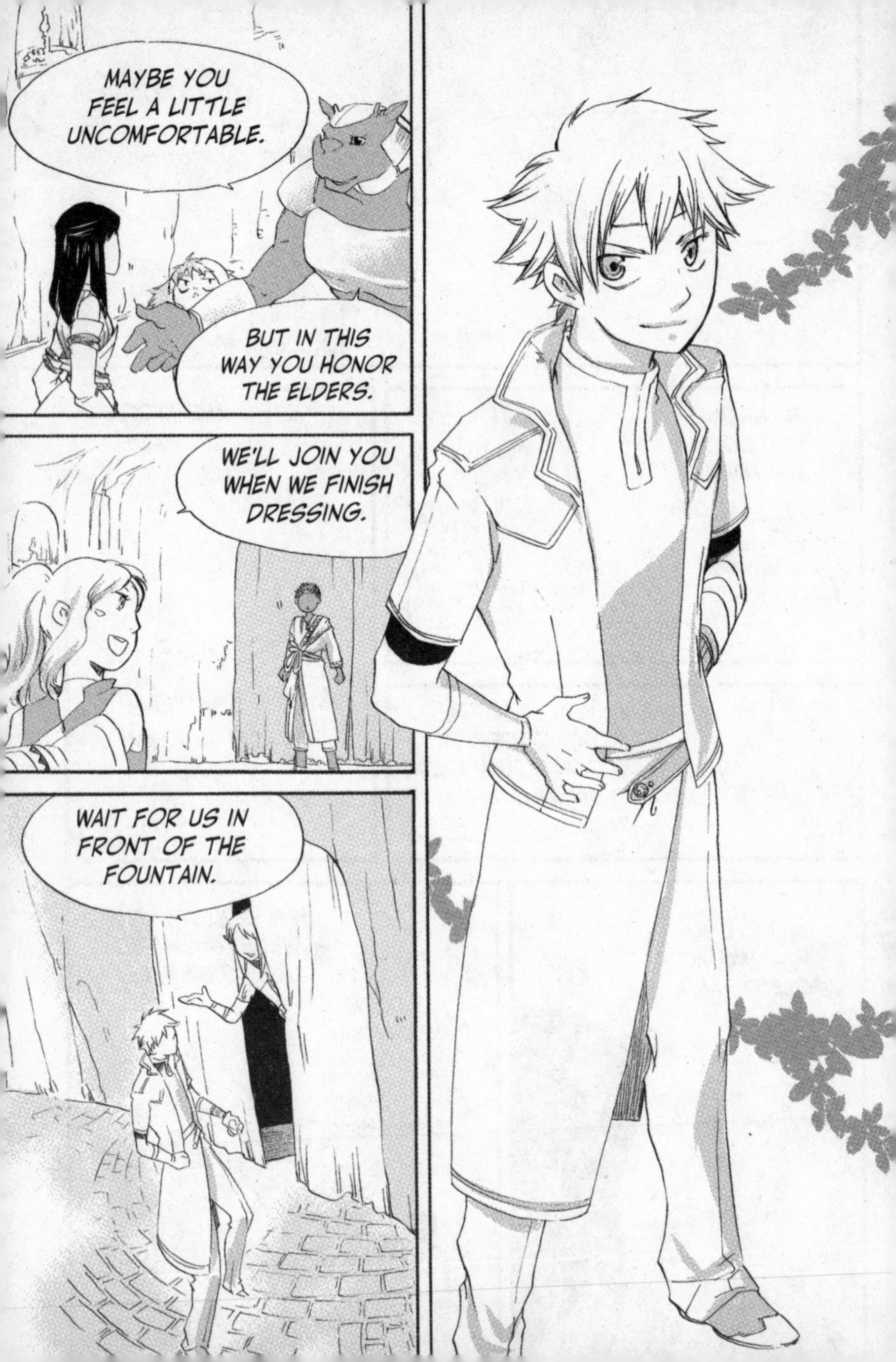
MAYBE YOU FEEL A LITTLE UNCOMFORTABLE.
BUT IN THIS WAY YOU HONOR THE ELDERS.
WE'LL JOIN YOU WHEN WE FINISH DRESSING.
WAIT FOR US IN FRONT OF THE FOUNTAIN.

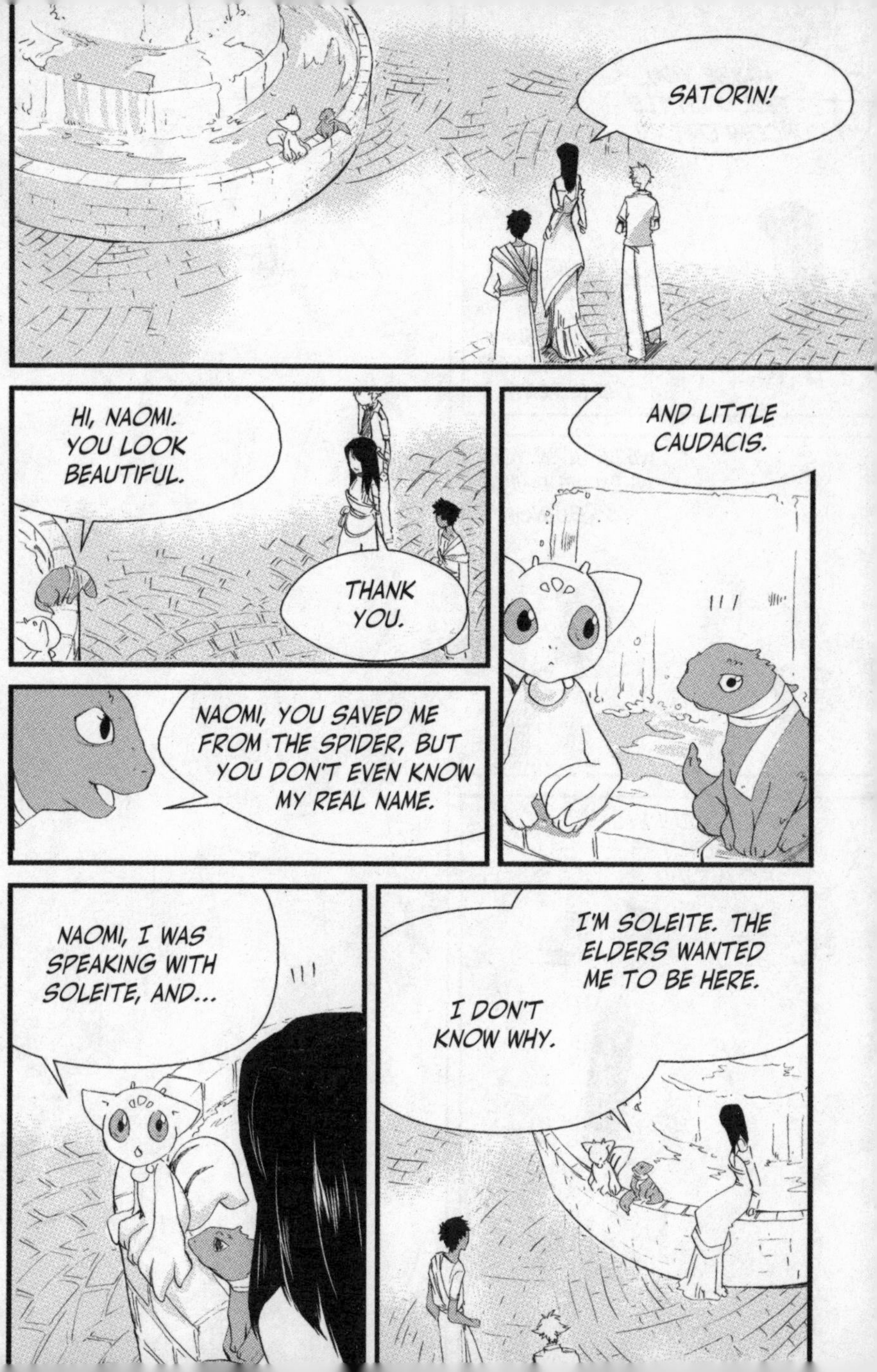
SATORIN!
AND LITTLE CAUDACIS.
HI, NAOMI. YOU LOOK BEAUTIFUL.
THANK YOU.
NAOMI, YOU SAVED ME FROM THE SPIDER, BUT YOU DON'T EVEN KNOW MY REAL NAME.
I'M SOLEITE. THE ELDERS WANTED ME TO BE HERE.
I DON'T KNOW WHY.
NAOMI, I WAS SPEAKING WITH SOLEITE, AND...

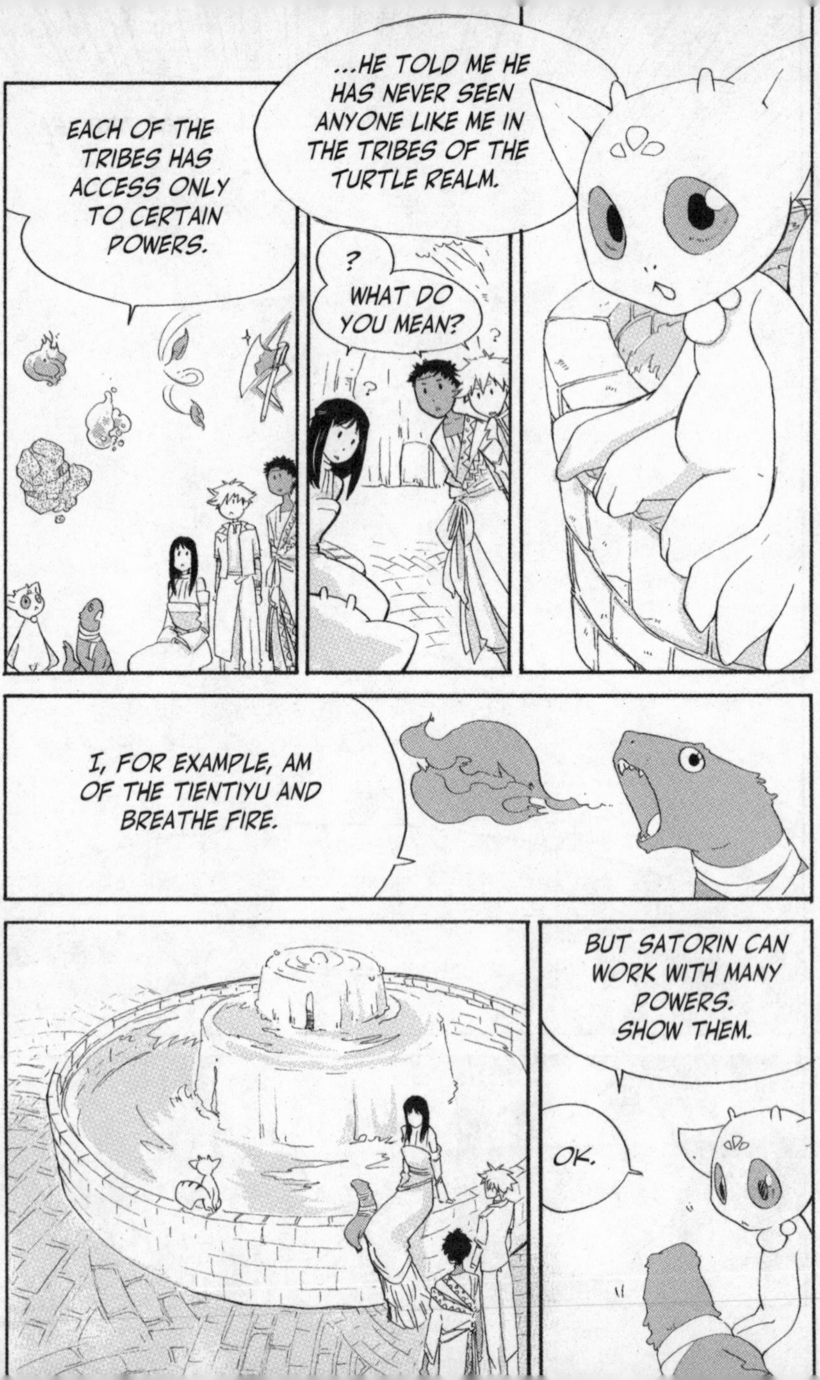
...HE TOLD ME HE HAS NEVER SEEN ANYONE LIKE ME IN THE TRIBES OF THE TURTLE REALM.
?
WHAT DO YOU MEAN?
?
?
EACH OF THE TRIBES HAS ACCESS ONLY TO CERTAIN POWERS.
I, FOR EXAMPLE, AM OF THE TIENTIYU AND BREATHE FIRE.
BUT SATORIN CAN WORK WITH MANY POWERS. SHOW THEM.
OK.

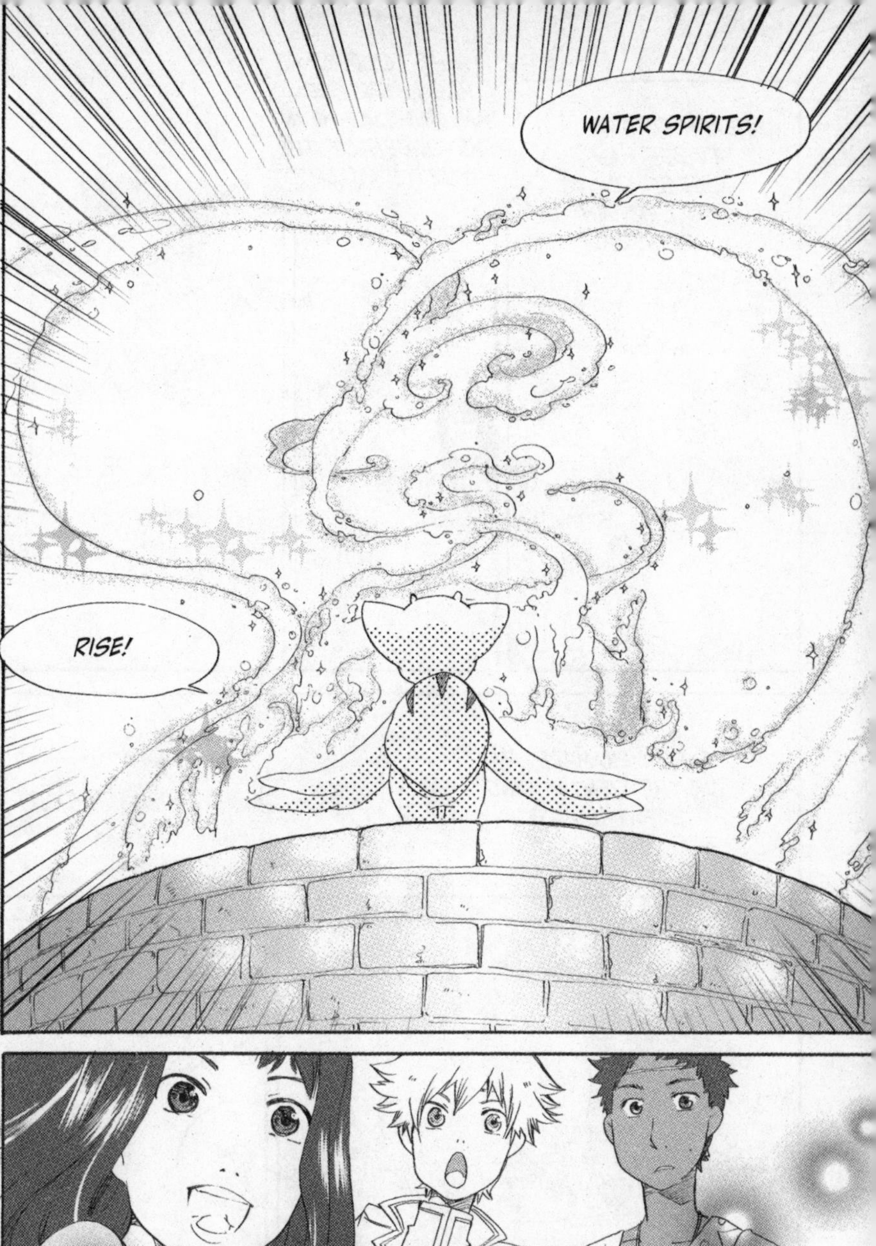
WATER SPIRITS!
RISE!

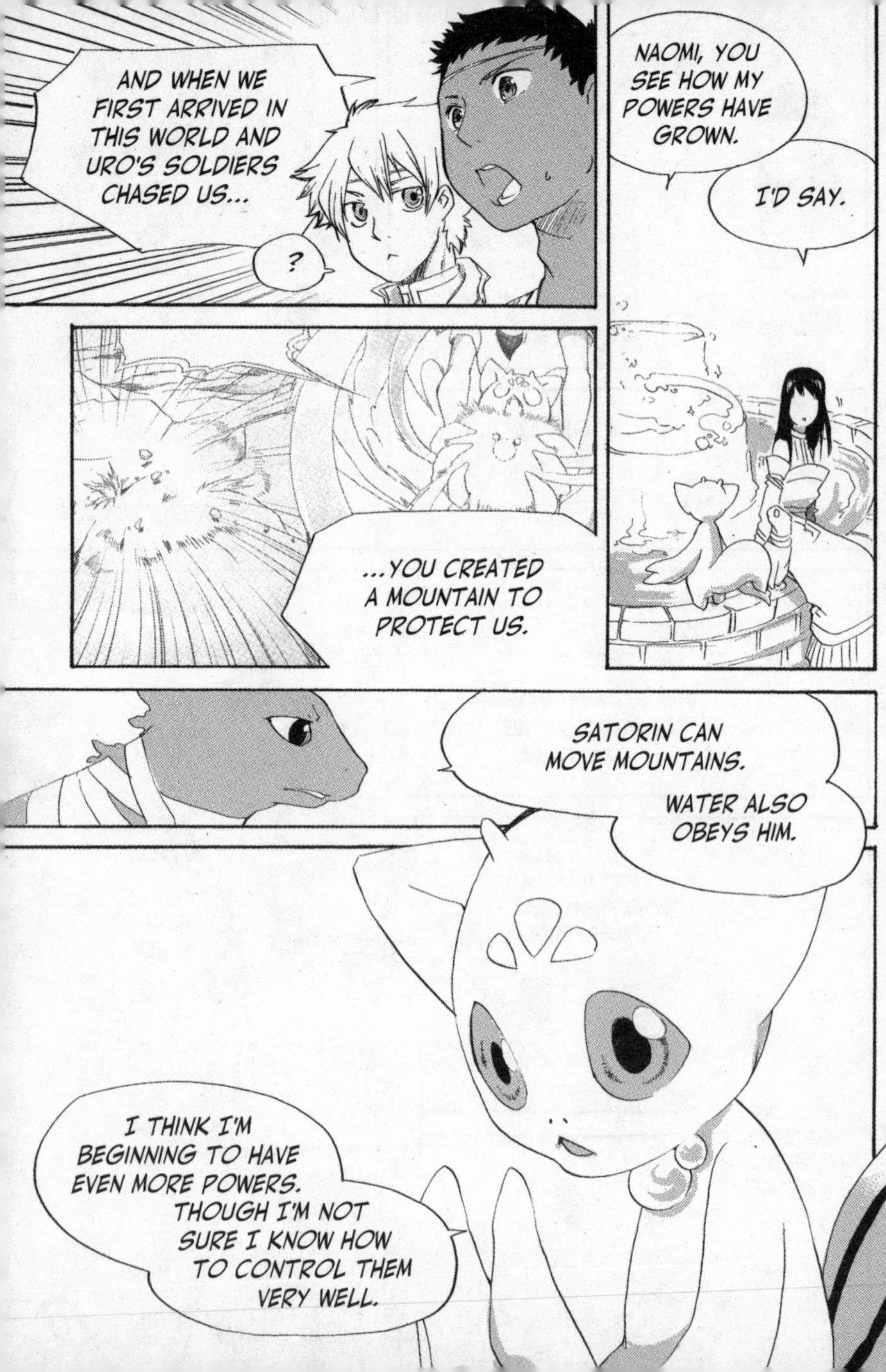

NAOMI, YOU SEE HOW MY POWERS HAVE GROWN.
I'D SAY.
AND WHEN WE FIRST ARRIVED IN THIS WORLD AND URO'S SOLDIERS CHASED US...
?
...YOU CREATED A MOUNTAIN TO PROTECT US.
SATORIN CAN MOVE MOUNTAINS.
WATER ALSO OBEYS HIM.
I THINK I'M BEGINNING TO HAVE EVEN MORE POWERS.
THOUGH I'M NOT SURE I KNOW HOW TO CONTROL THEM VERY WELL.

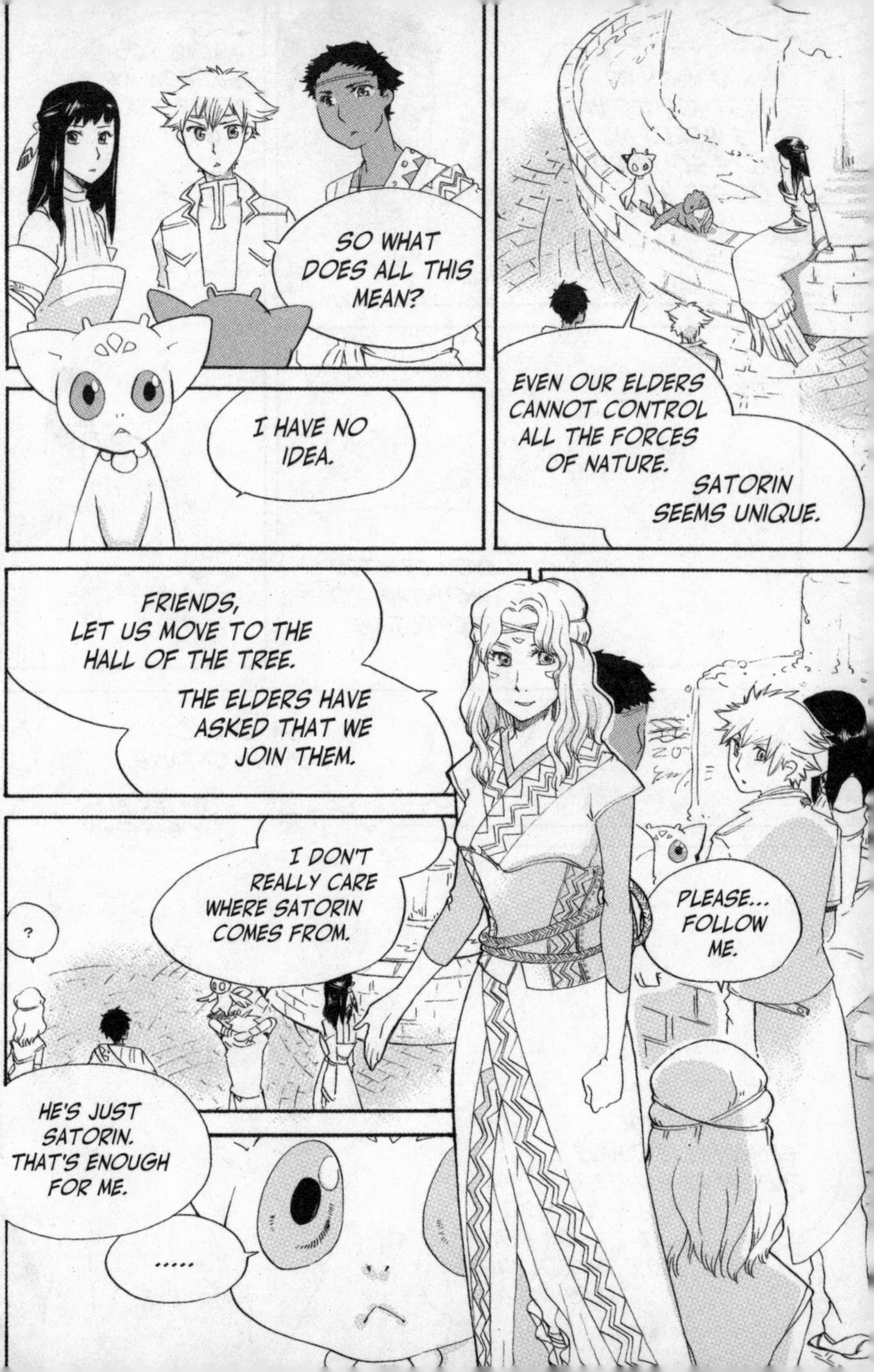

EVEN OUR ELDERS CANNOT CONTROL ALL THE FORCES OF NATURE.
SATORIN SEEMS UNIQUE.
SO WHAT DOES ALL THIS MEAN?
I HAVE NO IDEA.
PLEASE... FOLLOW ME.
FRIENDS, LET US MOVE TO THE HALL OF THE TREE.
THE ELDERS HAVE ASKED THAT WE JOIN THEM.
I DON'T REALLY CARE WHERE SATORIN COMES FROM.
?
HE'S JUST SATORIN. THAT'S ENOUGH FOR ME.
.....

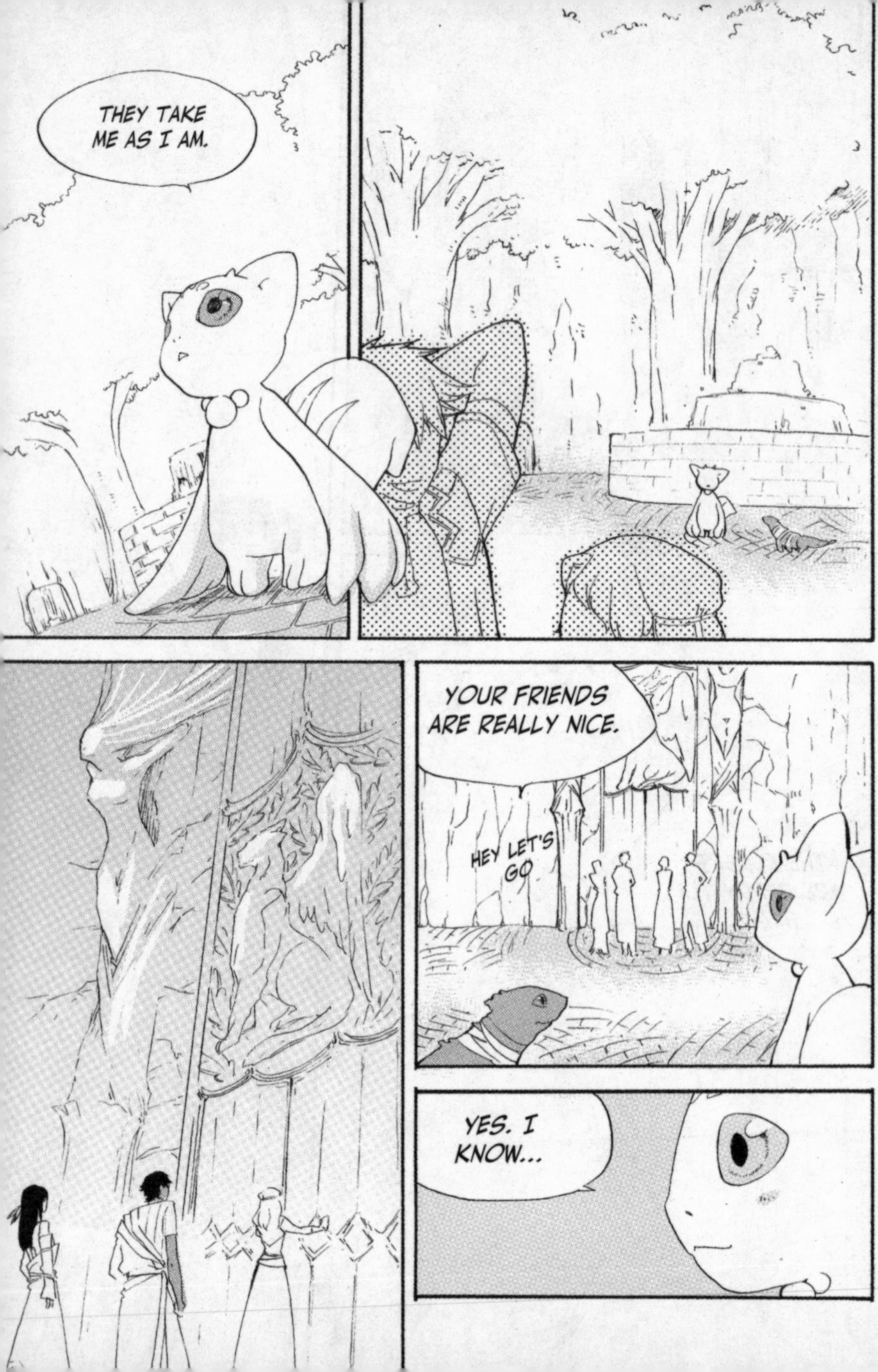
THEY TAKE ME AS I AM.
YOUR FRIENDS ARE REALLY NICE.
HEY LET'S GO
YES. I KNOW...

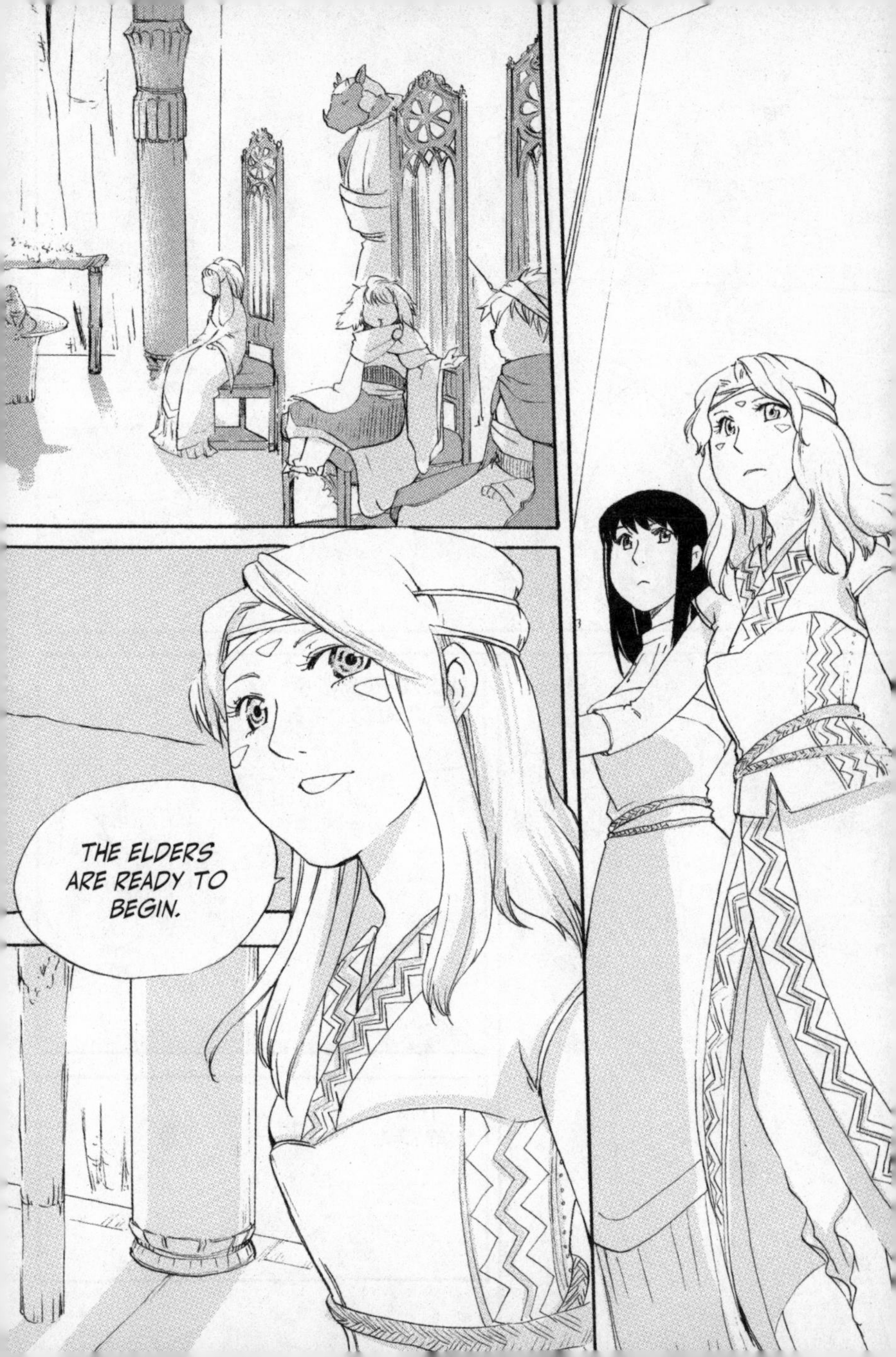
THE ELDERS ARE READY TO BEGIN.

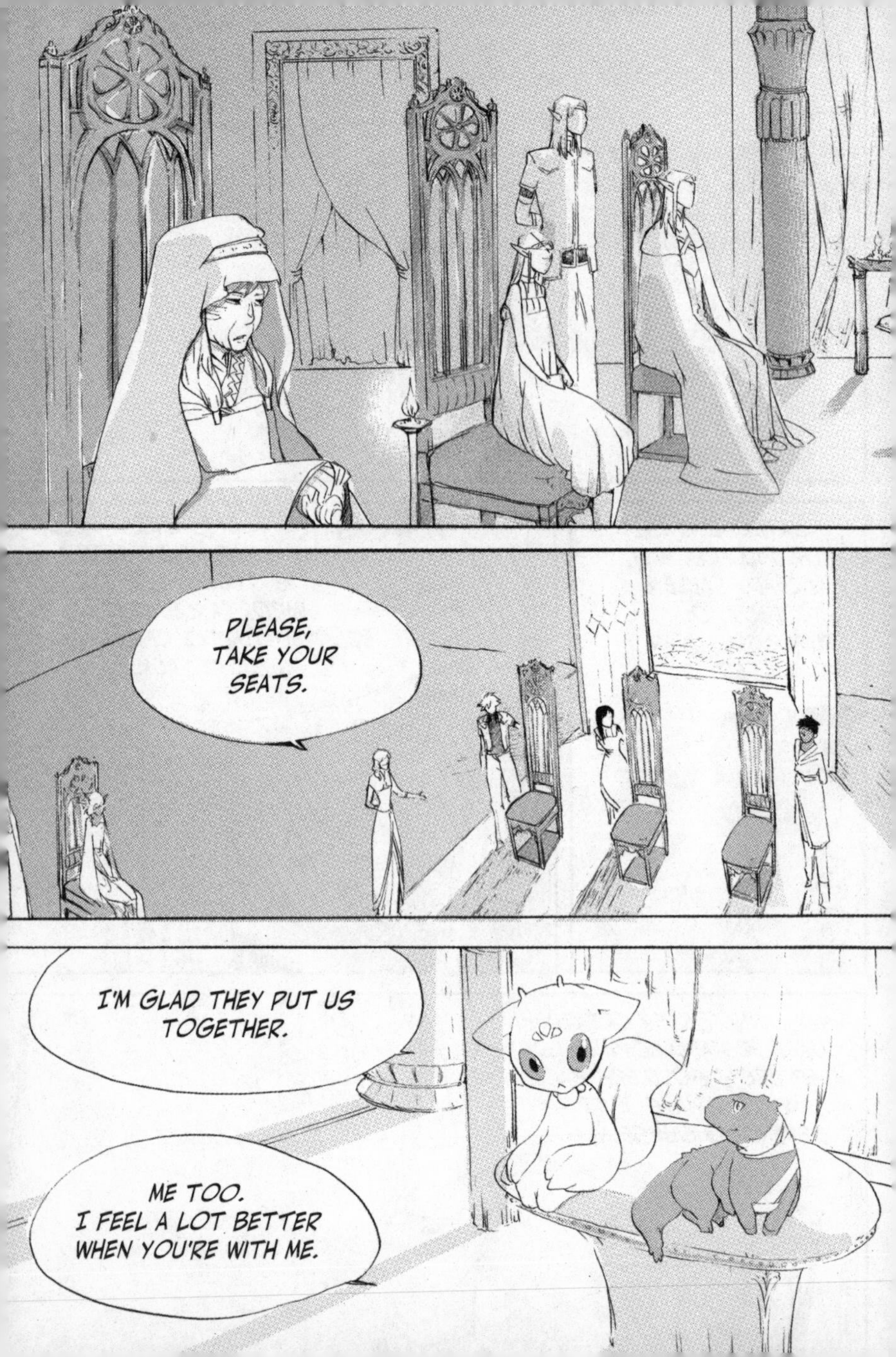
PLEASE, TAKE YOUR SEATS.
I'M GLAD THEY PUT US TOGETHER.
ME TOO. I FEEL A LOT BETTER WHEN YOU'RE WITH ME.

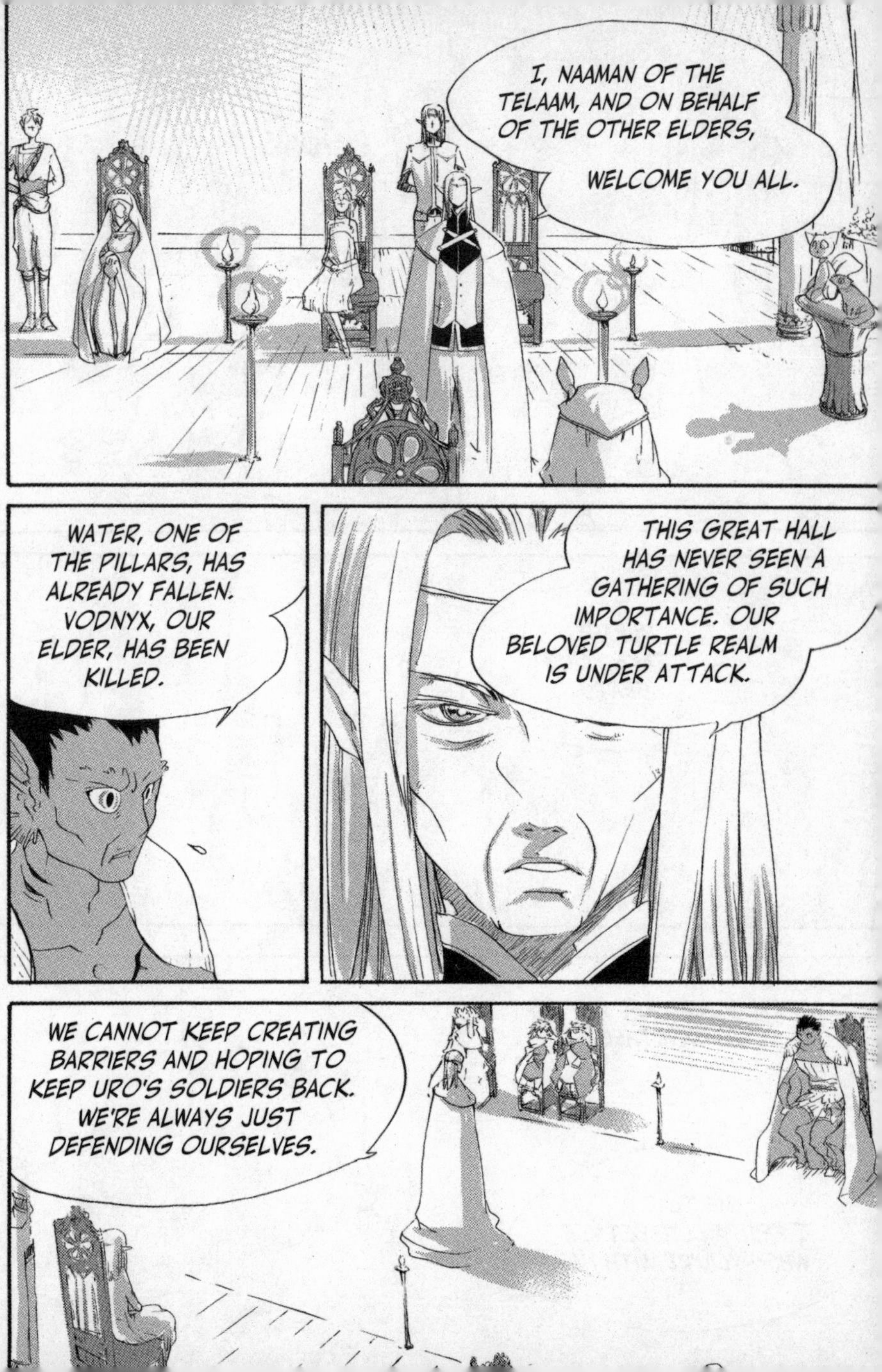
I, NAAMAN OF THE TELAAM, AND ON BEHALF OF THE OTHER ELDERS,
WELCOME YOU ALL.
THIS GREAT HALL HAS NEVER SEEN A GATHERING OF SUCH IMPORTANCE. OUR BELOVED TURTLE REALM IS UNDER ATTACK.
WATER, ONE OF THE PILLARS, HAS ALREADY FALLEN. VODNYX, OUR ELDER, HAS BEEN KILLED.
WE CANNOT KEEP CREATING BARRIERS AND HOPING TO KEEP URO'S SOLDIERS BACK. WE'RE ALWAYS JUST DEFENDING OURSELVES.

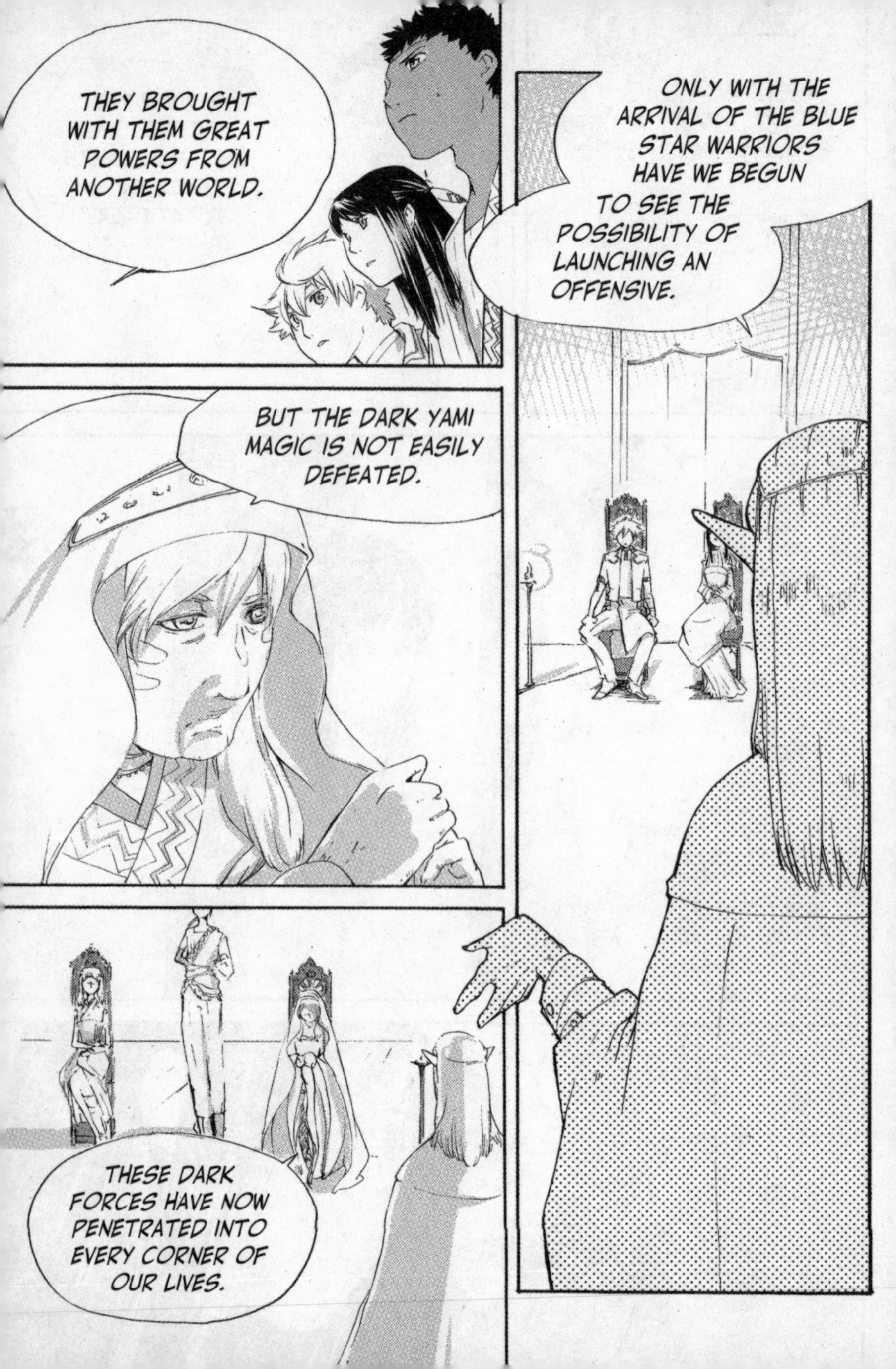
ONLY WITH THE ARRIVAL OF THE BLUE STAR WARRIORS HAVE WE BEGUN TO SEE THE POSSIBILITY OF LAUNCHING AN OFFENSIVE.
THEY BROUGHT WITH THEM GREAT POWERS FROM ANOTHER WORLD.
BUT THE DARK YAMI MAGIC IS NOT EASILY DEFEATED.
THESE DARK FORCES HAVE NOW PENETRATED INTO EVERY CORNER OF OUR LIVES.

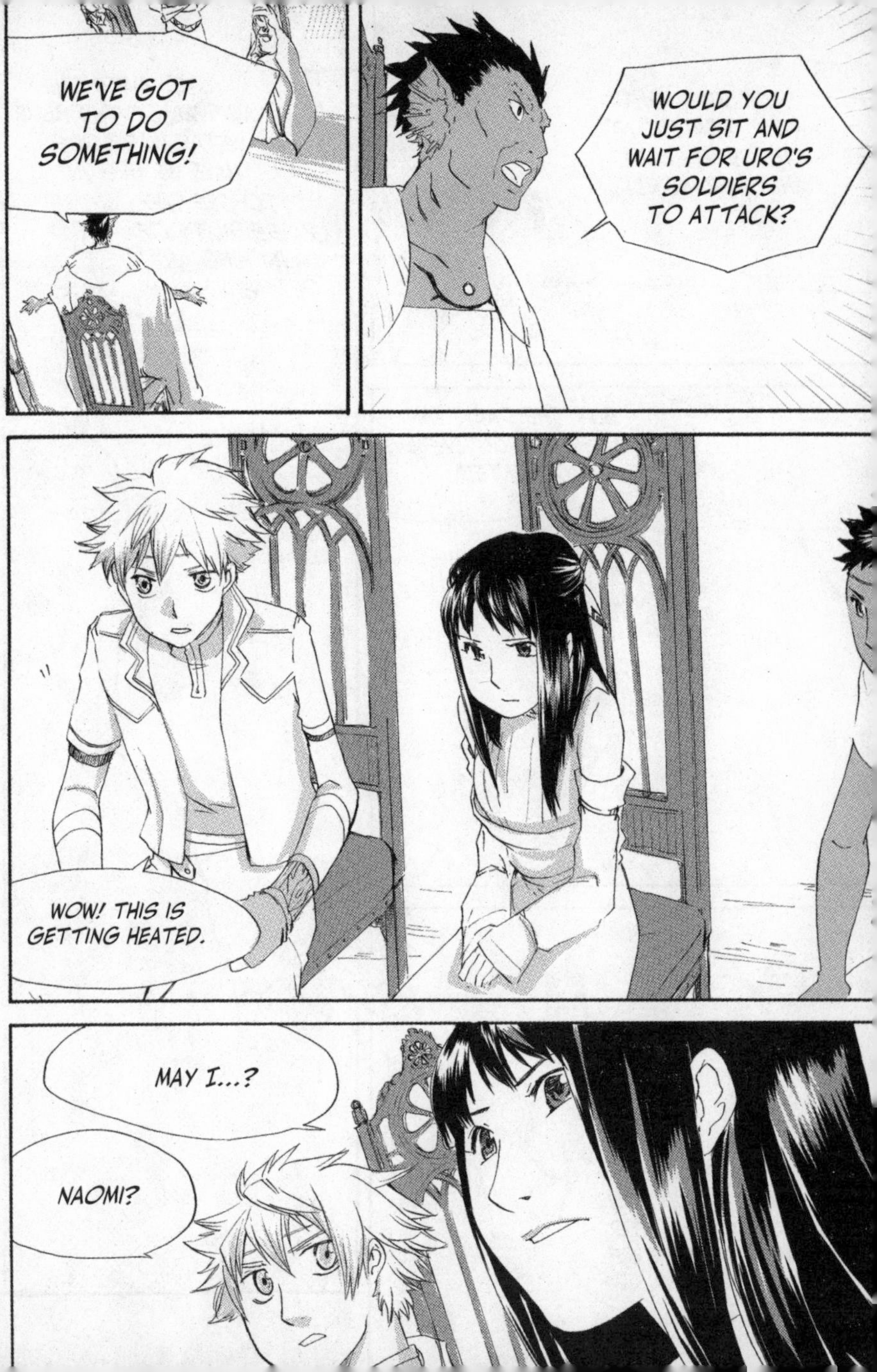
WOULD YOU JUST SIT AND WAIT FOR URO'S SOLDIERS TO ATTACK?
WE'VE GOT TO DO SOMETHING!
WOW! THIS IS GETTING HEATED.
MAY I...?
NAOMI?

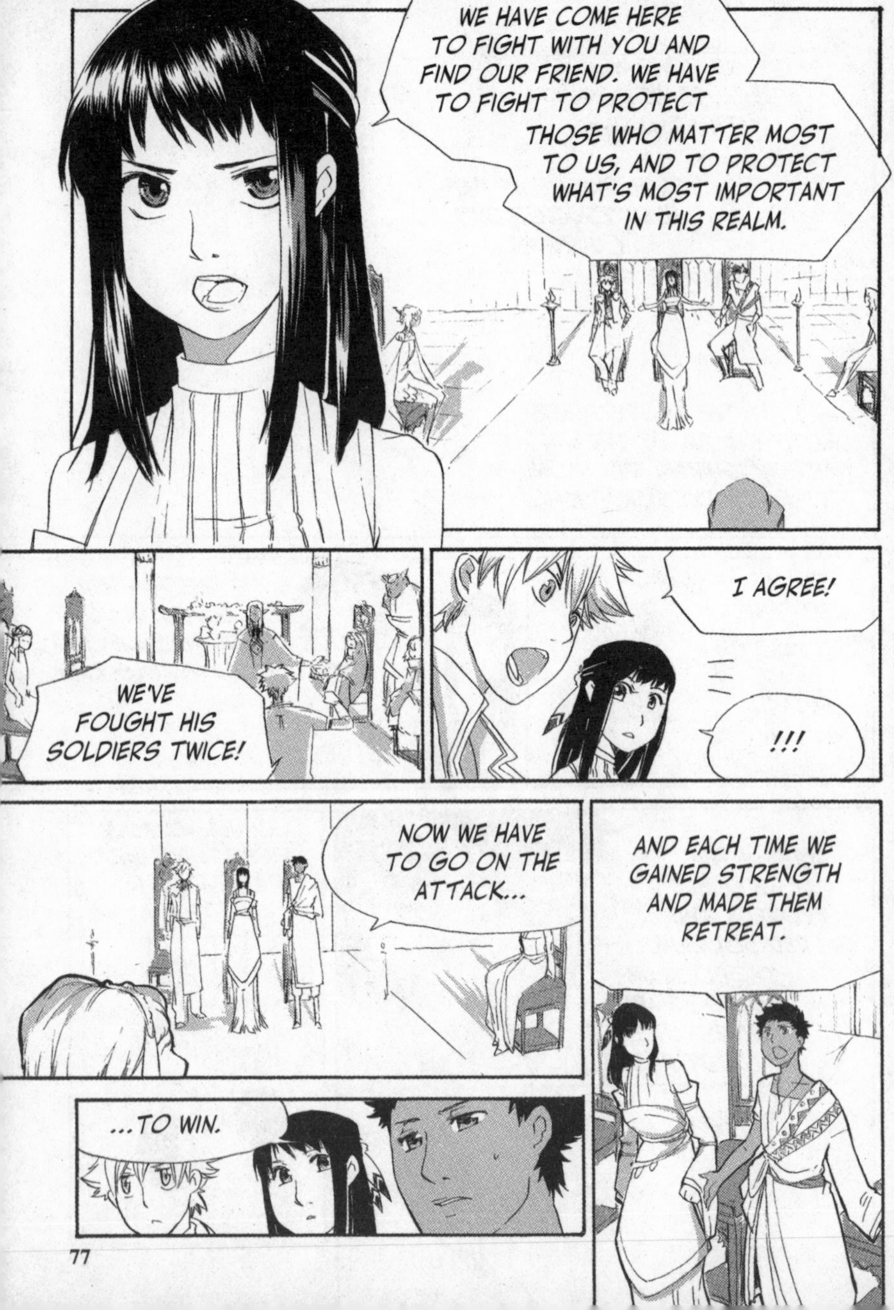
WE HAVE COME HERE TO FIGHT WITH YOU AND FIND OUR FRIEND. WE HAVE TO FIGHT TO PROTECT
THOSE WHO MATTER MOST TO US, AND TO PROTECT WHAT'S MOST IMPORTANT IN THIS REALM.
I AGREE!
!!!
WE'VE FOUGHT HIS SOLDIERS TWICE!
AND EACH TIME WE GAINED STRENGTH AND MADE THEM RETREAT.
NOW WE HAVE TO GO ON THE ATTACK...
...TO WIN.

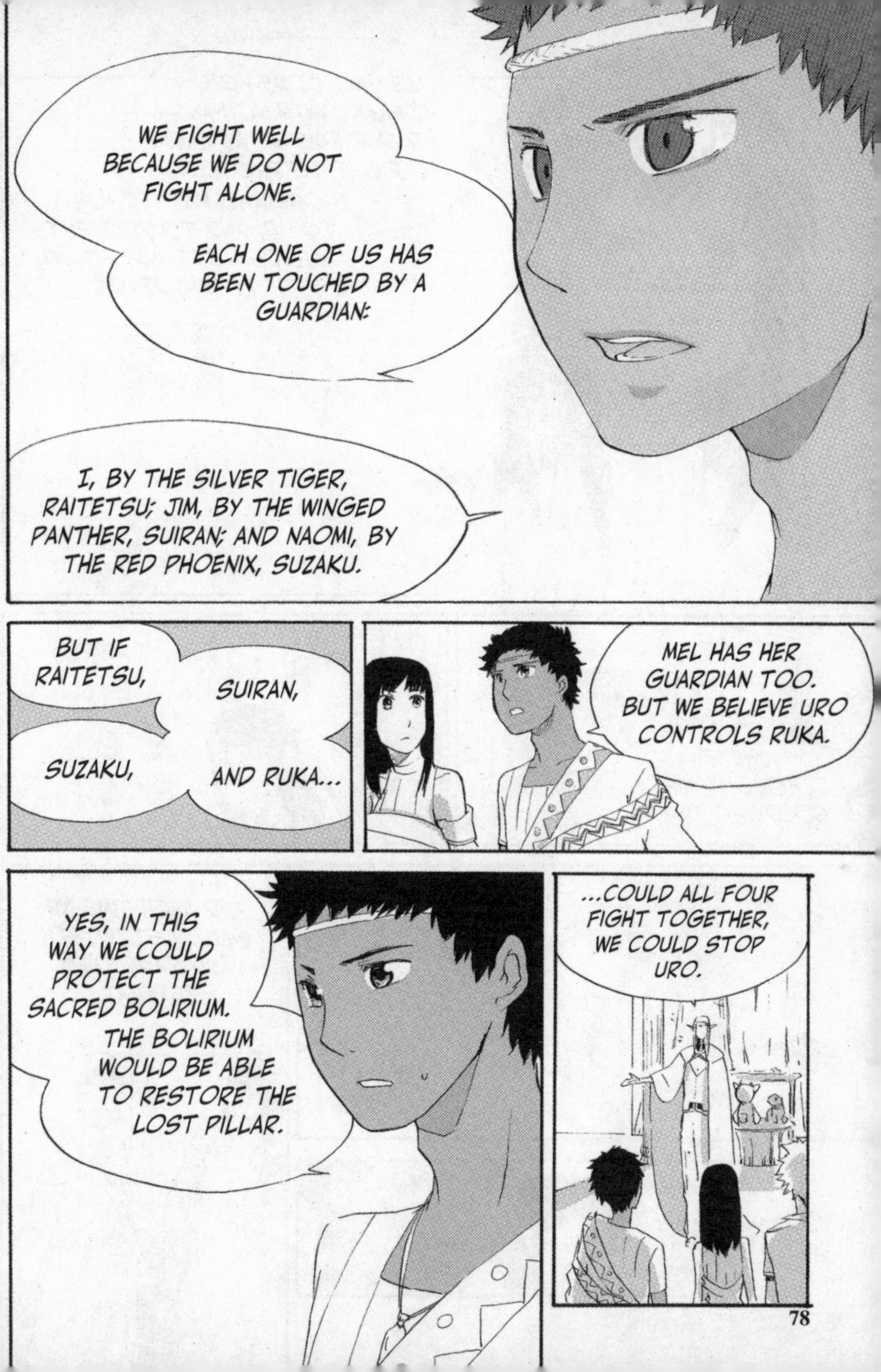
WE FIGHT WELL BECAUSE WE DO NOT FIGHT ALONE.
EACH ONE OF US HAS BEEN TOUCHED BY A GUARDIAN:
I, BY THE SILVER TIGER, RAITETSU; JIM, BY THE WINGED PANTHER, SUIRAN; AND NAOMI, BY THE RED PHOENIX, SUZAKU.
MEL HAS HER GUARDIAN TOO. BUT WE BELIEVE URO CONTROLS RUKA.
BUT IF RAITETSU,
SUIRAN,
SUZAKU,
AND RUKA...
...COULD ALL FOUR FIGHT TOGETHER, WE COULD STOP URO.
YES, IN THIS WAY WE COULD PROTECT THE SACRED BOLIRIUM.
THE BOLIRIUM WOULD BE ABLE TO RESTORE THE LOST PILLAR.

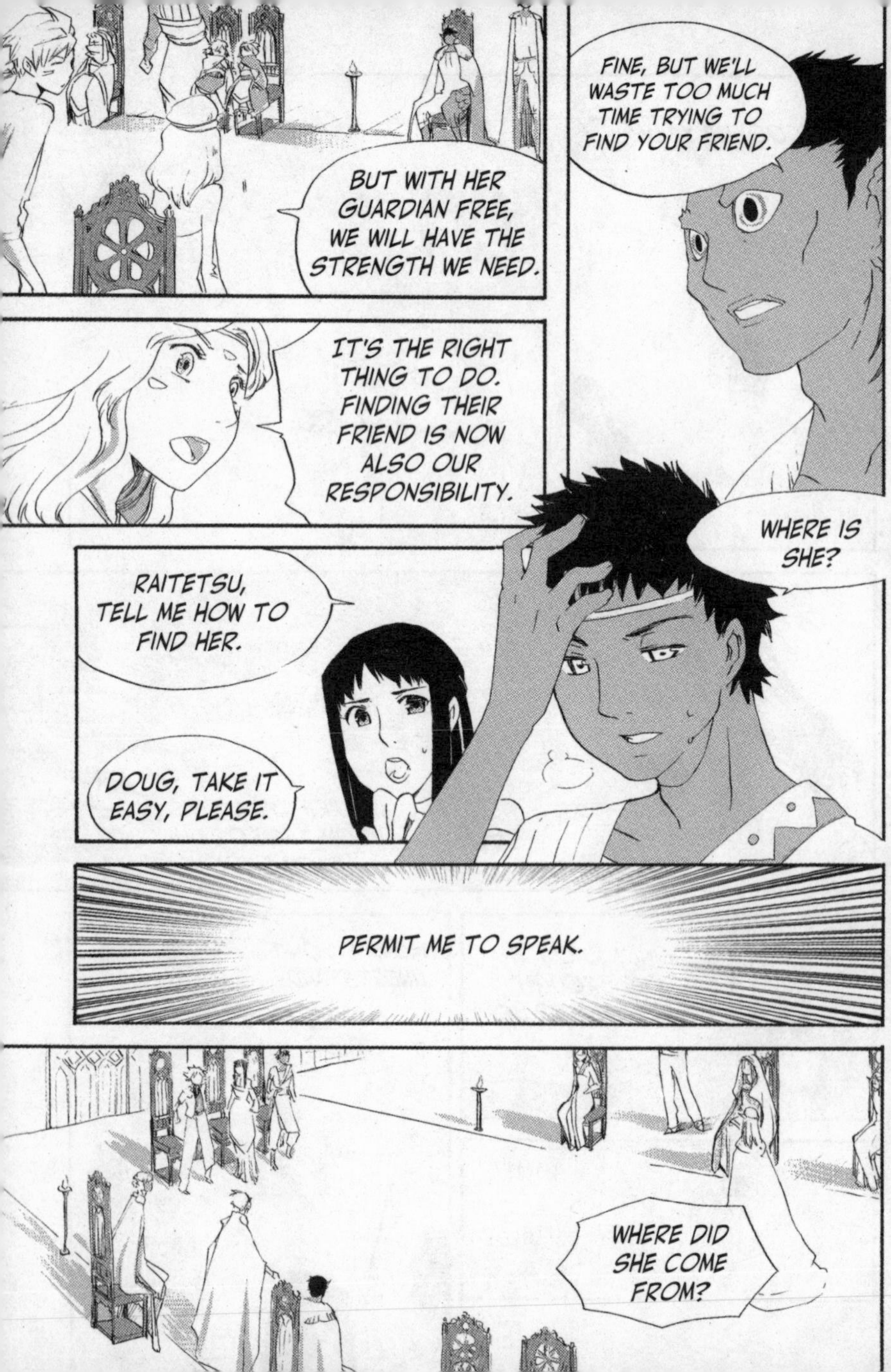
FINE, BUT WE'LL WASTE TOO MUCH TIME TRYING TO FIND YOUR FRIEND.
BUT WITH HER GUARDIAN FREE, WE WILL HAVE THE STRENGTH WE NEED.
IT'S THE RIGHT THING TO DO. FINDING THEIR FRIEND IS NOW ALSO OUR RESPONSIBILITY.
WHERE IS SHE?
RAITETSU, TELL ME HOW TO FIND HER.
DOUG, TAKE IT EASY, PLEASE.
PERMIT ME TO SPEAK.
WHERE DID SHE COME FROM?

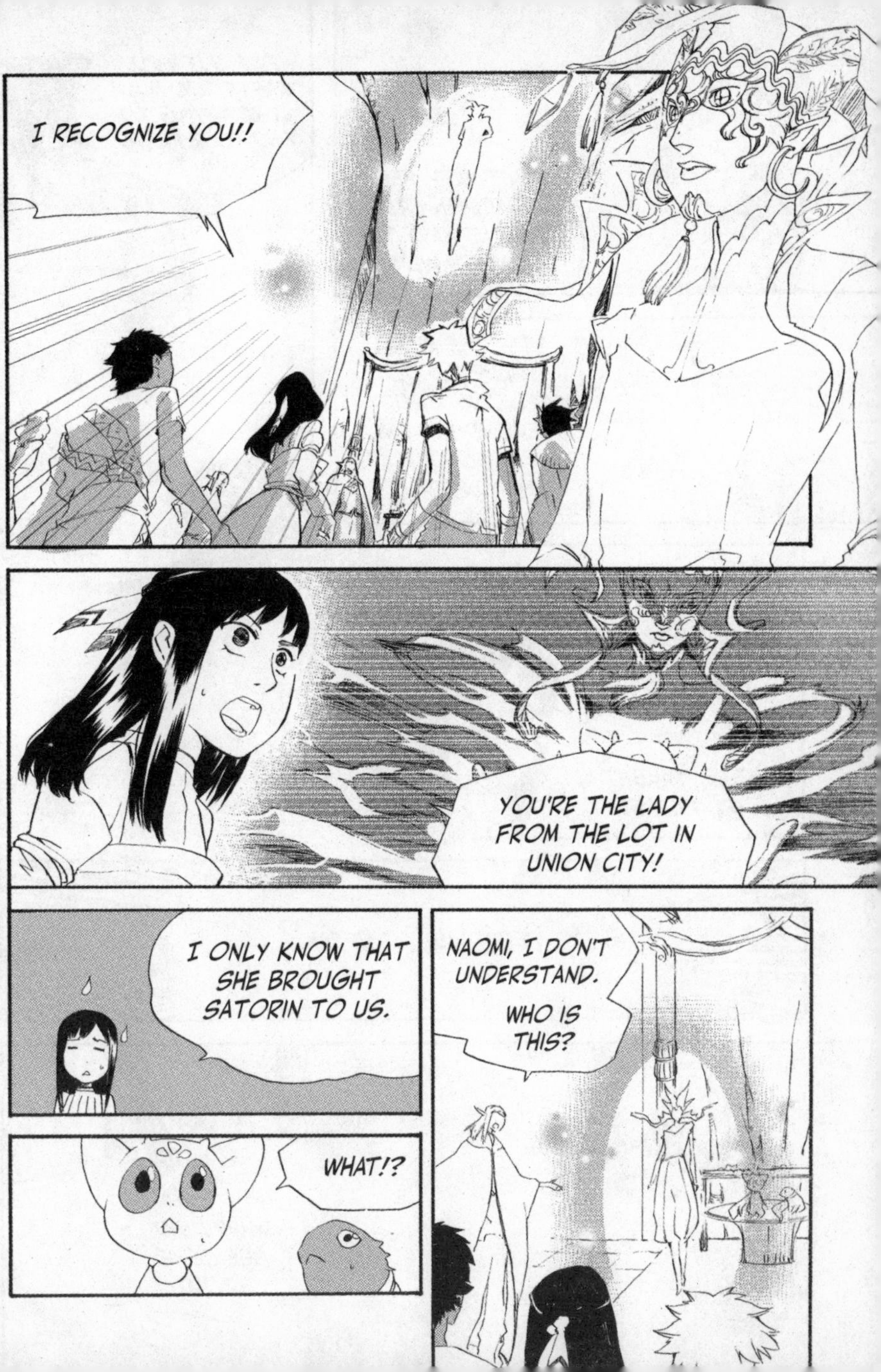
I RECOGNIZE YOU!!
YOU'RE THE LADY FROM THE LOT IN UNION CITY!
NAOMI, I DON'T UNDERSTAND.
WHO IS THIS?
I ONLY KNOW THAT SHE BROUGHT SATORIN TO US.
WHAT!?

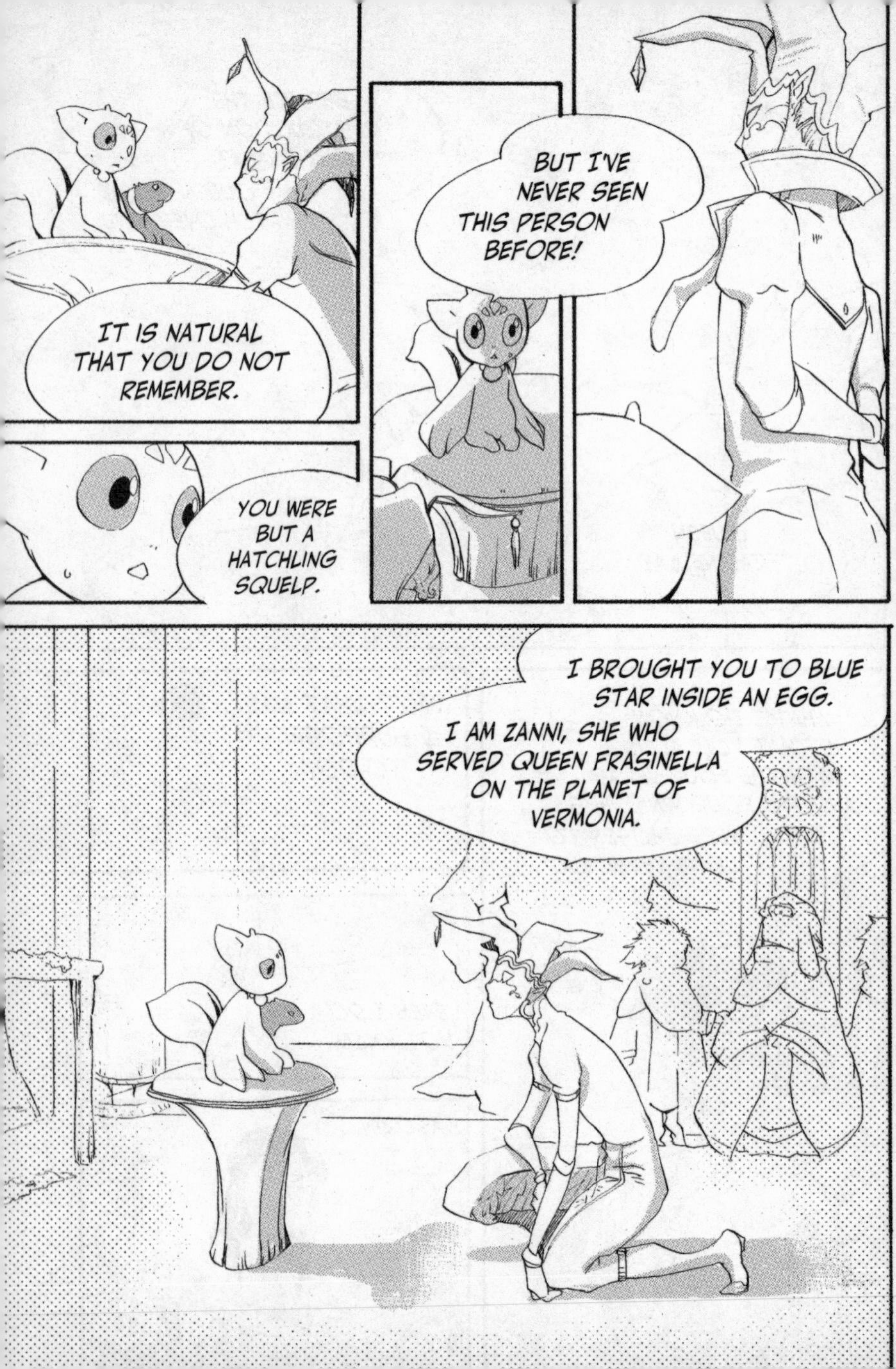
BUT I'VE NEVER SEEN THIS PERSON BEFORE!
IT IS NATURAL THAT YOU DO NOT REMEMBER.
YOU WERE BUT A HATCHLING SQUELP.
I BROUGHT YOU TO BLUE STAR INSIDE AN EGG.
I AM ZANNI, SHE WHO SERVED QUEEN FRASINELLA ON THE PLANET OF VERMONIA.

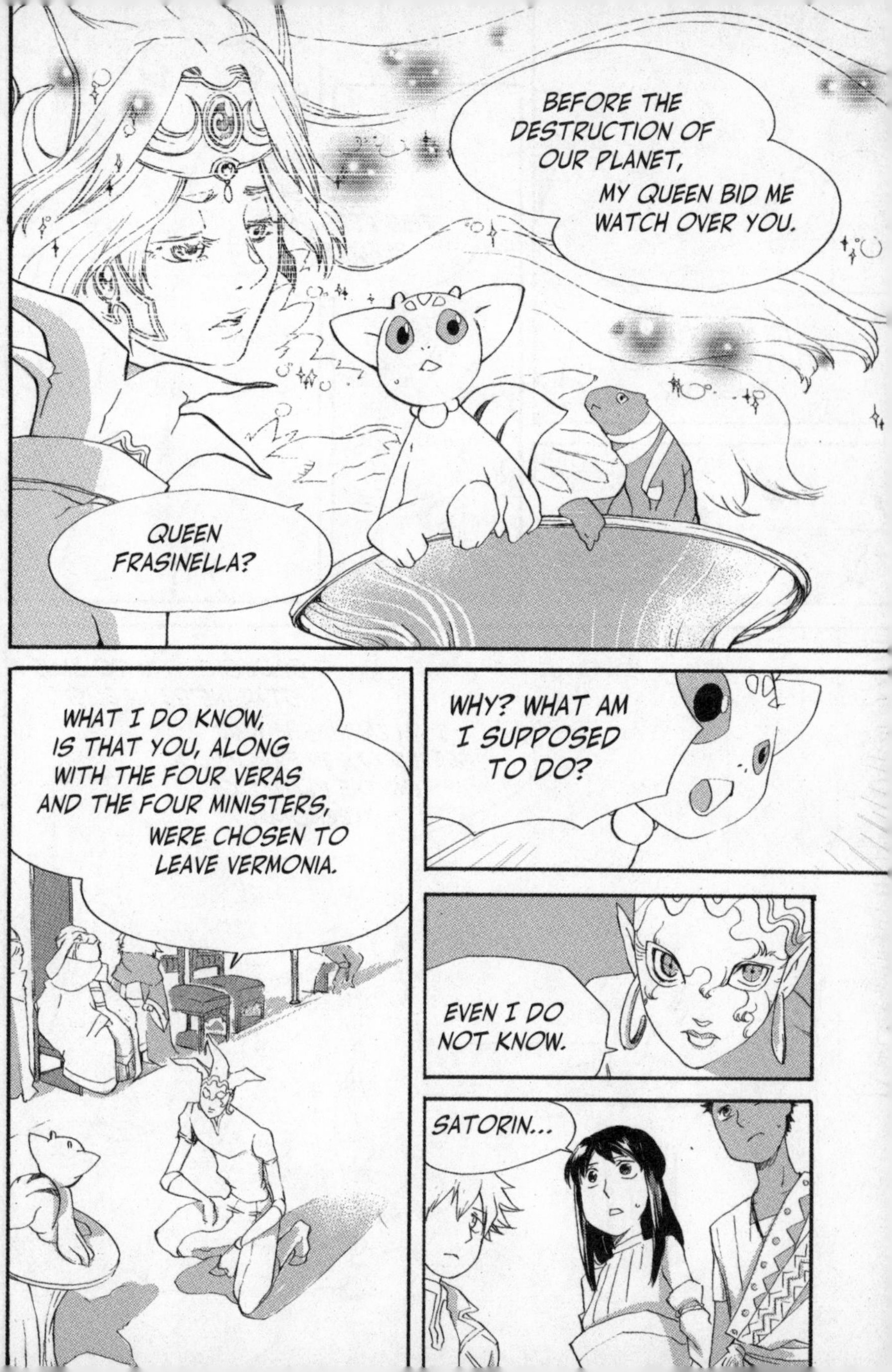
BEFORE THE DESTRUCTION OF OUR PLANET, MY QUEEN BID ME WATCH OVER YOU.
QUEEN FRASINELLA?
WHY? WHAT AM I SUPPOSED TO DO?
EVEN I DO NOT KNOW.
SATORIN...
WHAT I DO KNOW, IS THAT YOU, ALONG WITH THE FOUR VERAS AND THE FOUR MINISTERS, WERE CHOSEN TO LEAVE VERMONIA.

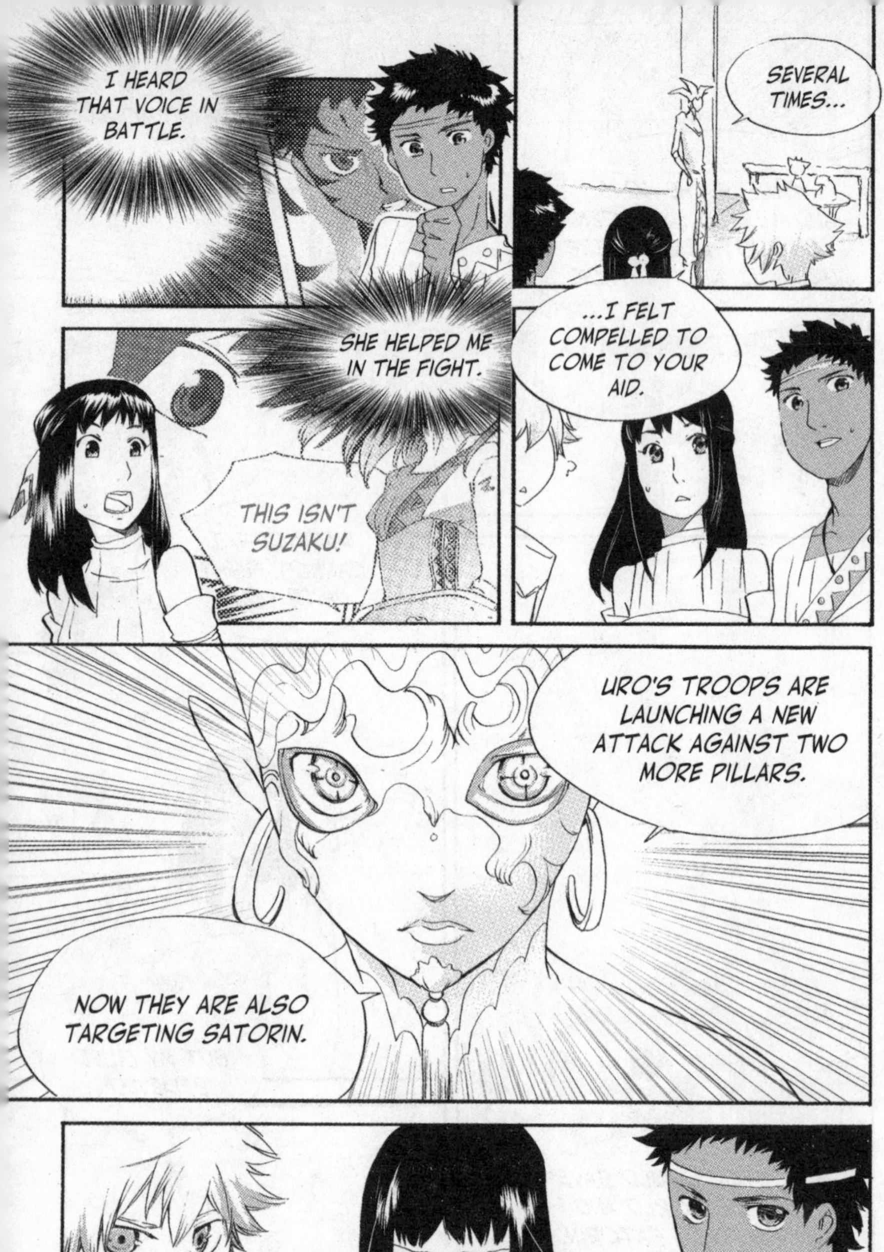
SEVERAL TIMES...
I HEARD THAT VOICE IN BATTLE.
...I FELT COMPELLED TO COME TO YOUR AID.
SHE HELPED ME IN THE FIGHT.
THIS ISN'T SUZAKU!
URO'S TROOPS ARE LAUNCHING A NEW ATTACK AGAINST TWO MORE PILLARS.
NOW THEY ARE ALSO TARGETING SATORIN.

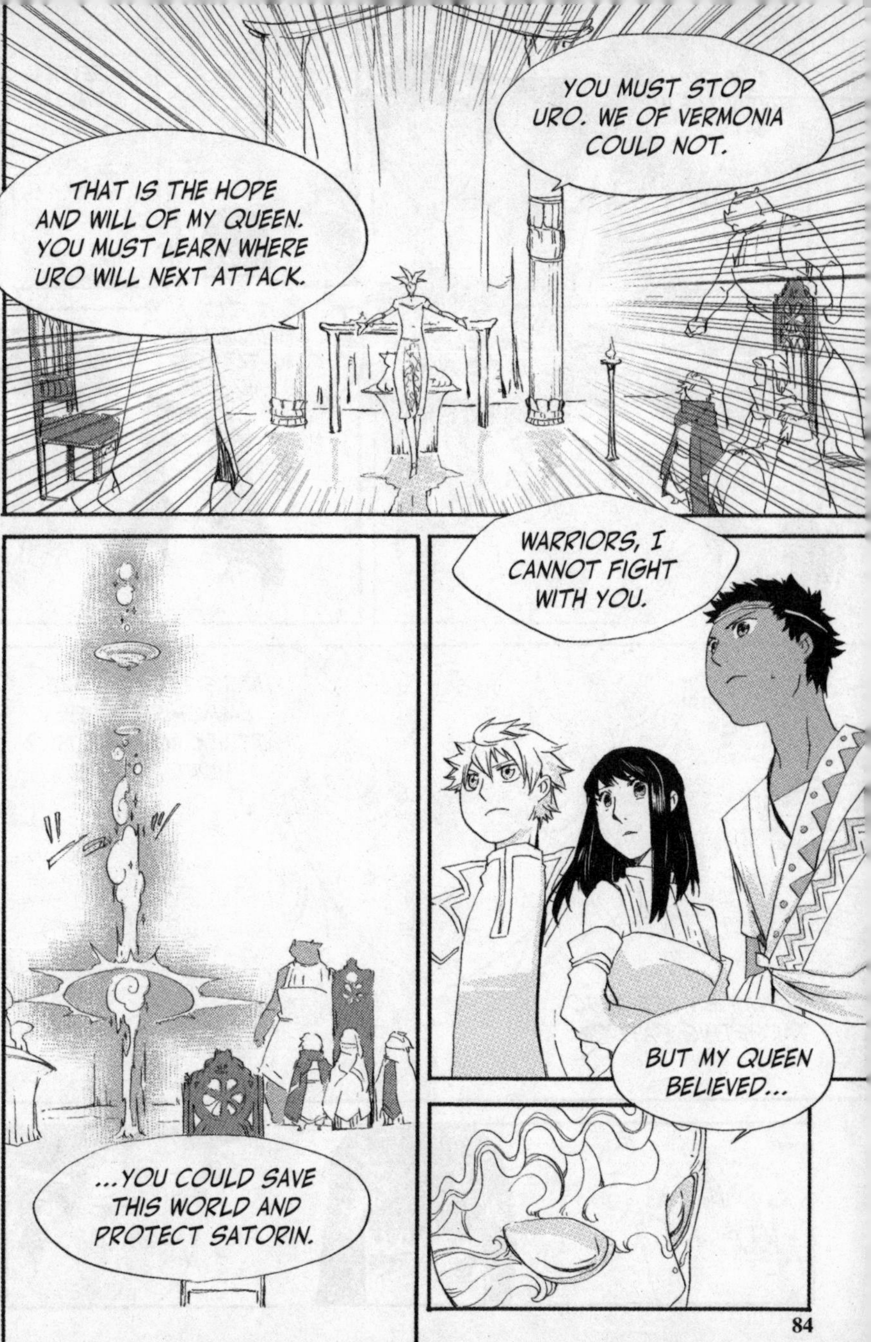
YOU MUST STOP URO. WE OF VERMONIA COULD NOT.
THAT IS THE HOPE AND WILL OF MY QUEEN. YOU MUST LEARN WHERE URO WILL NEXT ATTACK.
WARRIORS, I CANNOT FIGHT WITH YOU.
BUT MY QUEEN BELIEVED...
...YOU COULD SAVE THIS WORLD AND PROTECT SATORIN.

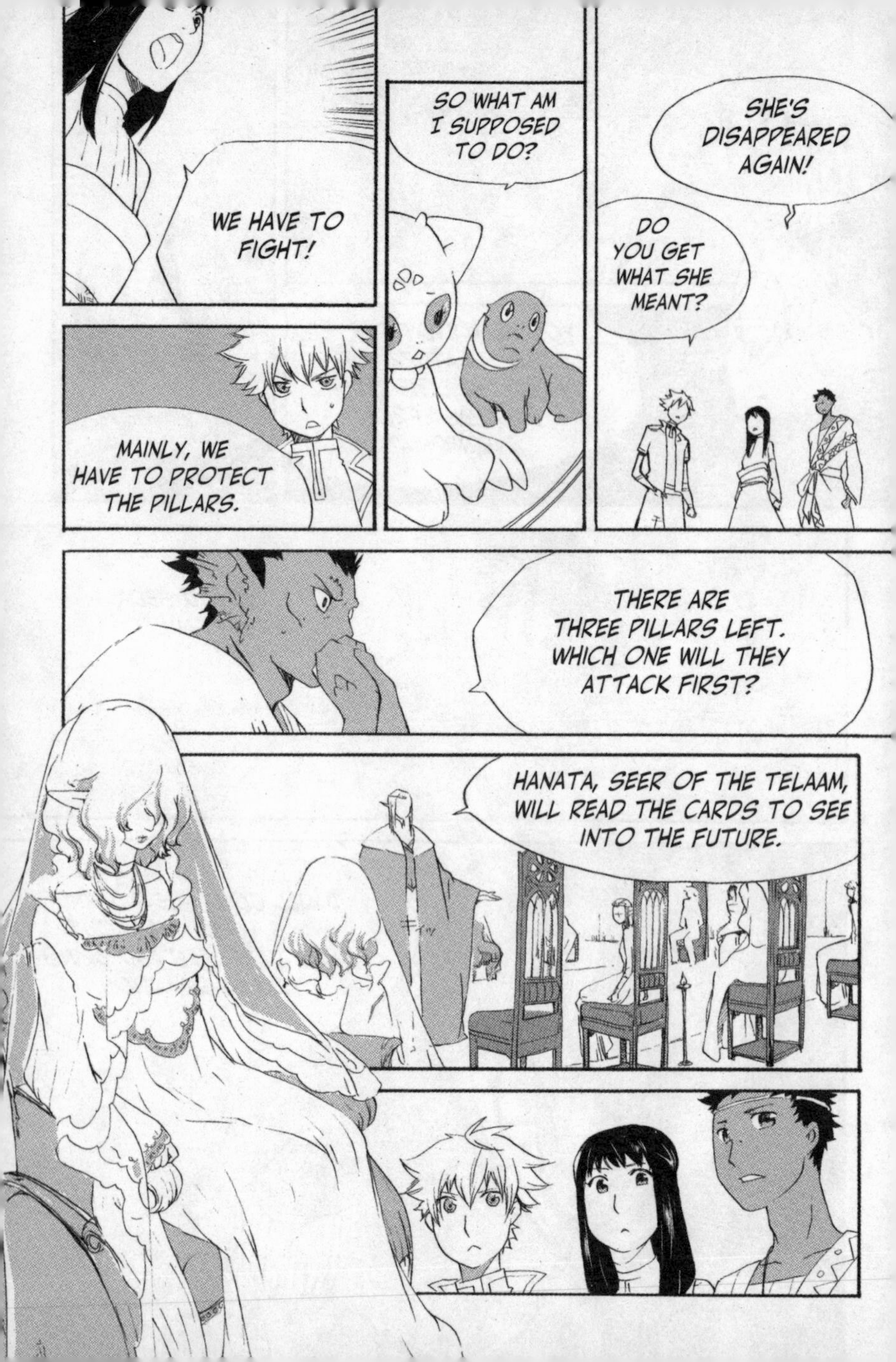
SHE'S DISAPPEARED AGAIN!
DO YOU GET WHAT SHE MEANT?
SO WHAT AM I SUPPOSED TO DO?
WE HAVE TO FIGHT!
MAINLY, WE HAVE TO PROTECT THE PILLARS.
THERE ARE THREE PILLARS LEFT. WHICH ONE WILL THEY ATTACK FIRST?
HANATA, SEER OF THE TELAAM, WILL READ THE CARDS TO SEE INTO THE FUTURE.

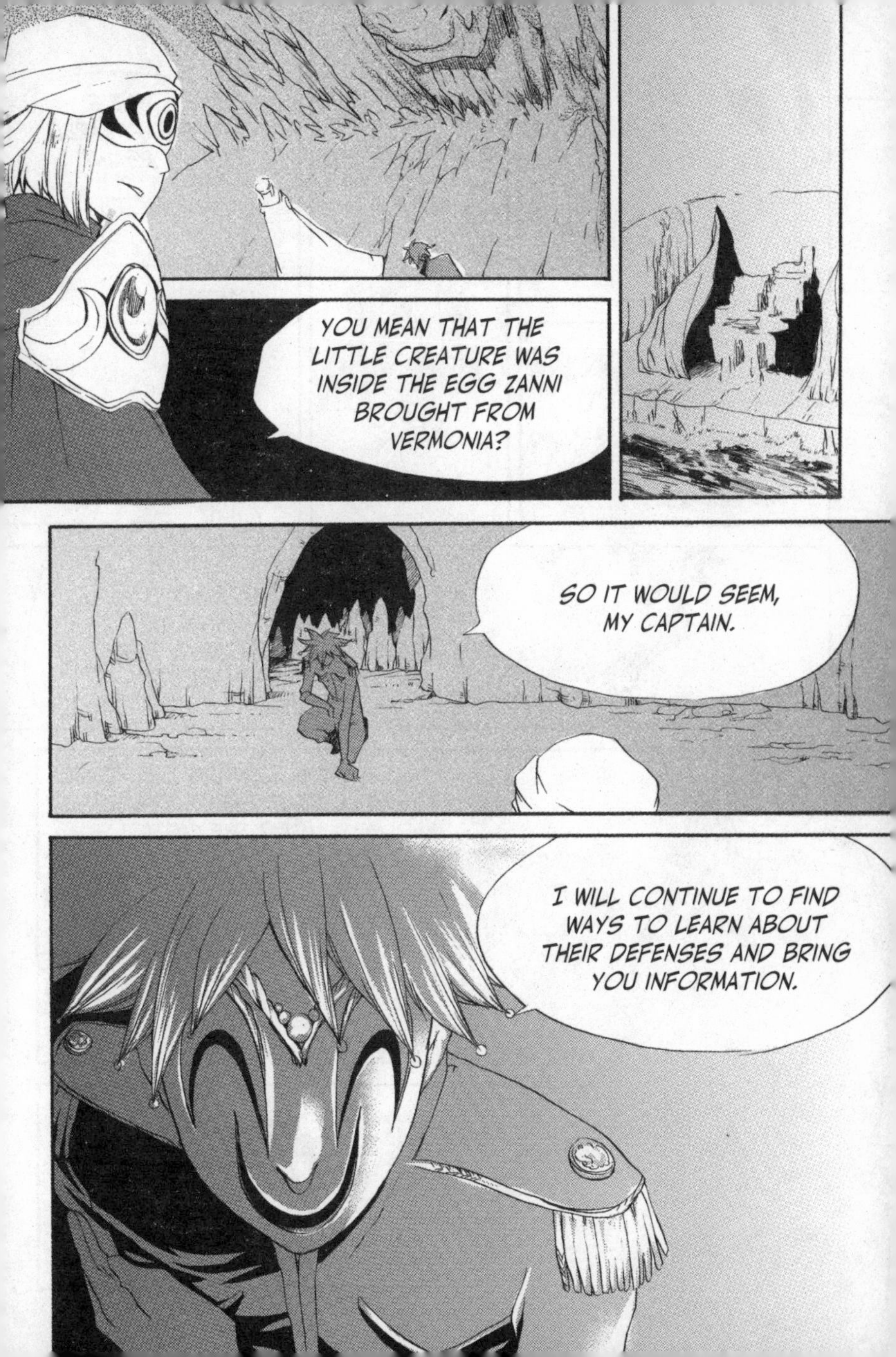
YOU MEAN THAT THE LITTLE CREATURE WAS INSIDE THE EGG ZANNI BROUGHT FROM VERMONIA?
SO IT WOULD SEEM, MY CAPTAIN.
I WILL CONTINUE TO FIND WAYS TO LEARN ABOUT THEIR DEFENSES AND BRING YOU INFORMATION.

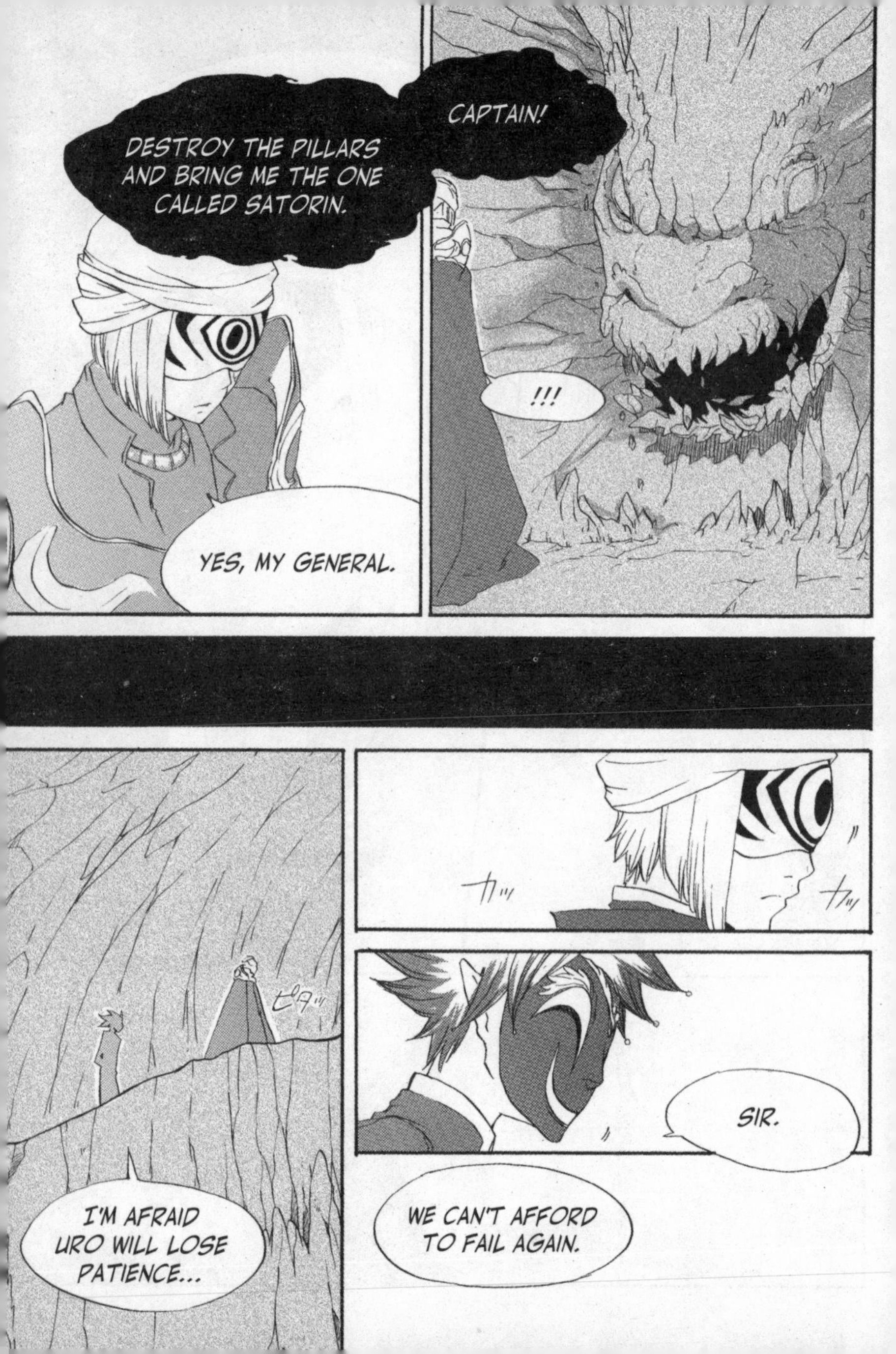
CAPTAIN!
DESTROY THE PILLARS AND BRING ME THE ONE CALLED SATORIN.
!!!
YES, MY GENERAL.
カッ
カッ
SIR.
WE CAN'T AFFORD TO FAIL AGAIN.
ピタッ
I'M AFRAID URO WILL LOSE PATIENCE...

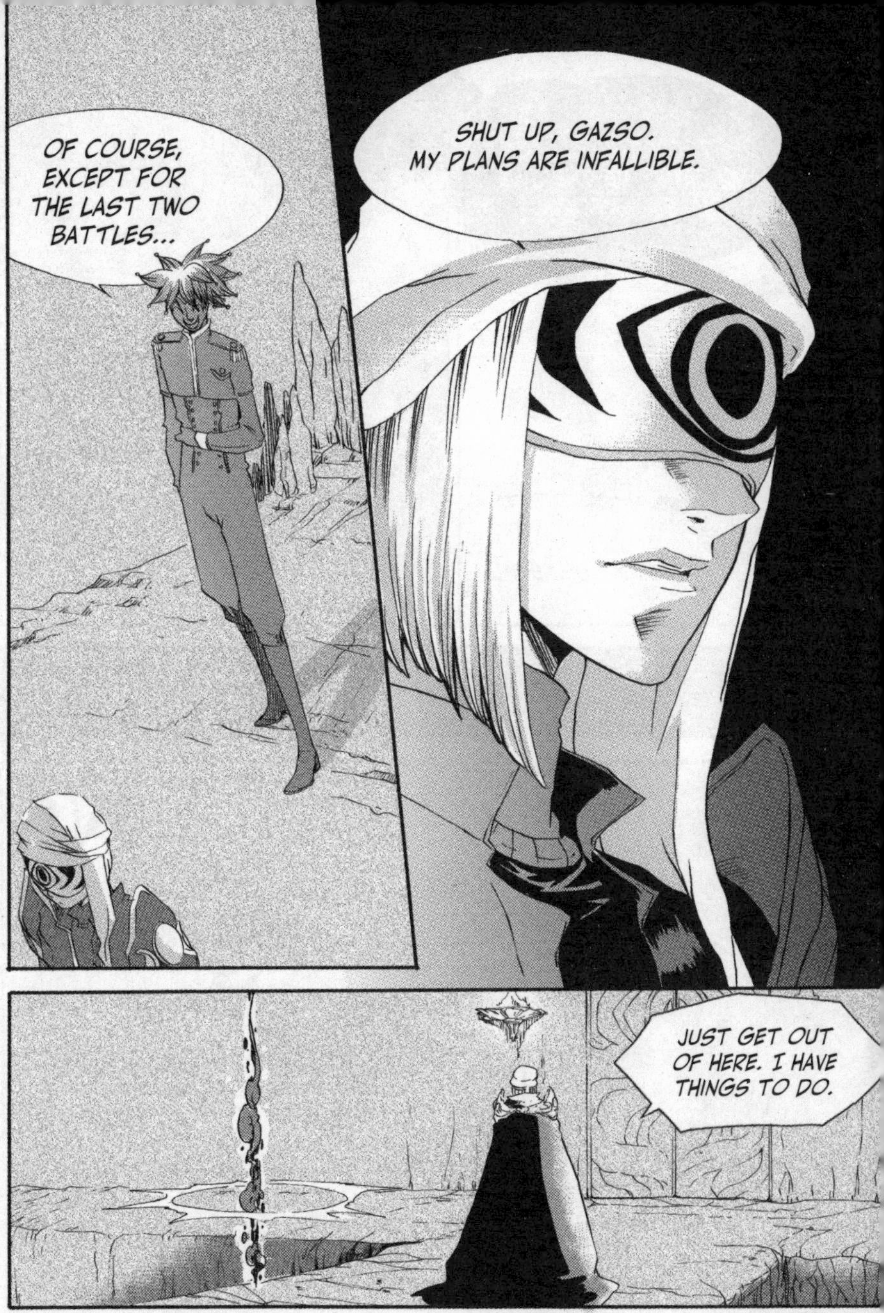
SHUT UP, GAZSO. MY PLANS ARE INFALLIBLE.
OF COURSE, EXCEPT FOR THE LAST TWO BATTLES...
JUST GET OUT OF HERE. I HAVE THINGS TO DO.

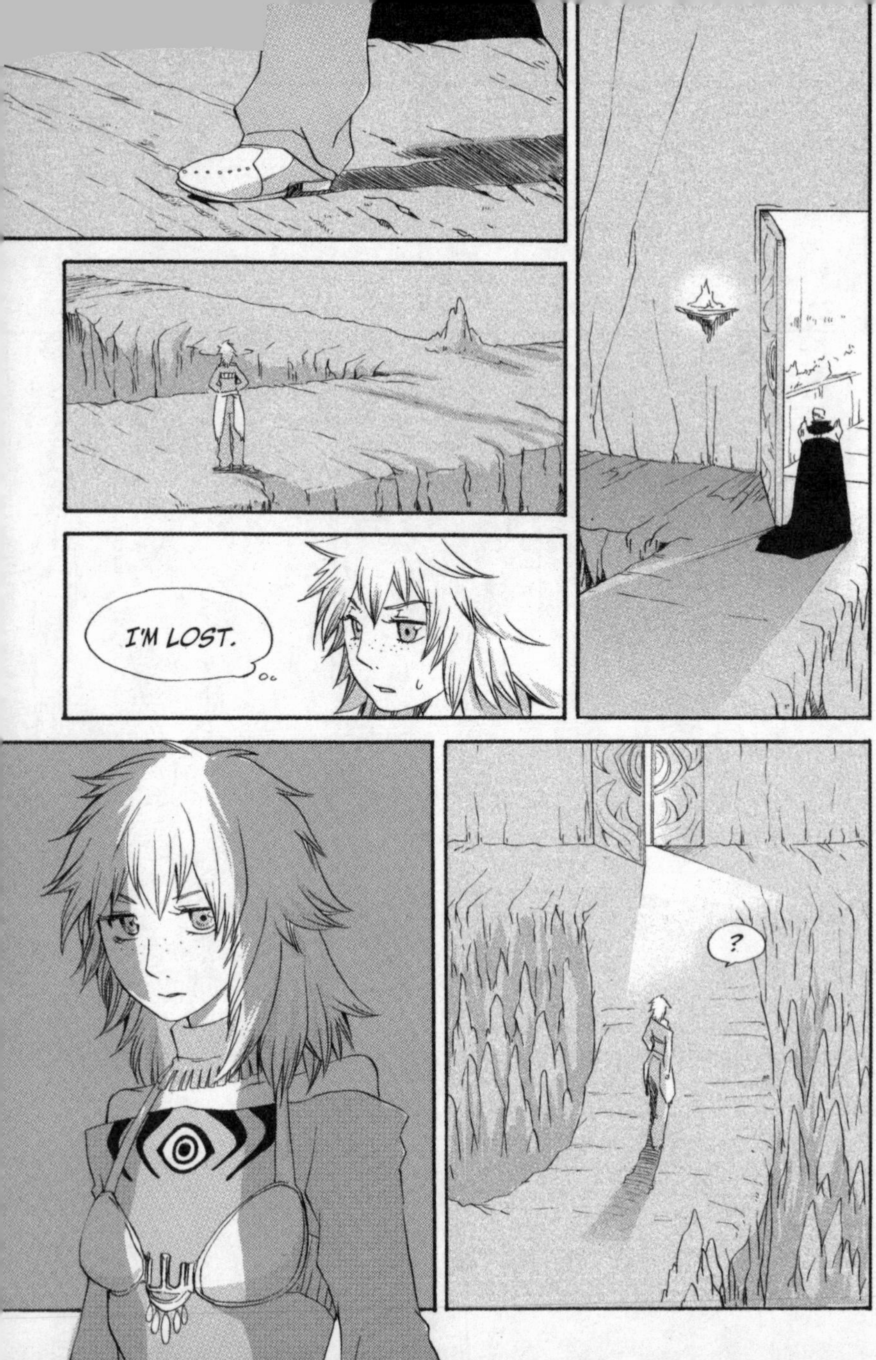
I'M LOST.
?

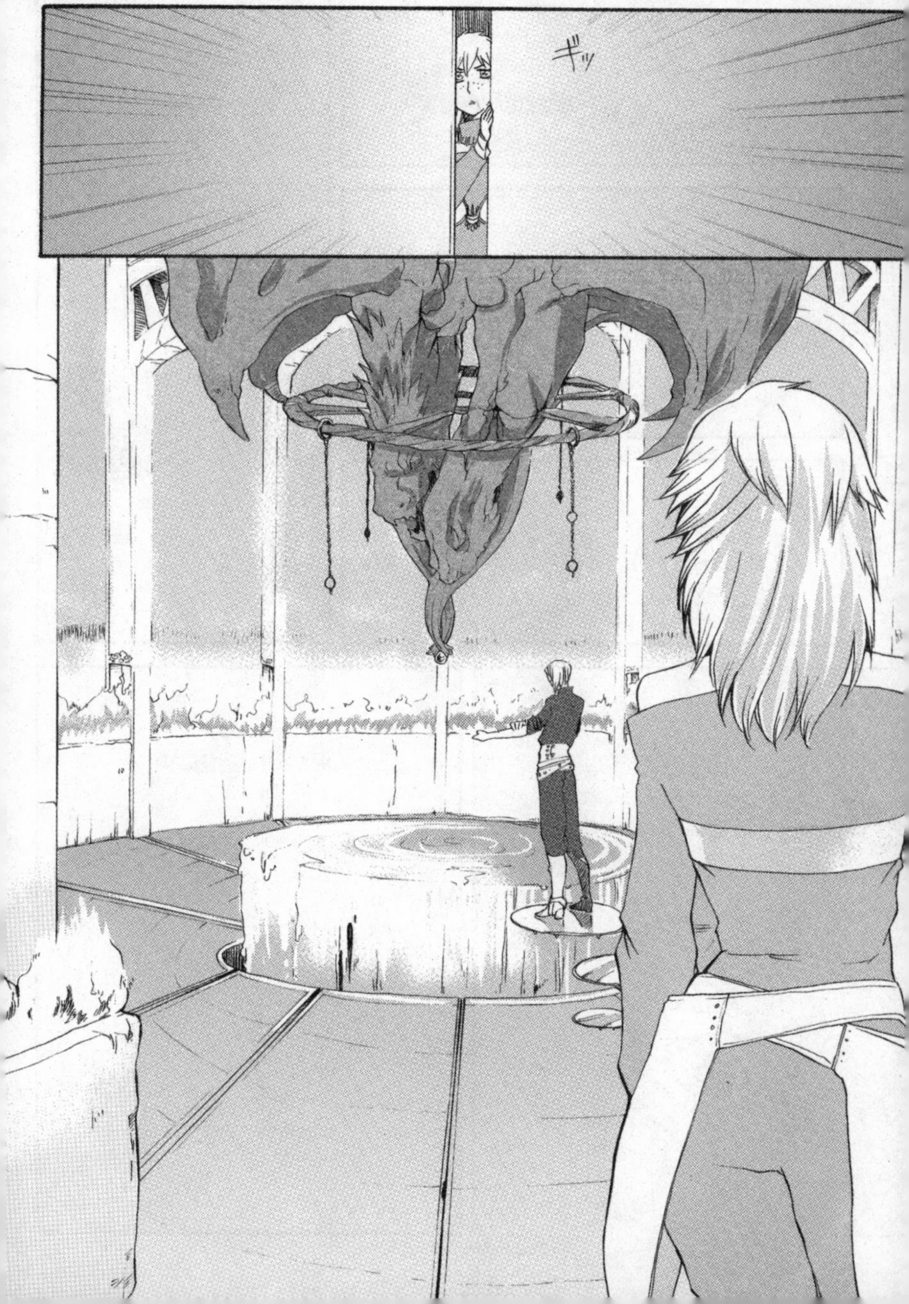
ギッ

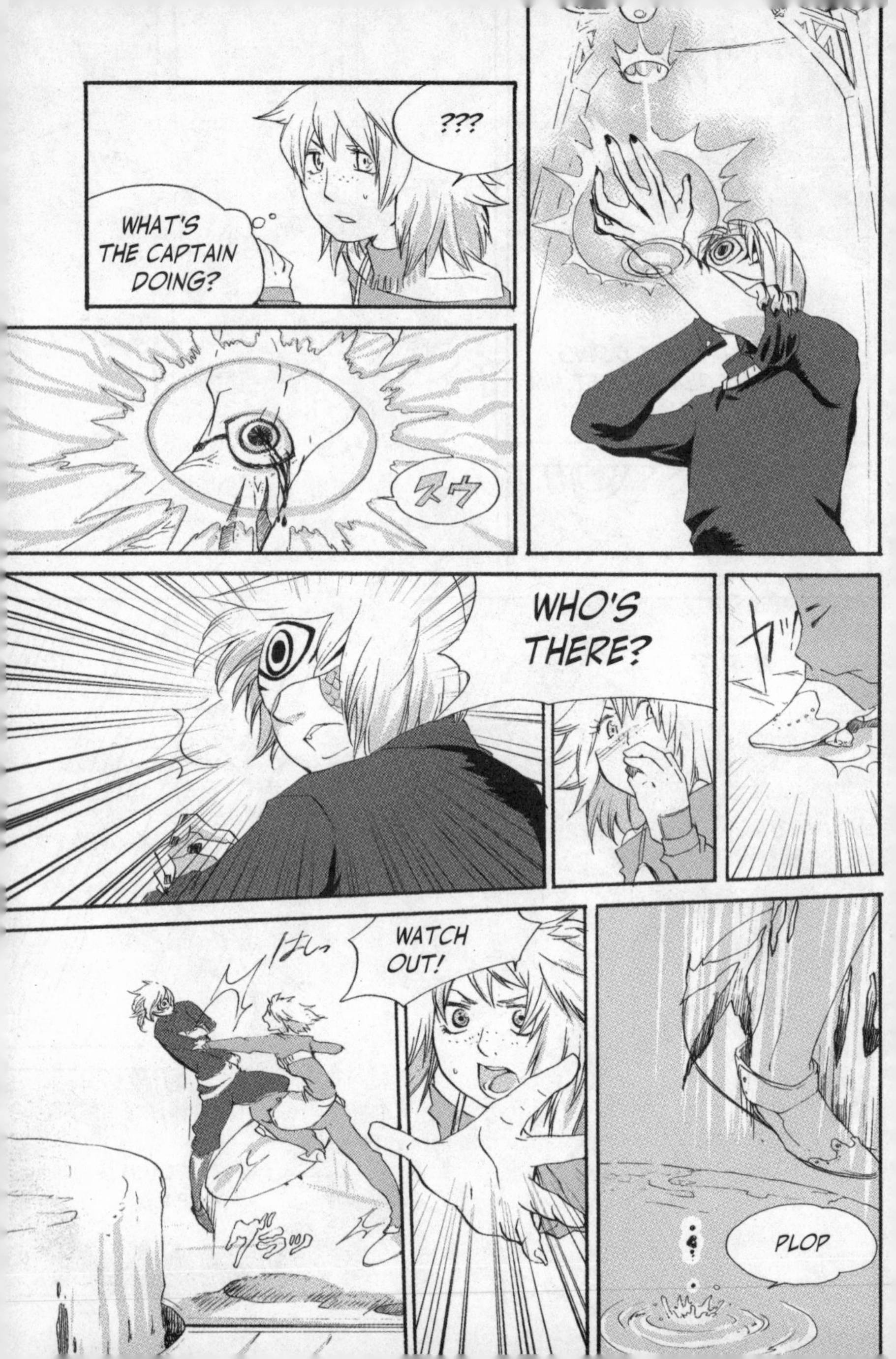
???
WHAT'S THE CAPTAIN DOING?
スウ
WHO'S THERE?
PLOP
WATCH OUT!
はっ
グラッ

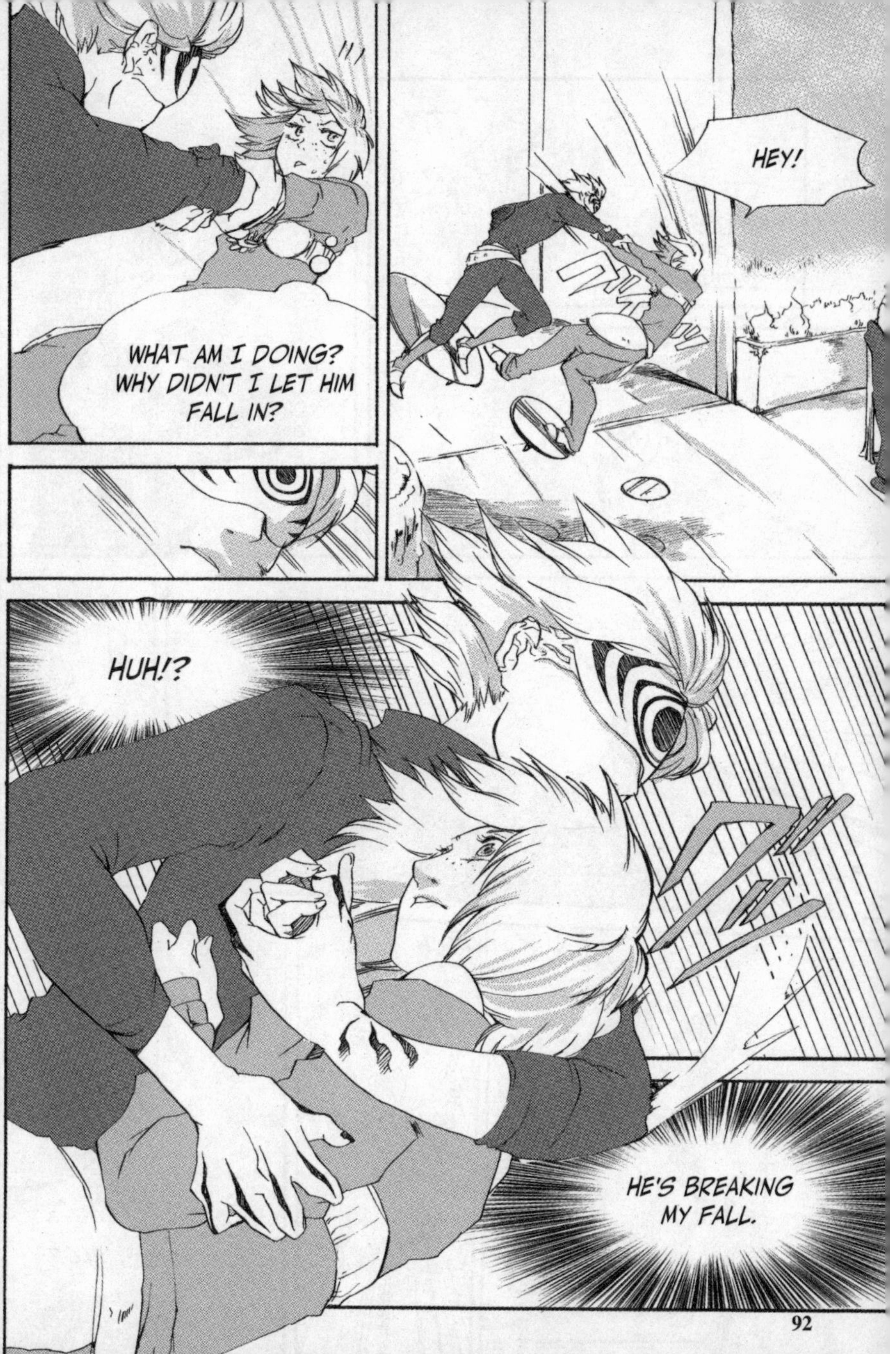
HEY!
WHAT AM I DOING? WHY DIDN'T I LET HIM FALL IN?
HUH!?
HE'S BREAKING MY FALL.

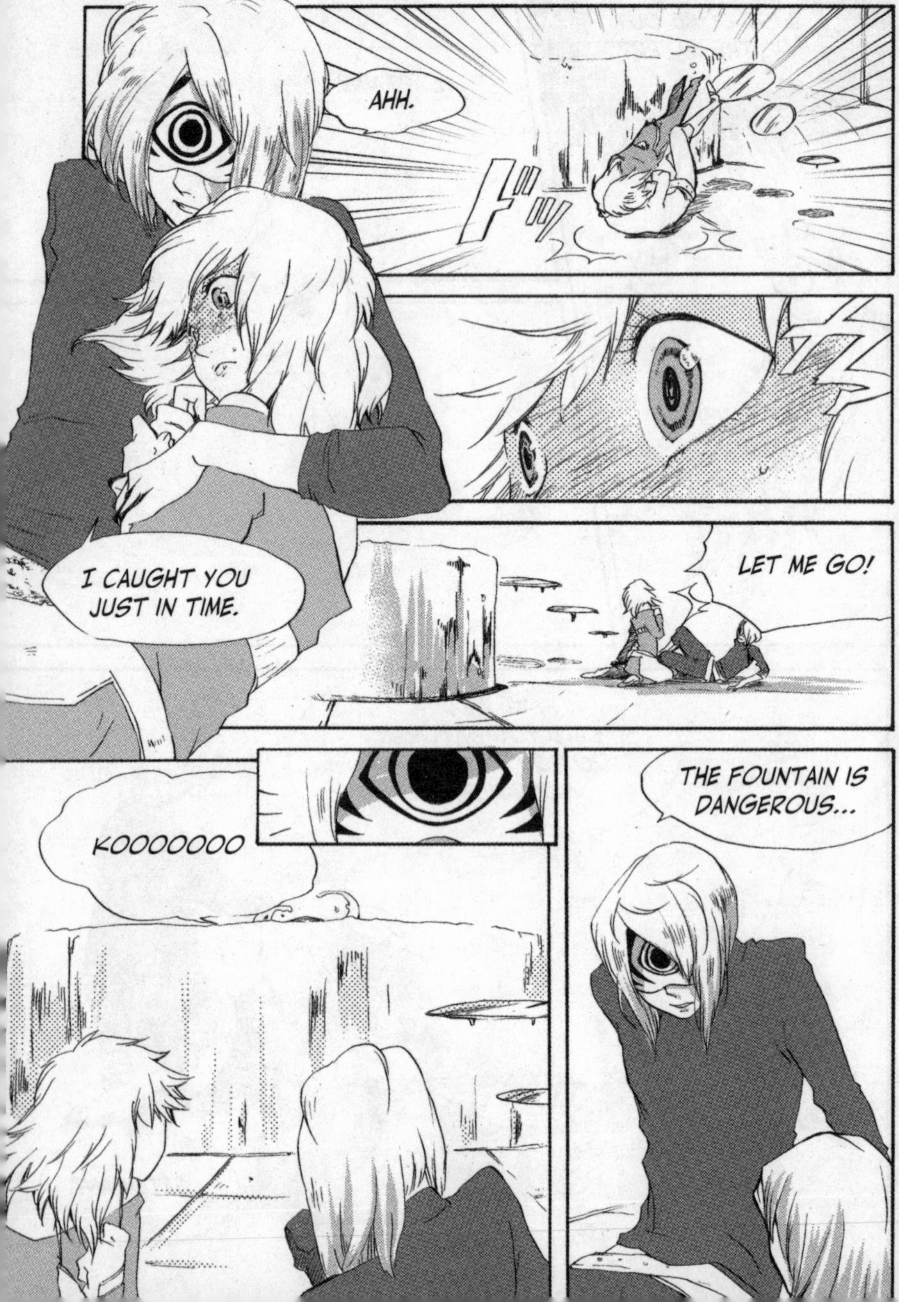
AHH.
LET ME GO!
I CAUGHT YOU JUST IN TIME.
THE FOUNTAIN IS DANGEROUS...
KOOOOOOO

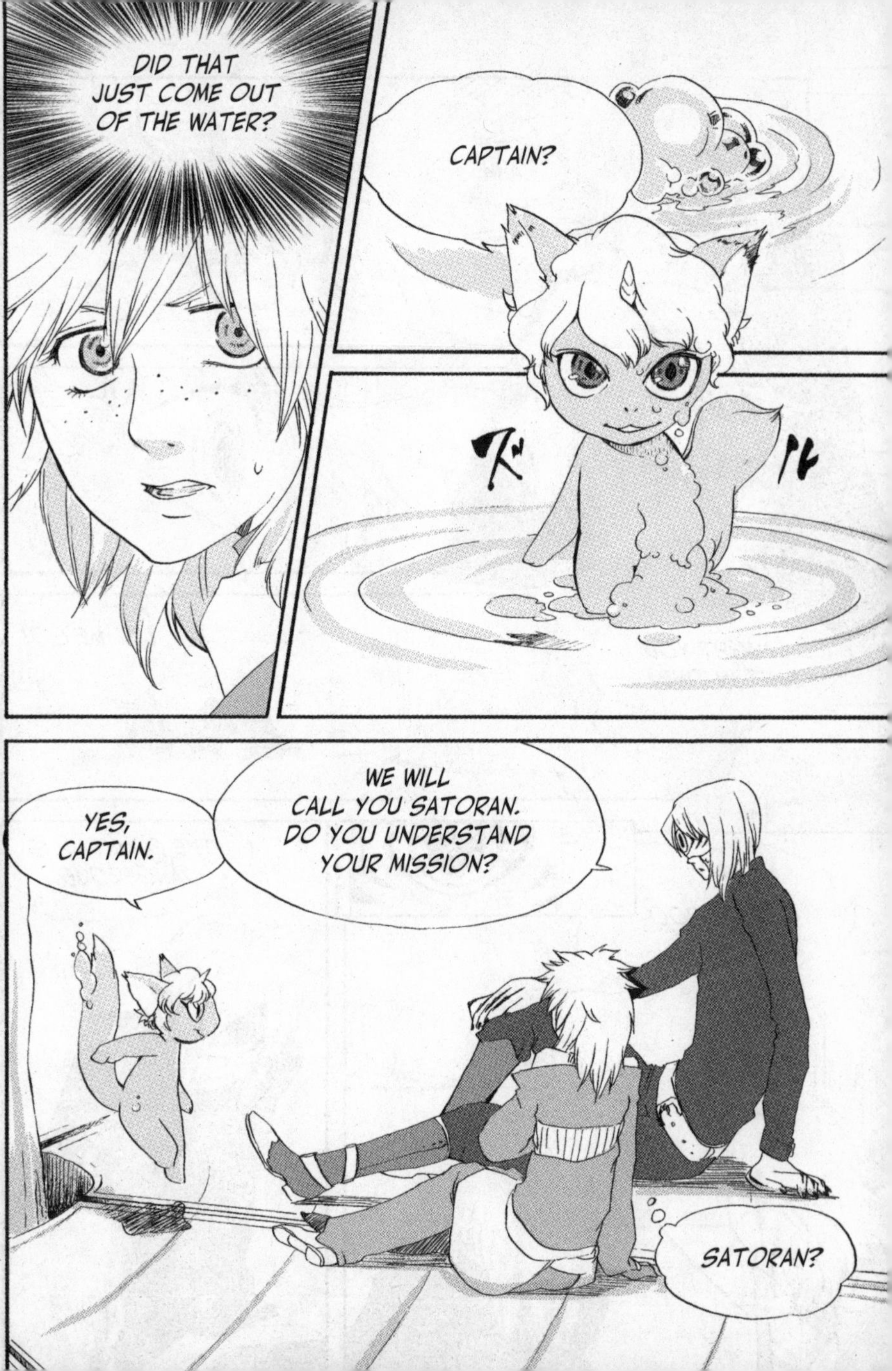
CAPTAIN?
DID THAT JUST COME OUT OF THE WATER?
WE WILL CALL YOU SATORAN. DO YOU UNDERSTAND YOUR MISSION?
YES, CAPTAIN.
SATORAN?

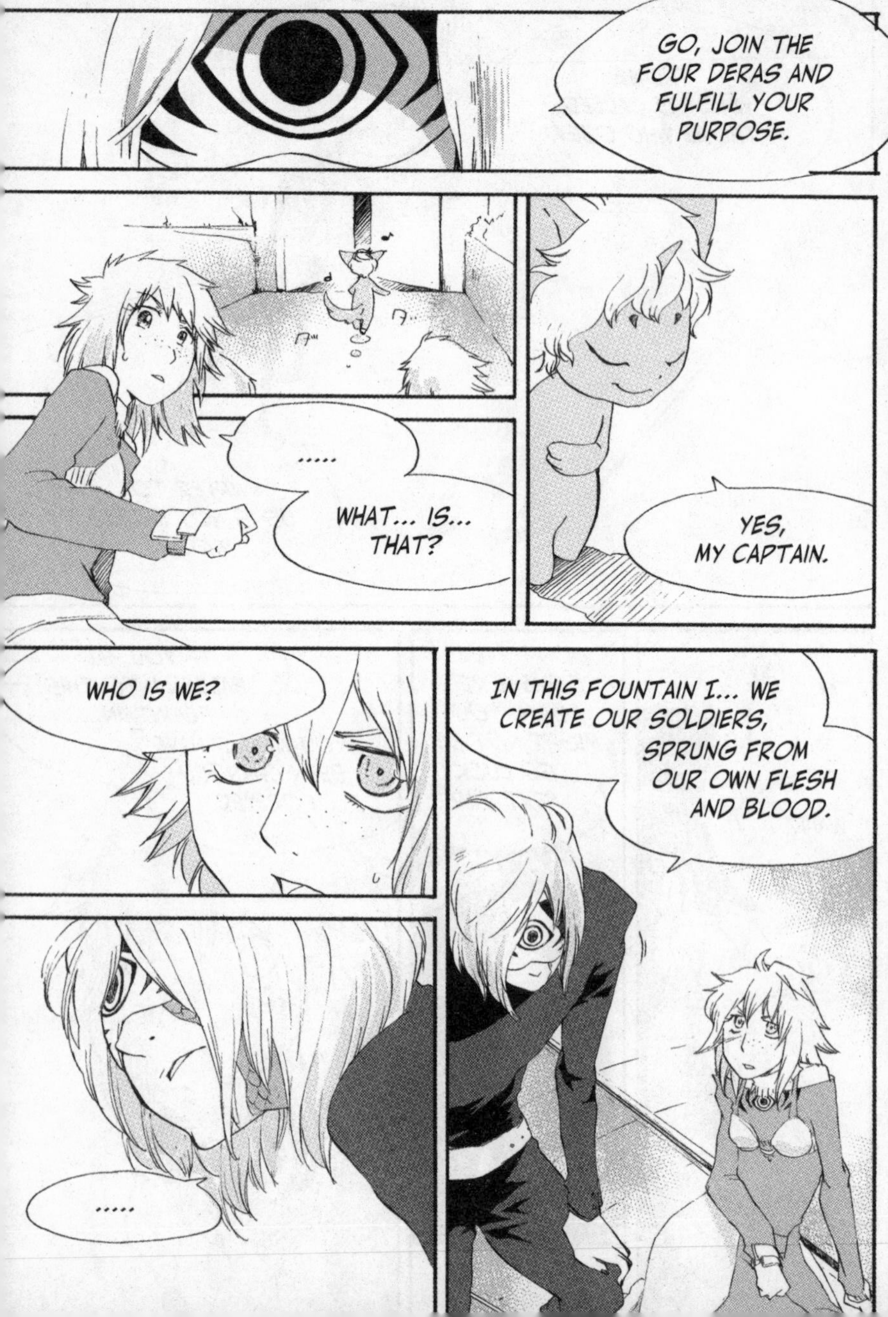
GO, JOIN THE FOUR DERAS AND FULFILL YOUR PURPOSE.
YES, MY CAPTAIN.
.....
WHAT... IS... THAT?
IN THIS FOUNTAIN I... WE CREATE OUR SOLDIERS, SPRUNG FROM OUR OWN FLESH AND BLOOD.
WHO IS WE?
.....

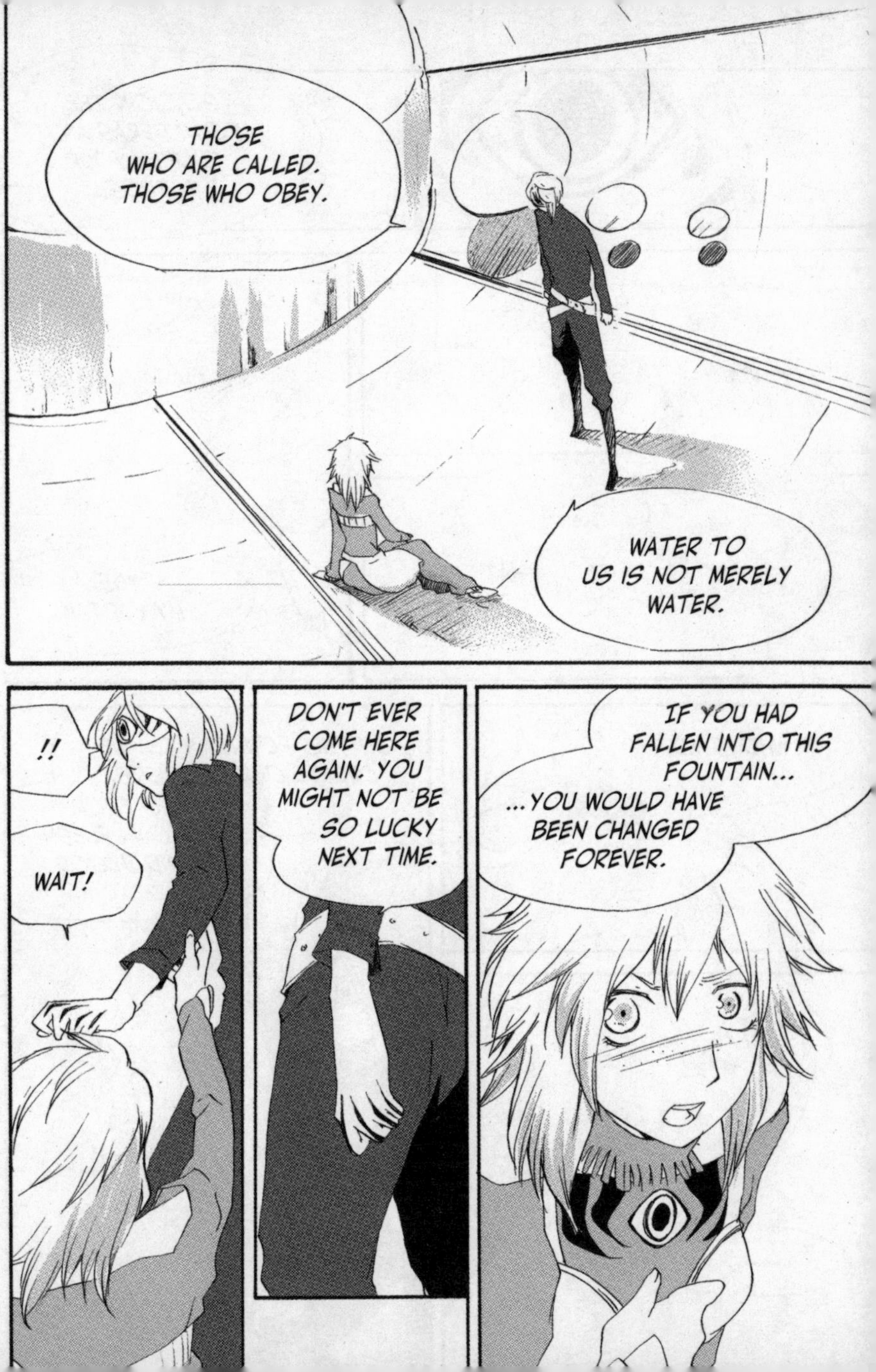
THOSE WHO ARE CALLED. THOSE WHO OBEY.
WATER TO US IS NOT MERELY WATER.
IF YOU HAD FALLEN INTO THIS FOUNTAIN...
...YOU WOULD HAVE BEEN CHANGED FOREVER.
DON'T EVER COME HERE AGAIN. YOU MIGHT NOT BE SO LUCKY NEXT TIME.
!!
WAIT!

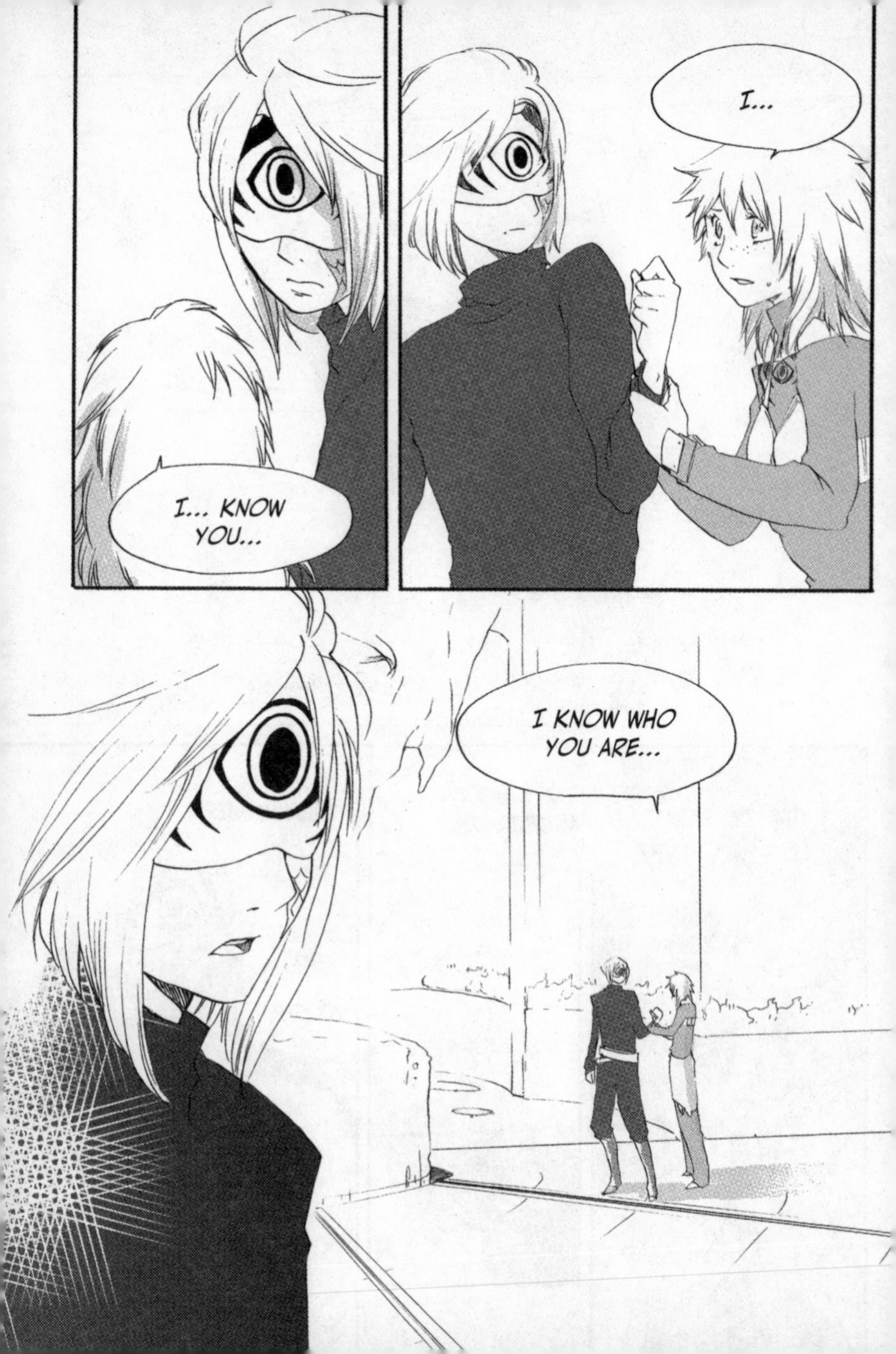
I...
I... KNOW YOU...
I KNOW WHO YOU ARE...

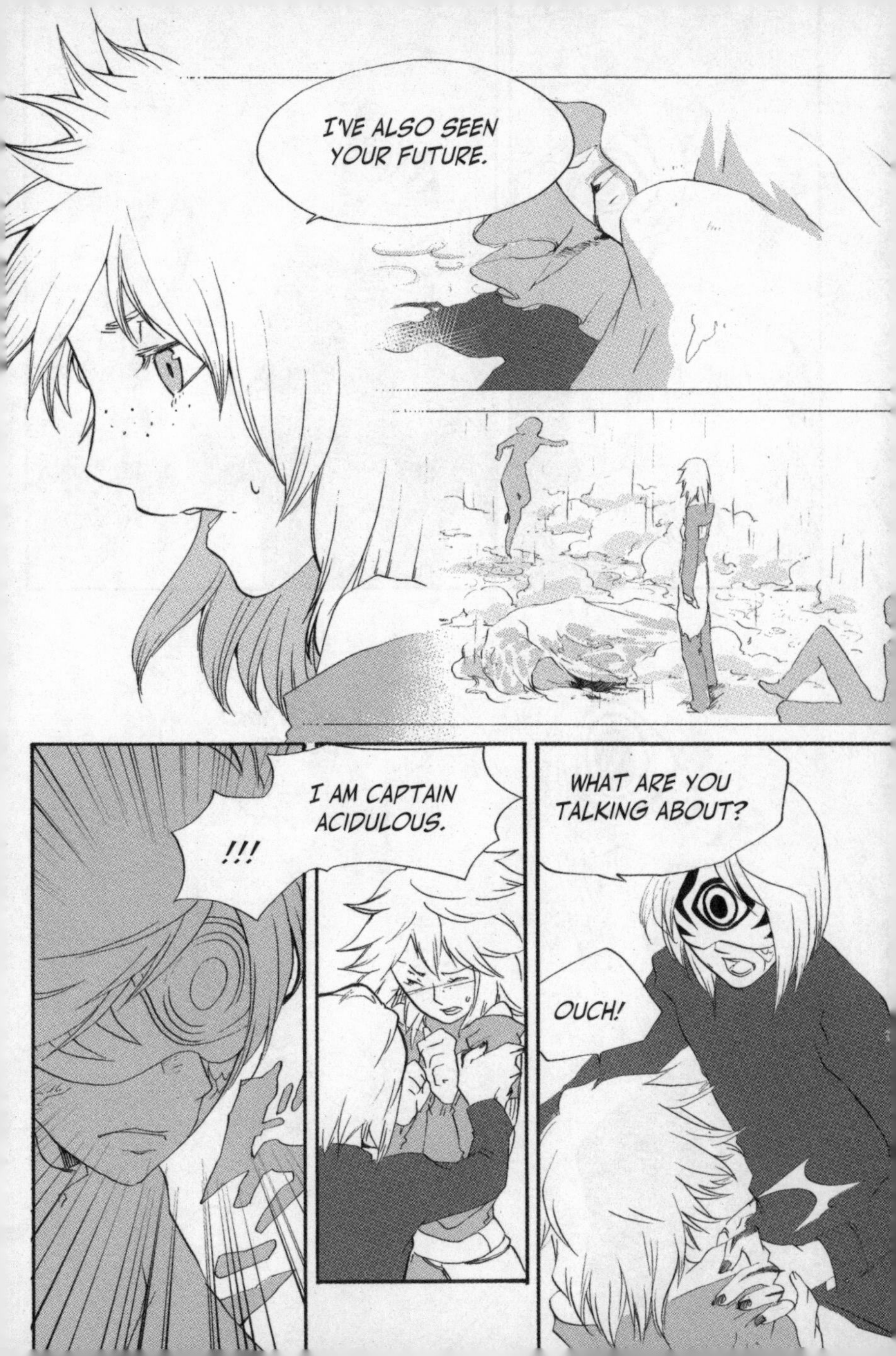
I'VE ALSO SEEN YOUR FUTURE.
WHAT ARE YOU TALKING ABOUT?
OUCH!
I AM CAPTAIN ACIDULOUS.
!!!

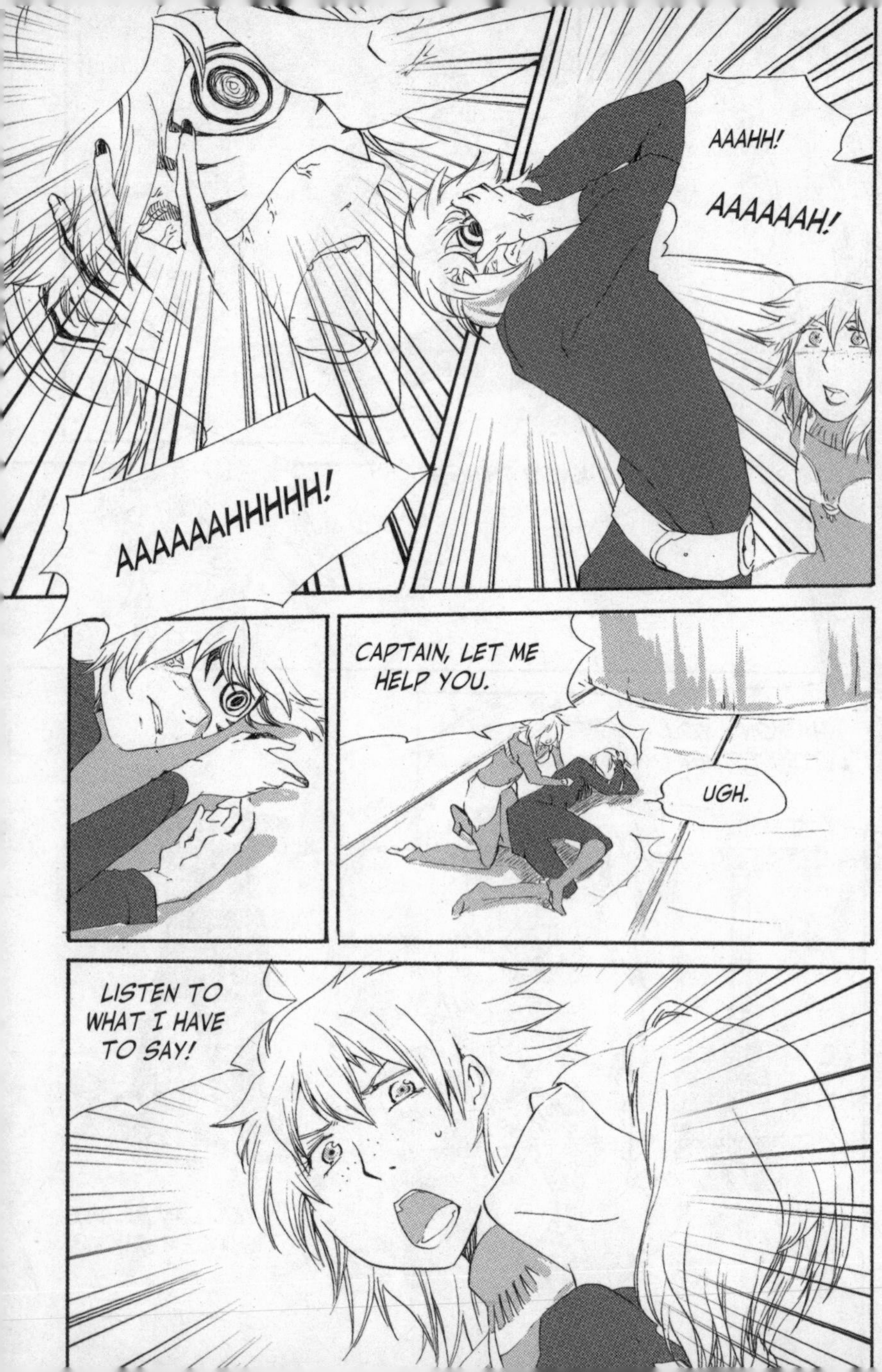
AAAHH!
AAAAAAH!
AAAAAAHHHHH!
CAPTAIN, LET ME HELP YOU.
UGH.
LISTEN TO WHAT I HAVE TO SAY!

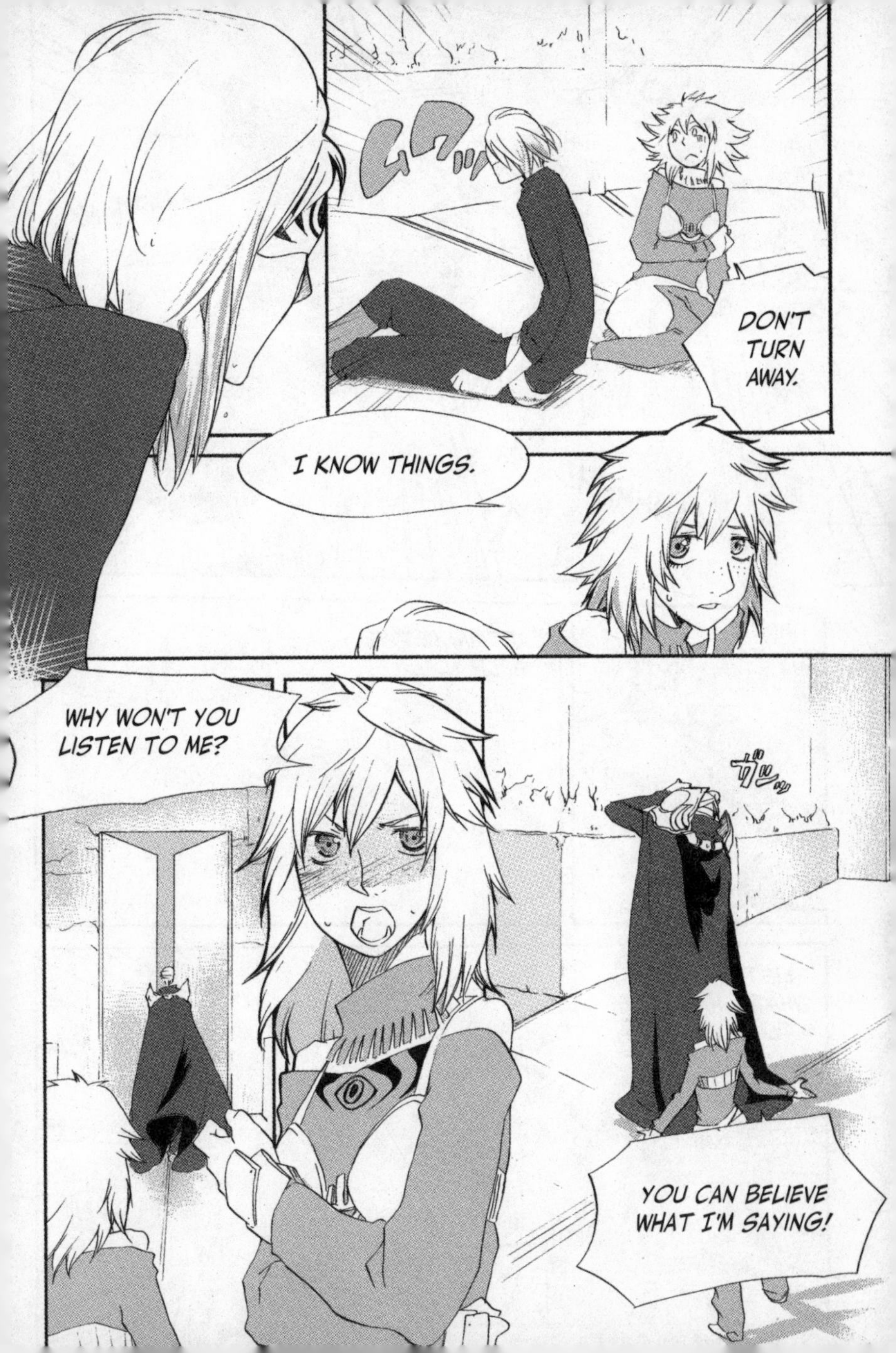
DON'T TURN AWAY.
I KNOW THINGS.
WHY WON'T YOU LISTEN TO ME?
YOU CAN BELIEVE WHAT I'M SAYING!

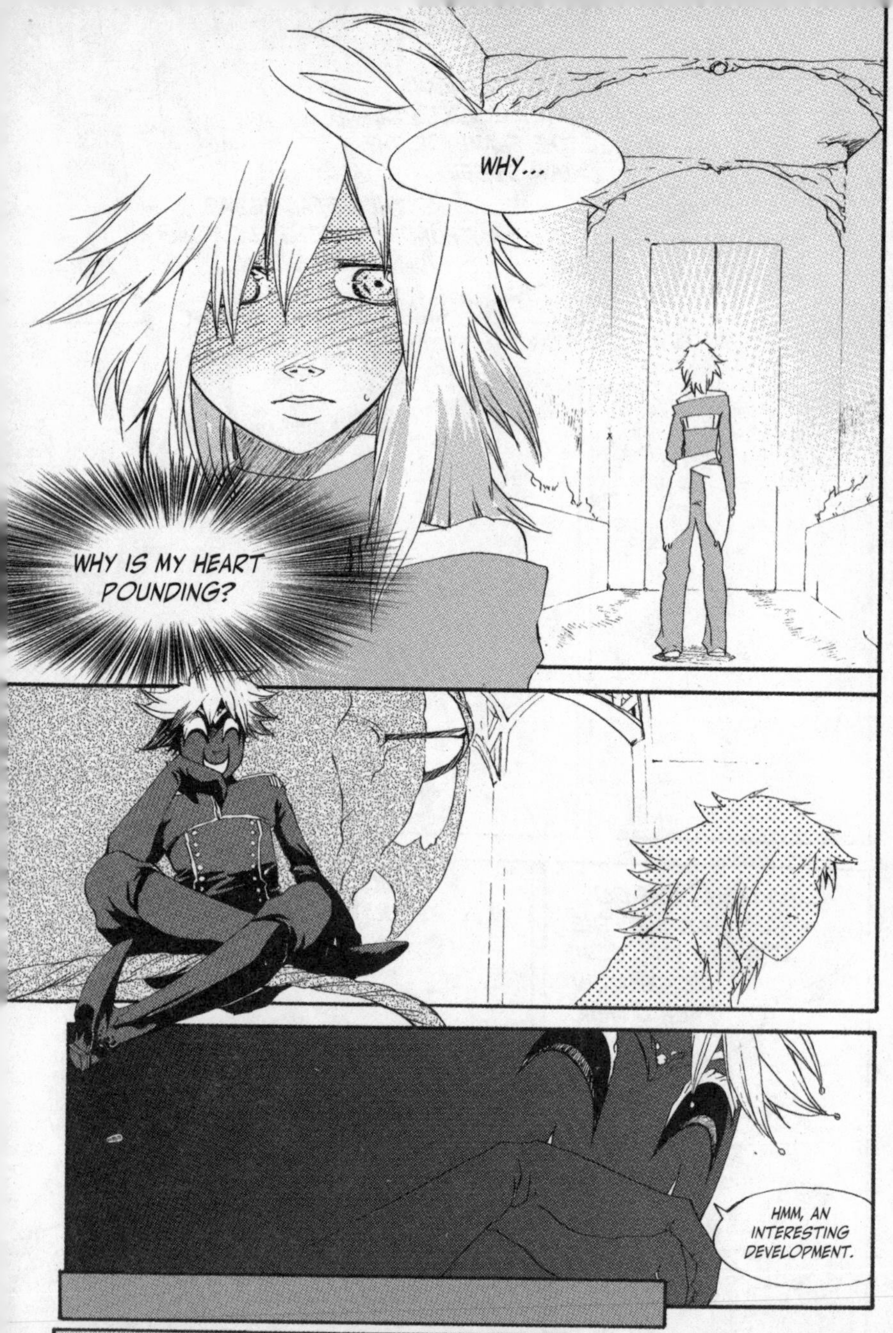
WHY...
WHY IS MY HEART POUNDING?
HMM, AN INTERESTING DEVELOPMENT.

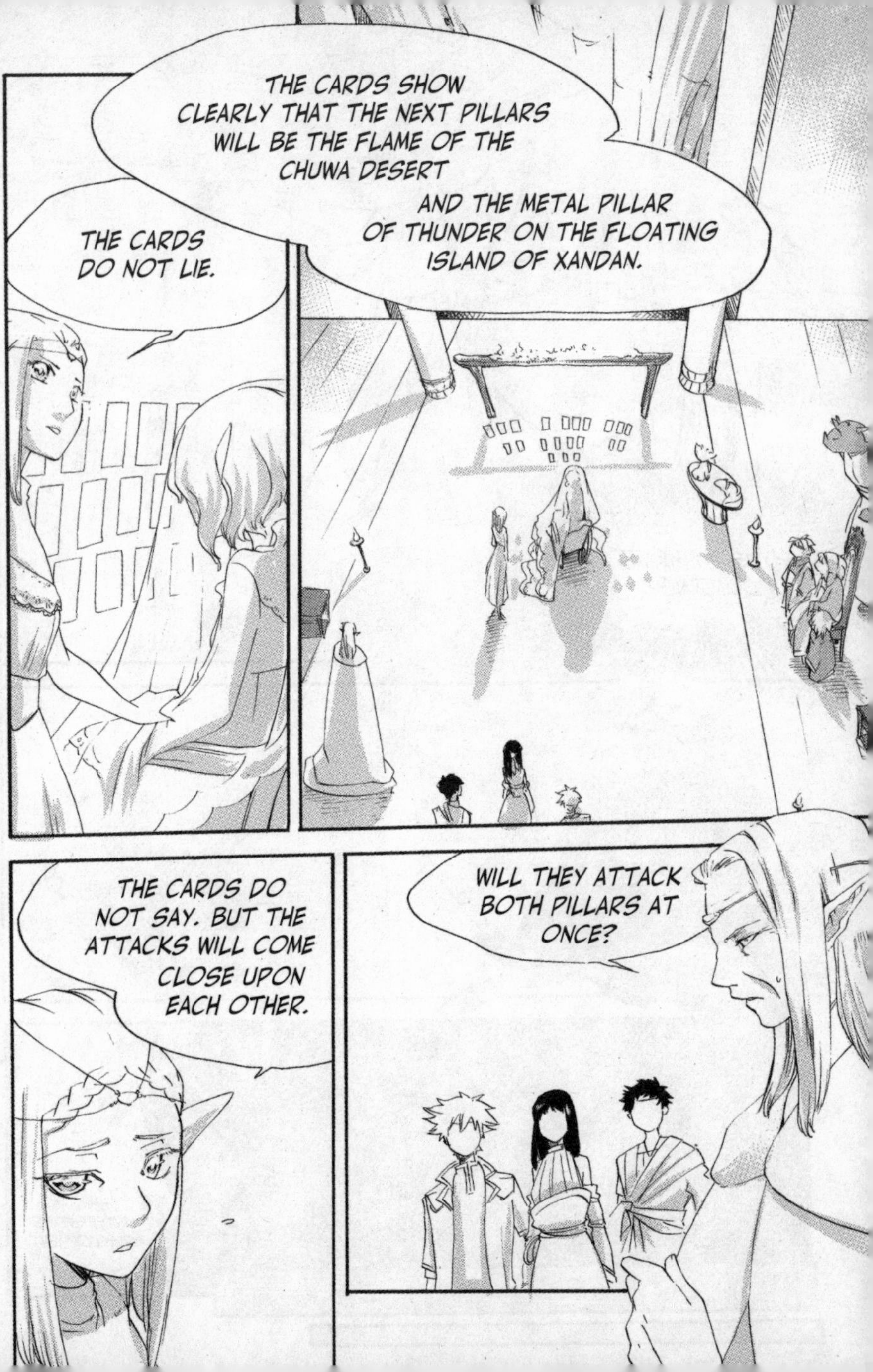
THE CARDS SHOW CLEARLY THAT THE NEXT PILLARS WILL BE THE FLAME OF THE CHUWA DESERT
AND THE METAL PILLAR OF THUNDER ON THE FLOATING ISLAND OF XANDAN.
THE CARDS DO NOT LIE.
WILL THEY ATTACK BOTH PILLARS AT ONCE?
THE CARDS DO NOT SAY. BUT THE ATTACKS WILL COME CLOSE UPON EACH OTHER.

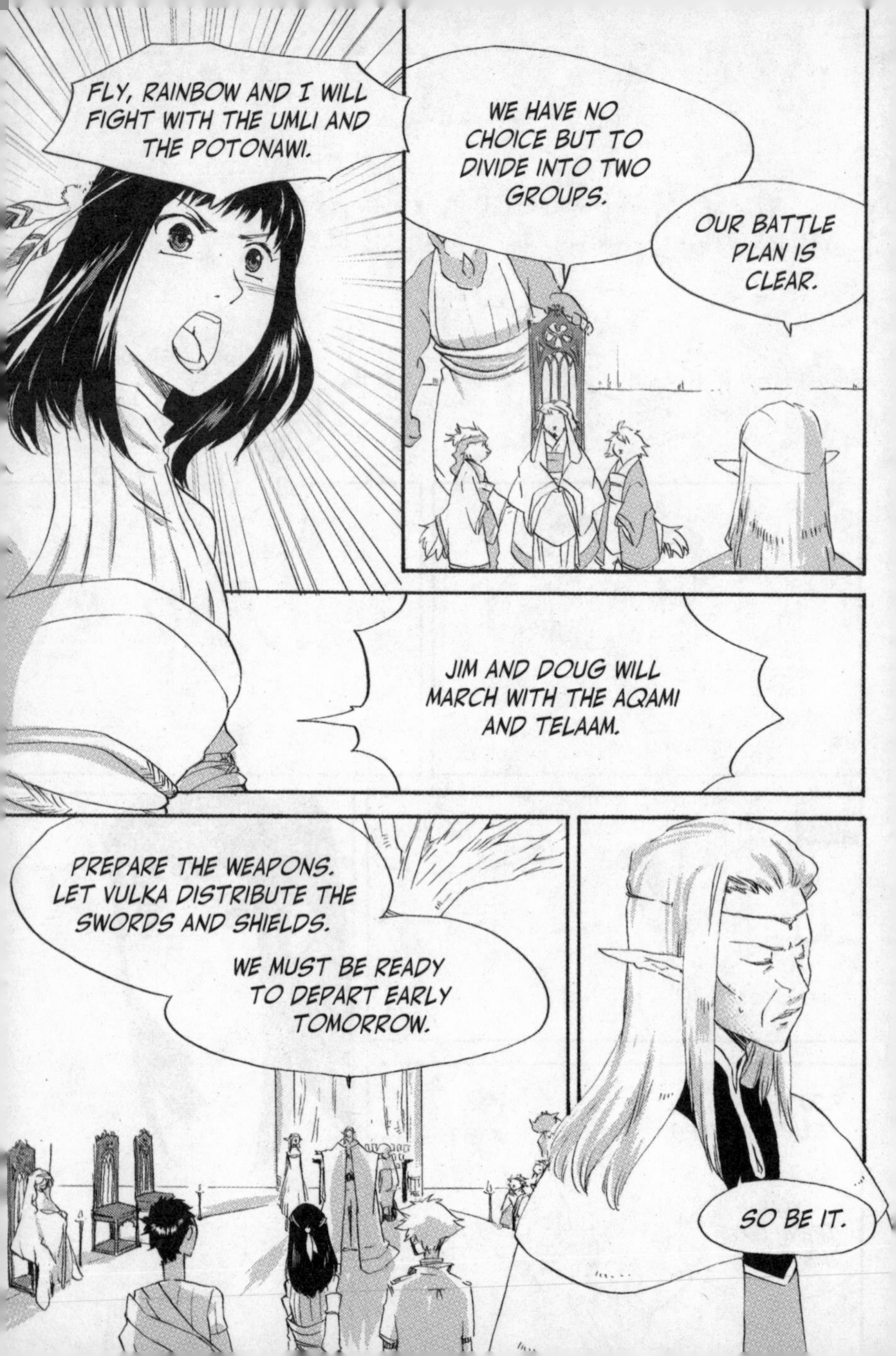
WE HAVE NO CHOICE BUT TO DIVIDE INTO TWO GROUPS.
OUR BATTLE PLAN IS CLEAR.
JIM AND DOUG WILL MARCH WITH THE AQAMI AND TELAAM.
FLY, RAINBOW AND I WILL FIGHT WITH THE UMLI AND THE POTONAWI.
SO BE IT.
PREPARE THE WEAPONS. LET VULKA DISTRIBUTE THE SWORDS AND SHIELDS.
WE MUST BE READY TO DEPART EARLY TOMORROW.

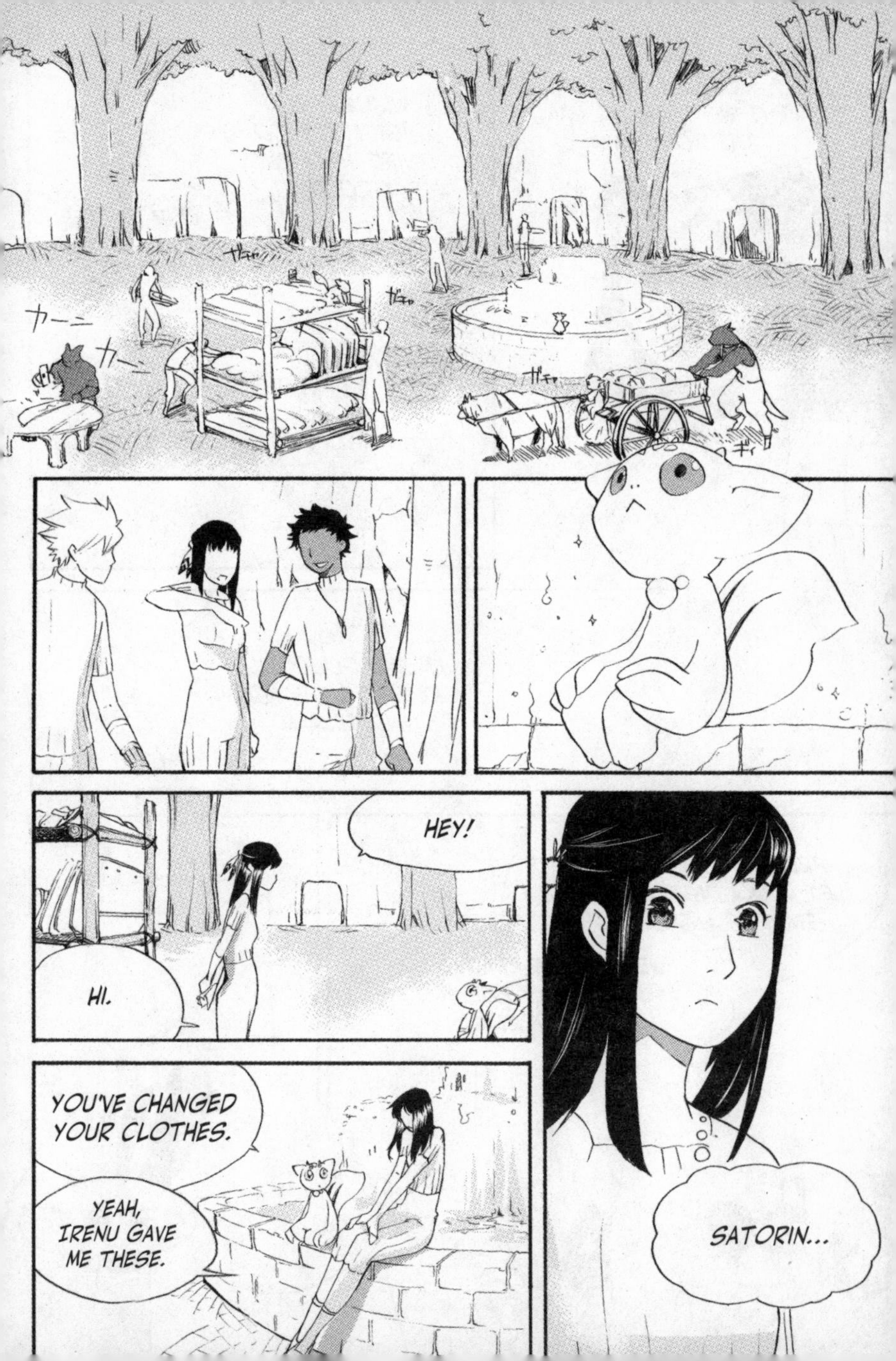
SATORIN...
HEY!
HI.
YOU'VE CHANGED YOUR CLOTHES.
YEAH, IRENU GAVE ME THESE.

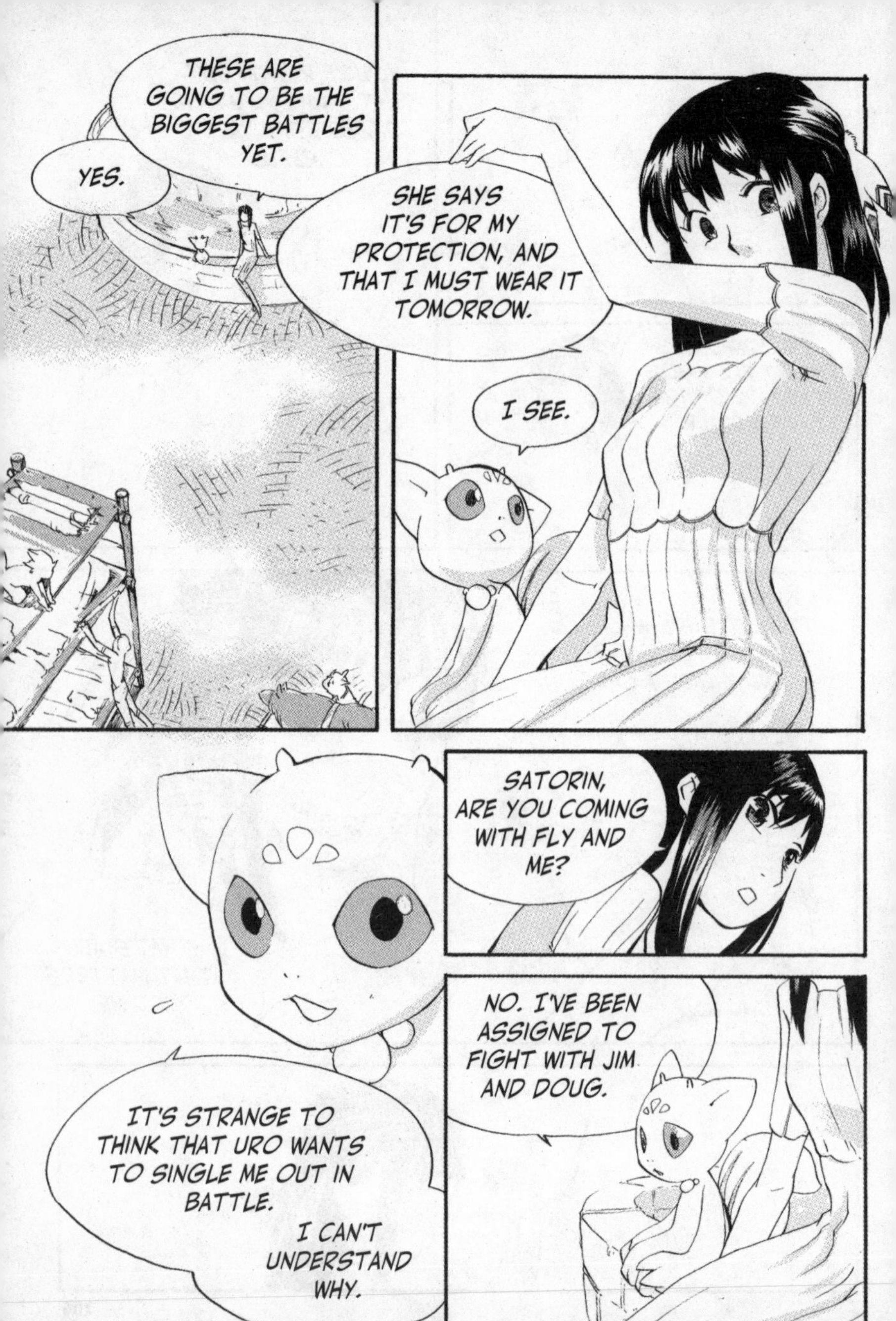
SHE SAYS IT'S FOR MY PROTECTION, AND THAT I MUST WEAR IT TOMORROW.
I SEE.
THESE ARE GOING TO BE THE BIGGEST BATTLES YET.
YES.
SATORIN, ARE YOU COMING WITH FLY AND ME?
NO. I'VE BEEN ASSIGNED TO FIGHT WITH JIM AND DOUG.
IT'S STRANGE TO THINK THAT URO WANTS TO SINGLE ME OUT IN BATTLE.
I CAN'T UNDERSTAND WHY.

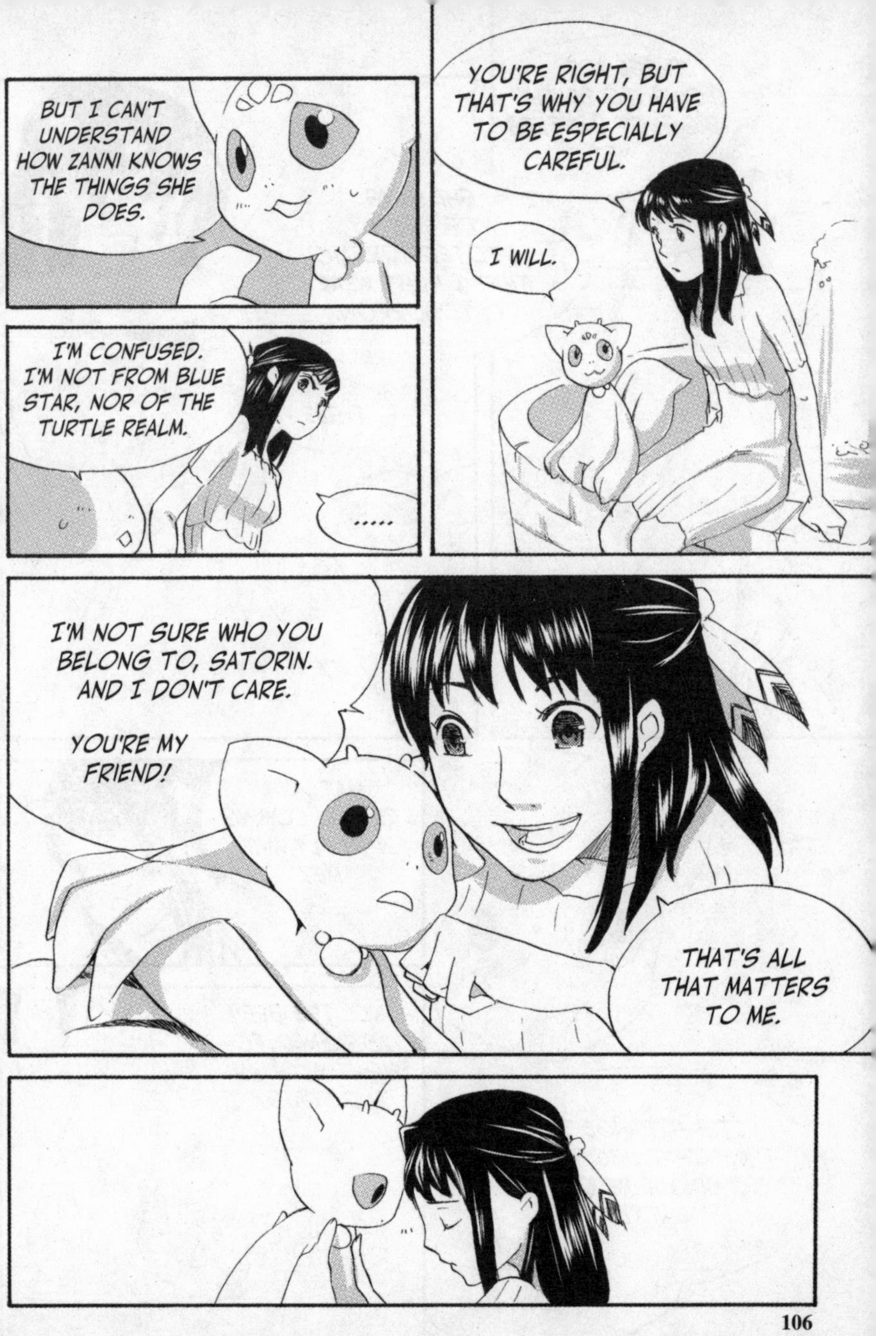
YOU'RE RIGHT, BUT THAT'S WHY YOU HAVE TO BE ESPECIALLY CAREFUL.
I WILL.
BUT I CAN'T UNDERSTAND HOW ZANNI KNOWS THE THINGS SHE DOES.
I'M CONFUSED. I'M NOT FROM BLUE STAR, NOR OF THE TURTLE REALM.
......
I'M NOT SURE WHO YOU BELONG TO, SATORIN. AND I DON'T CARE.
YOU'RE MY FRIEND!
THAT'S ALL THAT MATTERS TO ME.

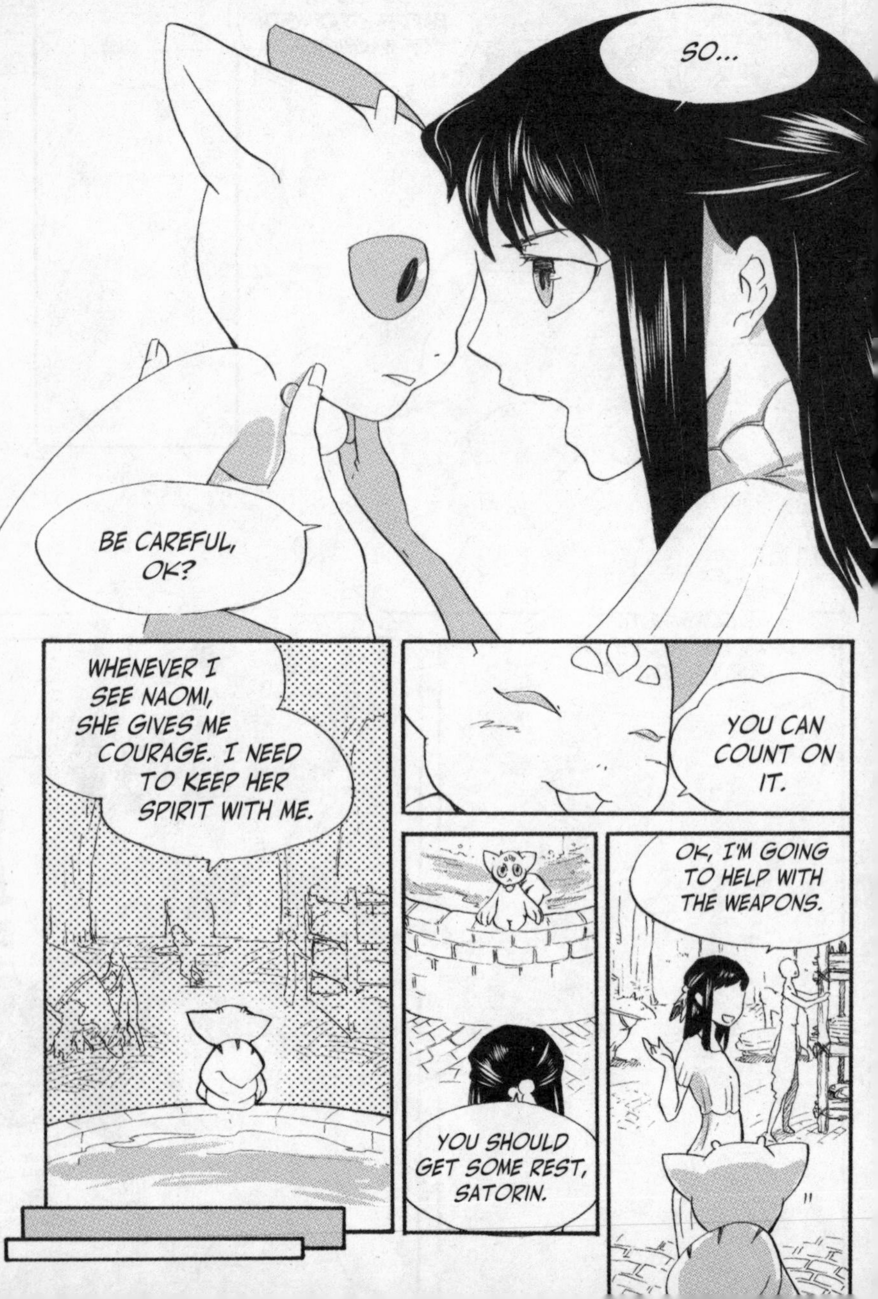
SO...
BE CAREFUL, OK?
YOU CAN COUNT ON IT.
OK, I'M GOING TO HELP WITH THE WEAPONS.
YOU SHOULD GET SOME REST, SATORIN.
WHENEVER I SEE NAOMI, SHE GIVES ME COURAGE. I NEED TO KEEP HER SPIRIT WITH ME.

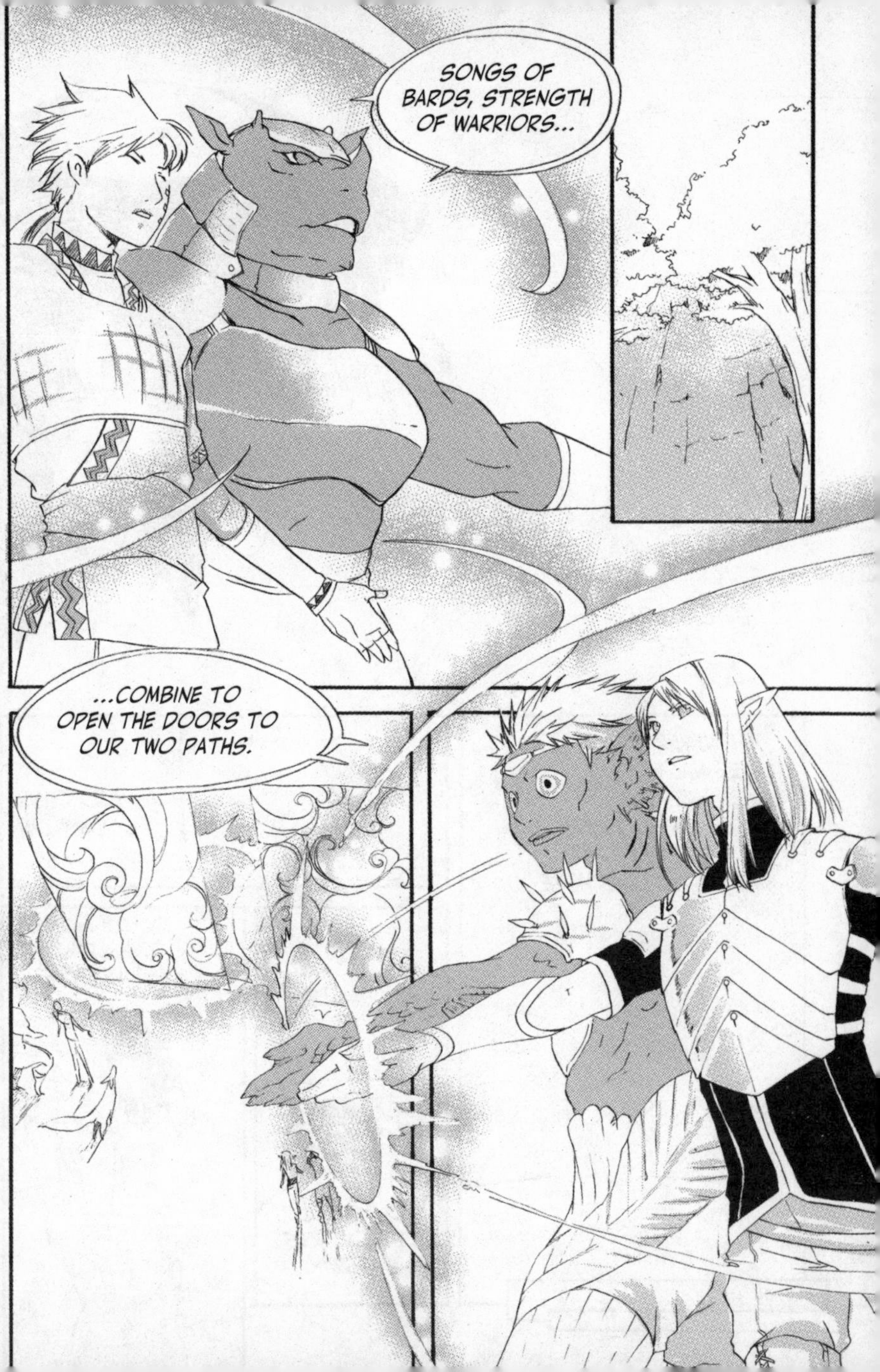
SONGS OF BARDS, STRENGTH OF WARRIORS...
...COMBINE TO OPEN THE DOORS TO OUR TWO PATHS.

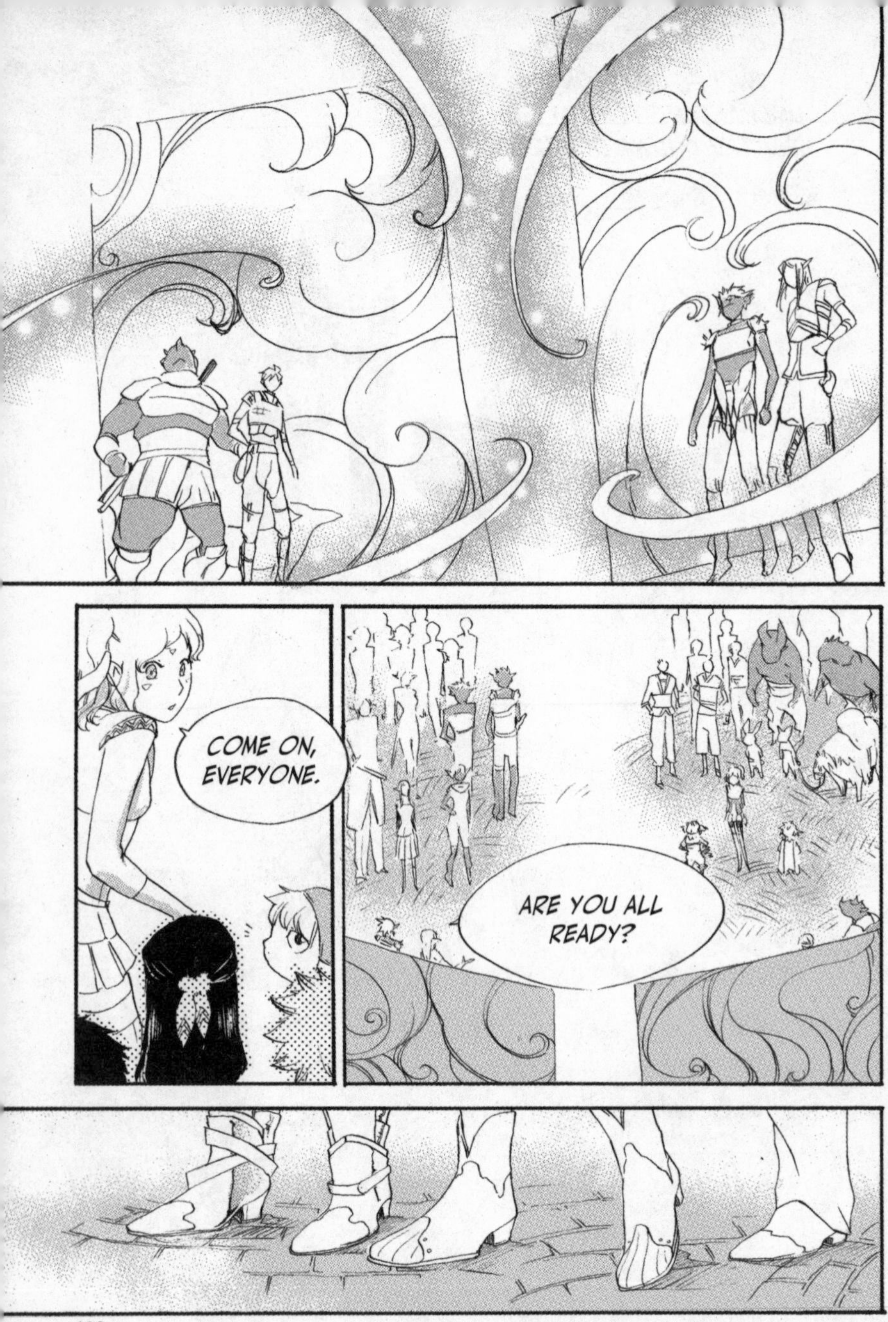
ARE YOU ALL READY?
COME ON, EVERYONE.

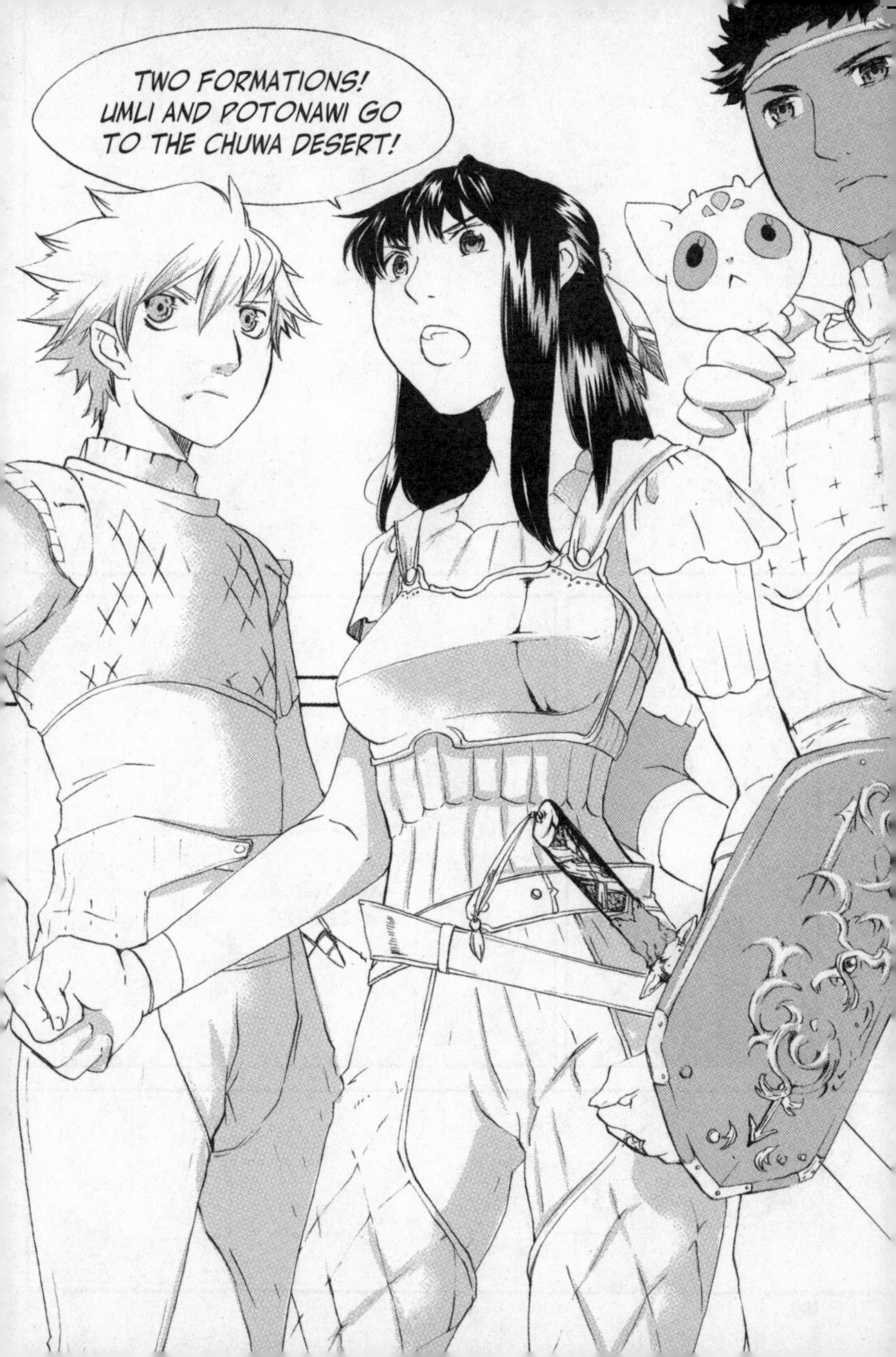
TWO FORMATIONS! UMLI AND POTONAWI GO TO THE CHUWA DESERT!

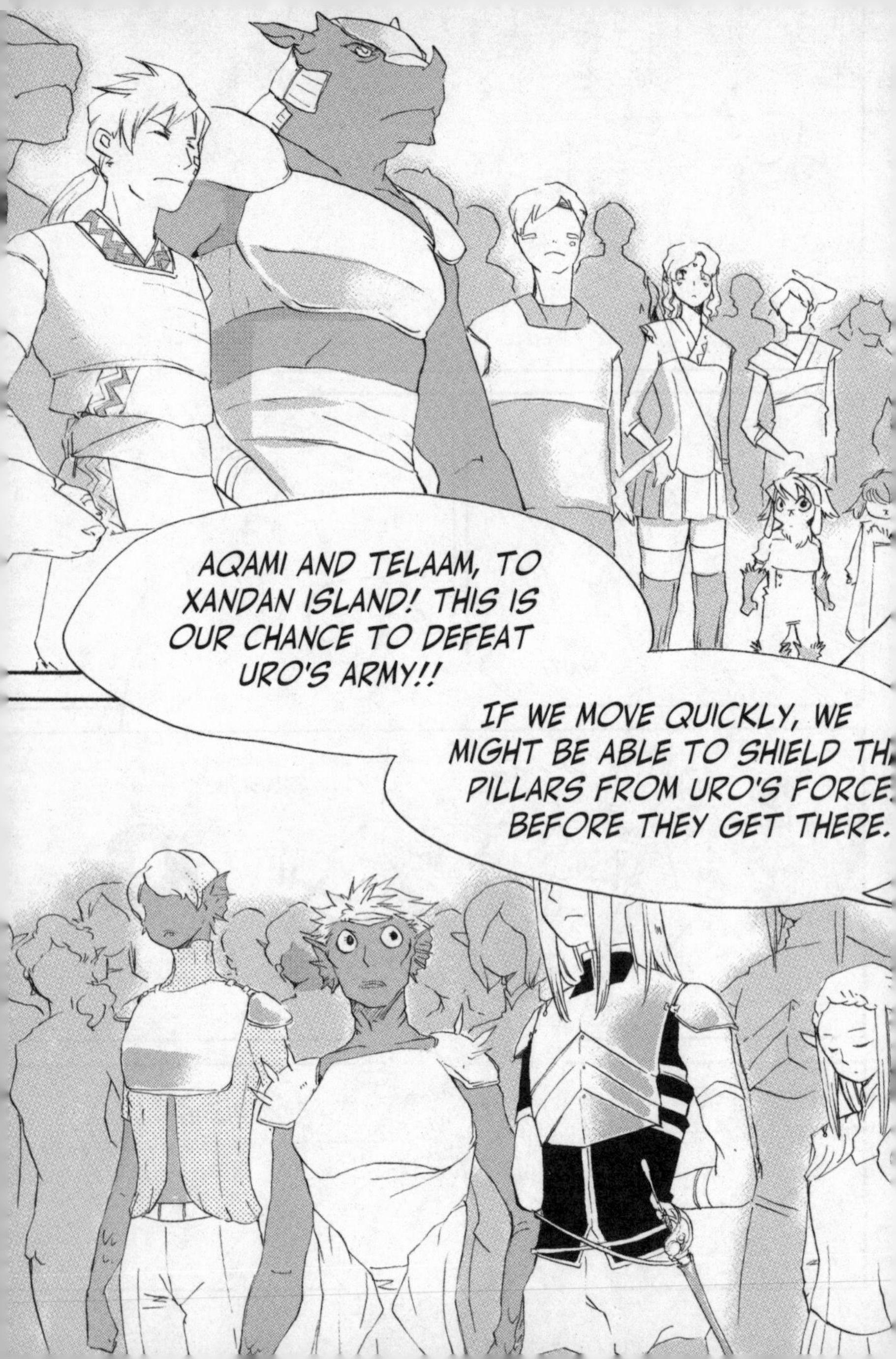
AQAMI AND TELAAM, TO XANDAN ISLAND! THIS IS OUR CHANCE TO DEFEAT URO'S ARMY!!
IF WE MOVE QUICKLY, WE MIGHT BE ABLE TO SHIELD TH PILLARS FROM URO'S FORCE BEFORE THEY GET THERE.

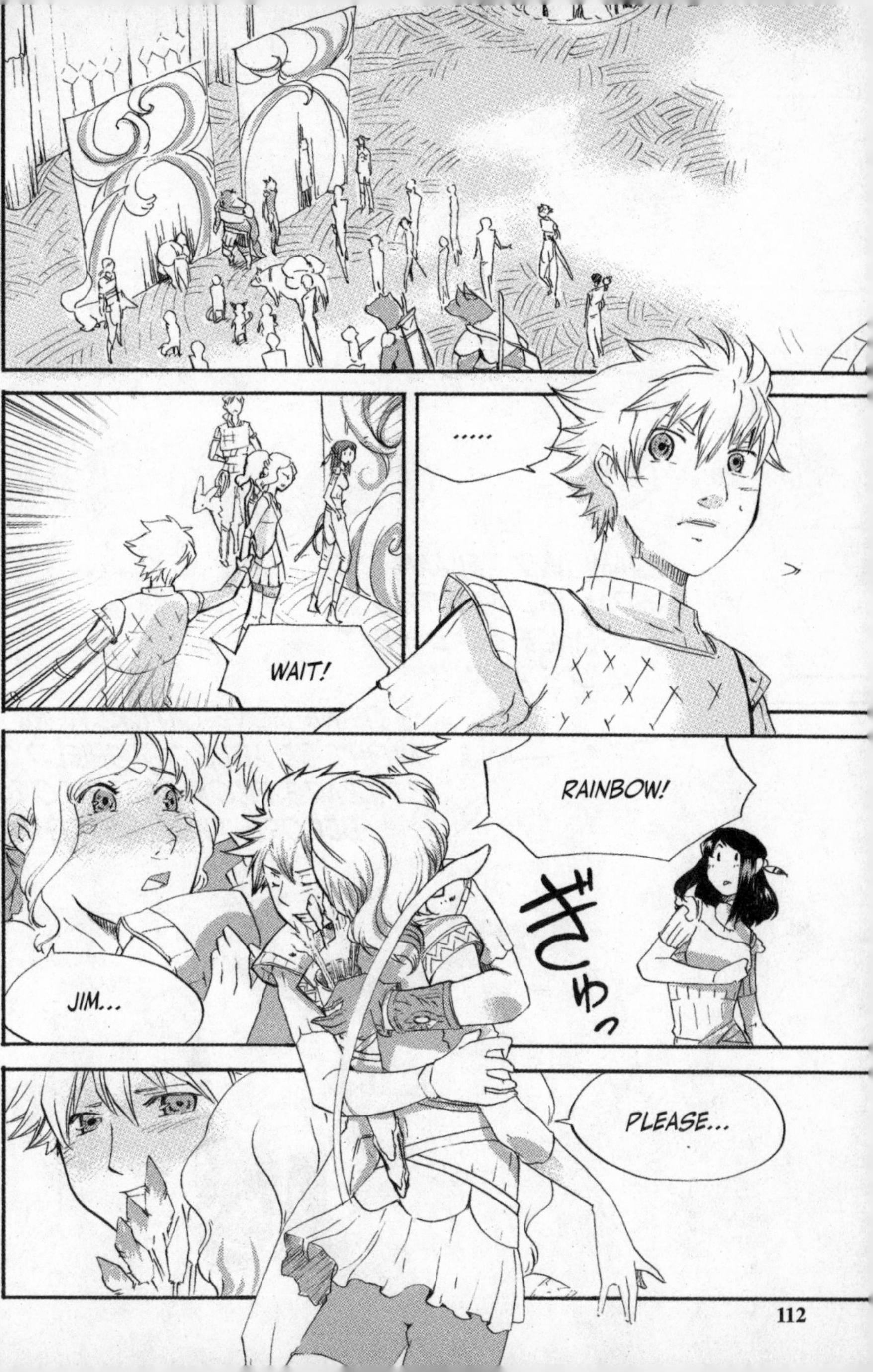
.....
WAIT!
RAINBOW!
ぎゅっ
JIM...
PLEASE...

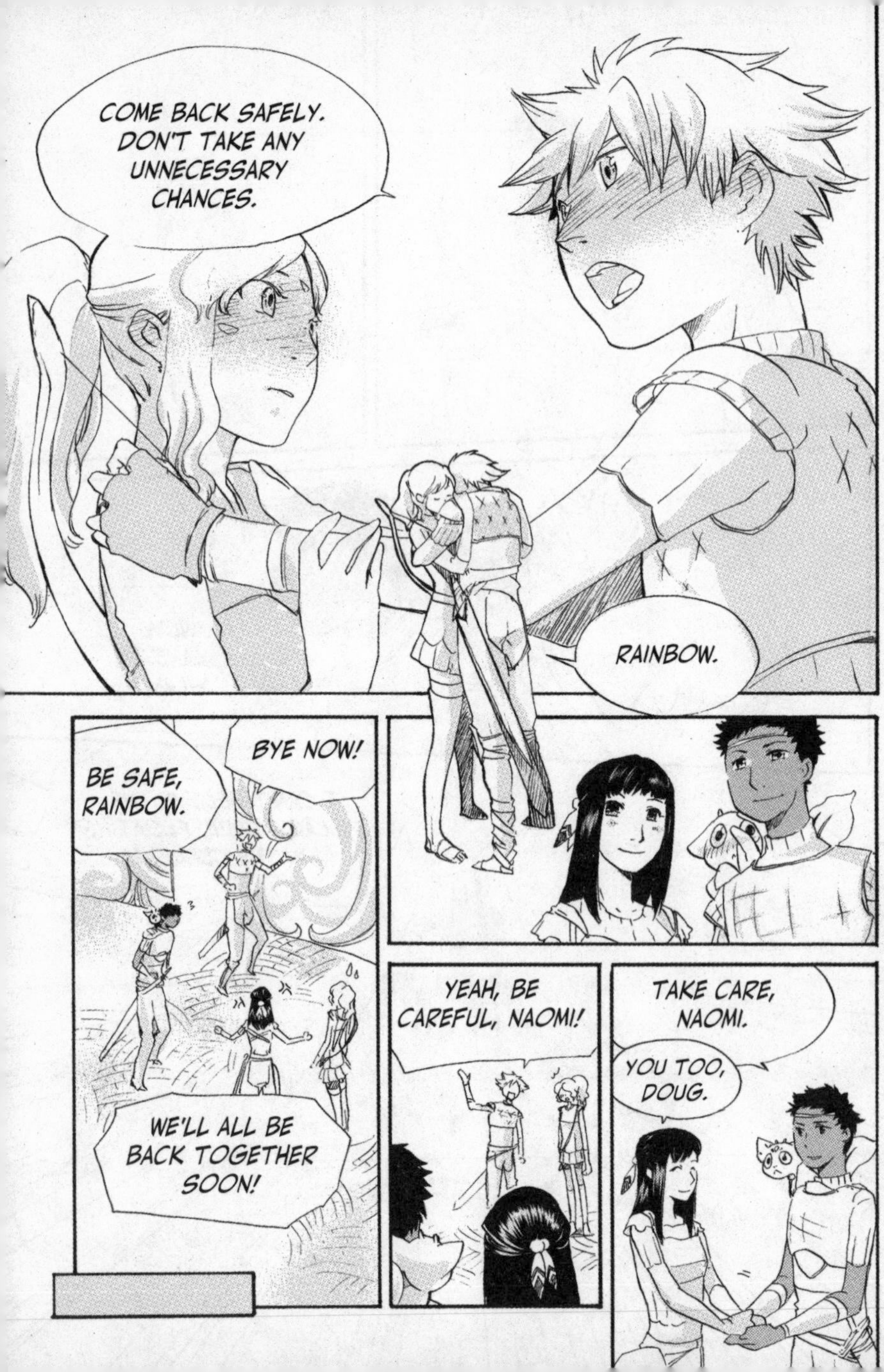
COME BACK SAFELY. DON'T TAKE ANY UNNECESSARY CHANCES.
RAINBOW.
TAKE CARE, NAOMI.
YOU TOO, DOUG.
YEAH, BE CAREFUL, NAOMI!
BYE NOW!
BE SAFE, RAINBOW.
WE'LL ALL BE BACK TOGETHER SOON!

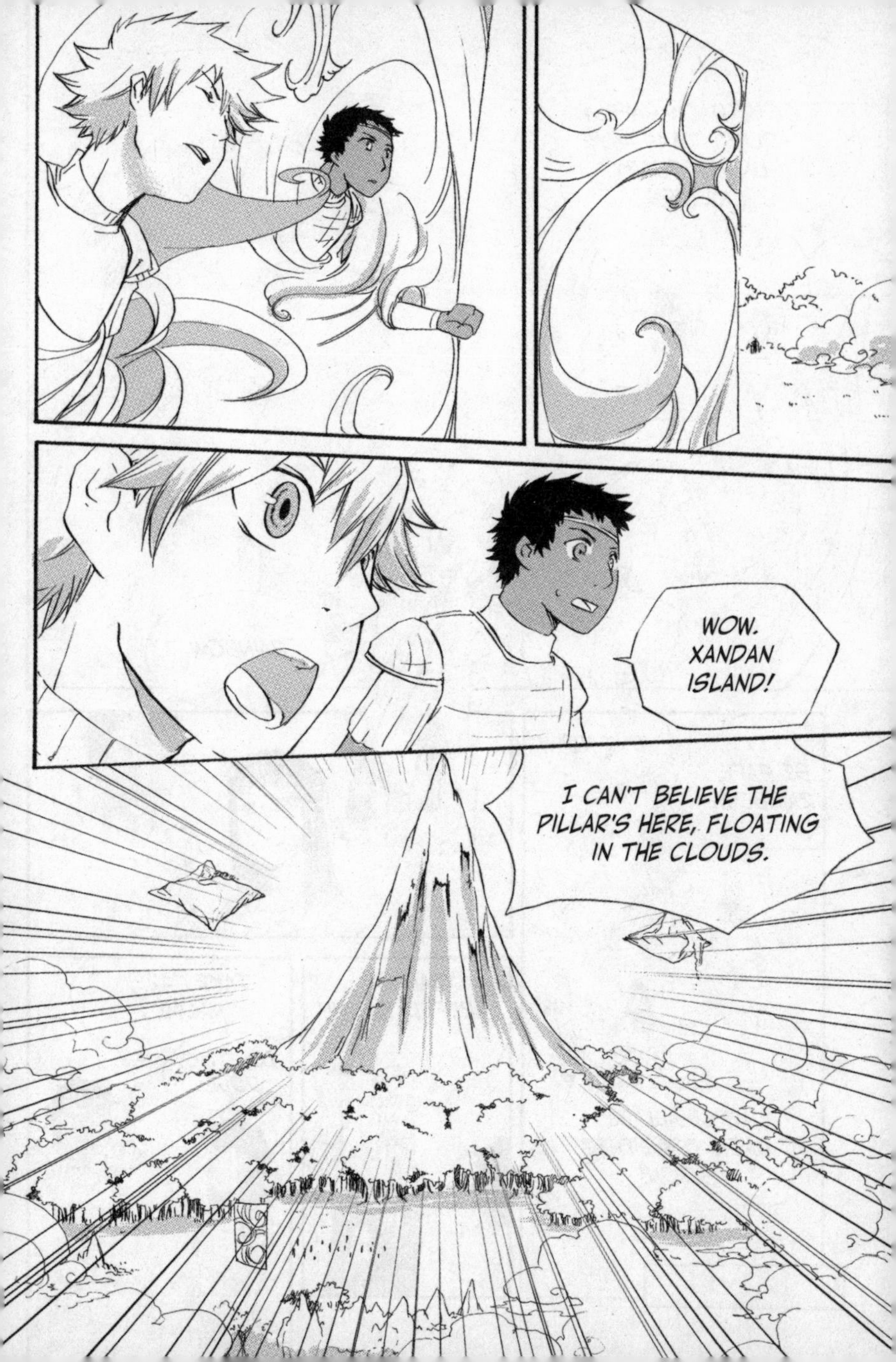
WOW. XANDAN ISLAND!
I CAN'T BELIEVE THE PILLAR'S HERE, FLOATING IN THE CLOUDS.

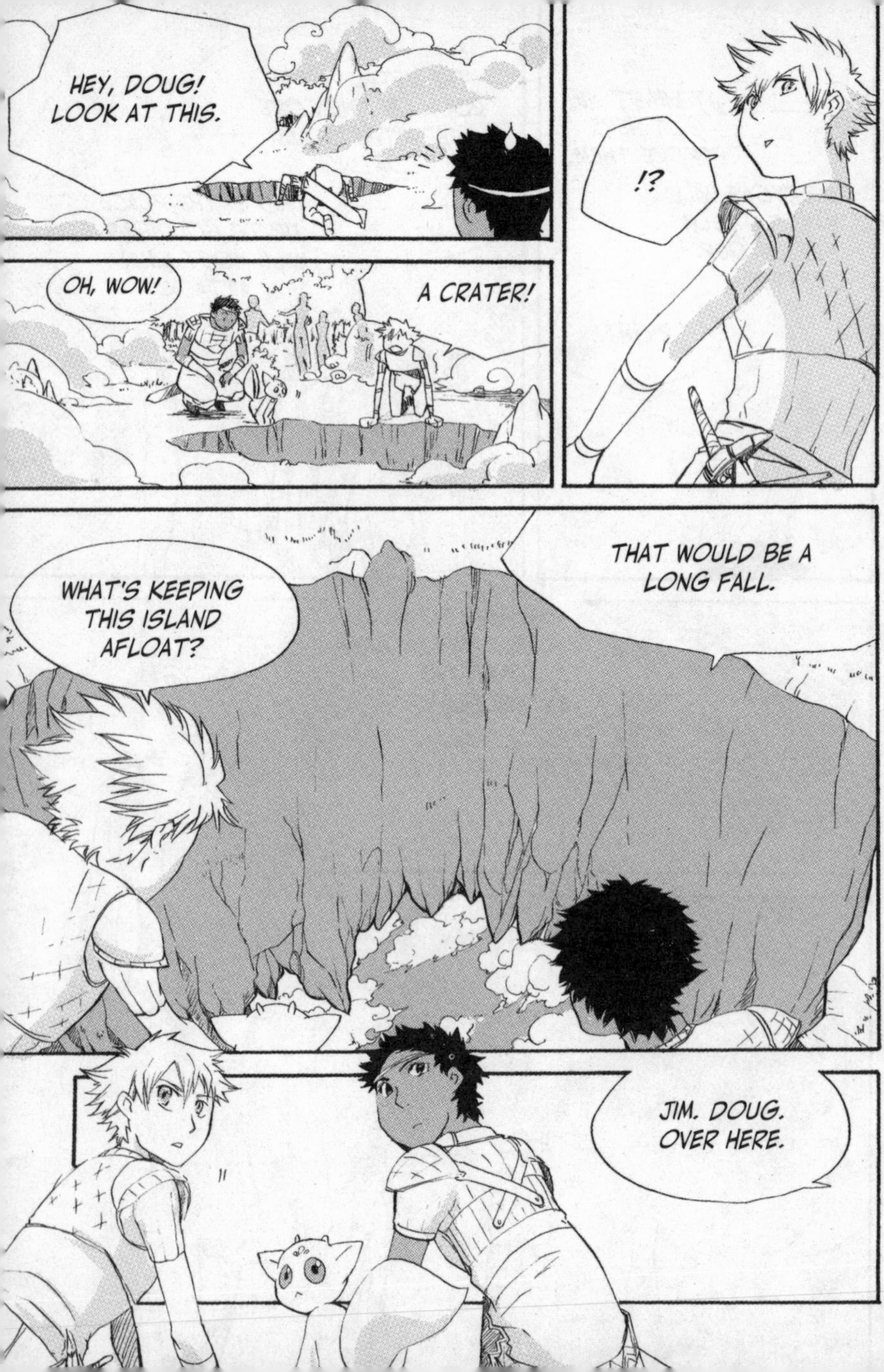

!?
HEY, DOUG! LOOK AT THIS.
A CRATER!
OH, WOW!
THAT WOULD BE A LONG FALL.
WHAT'S KEEPING THIS ISLAND AFLOAT?
JIM. DOUG. OVER HERE.

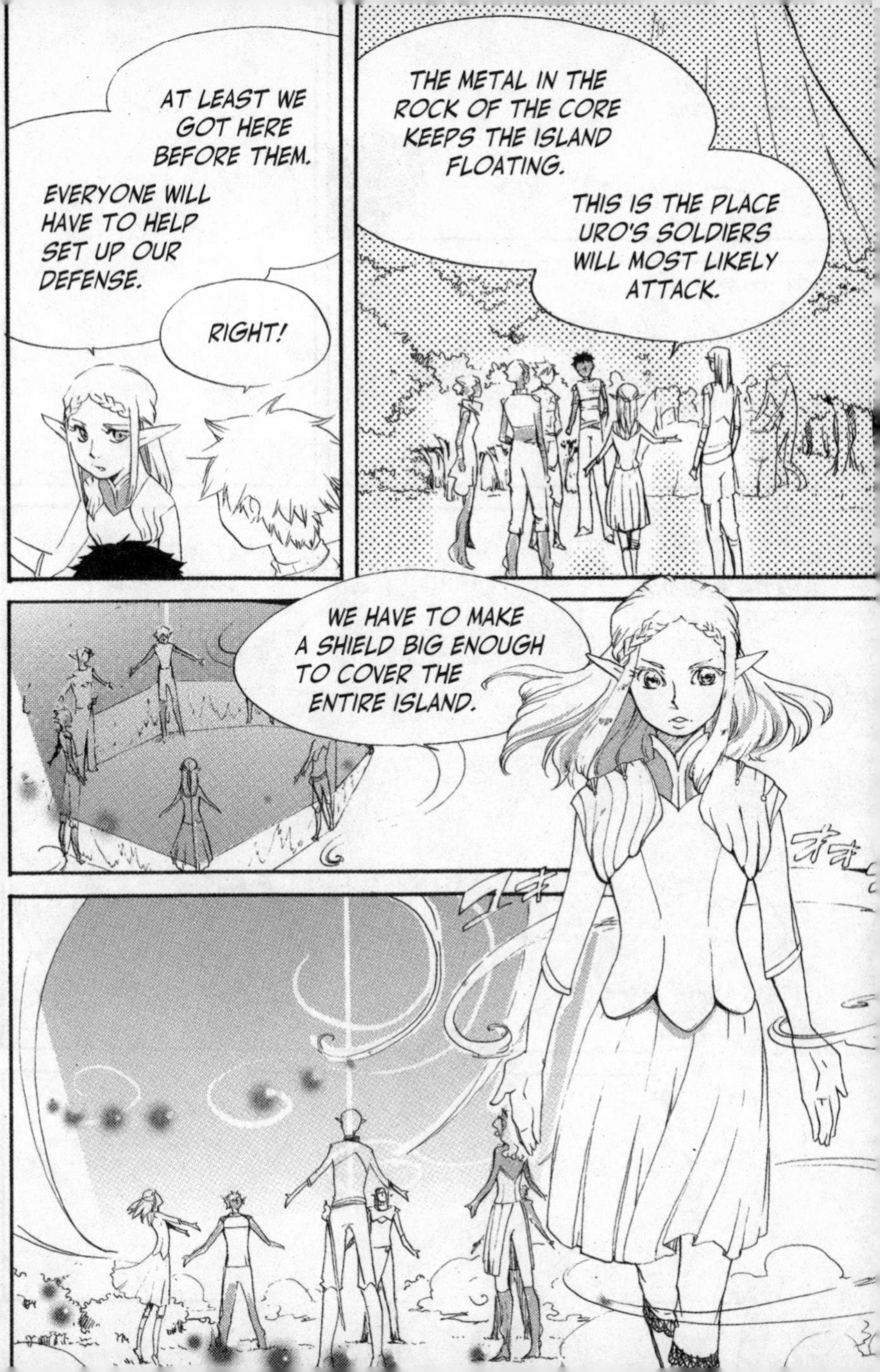
THE METAL IN THE ROCK OF THE CORE KEEPS THE ISLAND FLOATING.
THIS IS THE PLACE URO'S SOLDIERS WILL MOST LIKELY ATTACK.
AT LEAST WE GOT HERE BEFORE THEM.
EVERYONE WILL HAVE TO HELP SET UP OUR DEFENSE.
RIGHT!
WE HAVE TO MAKE A SHIELD BIG ENOUGH TO COVER THE ENTIRE ISLAND.

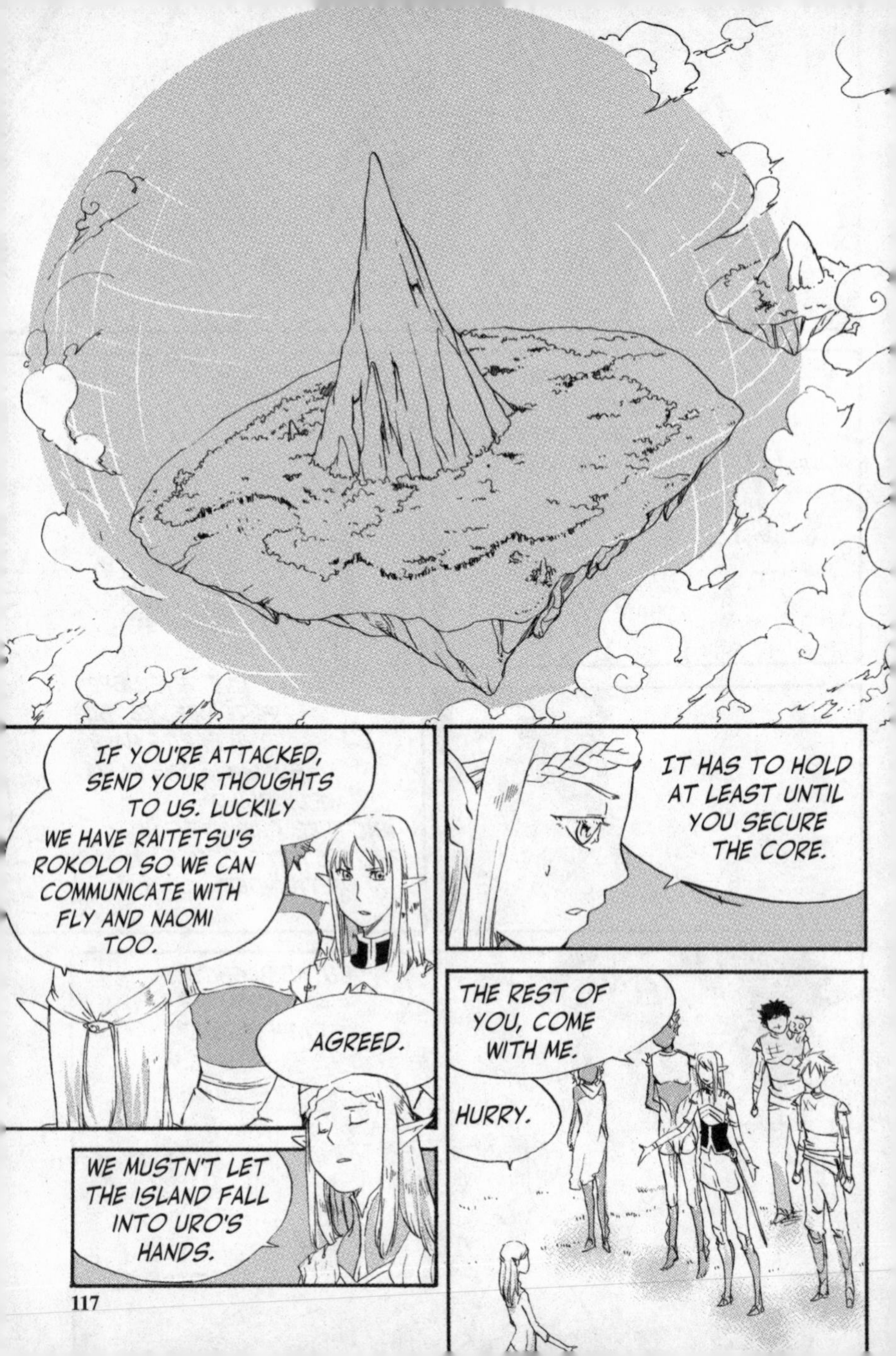
IT HAS TO HOLD AT LEAST UNTIL YOU SECURE THE CORE.
IF YOU'RE ATTACKED, SEND YOUR THOUGHTS TO US. LUCKILY WE HAVE RAITETSU'S ROKOLOI SO WE CAN COMMUNICATE WITH FLY AND NAOMI TOO.
AGREED.
THE REST OF YOU, COME WITH ME.
HURRY.
WE MUSTN'T LET THE ISLAND FALL INTO URO'S HANDS.

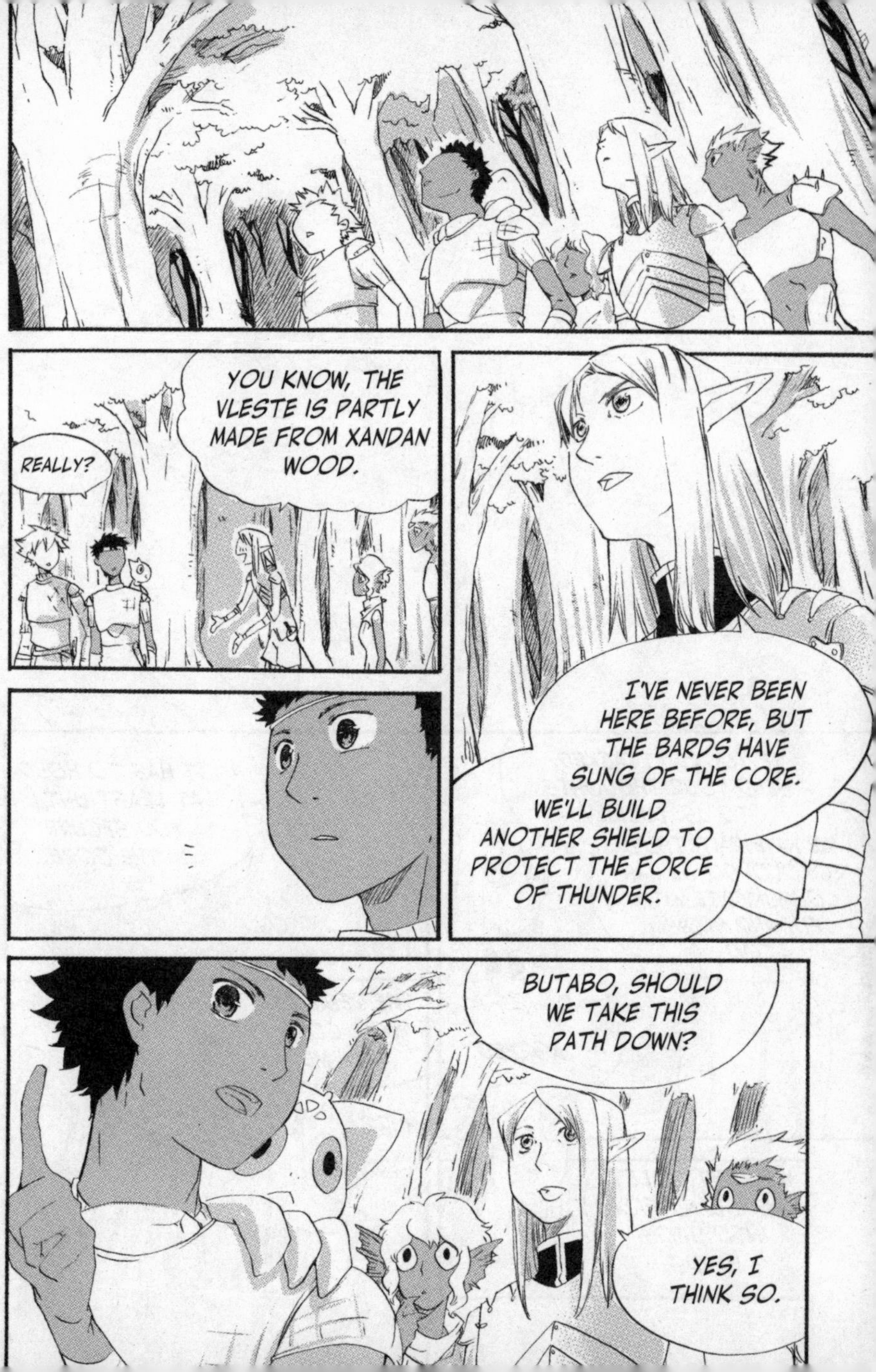
I'VE NEVER BEEN HERE BEFORE, BUT THE BARDS HAVE SUNG OF THE CORE.
WE'LL BUILD ANOTHER SHIELD TO PROTECT THE FORCE OF THUNDER.
YOU KNOW, THE VLESTE IS PARTLY MADE FROM XANDAN WOOD.
REALLY?
BUTABO, SHOULD WE TAKE THIS PATH DOWN?
YES, I THINK SO.

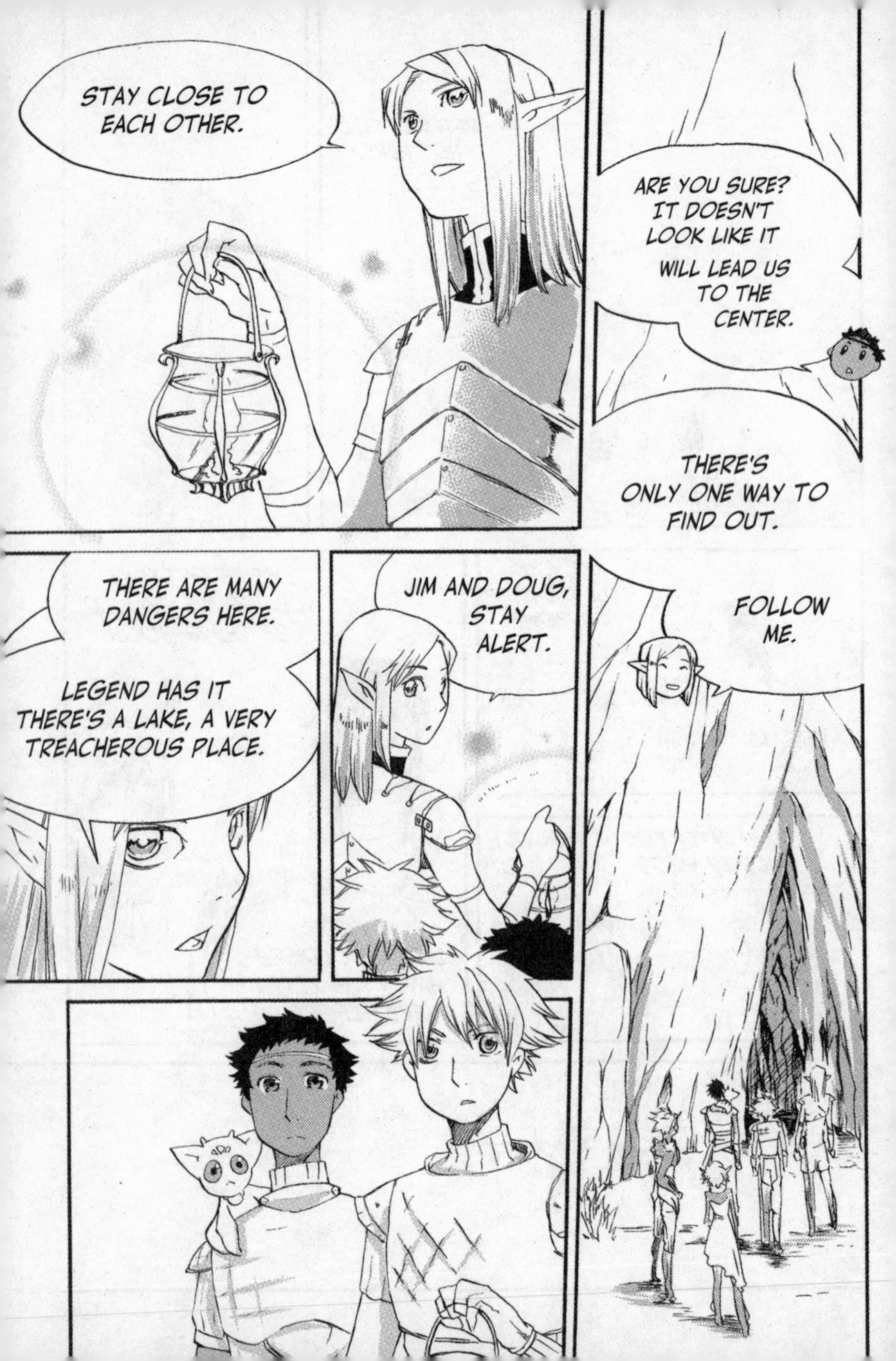
ARE YOU SURE? IT DOESN'T LOOK LIKE IT WILL LEAD US TO THE CENTER.
THERE'S ONLY ONE WAY TO FIND OUT.
FOLLOW ME.
STAY CLOSE TO EACH OTHER.
JIM AND DOUG, STAY ALERT.
THERE ARE MANY DANGERS HERE.
LEGEND HAS IT THERE'S A LAKE, A VERY TREACHEROUS PLACE.

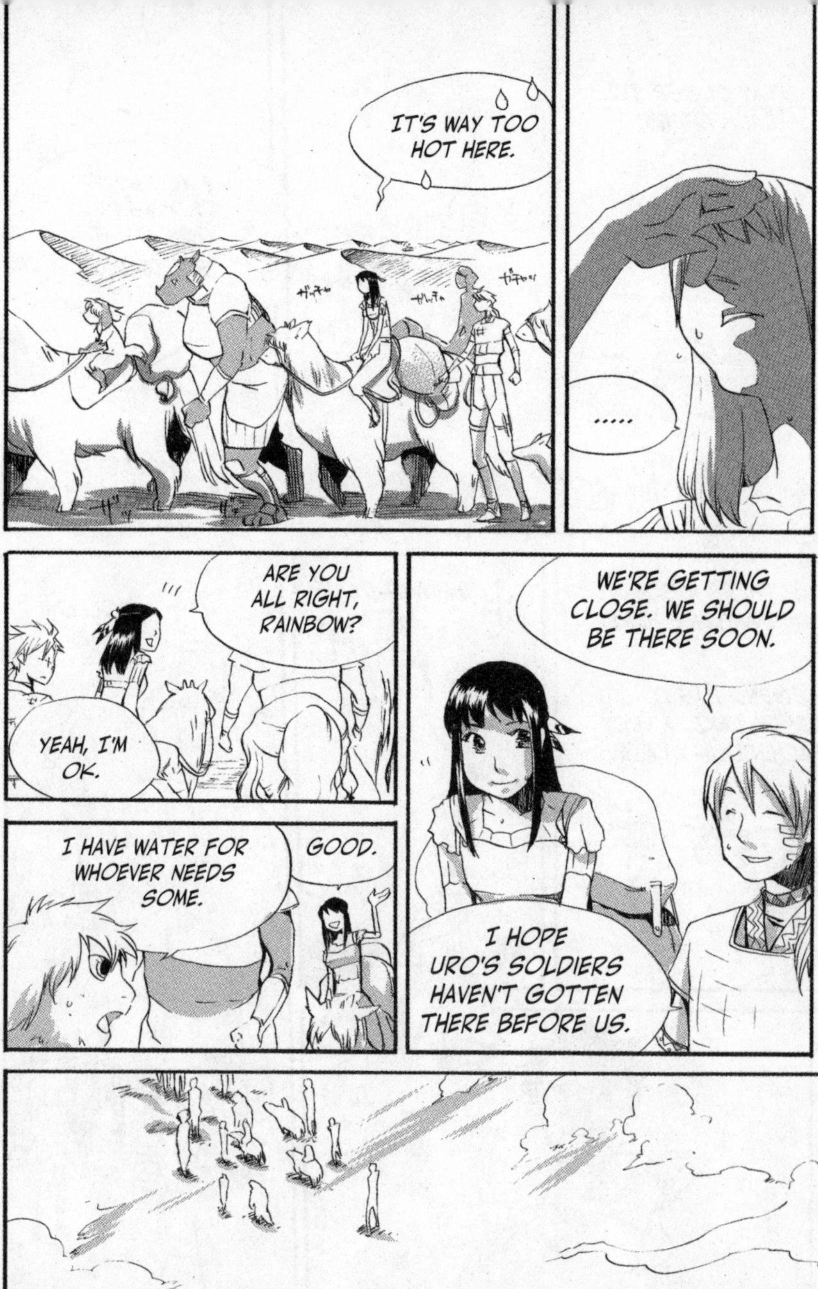
.....
IT'S WAY TOO HOT HERE.
WE'RE GETTING CLOSE. WE SHOULD BE THERE SOON.
I HOPE URO'S SOLDIERS HAVEN'T GOTTEN THERE BEFORE US.
ARE YOU ALL RIGHT, RAINBOW?
YEAH, I'M OK.
GOOD.
I HAVE WATER FOR WHOEVER NEEDS SOME.

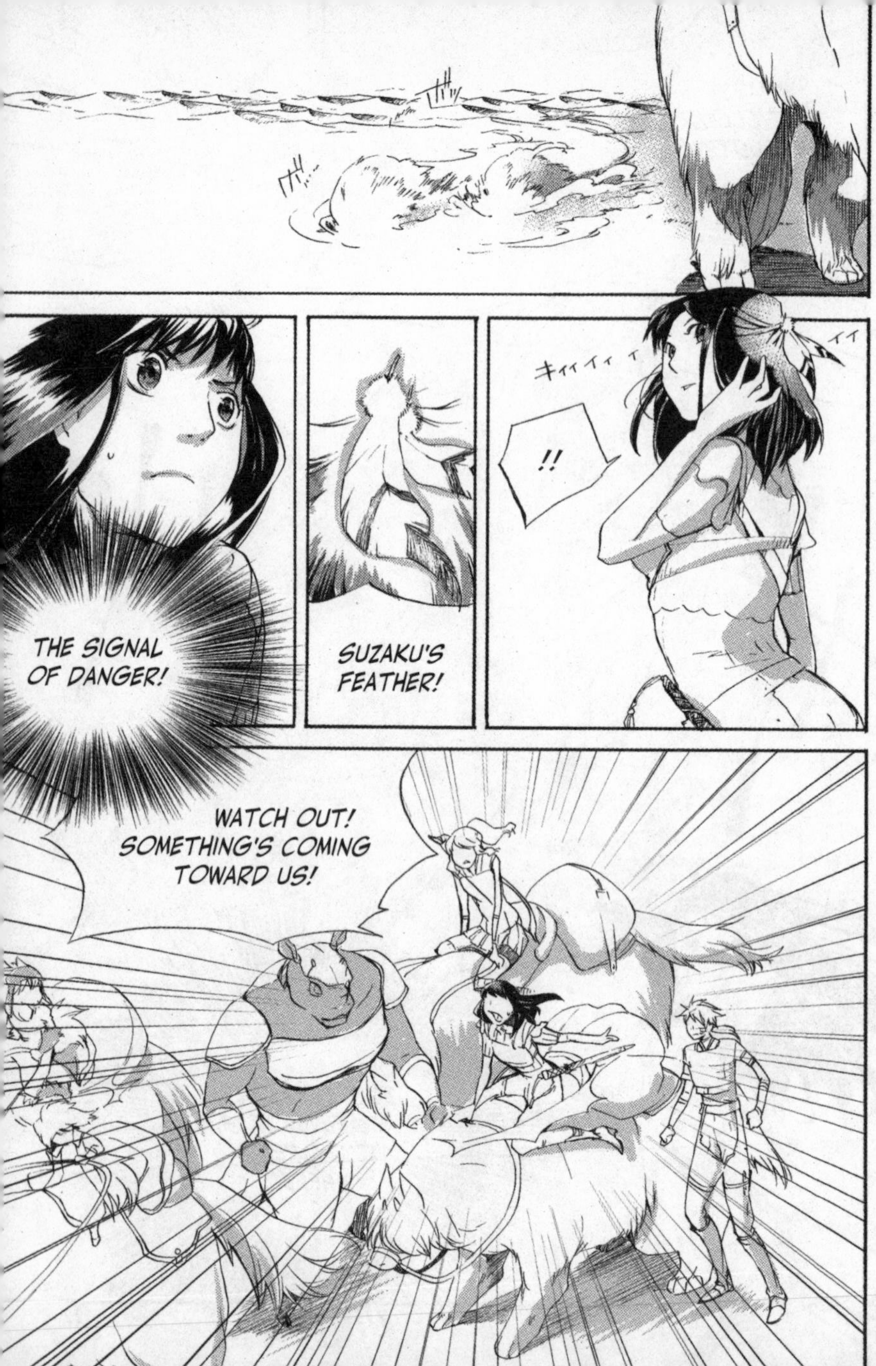

キィィィィ ィ
イイ
!!
SUZAKU'S FEATHER!
THE SIGNAL OF DANGER!
WATCH OUT! SOMETHING'S COMING TOWARD US!

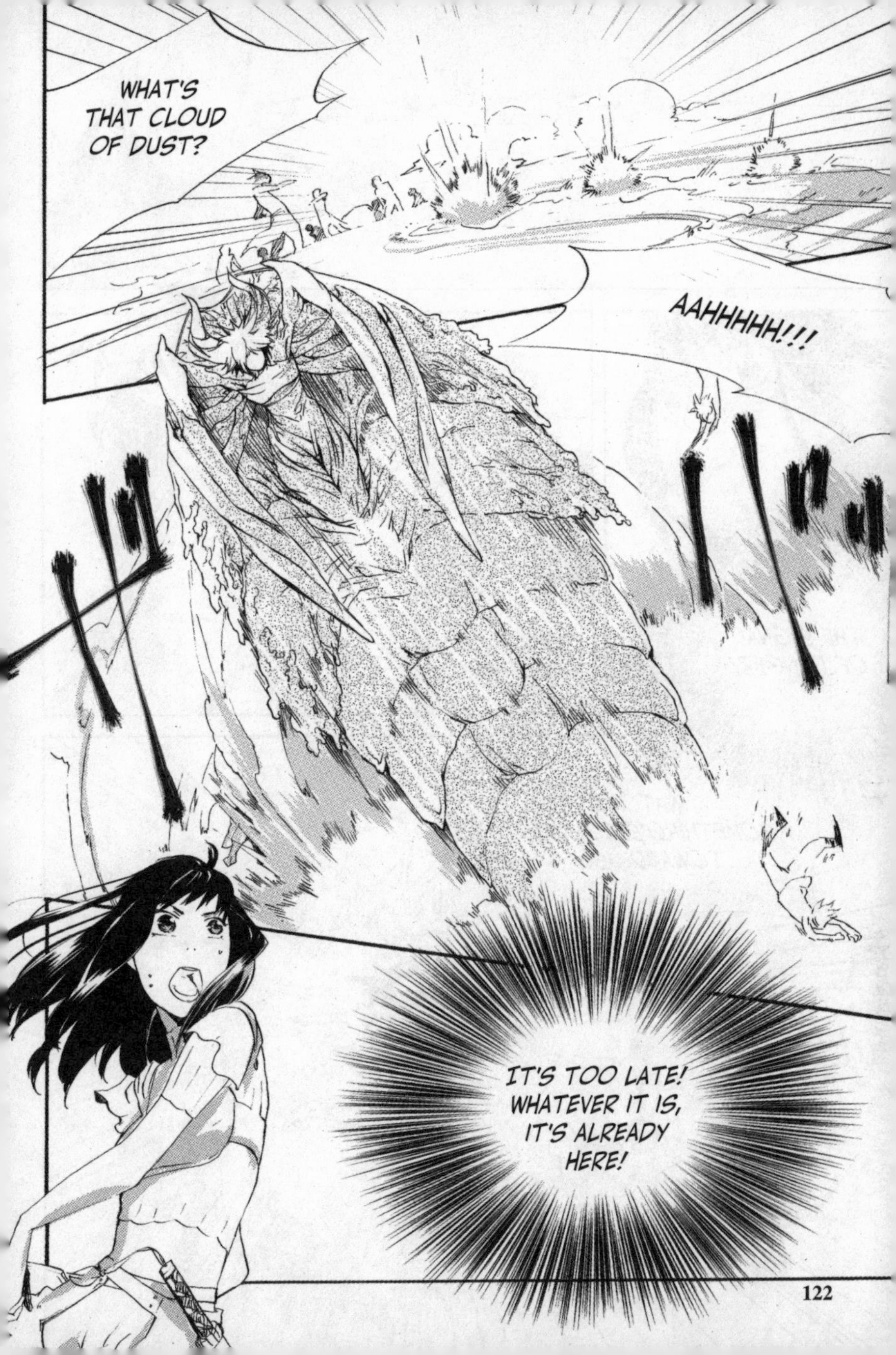
WHAT'S THAT CLOUD OF DUST?
AAHHHHH!!!
IT'S TOO LATE! WHATEVER IT IS, IT'S ALREADY HERE!

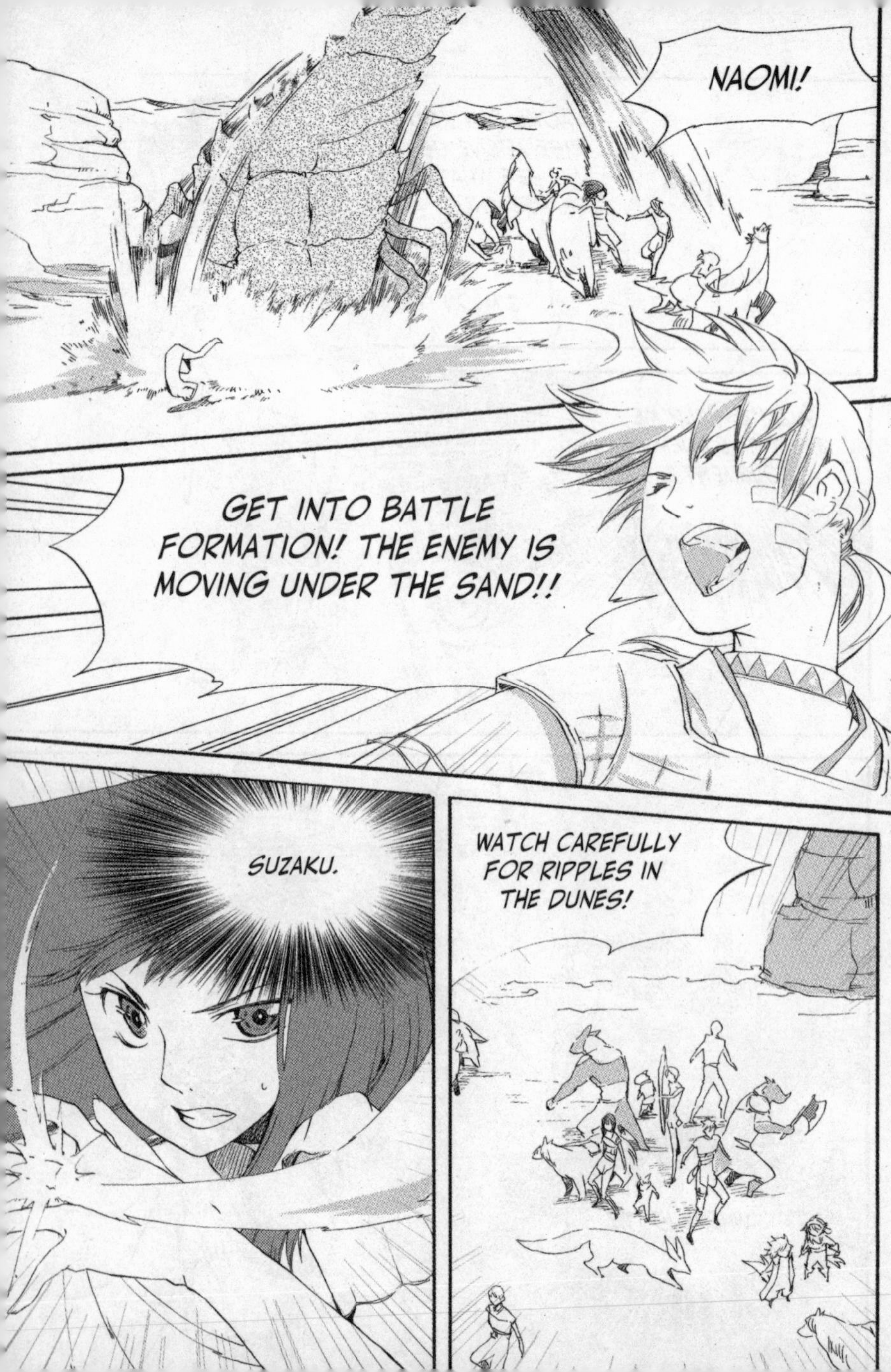
NAOMI!
GET INTO BATTLE FORMATION! THE ENEMY IS MOVING UNDER THE SAND!!
WATCH CAREFULLY FOR RIPPLES IN THE DUNES!
SUZAKU.

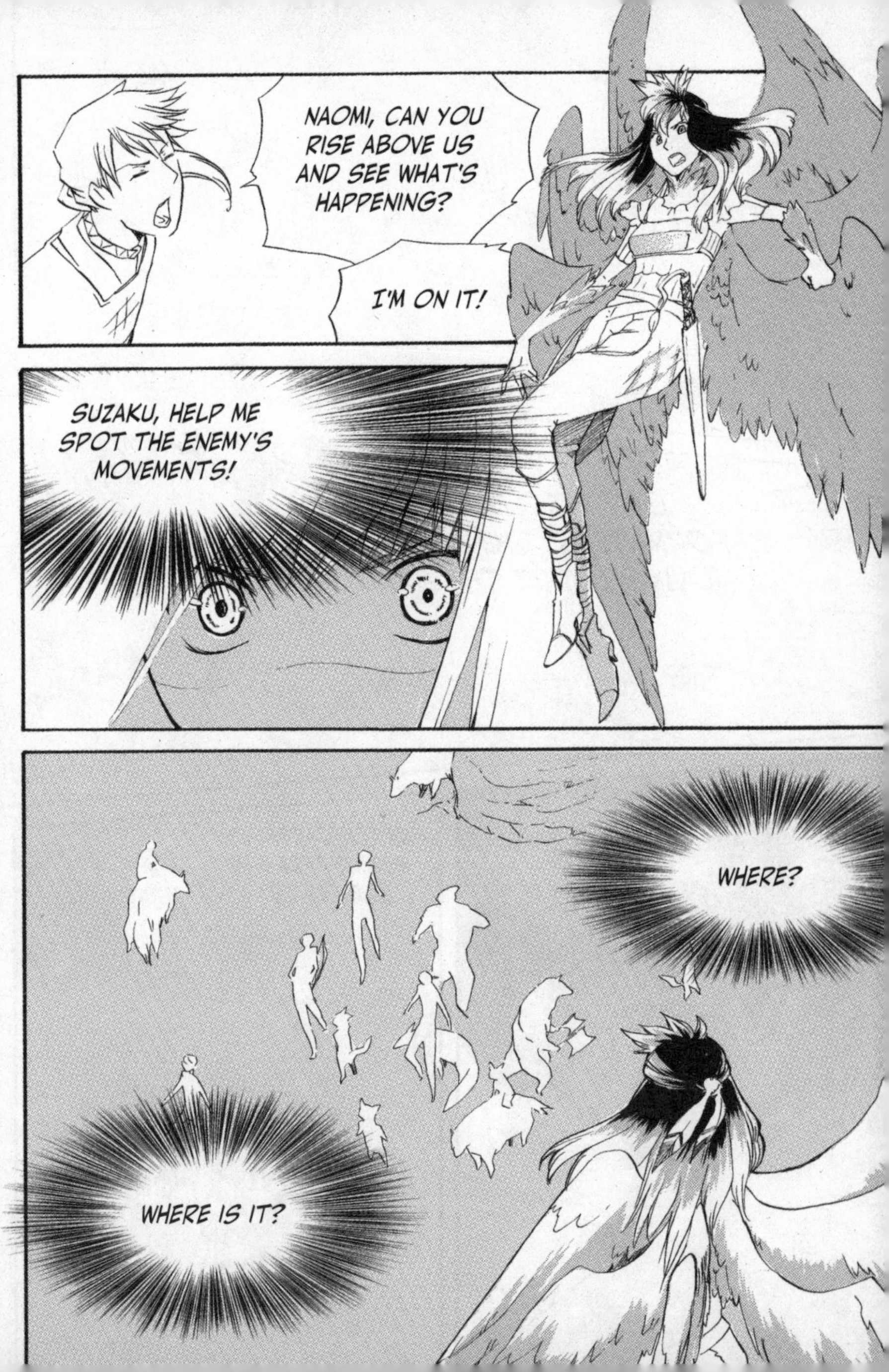
NAOMI, CAN YOU RISE ABOVE US AND SEE WHAT'S HAPPENING?
I'M ON IT!
SUZAKU, HELP ME SPOT THE ENEMY'S MOVEMENTS!
WHERE?
WHERE IS IT?

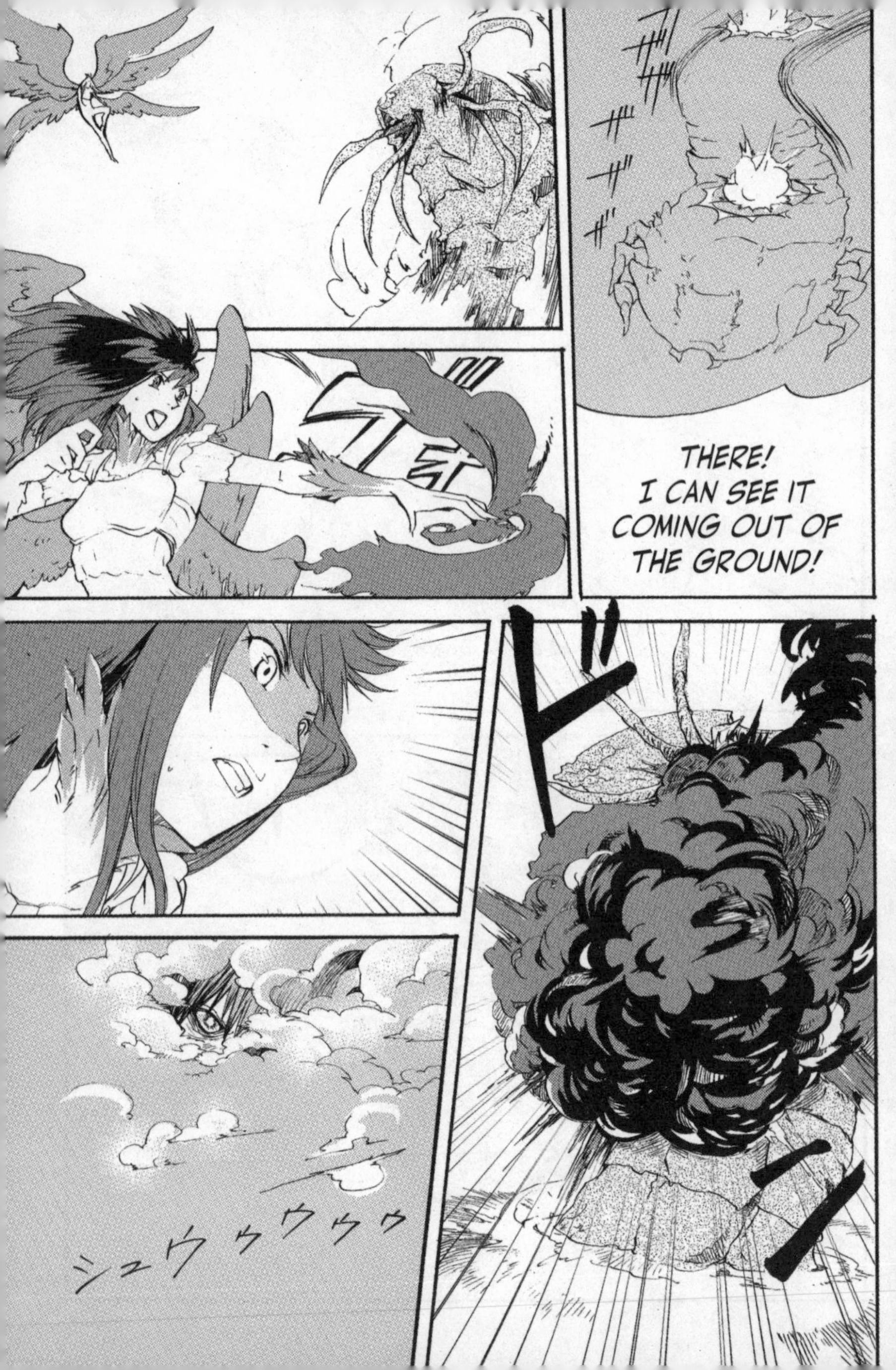
THERE! I CAN SEE IT COMING OUT OF THE GROUND!

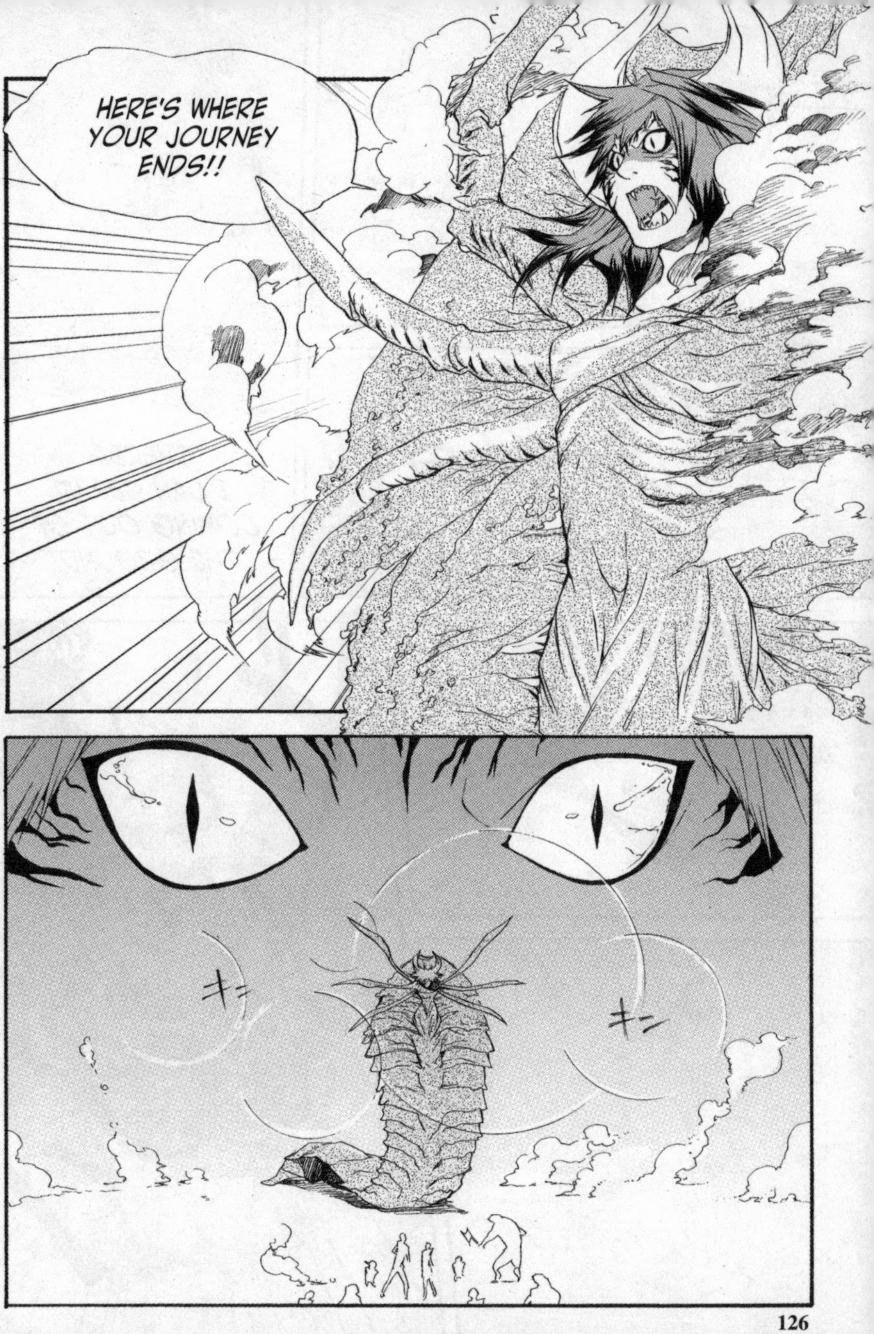
HERE'S WHERE YOUR JOURNEY ENDS!!

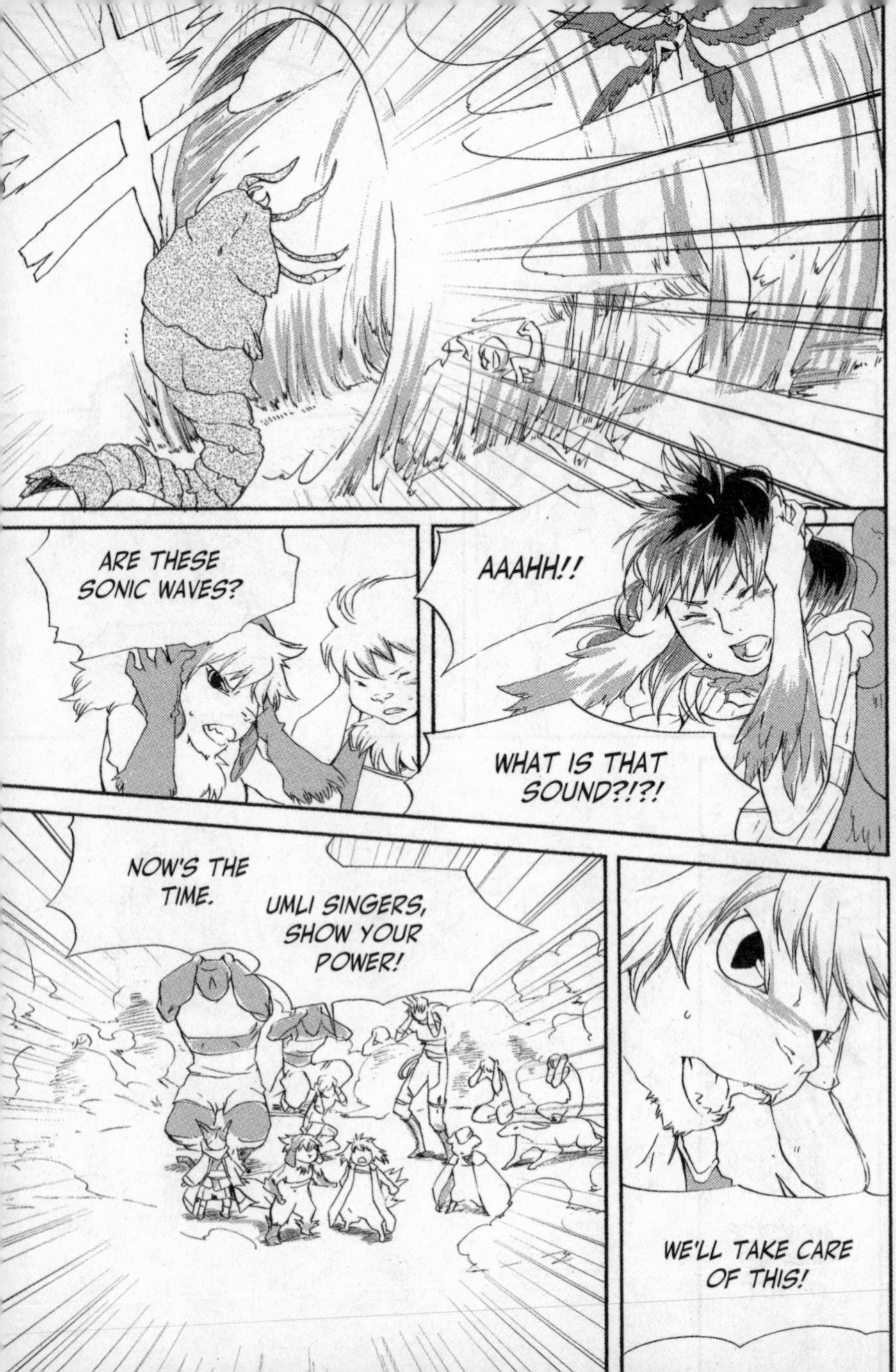
AAAHH!!
WHAT IS THAT SOUND?!?!
ARE THESE SONIC WAVES?
WE'LL TAKE CARE OF THIS!
NOW'S THE TIME.
UMLI SINGERS, SHOW YOUR POWER!

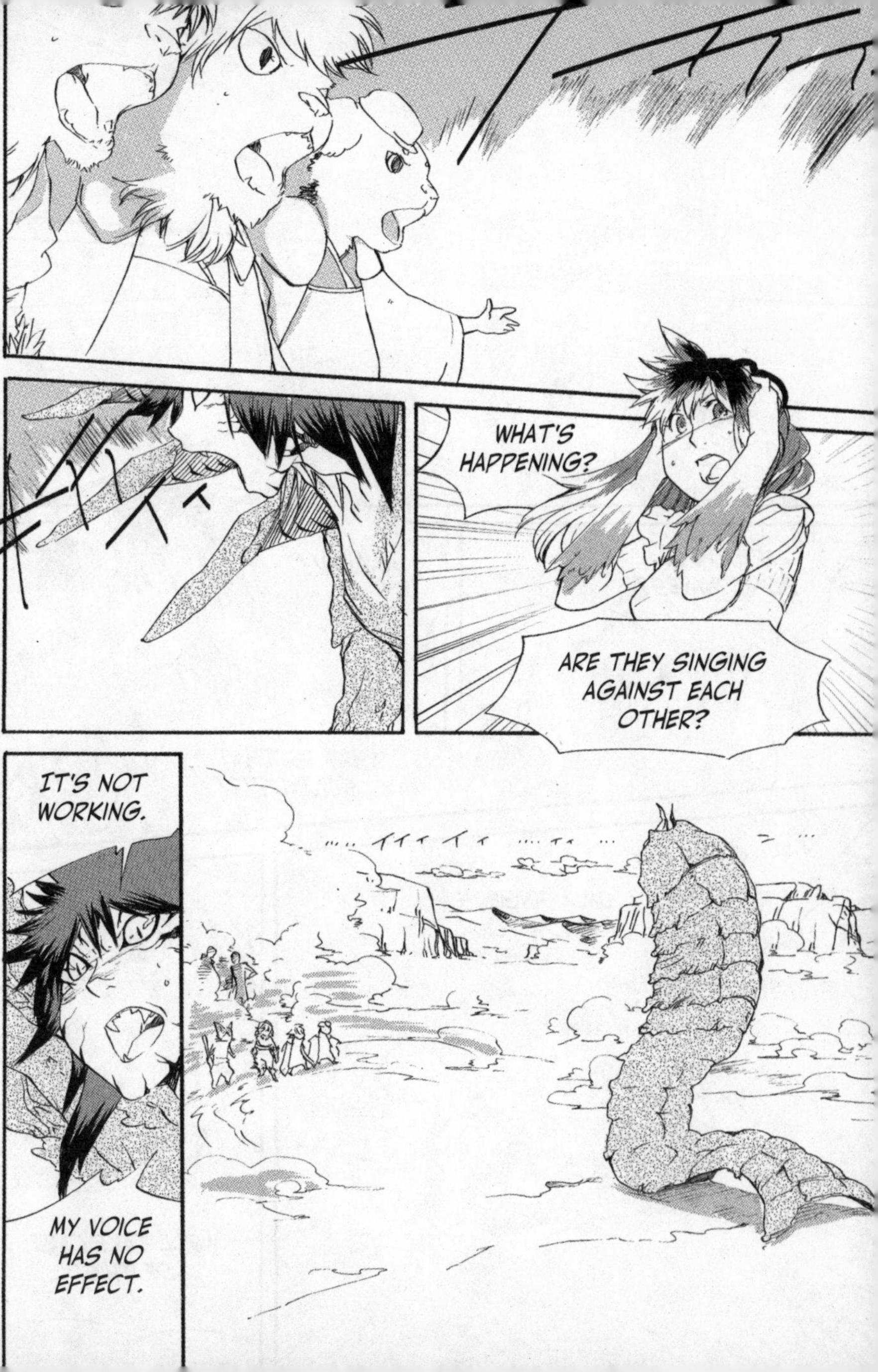
WHAT'S HAPPENING?
ARE THEY SINGING AGAINST EACH OTHER?
IT'S NOT WORKING.
MY VOICE HAS NO EFFECT.

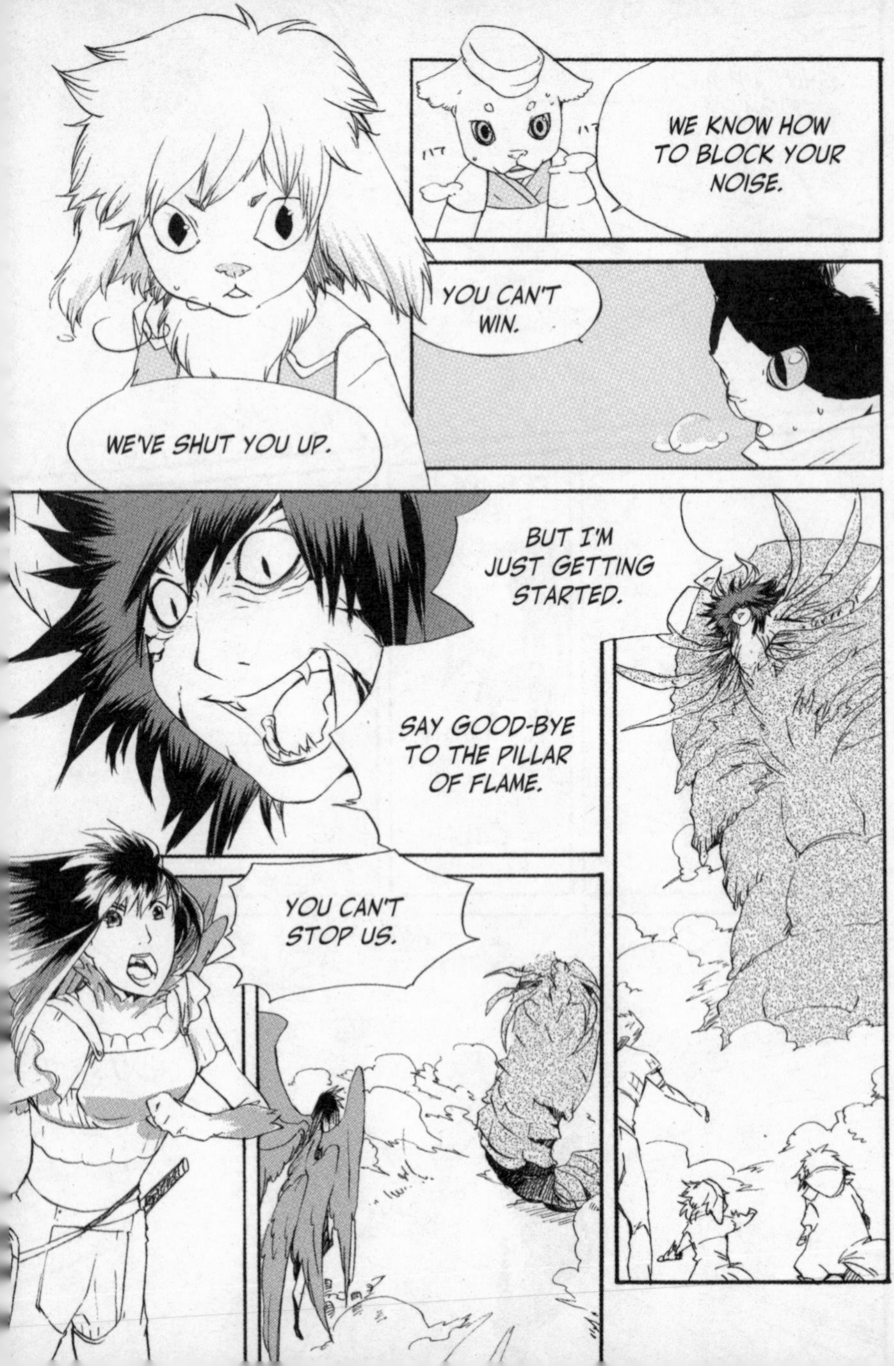

WE KNOW HOW TO BLOCK YOUR NOISE.
YOU CAN'T WIN.
WE'VE SHUT YOU UP.
BUT I'M JUST GETTING STARTED.
SAY GOOD-BYE TO THE PILLAR OF FLAME.
YOU CAN'T STOP US.

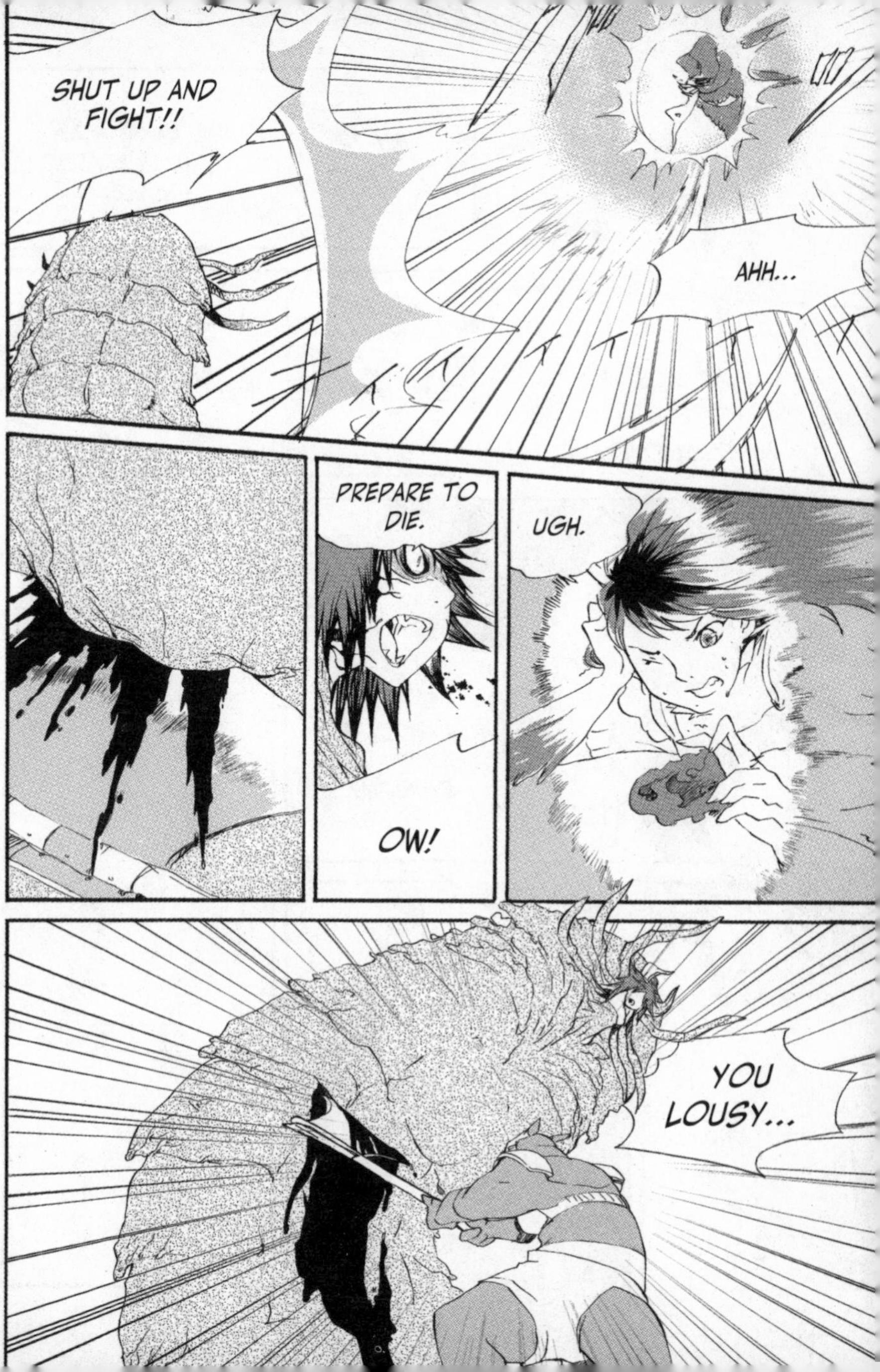
AHH...
SHUT UP AND FIGHT!!
UGH.
PREPARE TO DIE.
OW!
YOU LOUSY...

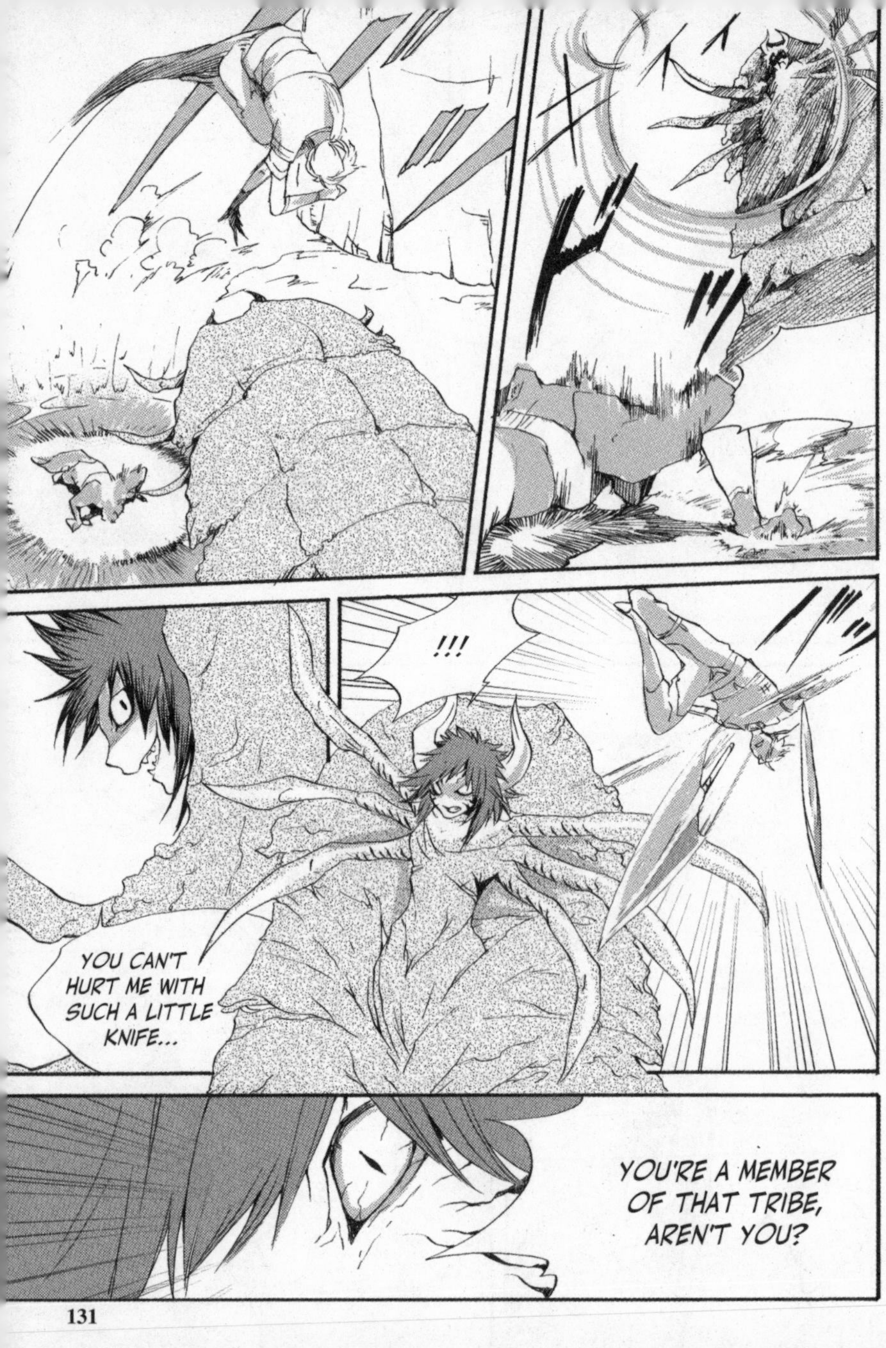
!!!
YOU CAN'T HURT ME WITH SUCH A LITTLE KNIFE...
YOU'RE A MEMBER OF THAT TRIBE, AREN'T YOU?

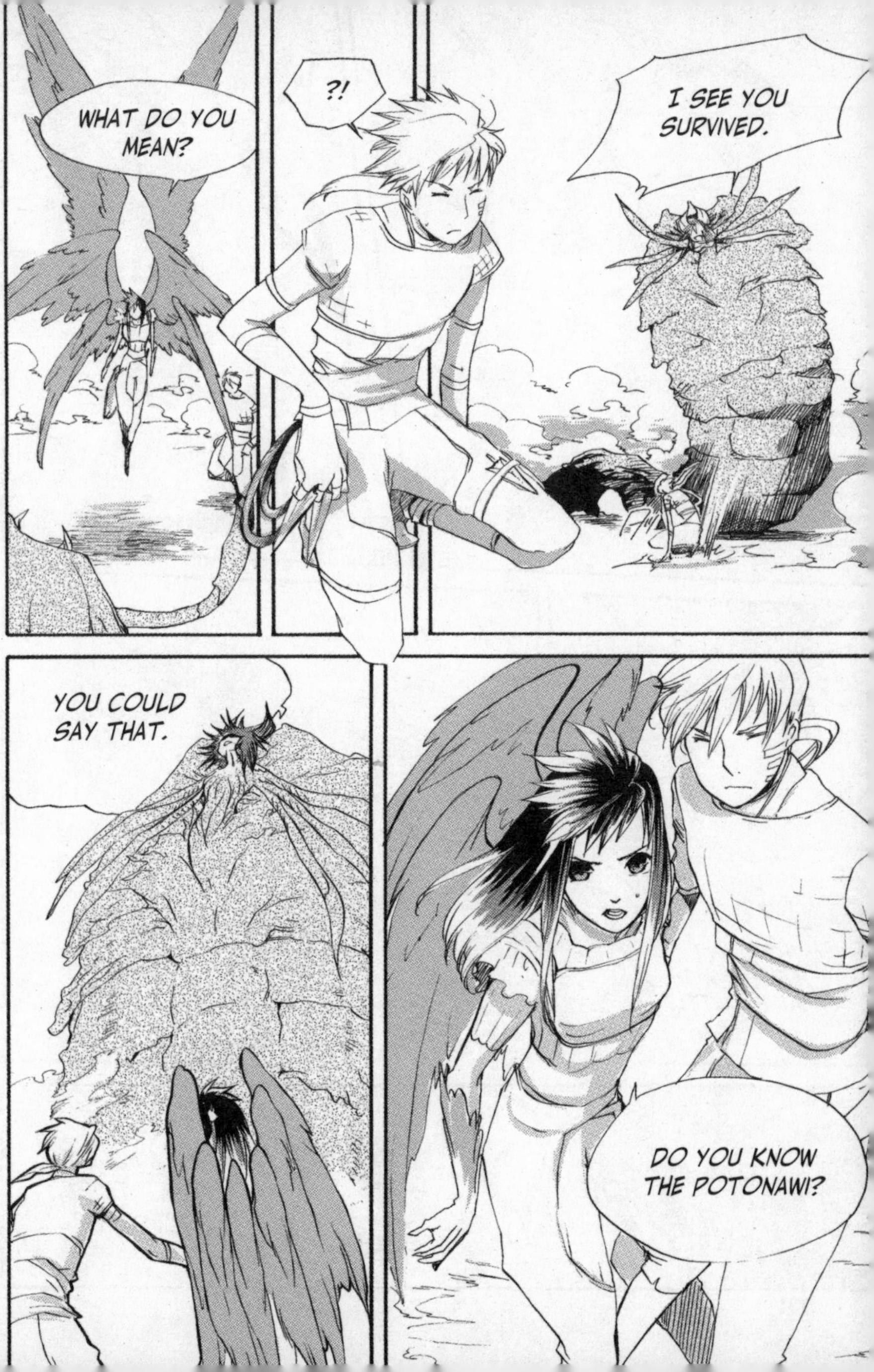
I SEE YOU SURVIVED.
?!
WHAT DO YOU MEAN?
DO YOU KNOW THE POTONAWI?
YOU COULD SAY THAT.

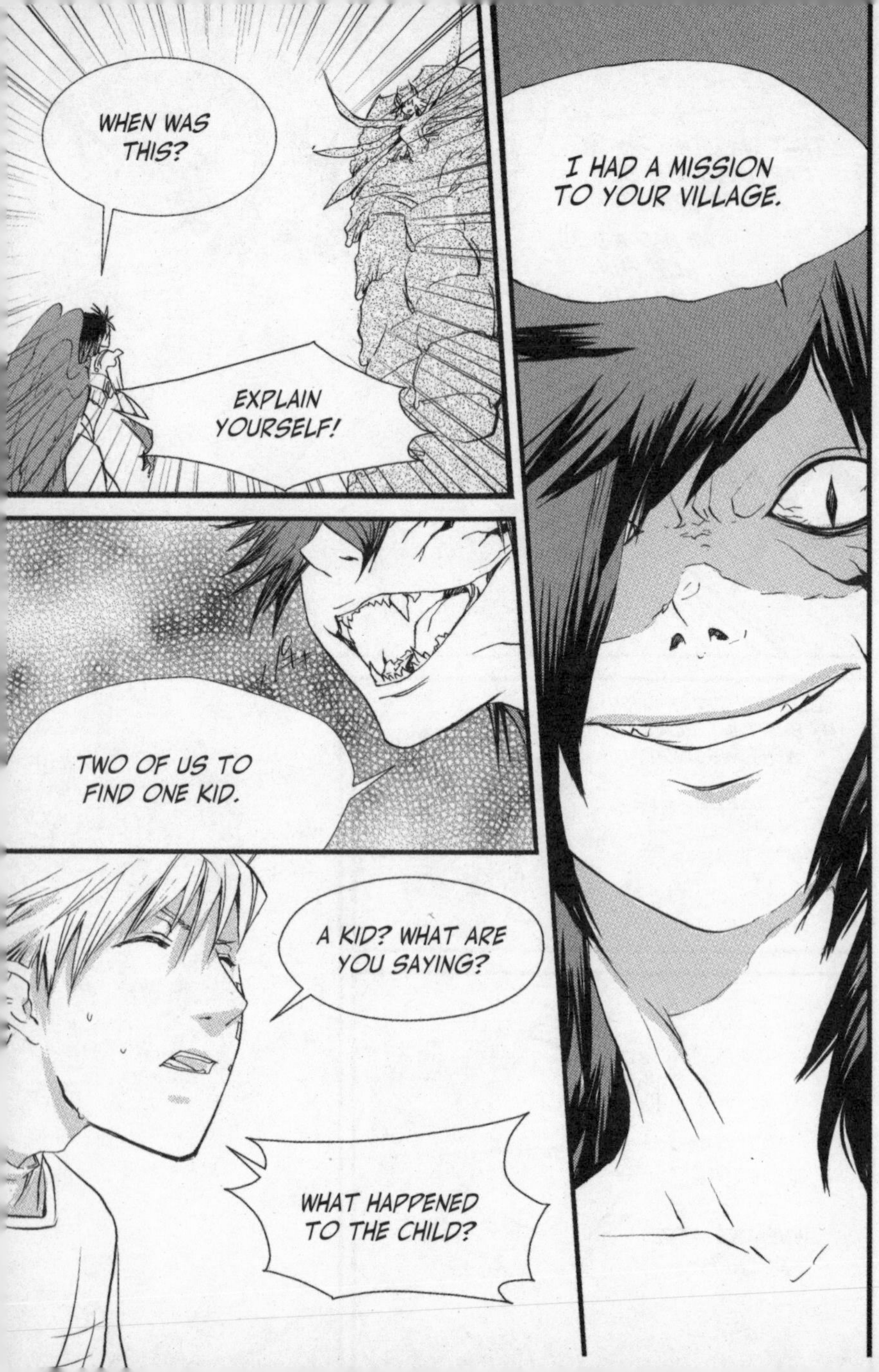
I HAD A MISSION TO YOUR VILLAGE.
WHEN WAS THIS?
EXPLAIN YOURSELF!
TWO OF US TO FIND ONE KID.
A KID? WHAT ARE YOU SAYING?
WHAT HAPPENED TO THE CHILD?

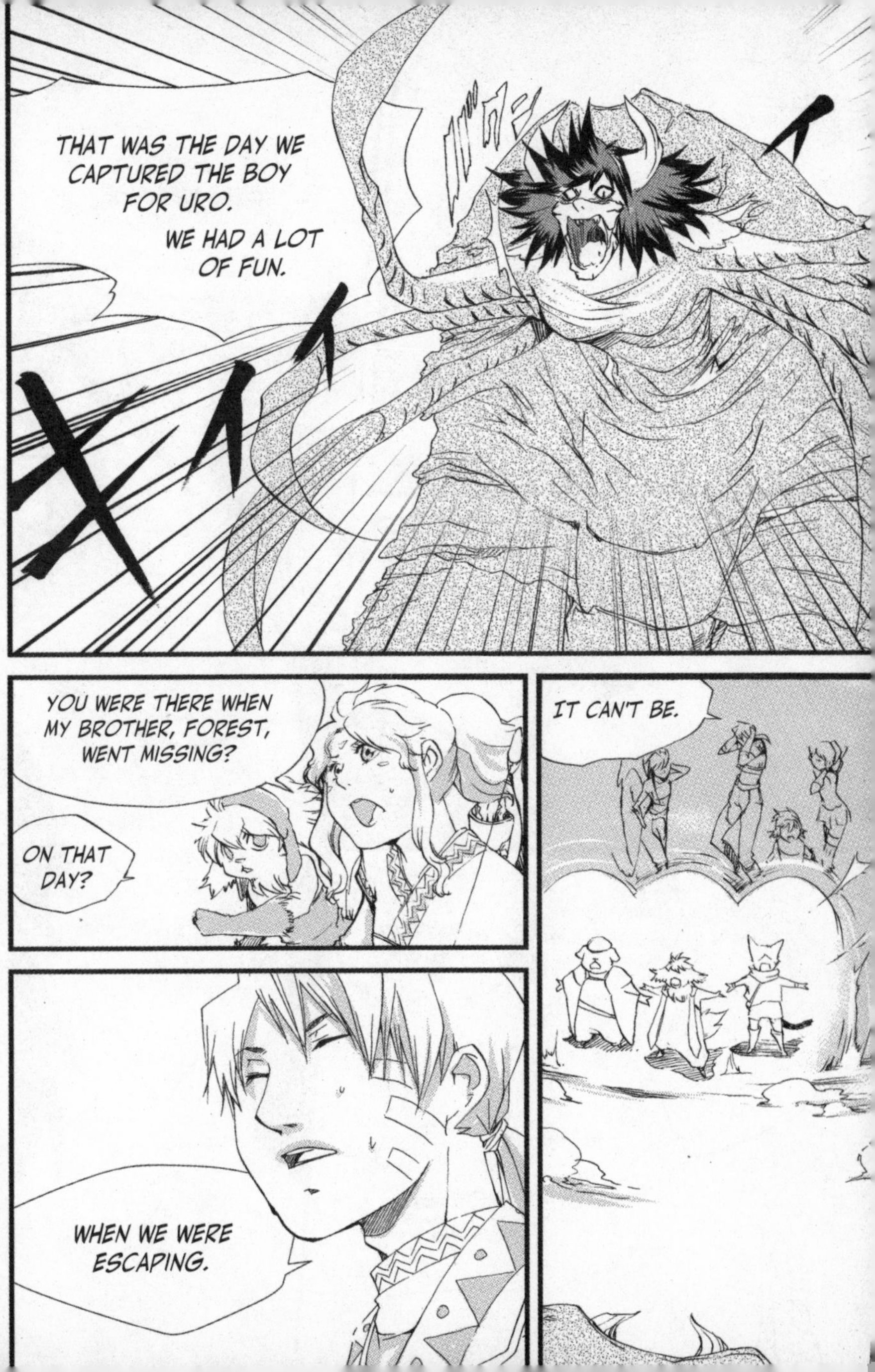
THAT WAS THE DAY WE CAPTURED THE BOY FOR URO.
WE HAD A LOT OF FUN.
IT CAN'T BE.
YOU WERE THERE WHEN MY BROTHER, FOREST, WENT MISSING?
ON THAT DAY?
WHEN WE WERE ESCAPING.

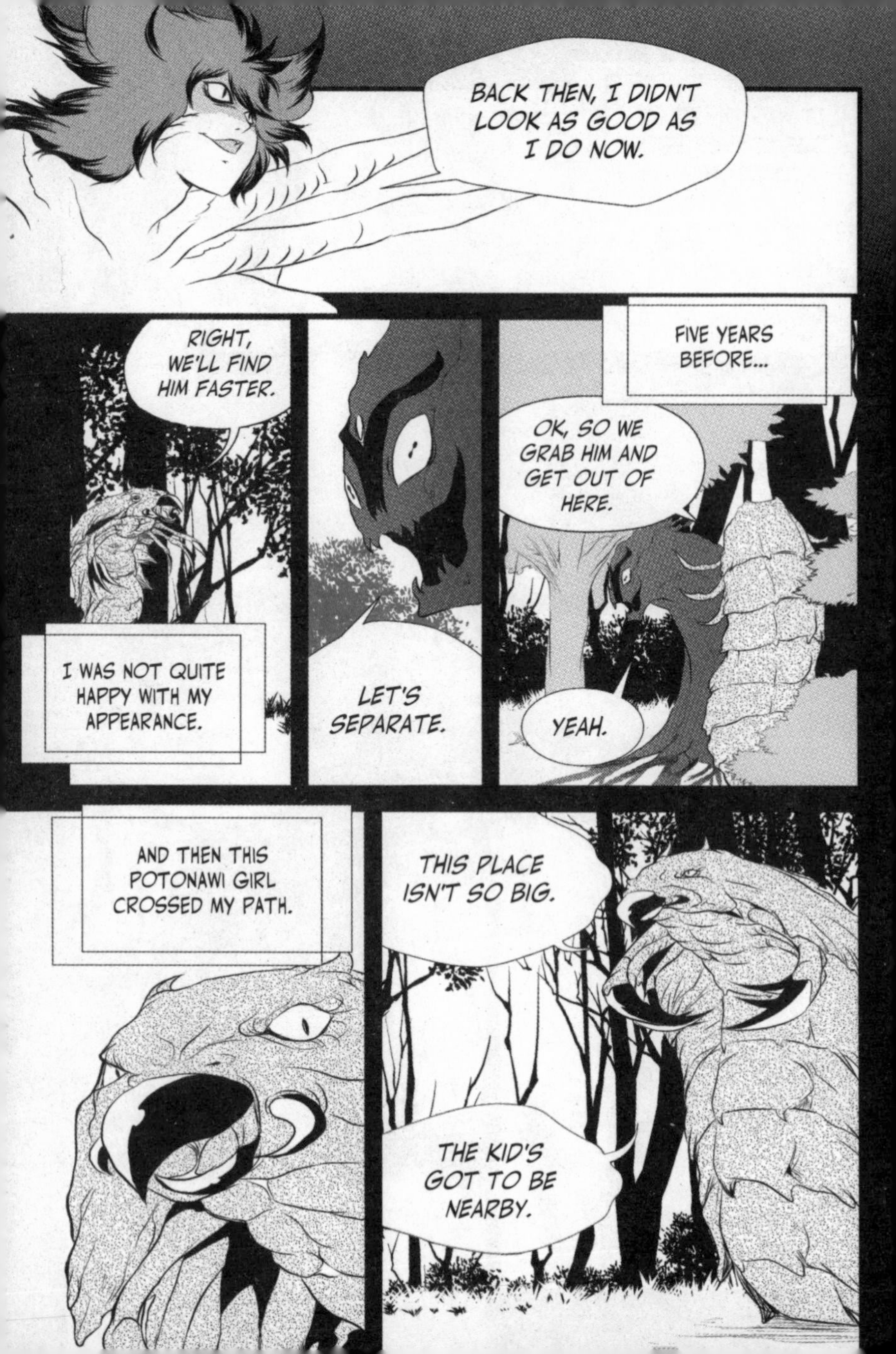
BACK THEN, I DIDN'T LOOK AS GOOD AS I DO NOW.
FIVE YEARS BEFORE...
OK, SO WE GRAB HIM AND GET OUT OF HERE.
YEAH.
LET'S SEPARATE.
RIGHT, WE'LL FIND HIM FASTER.
I WAS NOT QUITE HAPPY WITH MY APPEARANCE.
THIS PLACE ISN'T SO BIG.
THE KID'S GOT TO BE NEARBY.
AND THEN THIS POTONAWI GIRL CROSSED MY PATH.

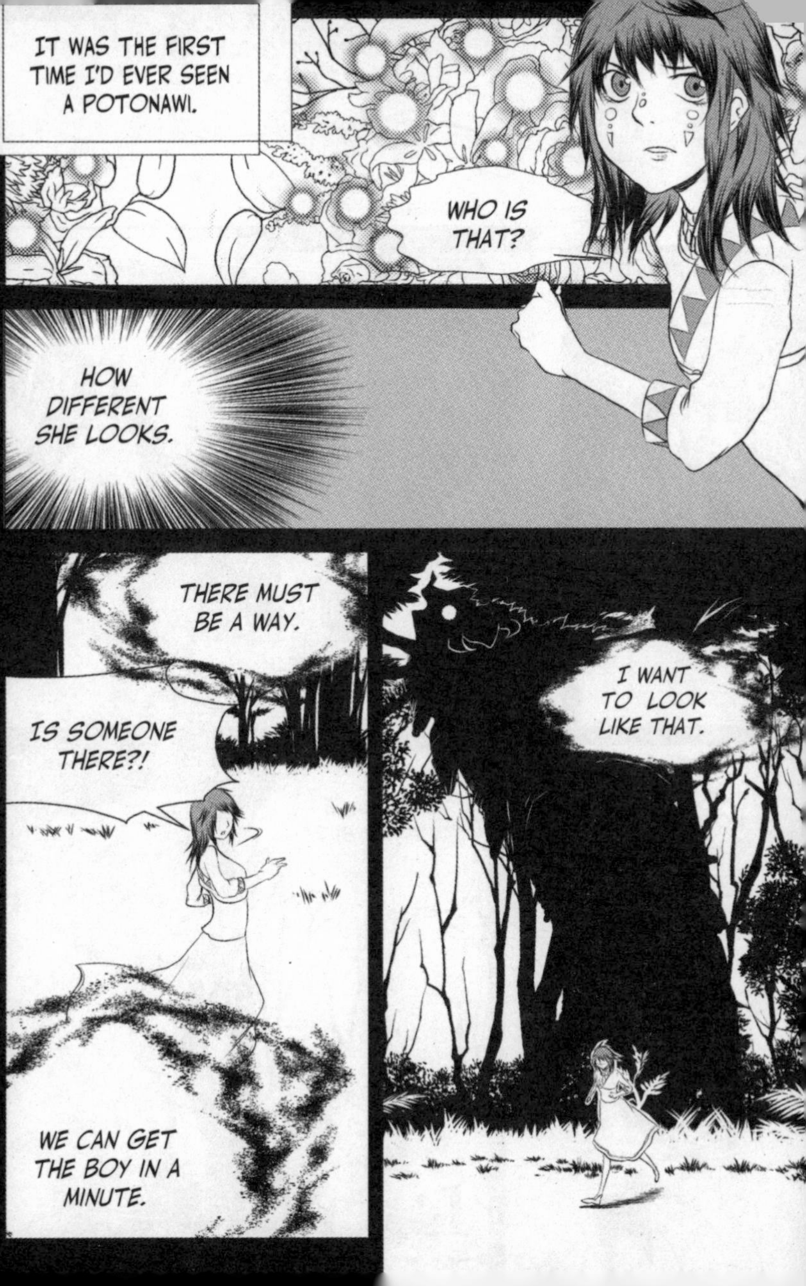
IT WAS THE FIRST TIME I'D EVER SEEN A POTONAWI.
WHO IS THAT?
HOW DIFFERENT SHE LOOKS.
I WANT TO LOOK LIKE THAT.
THERE MUST BE A WAY.
IS SOMEONE THERE?!
WE CAN GET THE BOY IN A MINUTE.

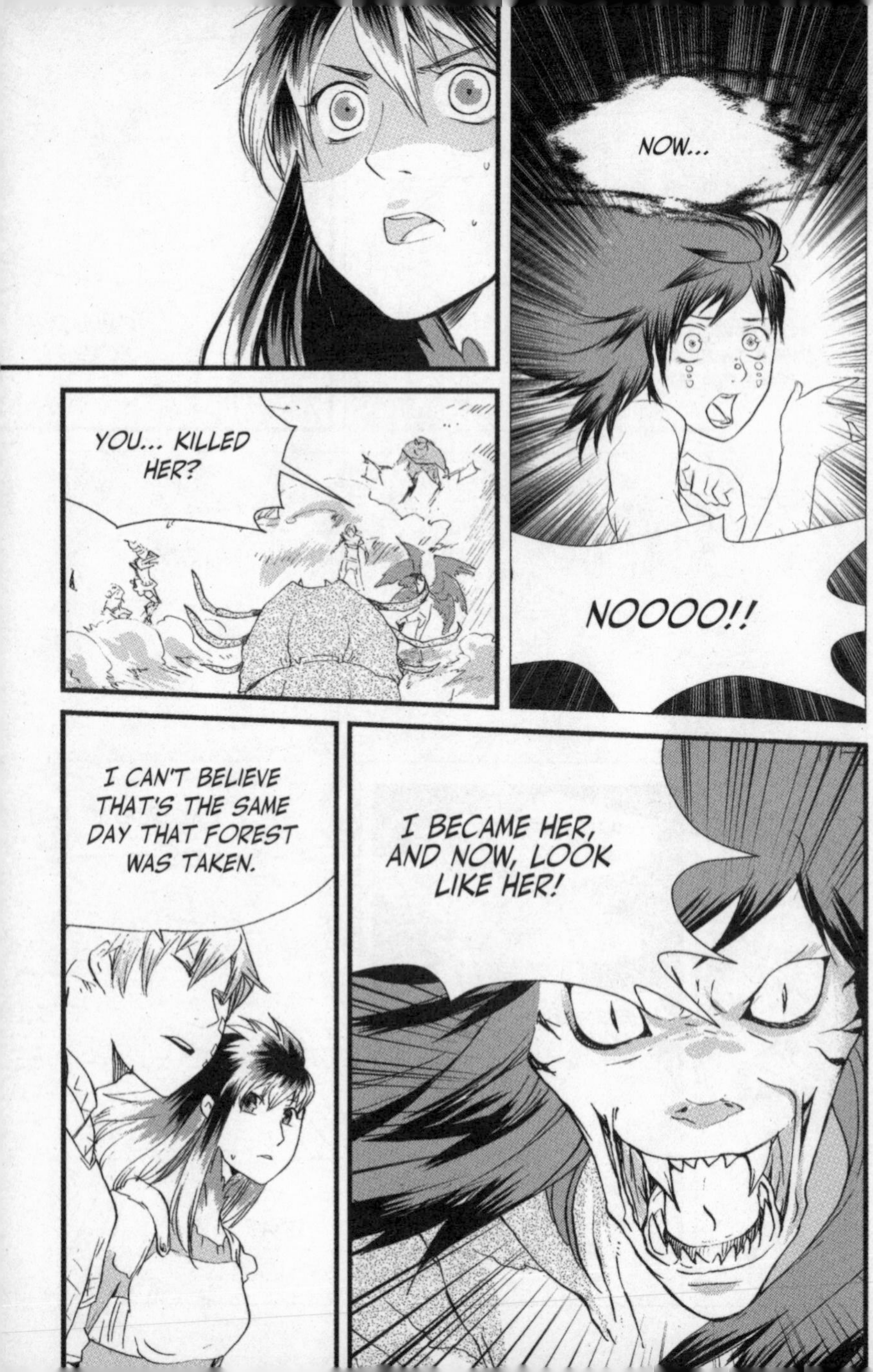
NOW...
NOOOO!!
YOU... KILLED HER?
I BECAME HER, AND NOW, LOOK LIKE HER!
I CAN'T BELIEVE THAT'S THE SAME DAY THAT FOREST WAS TAKEN.

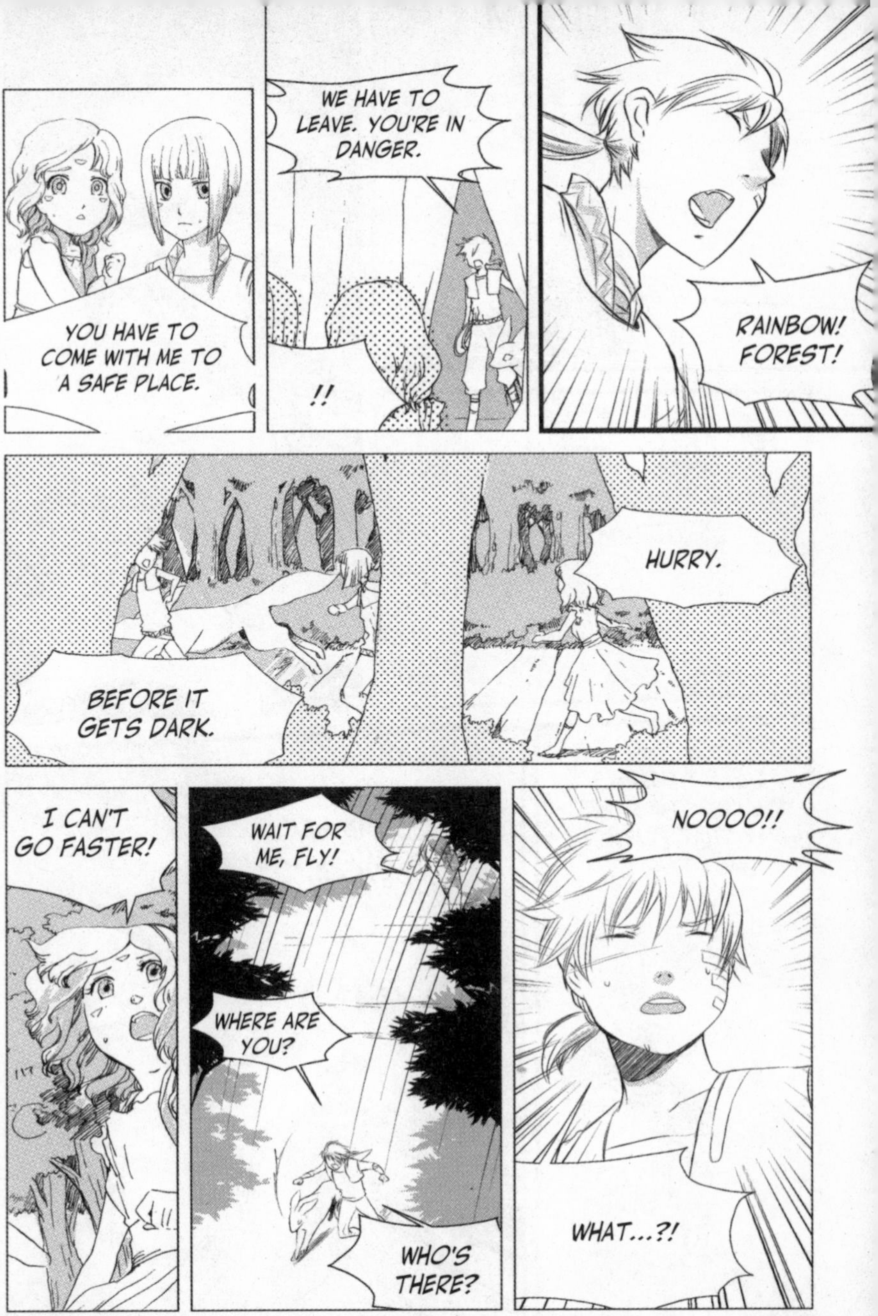
RAINBOW! FOREST!
WE HAVE TO LEAVE. YOU'RE IN DANGER.
!!
YOU HAVE TO COME WITH ME TO A SAFE PLACE.
HURRY.
BEFORE IT GETS DARK.
NOOOO!!
WHAT...?!
WAIT FOR ME, FLY!
WHERE ARE YOU?
WHO'S THERE?
I CAN'T GO FASTER!

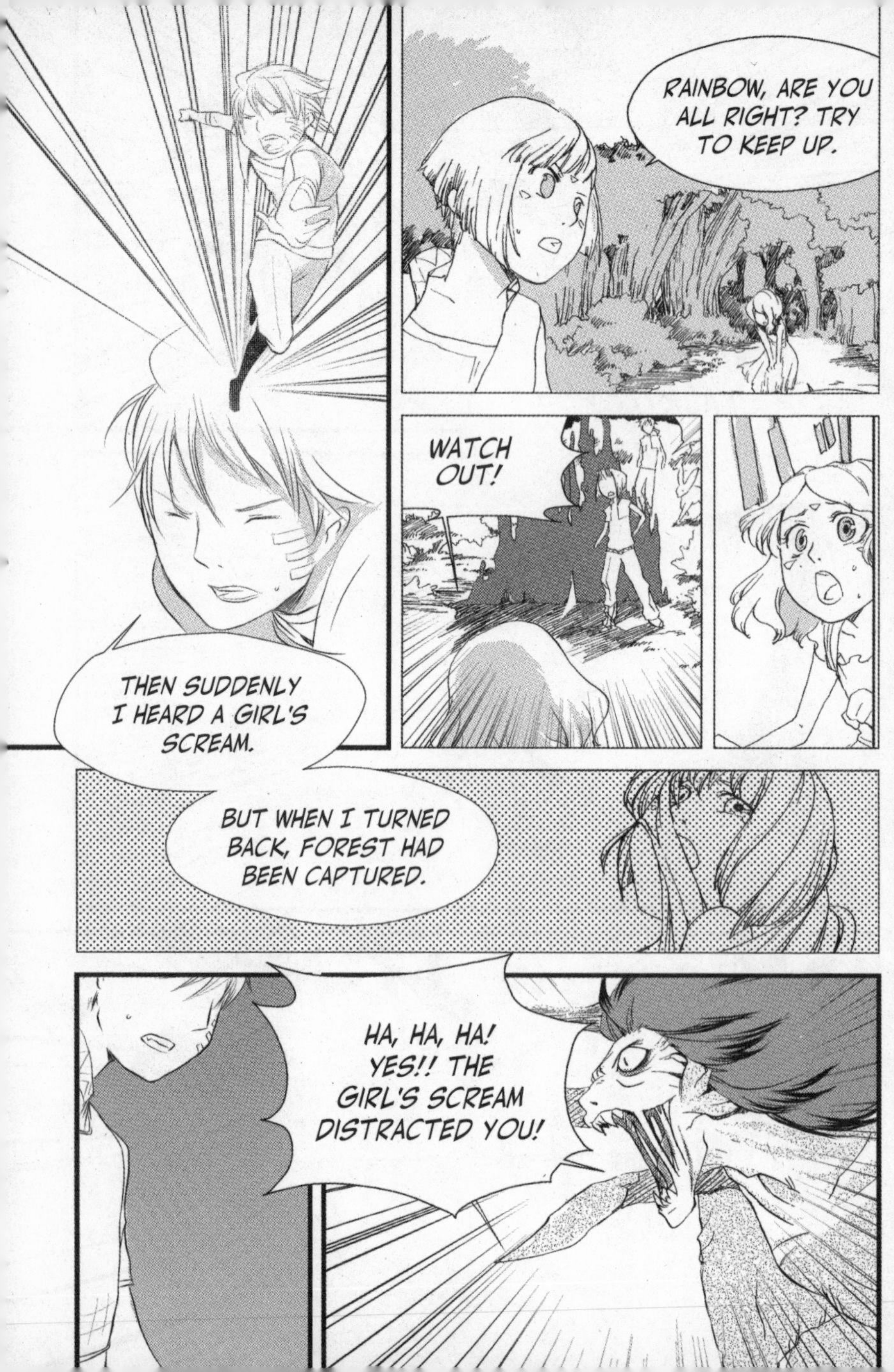
RAINBOW, ARE YOU ALL RIGHT? TRY TO KEEP UP.
WATCH OUT!
THEN SUDDENLY I HEARD A GIRL'S SCREAM.
BUT WHEN I TURNED BACK, FOREST HAD BEEN CAPTURED.
HA, HA, HA! YES!! THE GIRL'S SCREAM DISTRACTED YOU!

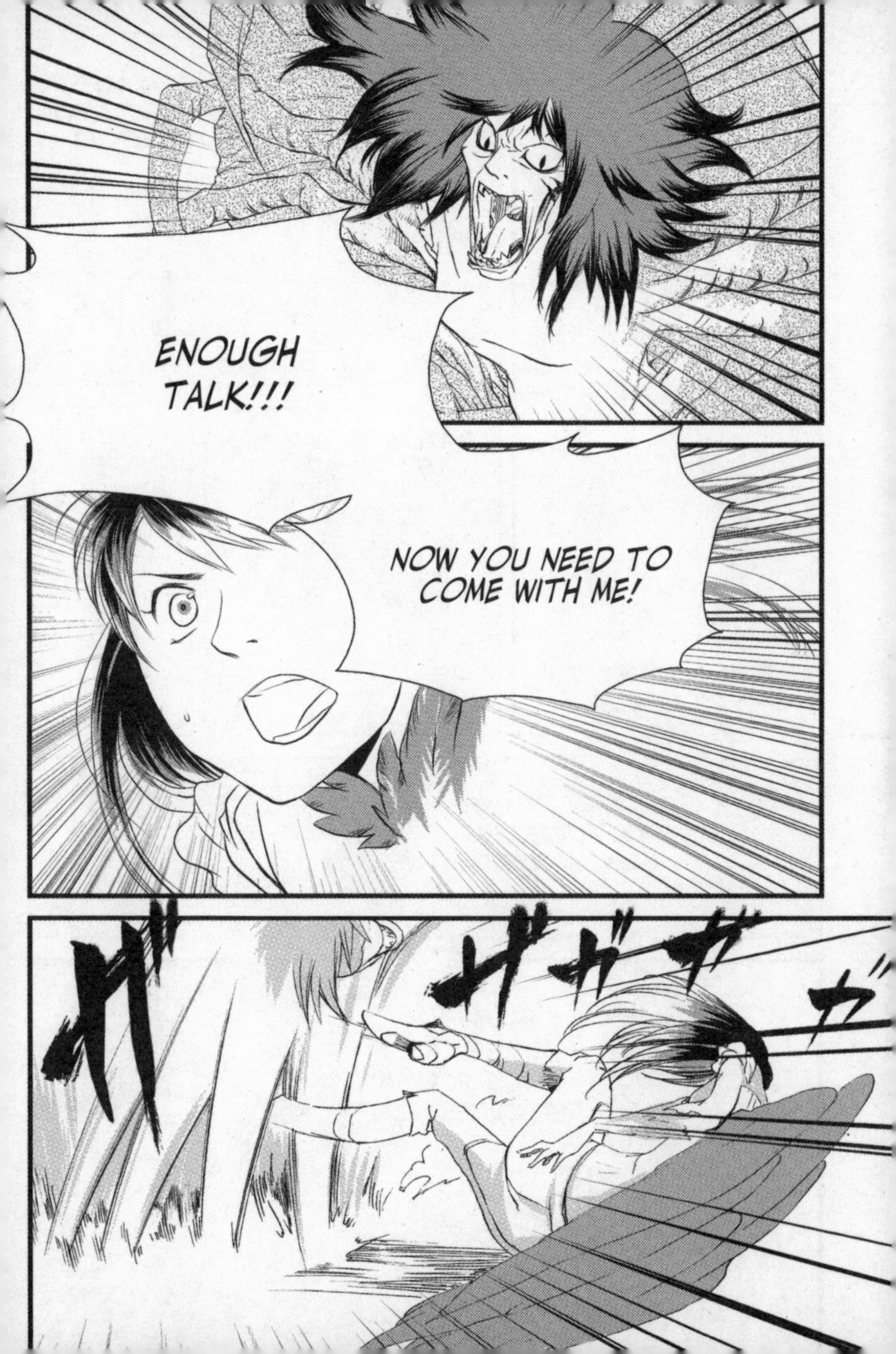
ENOUGH TALK!!!
NOW YOU NEED TO COME WITH ME!

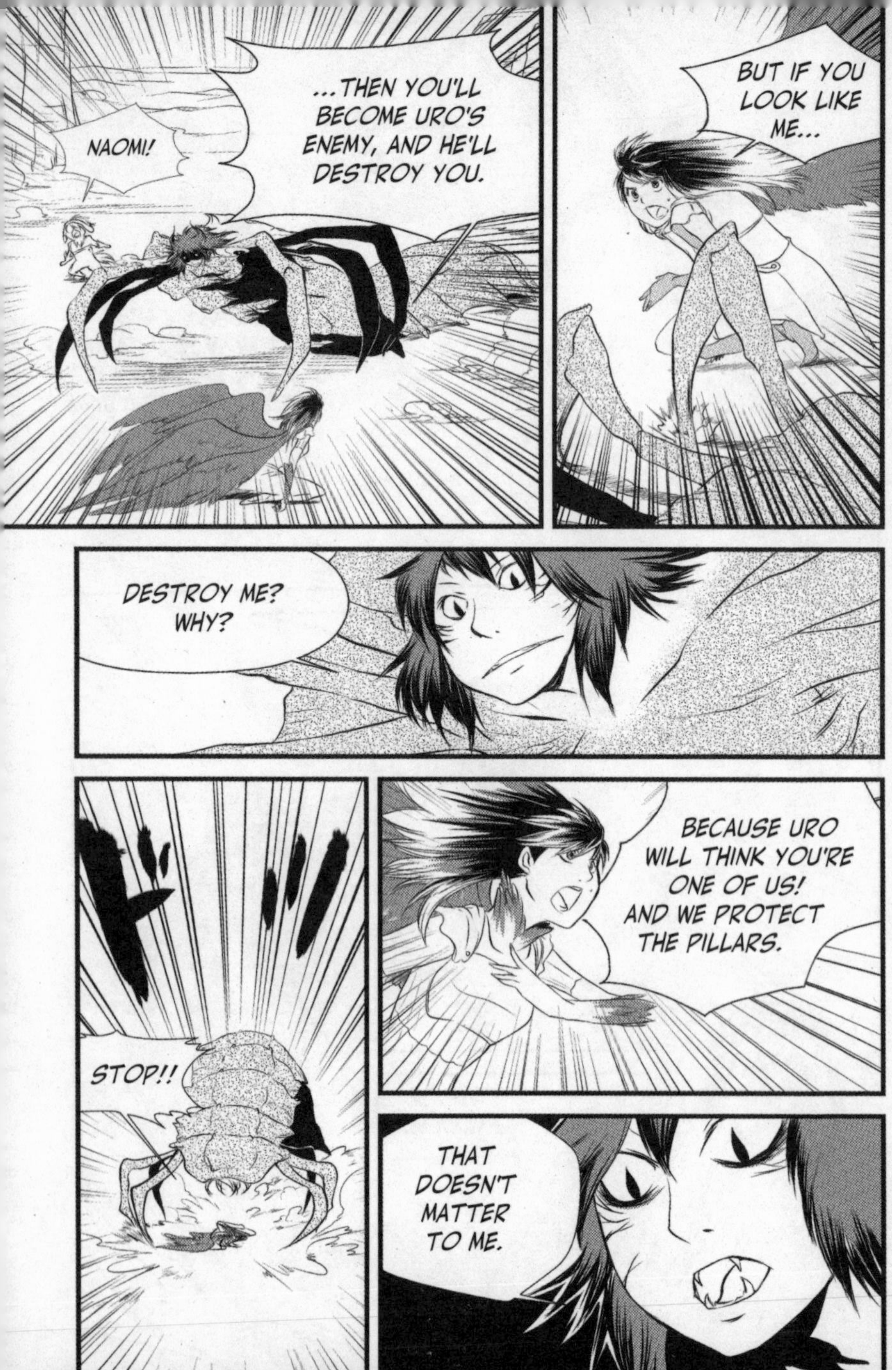
BUT IF YOU LOOK LIKE ME...
...THEN YOU'LL BECOME URO'S ENEMY, AND HE'LL DESTROY YOU.
NAOMI!
DESTROY ME? WHY?
BECAUSE URO WILL THINK YOU'RE ONE OF US! AND WE PROTECT THE PILLARS.
THAT DOESN'T MATTER TO ME.
STOP!!

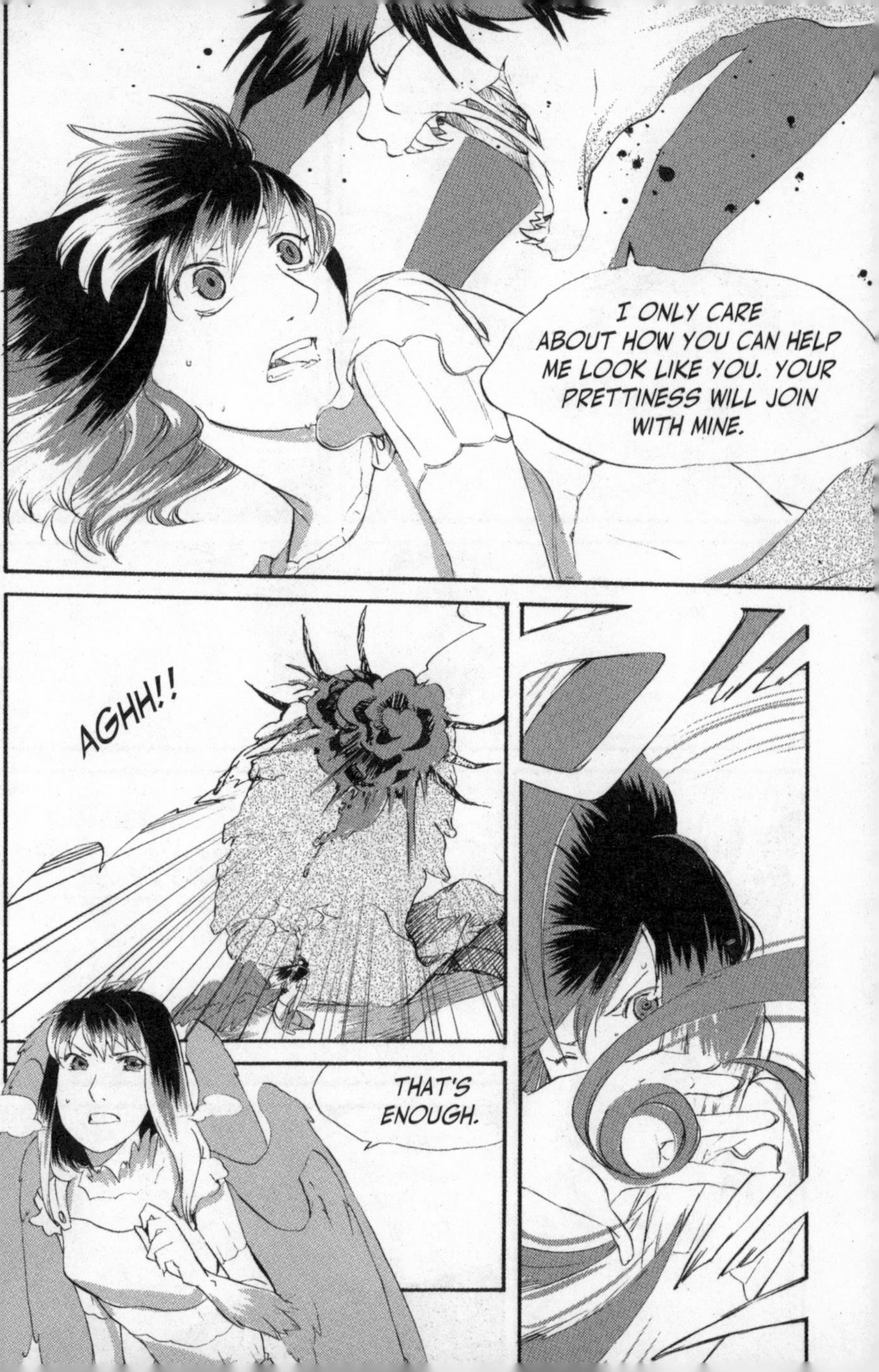
I ONLY CARE ABOUT HOW YOU CAN HELP ME LOOK LIKE YOU. YOUR PRETTINESS WILL JOIN WITH MINE.
AGHH!!
THAT'S ENOUGH.

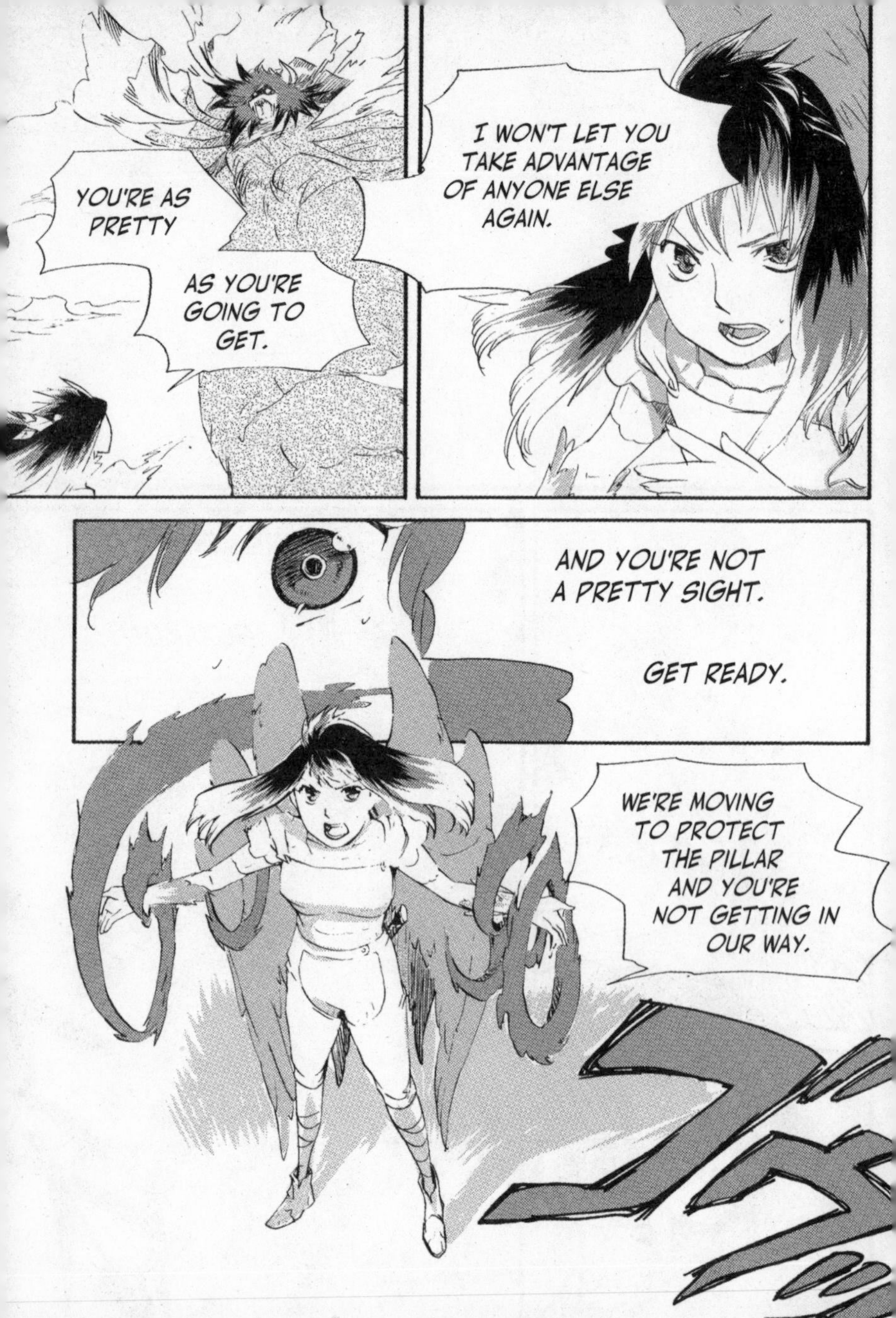
I WON'T LET YOU TAKE ADVANTAGE OF ANYONE ELSE AGAIN.
YOU'RE AS PRETTY
AS YOU'RE GOING TO GET.
AND YOU'RE NOT A PRETTY SIGHT.
GET READY.
WE'RE MOVING TO PROTECT THE PILLAR AND YOU'RE NOT GETTING IN OUR WAY.

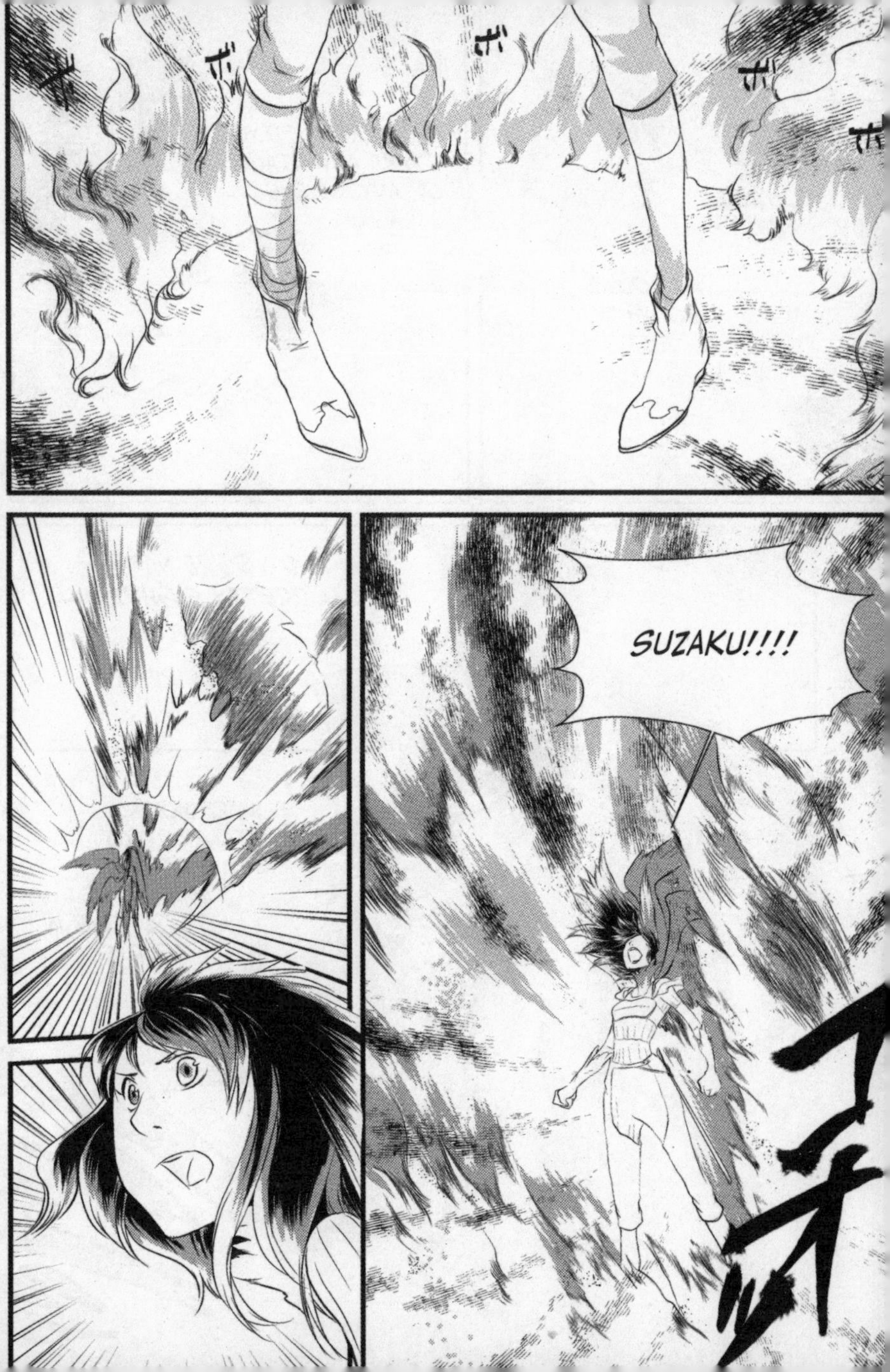
SUZAKU!!!!

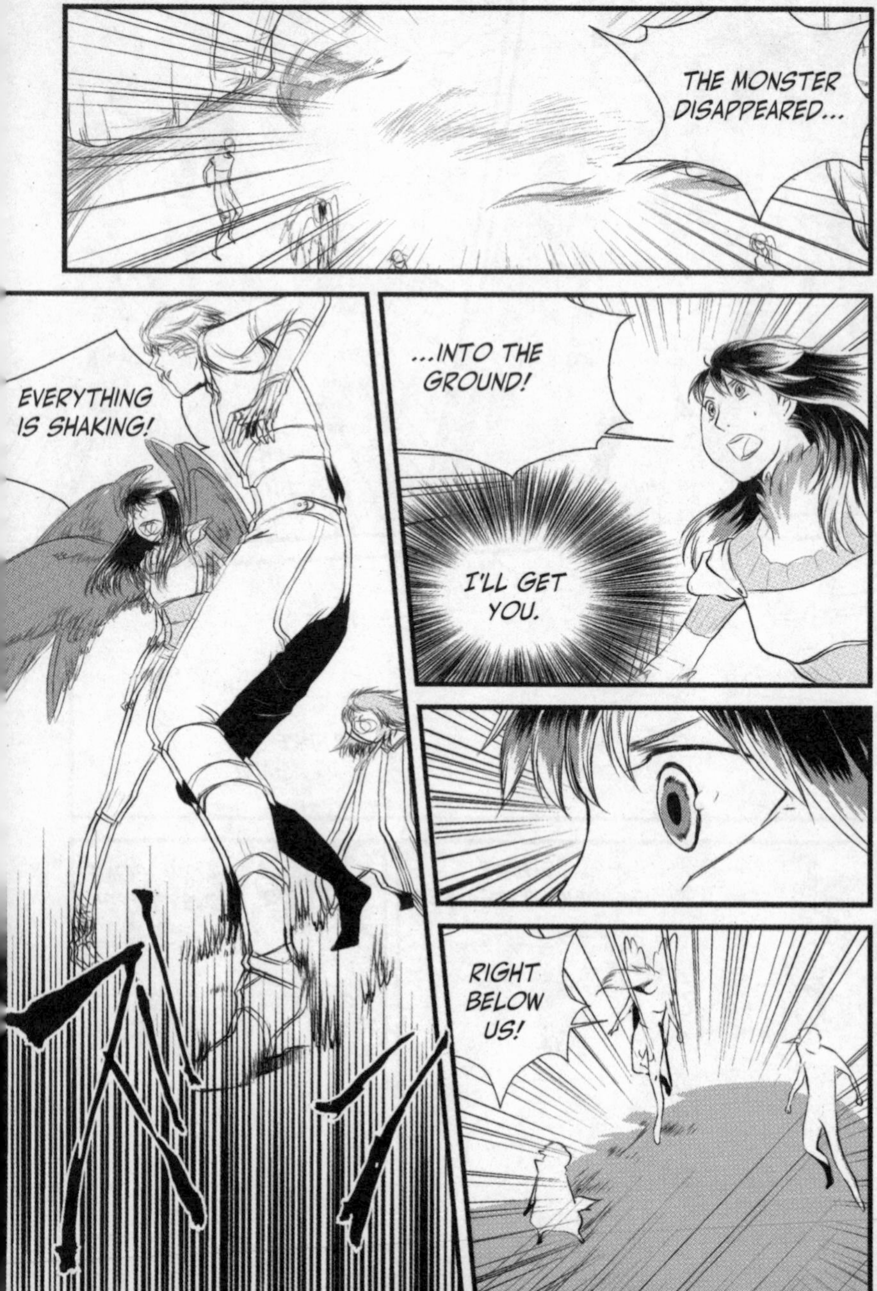
THE MONSTER DISAPPEARED...
...INTO THE GROUND!
I'LL GET YOU.
RIGHT BELOW US!
EVERYTHING IS SHAKING!

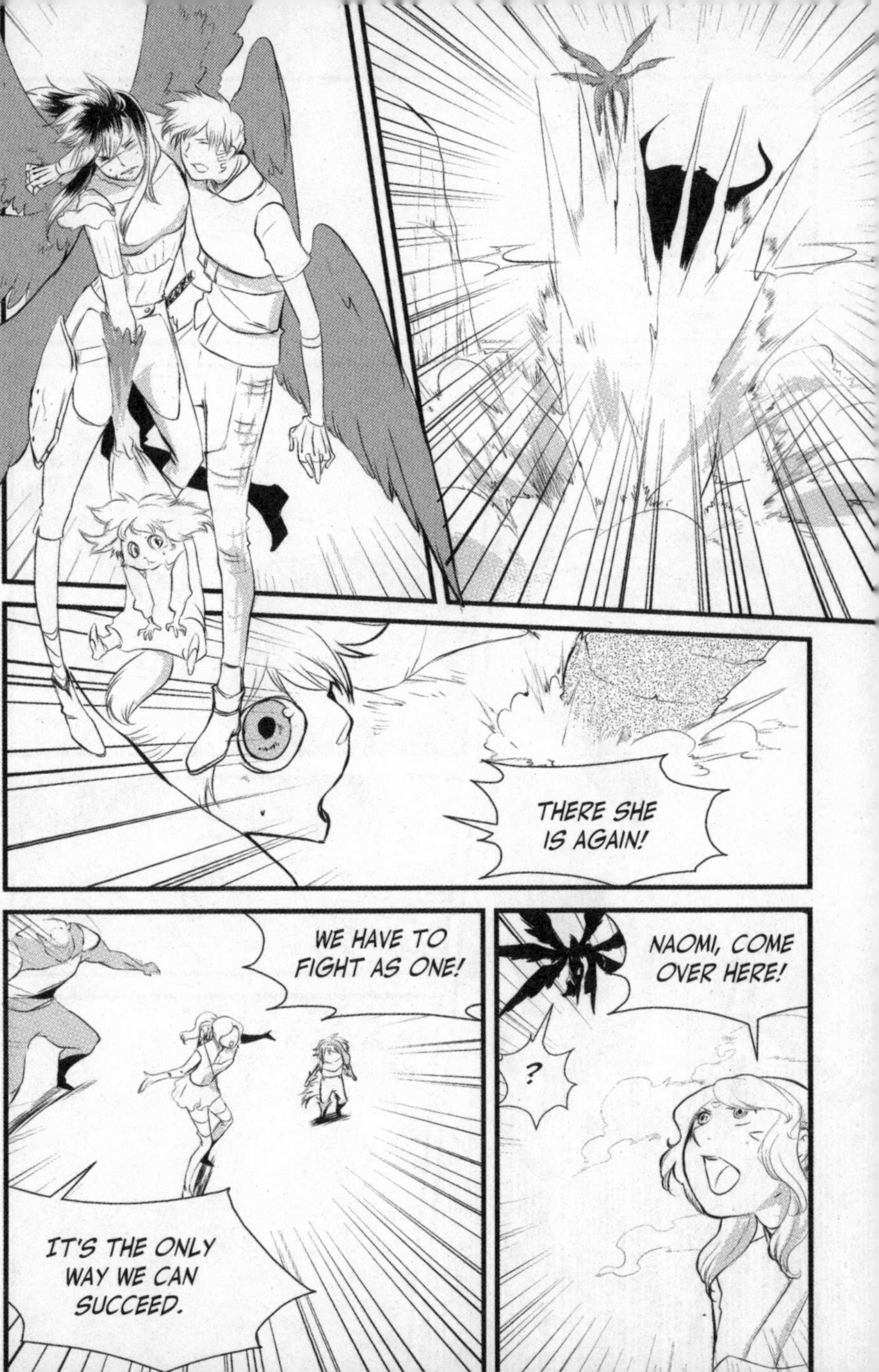
THERE SHE IS AGAIN!
NAOMI, COME OVER HERE!
?
WE HAVE TO FIGHT AS ONE!
IT'S THE ONLY WAY WE CAN SUCCEED.

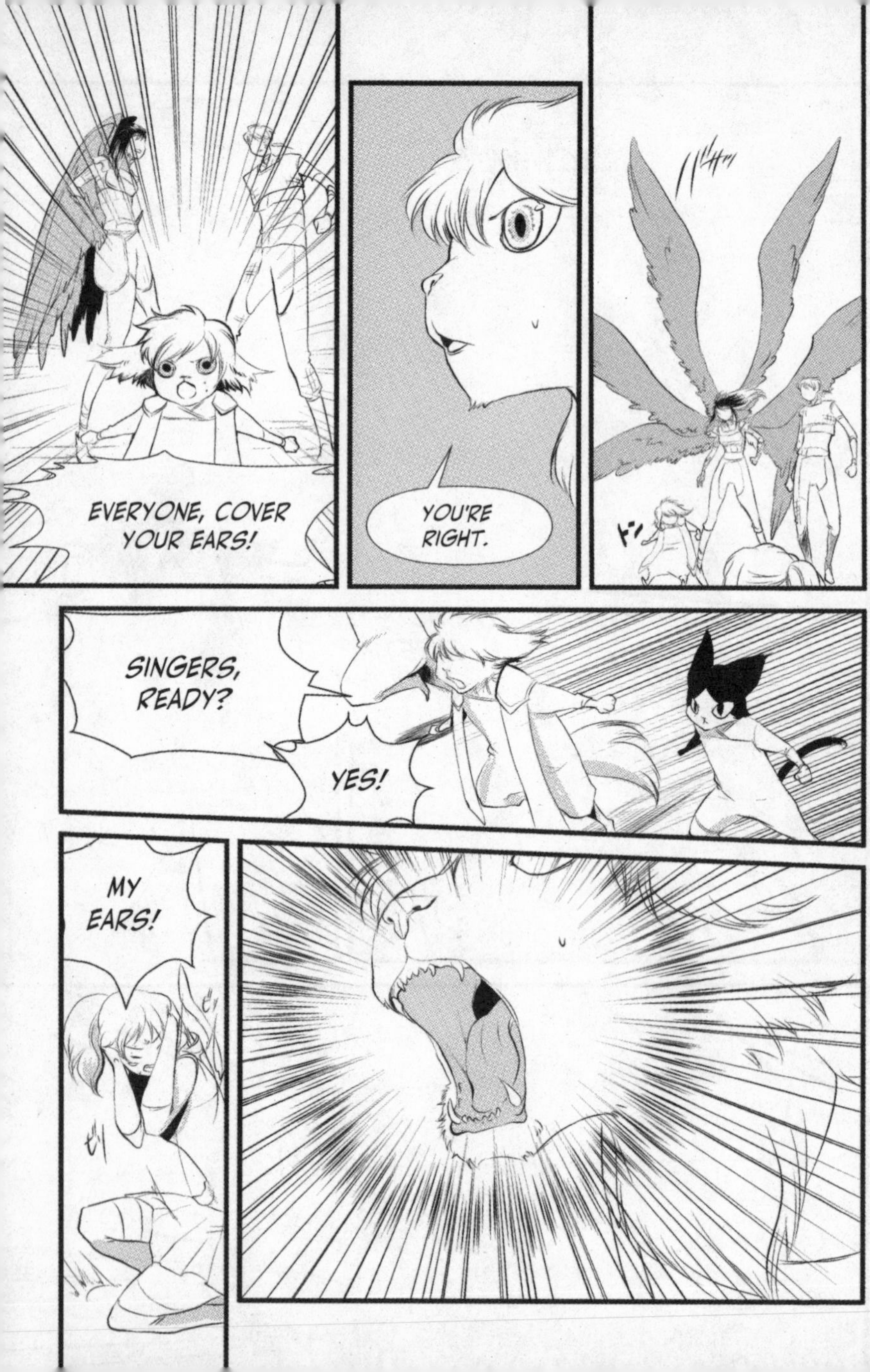
YOU'RE RIGHT.
EVERYONE, COVER YOUR EARS!
SINGERS, READY?
YES!
MY EARS!

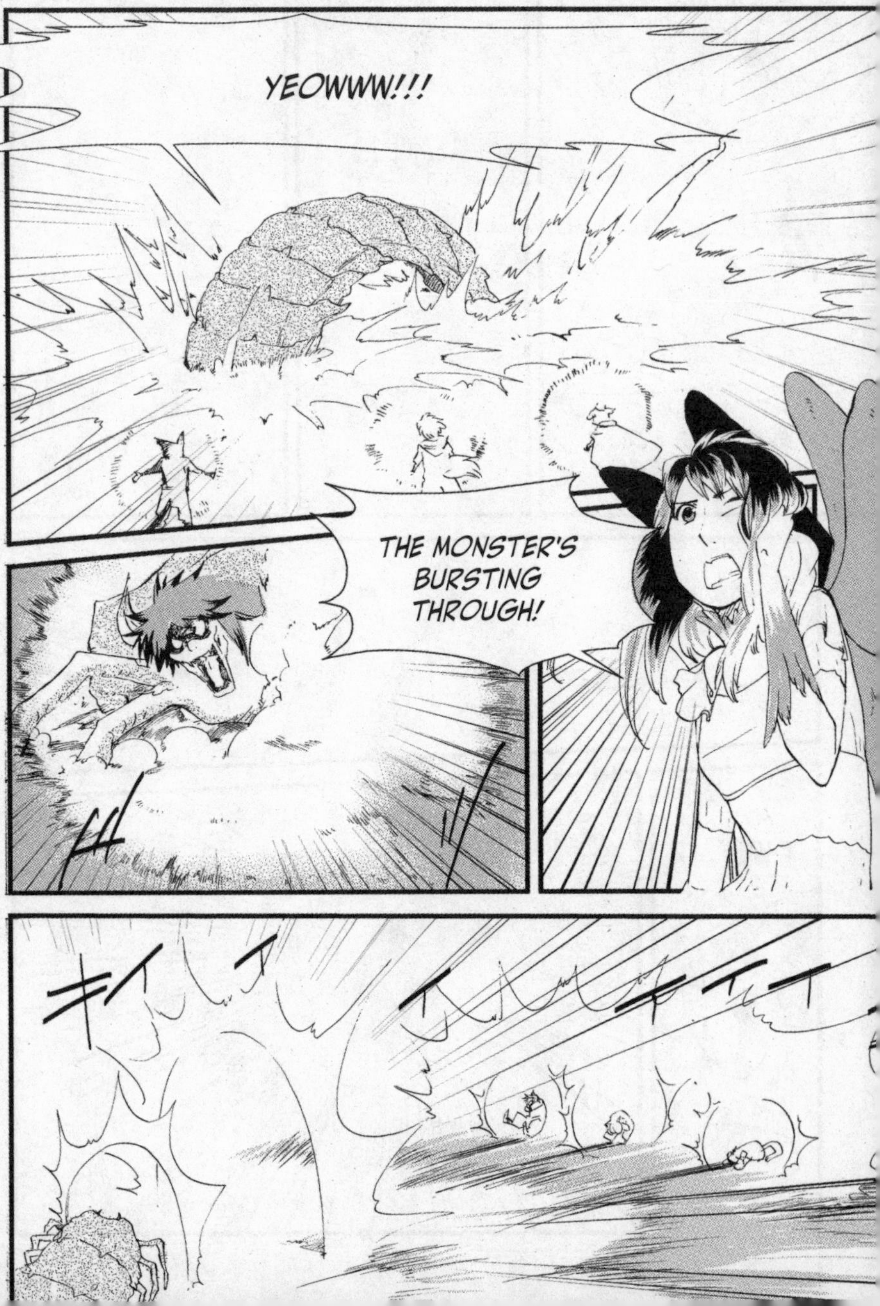
YEOWWW!!!
THE MONSTER'S BURSTING THROUGH!

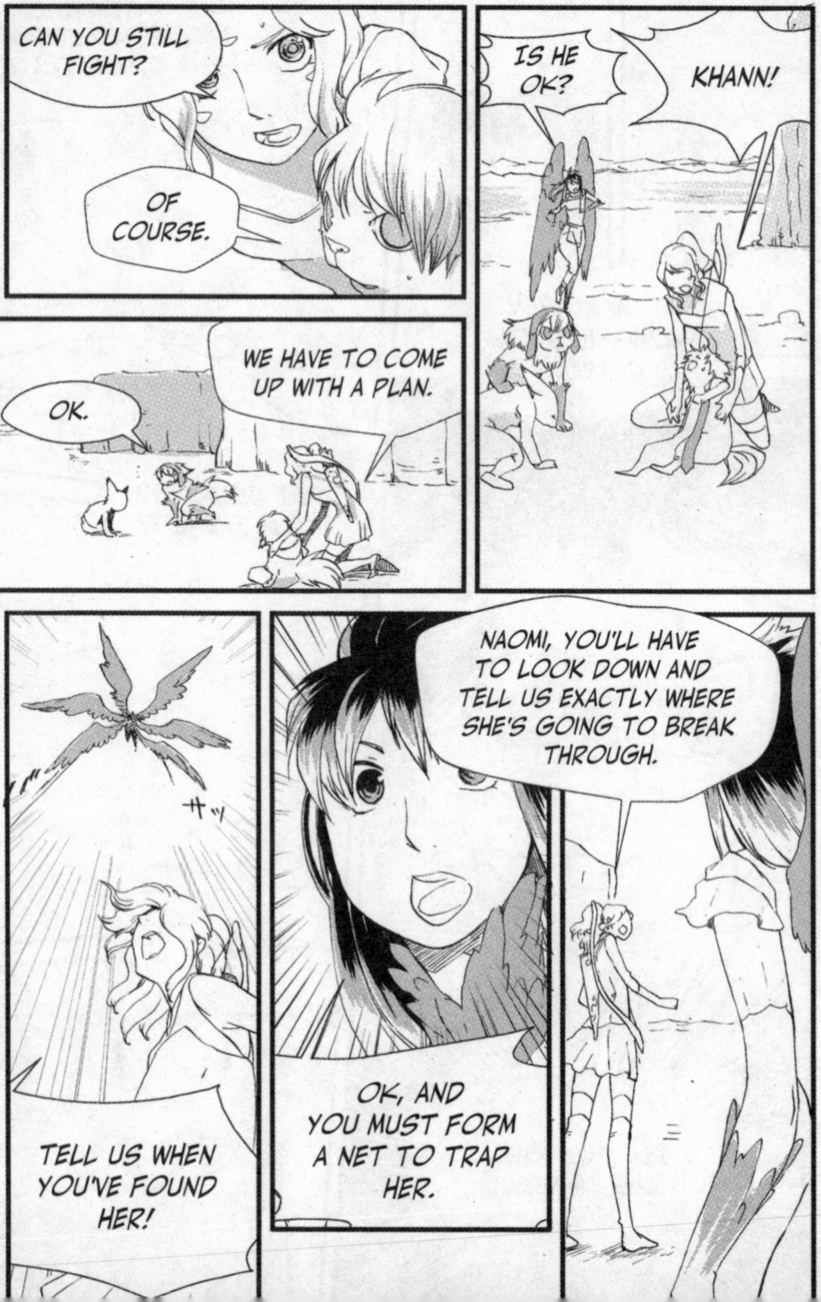
KHANN!
IS HE OK?
CAN YOU STILL FIGHT?
OF COURSE.
WE HAVE TO COME UP WITH A PLAN.
OK.
NAOMI, YOU'LL HAVE TO LOOK DOWN AND TELL US EXACTLY WHERE SHE'S GOING TO BREAK THROUGH.
OK, AND YOU MUST FORM A NET TO TRAP HER.
サッ
TELL US WHEN YOU'VE FOUND HER!

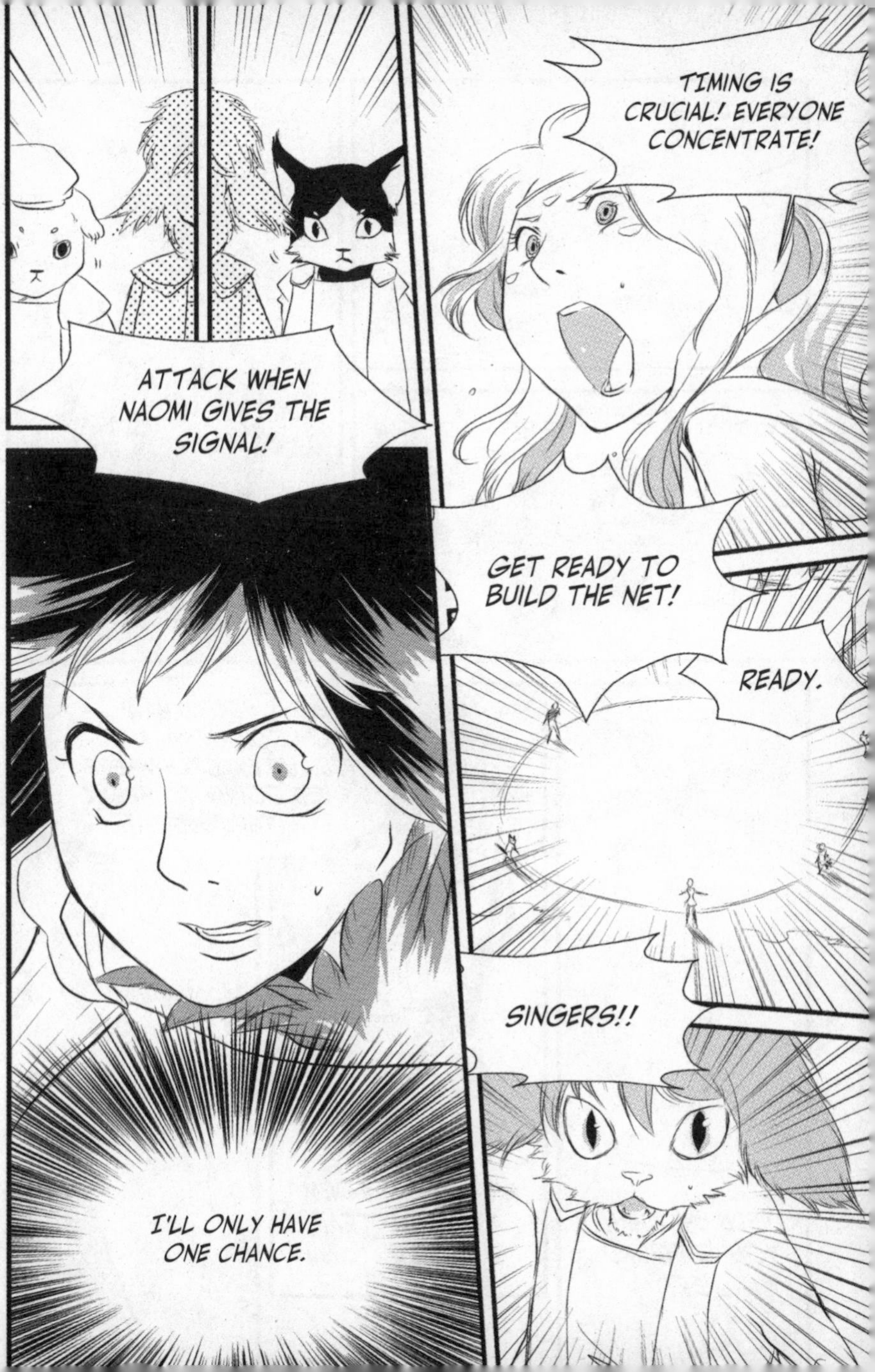
TIMING IS CRUCIAL! EVERYONE CONCENTRATE!
ATTACK WHEN NAOMI GIVES THE SIGNAL!
GET READY TO BUILD THE NET!
READY.
SINGERS!!
I'LL ONLY HAVE ONE CHANCE.

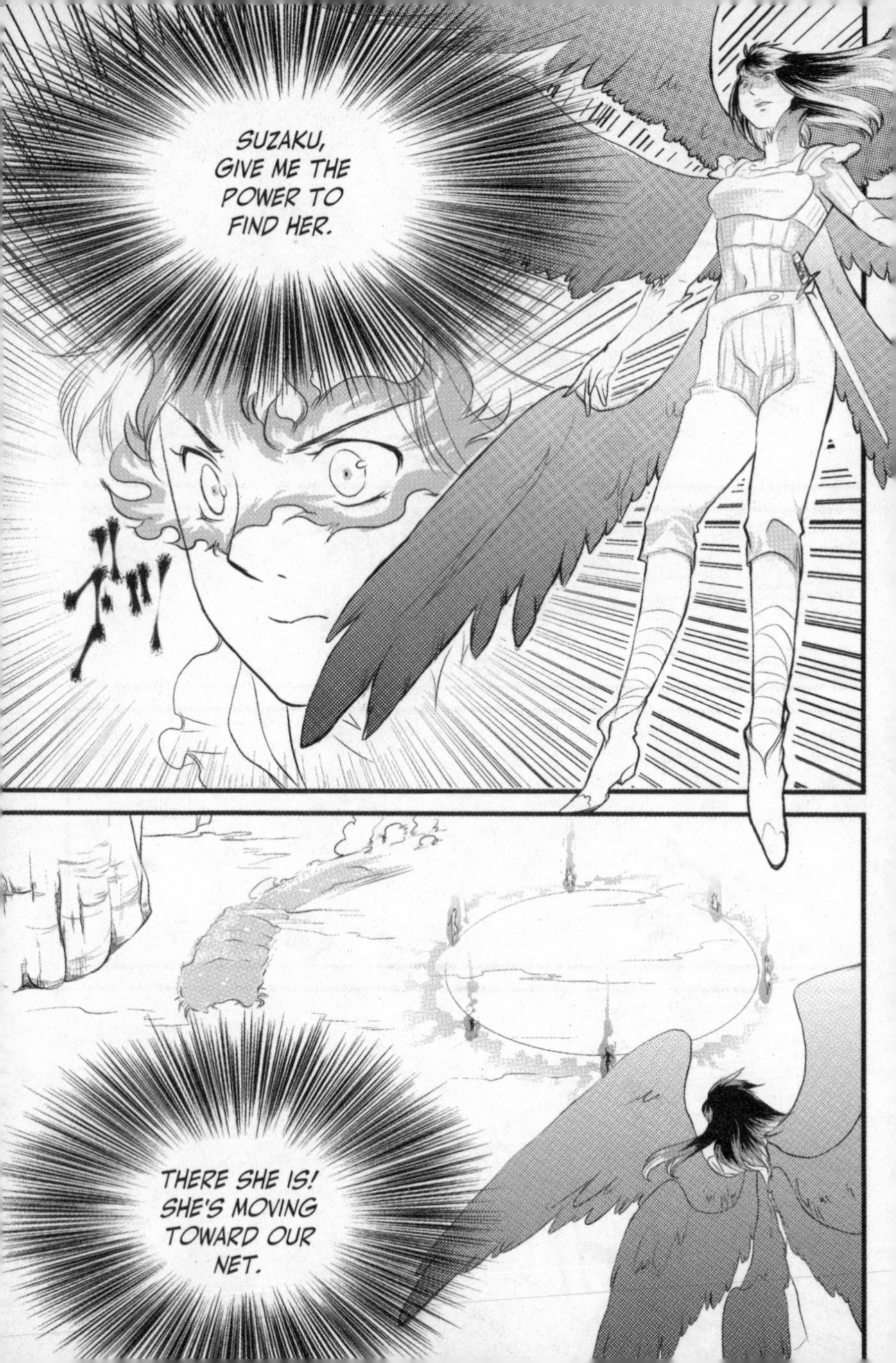
SUZAKU, GIVE ME THE POWER TO FIND HER.
THERE SHE IS! SHE'S MOVING TOWARD OUR NET.

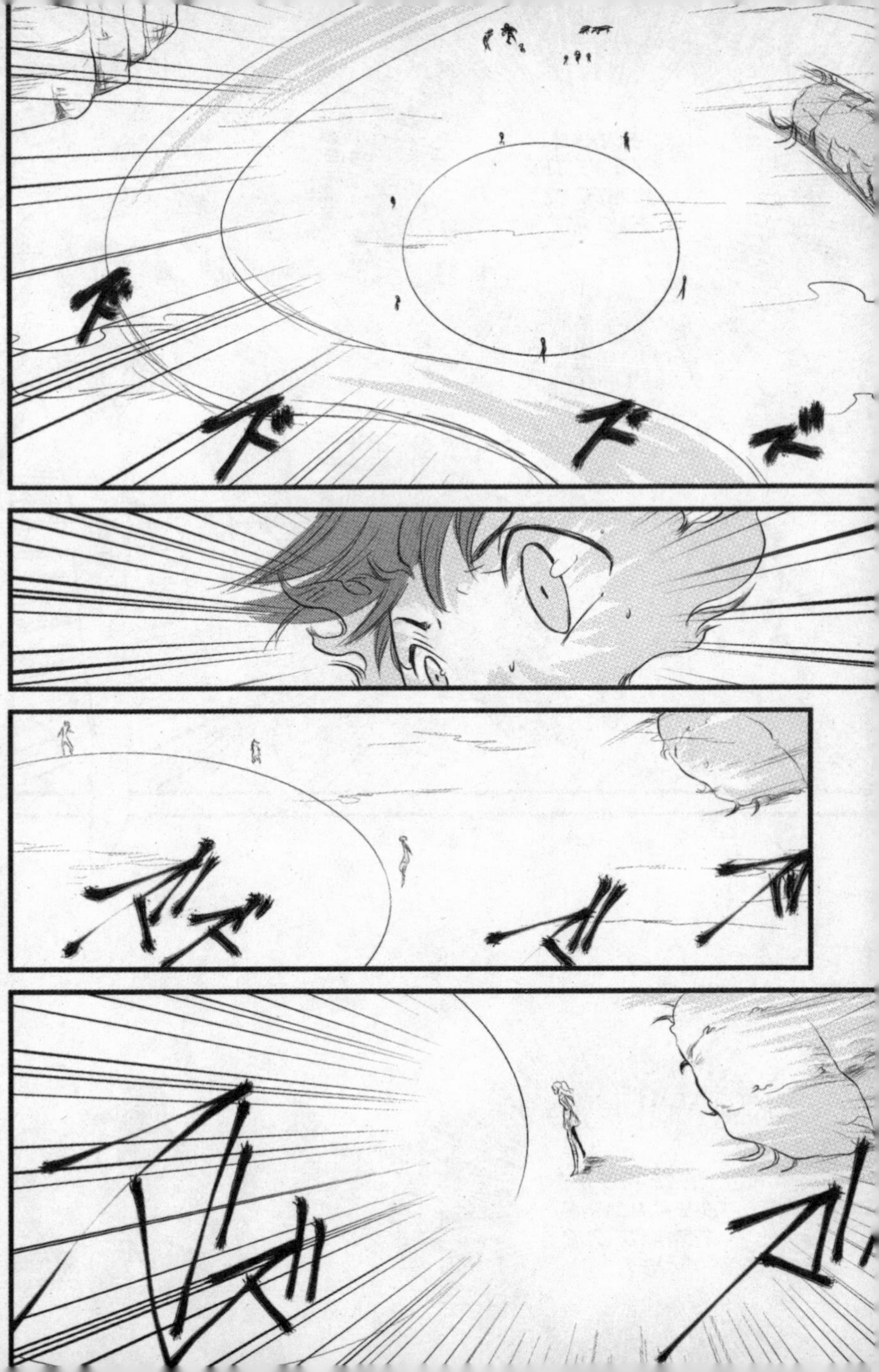

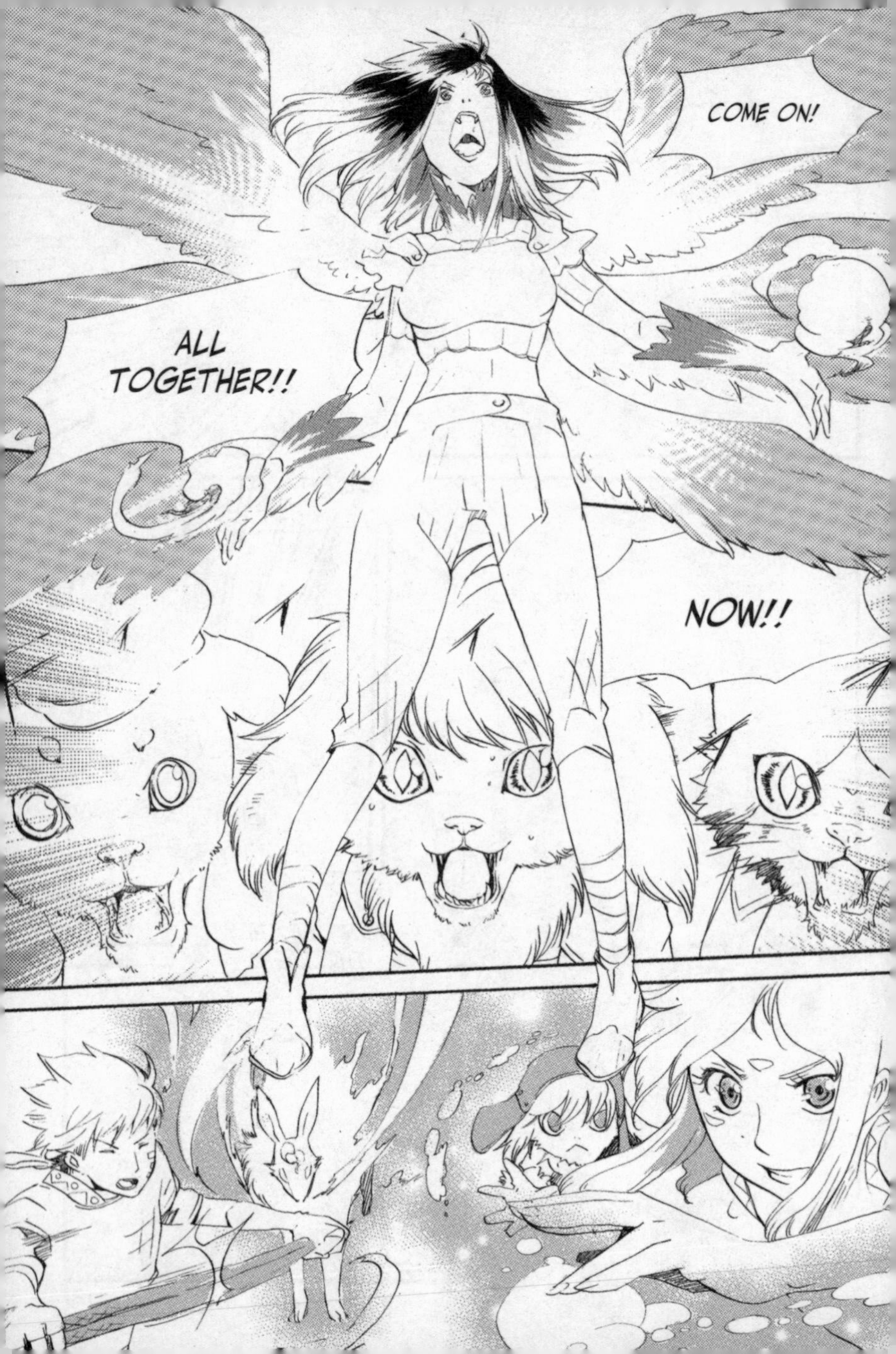
COME ON!
ALL TOGETHER!!
NOW!!

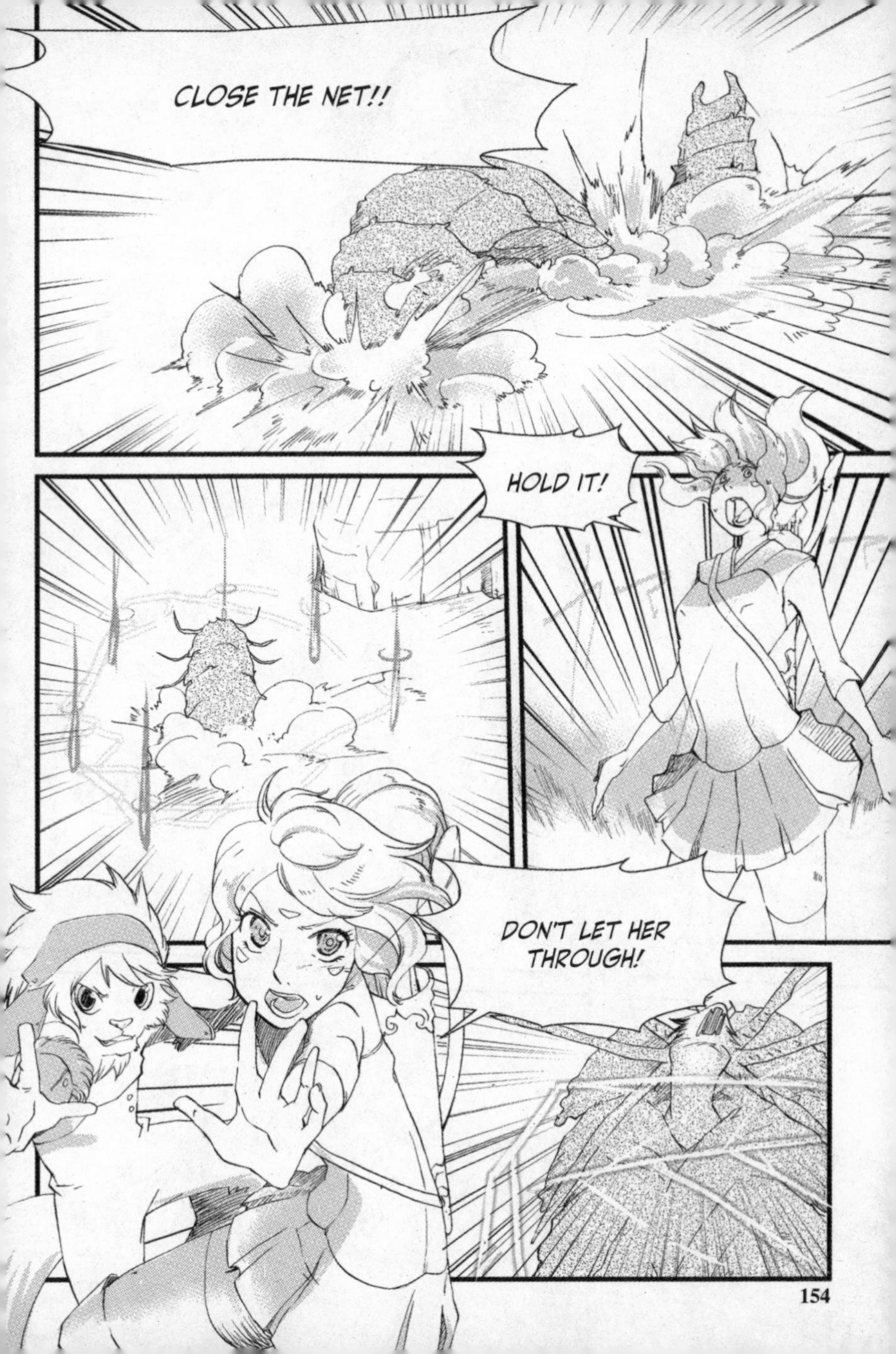
CLOSE THE NET!!
HOLD IT!
DON'T LET HER THROUGH!

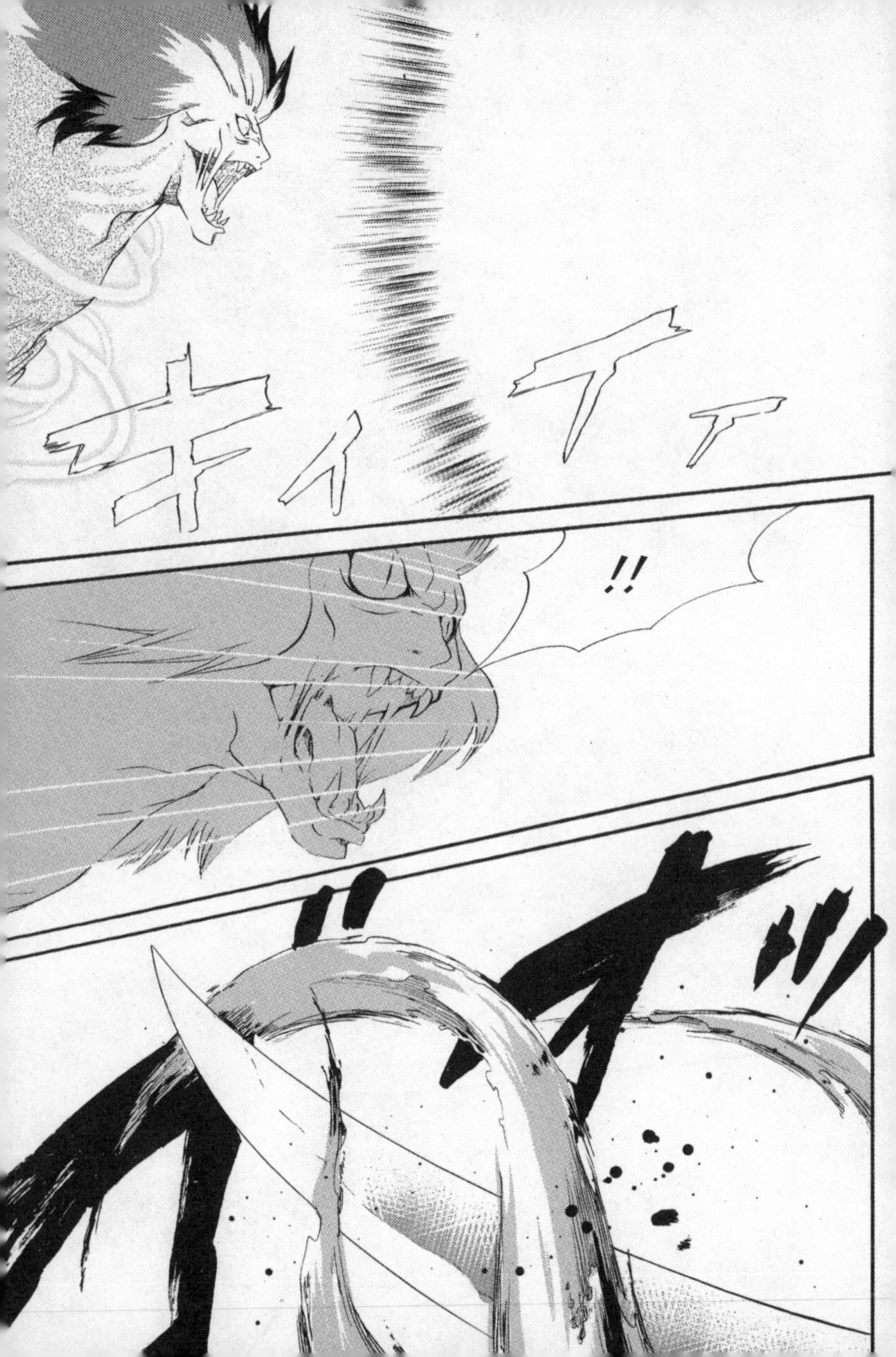
キイアァ
!!
ズッ

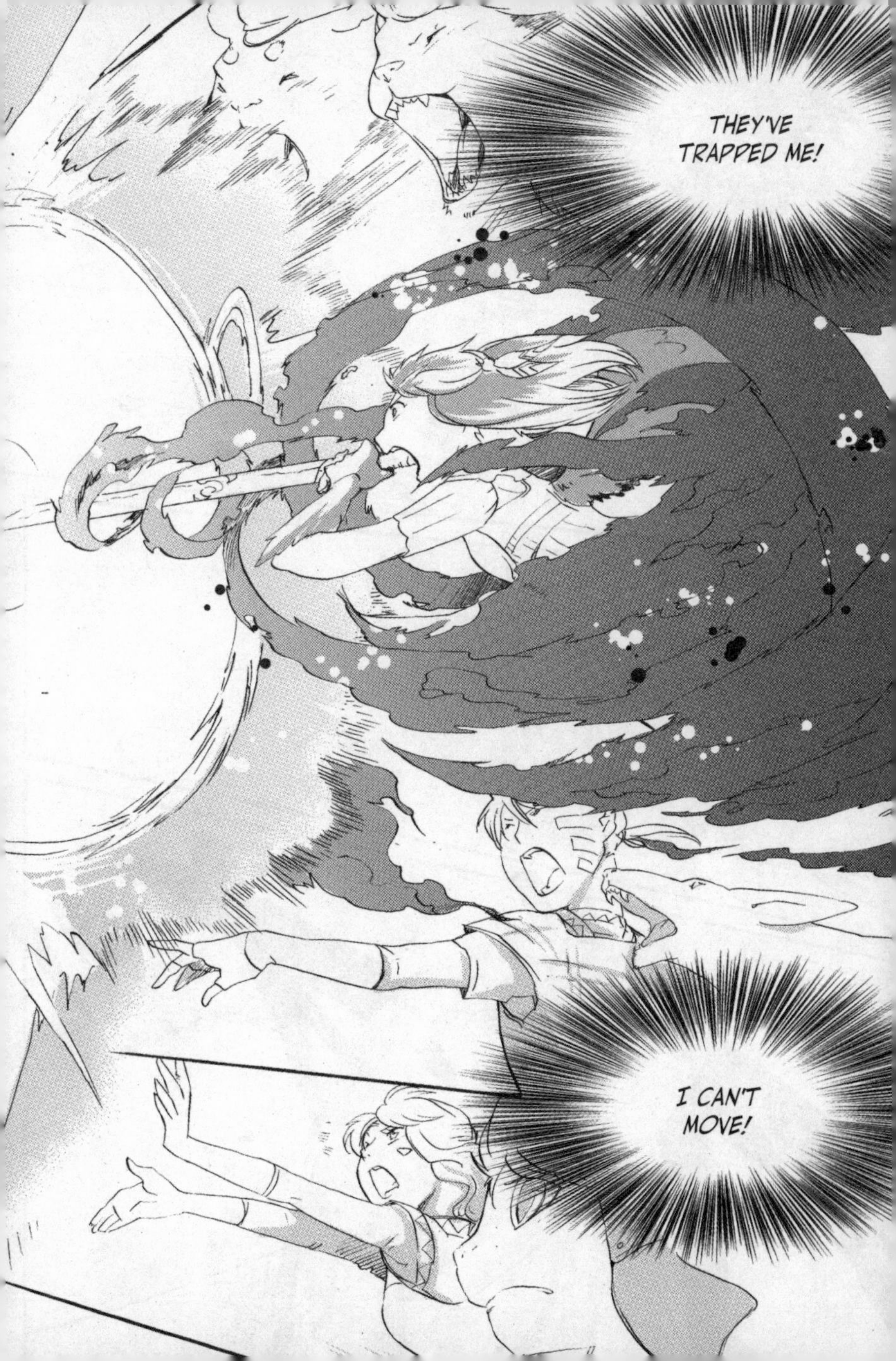
THEY'VE TRAPPED ME!
I CAN'T MOVE!

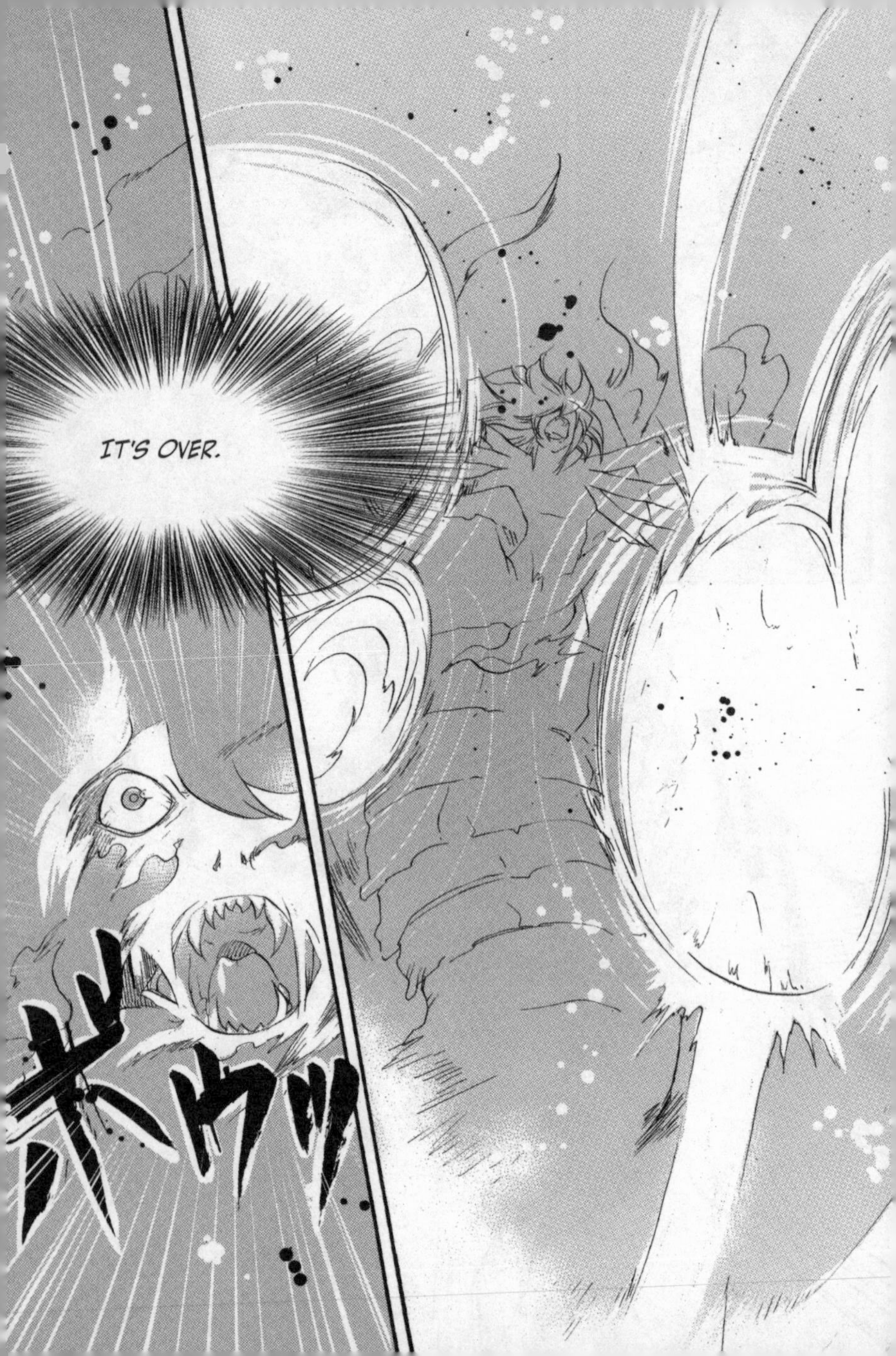
IT'S OVER.

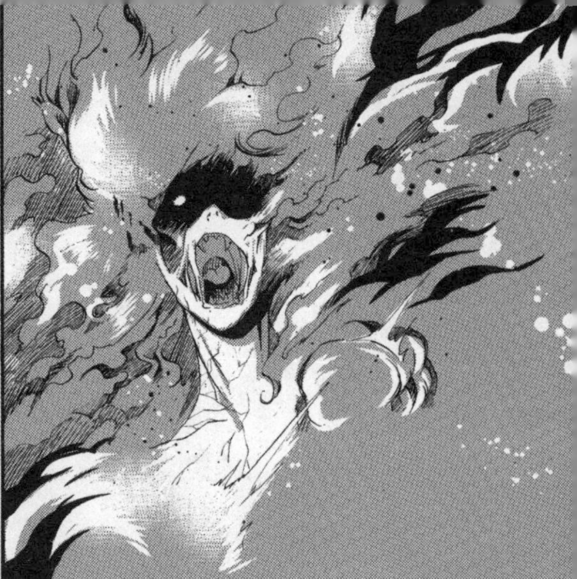

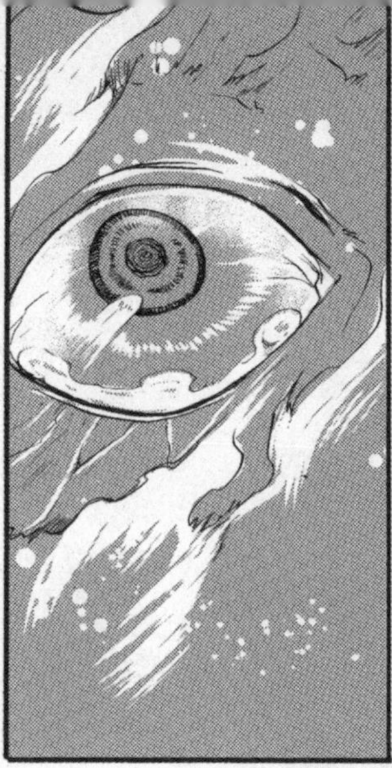

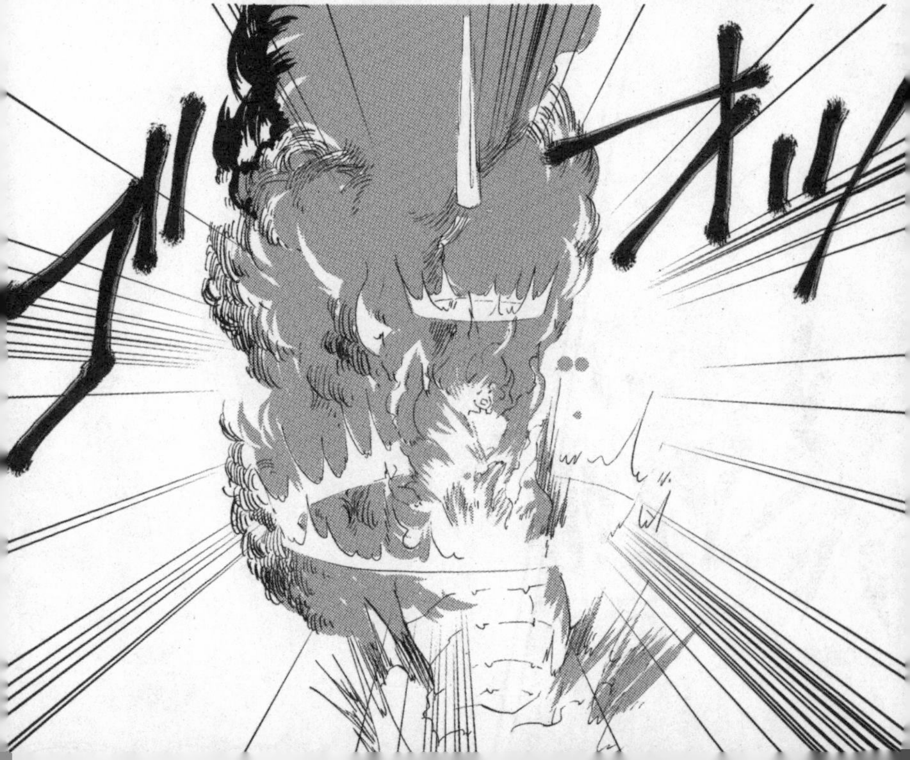
ゴオッ

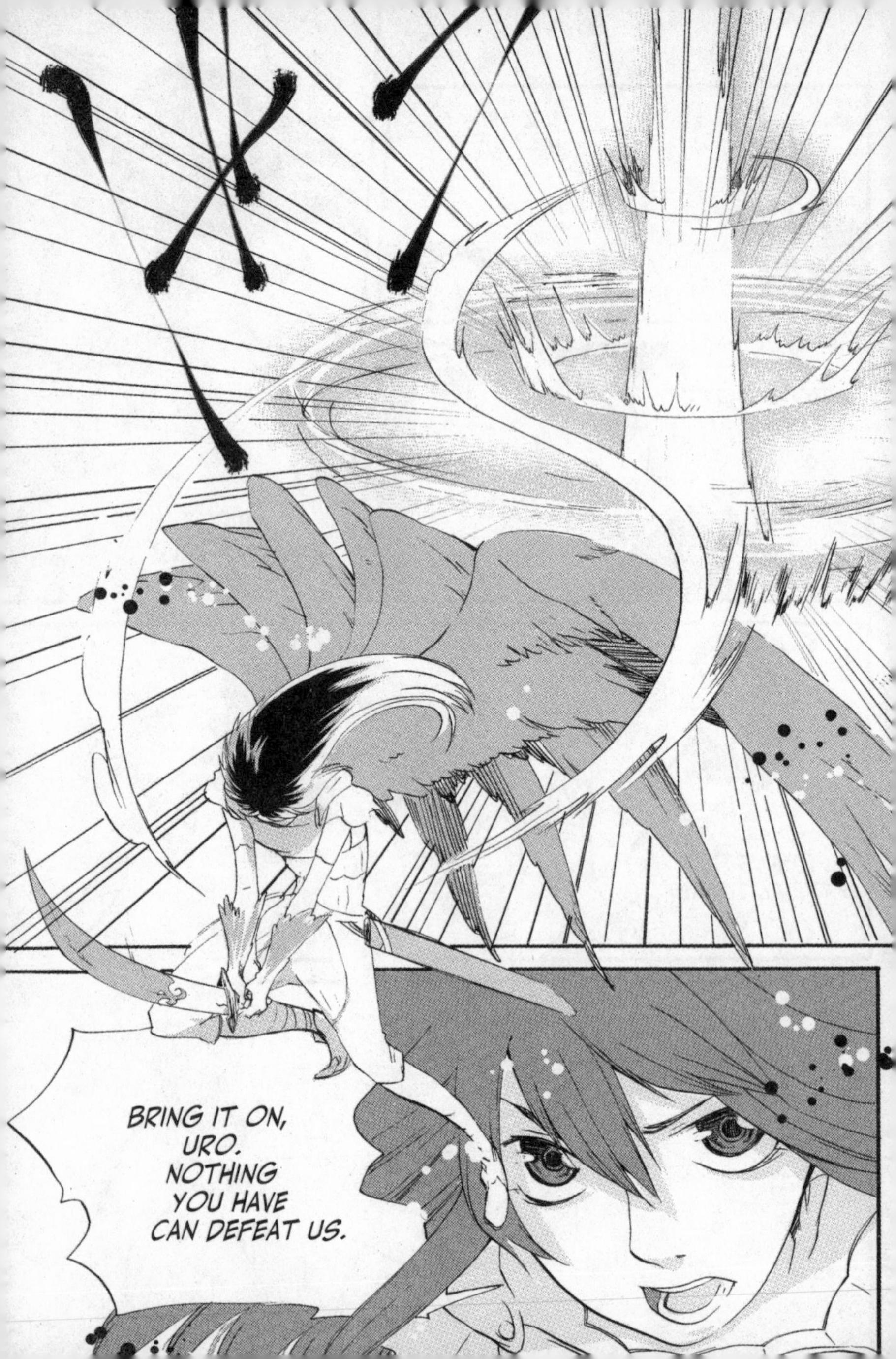
BRING IT ON, URO. NOTHING YOU HAVE CAN DEFEAT US.

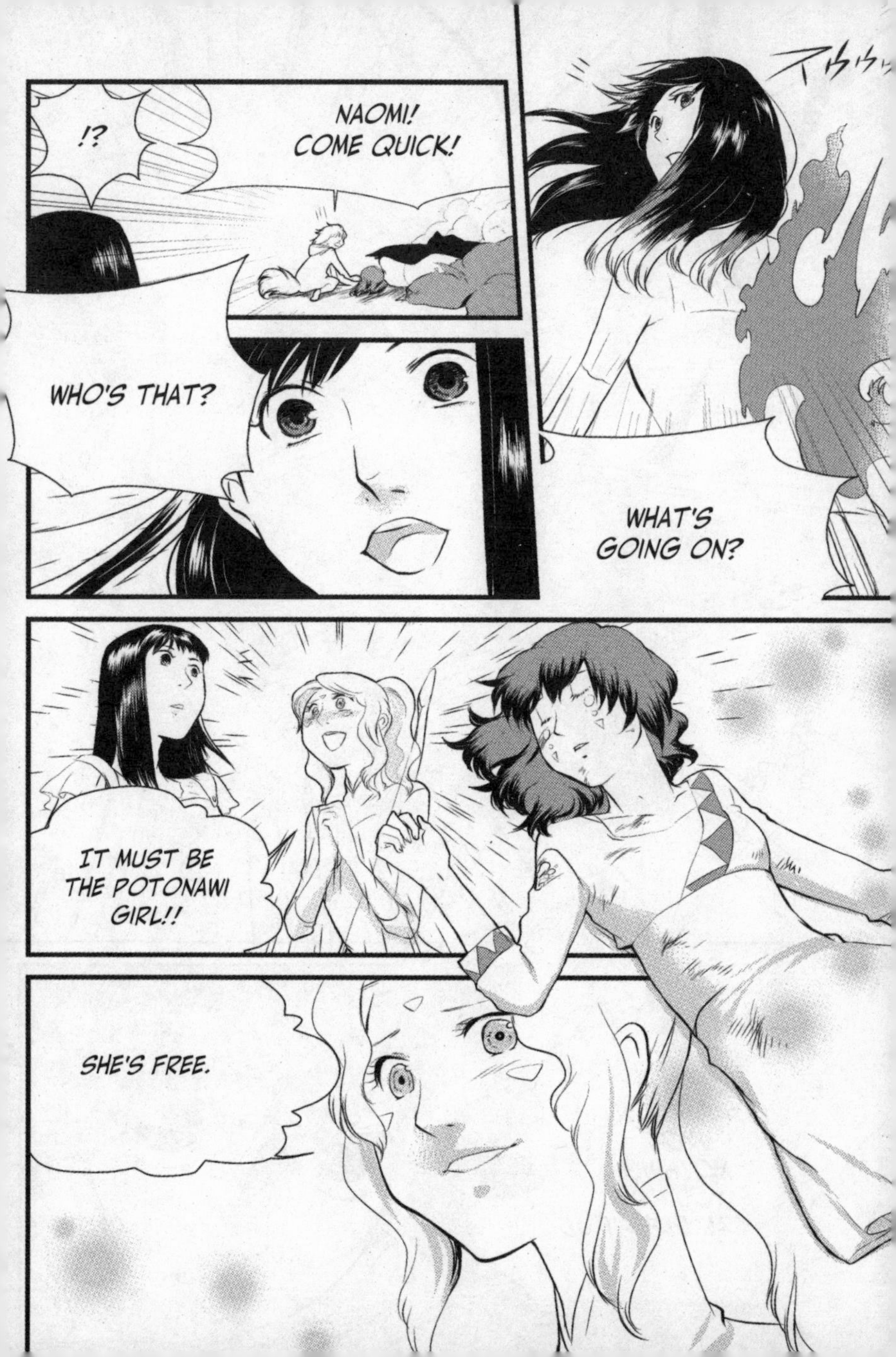

WHAT'S GOING ON?
NAOMI! COME QUICK!
!?
WHO'S THAT?
IT MUST BE THE POTONAWI GIRL!!
SHE'S FREE.

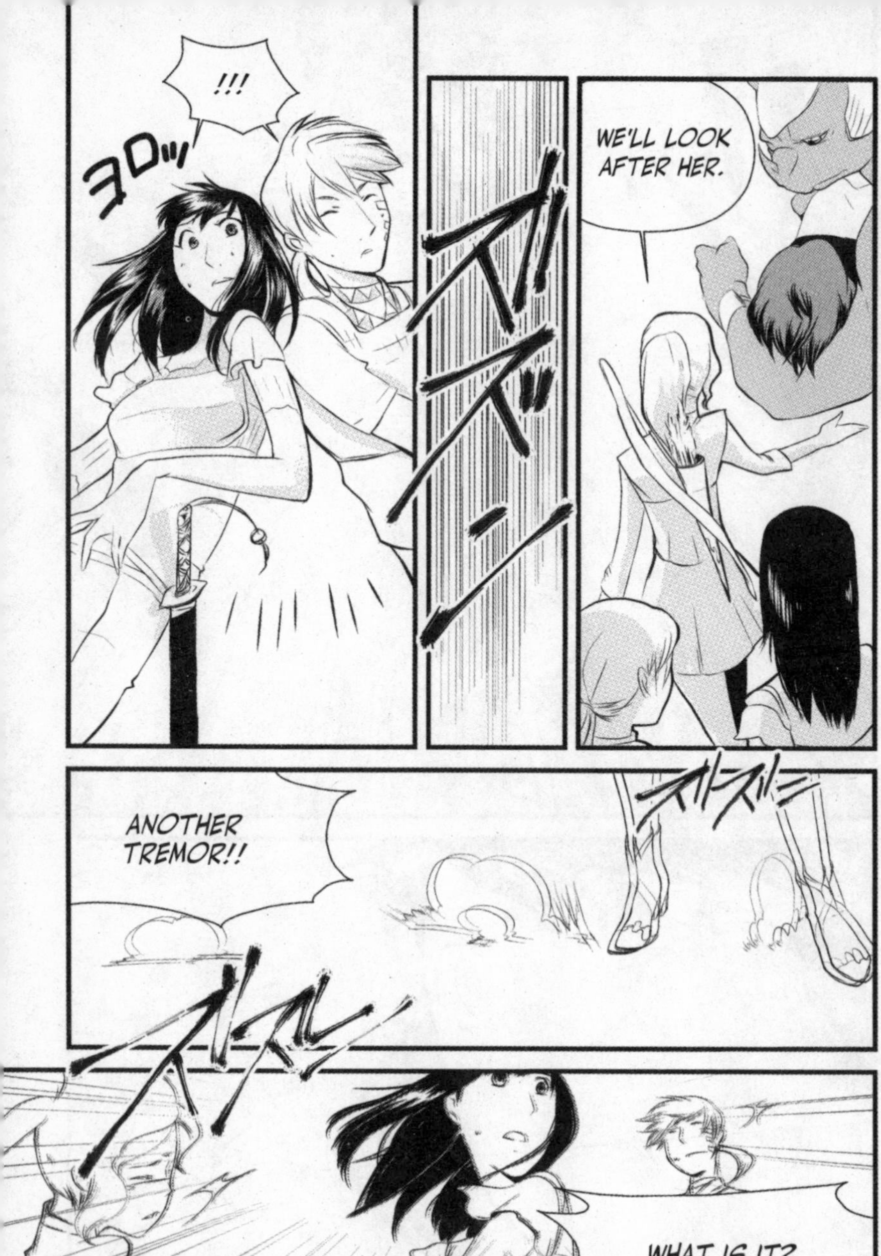
WE'LL LOOK AFTER HER.
!!!
ヨロッ
ANOTHER TREMOR!!
WHAT IS IT?

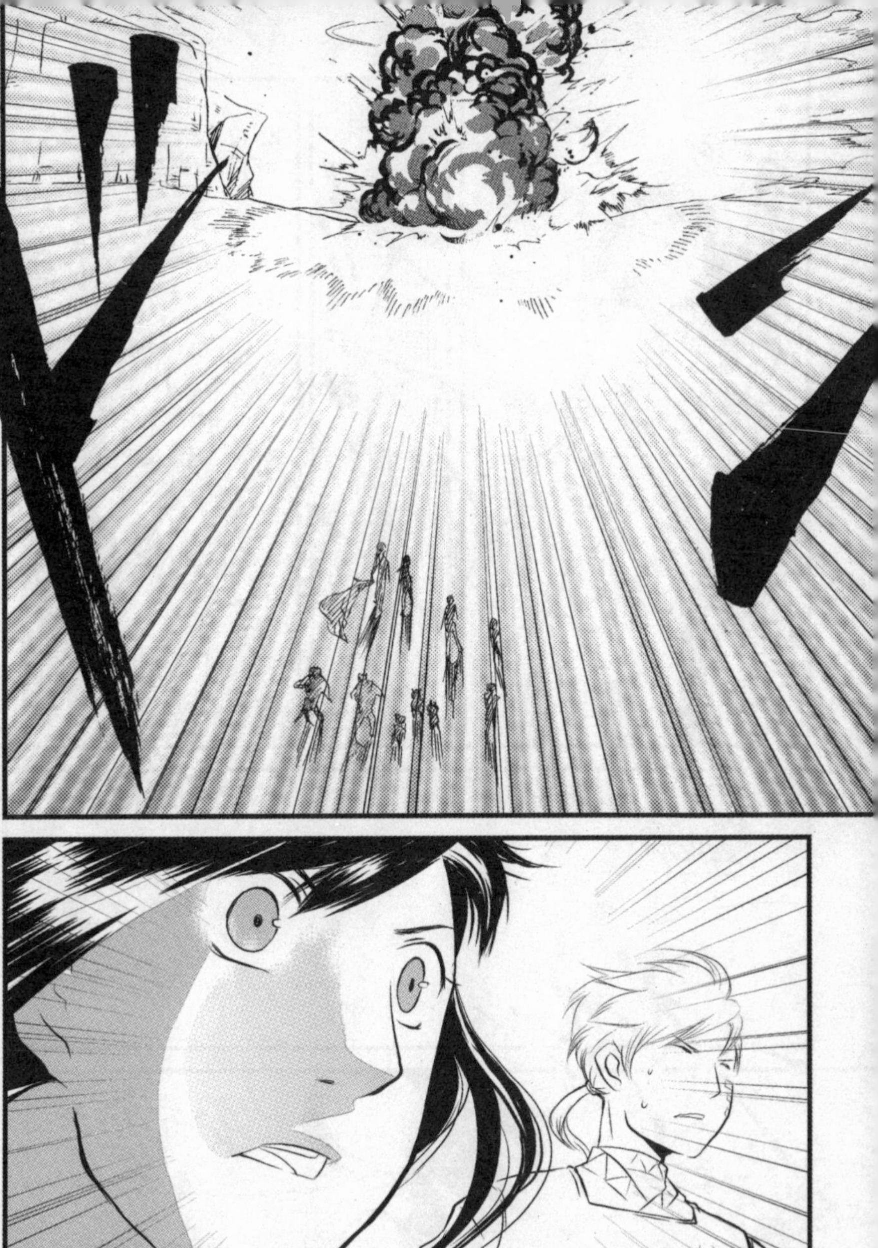

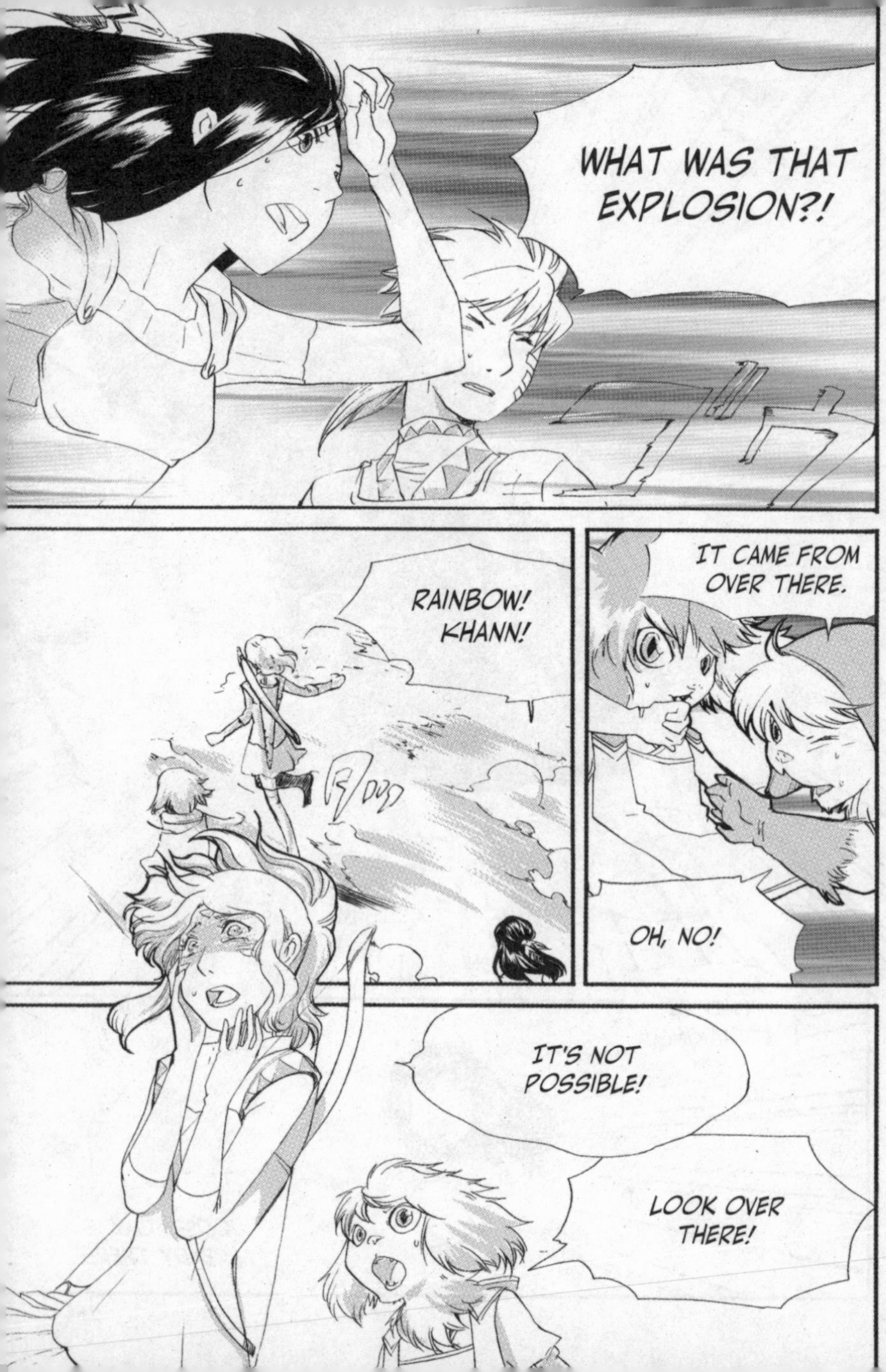
WHAT WAS THAT EXPLOSION?!
IT CAME FROM OVER THERE.
OH, NO!
RAINBOW! KHANN!
IT'S NOT POSSIBLE!
LOOK OVER THERE!

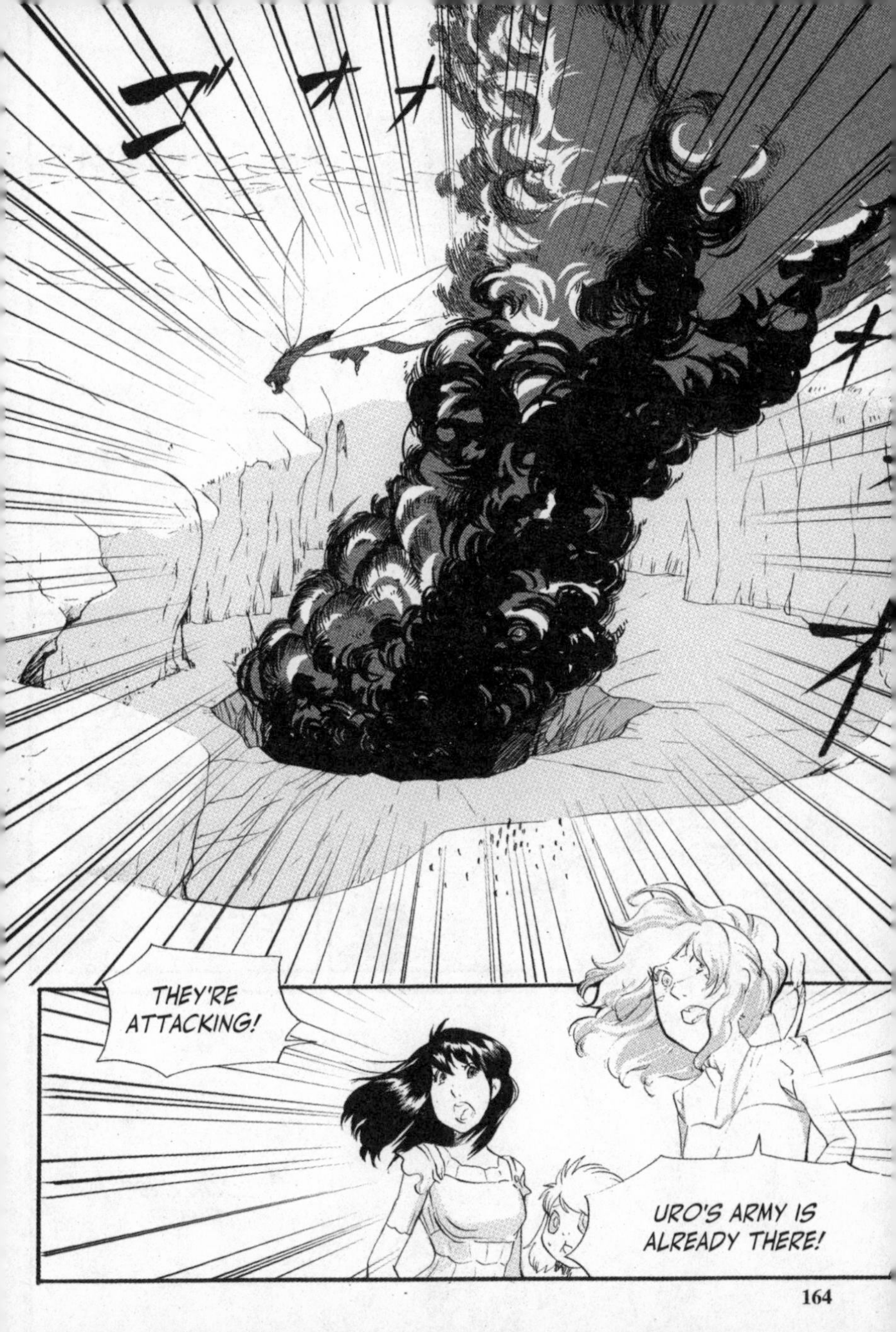
THEY'RE ATTACKING!
URO'S ARMY IS ALREADY THERE!

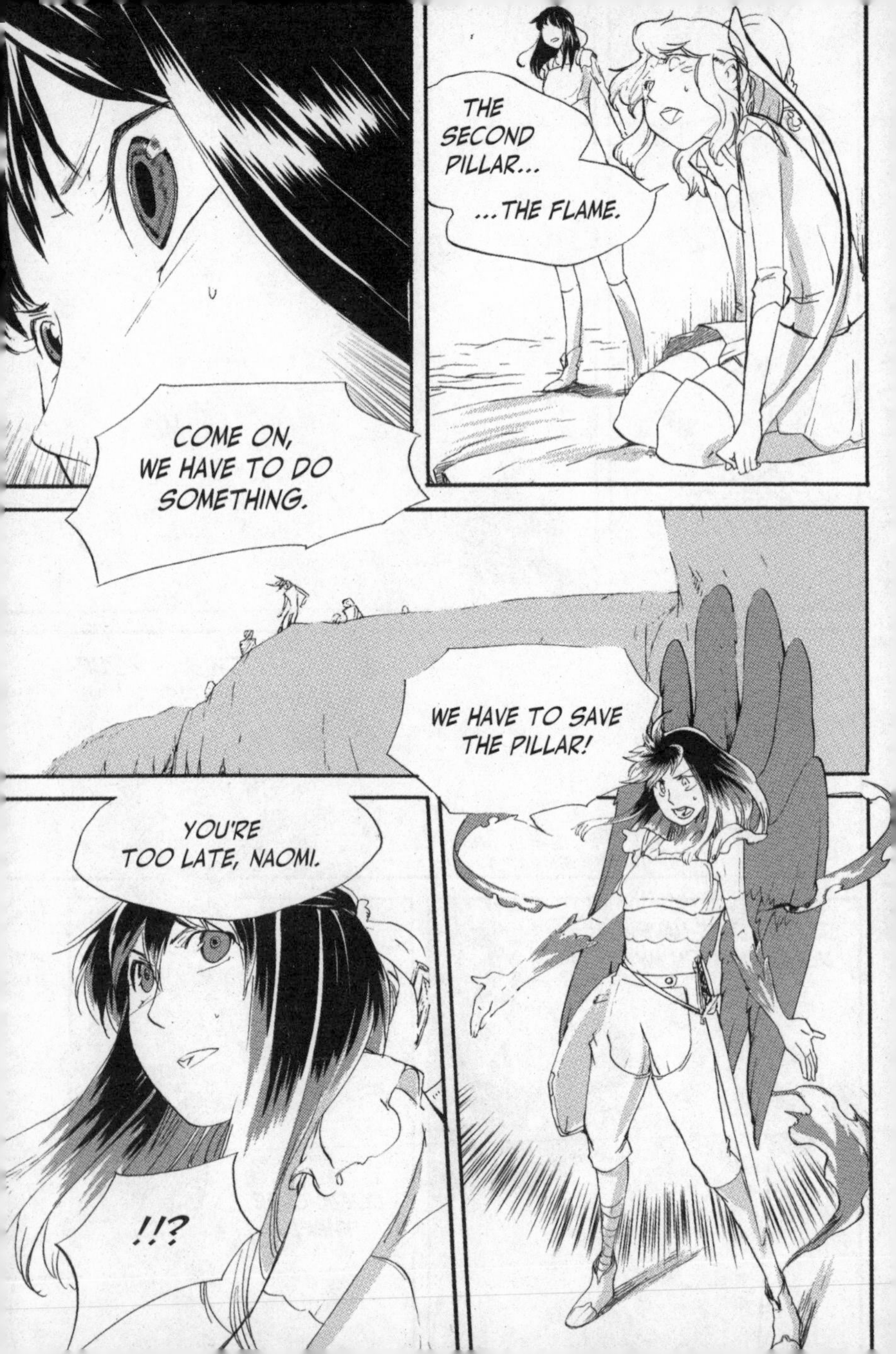
THE SECOND PILLAR...
...THE FLAME.
COME ON, WE HAVE TO DO SOMETHING.
WE HAVE TO SAVE THE PILLAR!
YOU'RE TOO LATE, NAOMI.
!!?

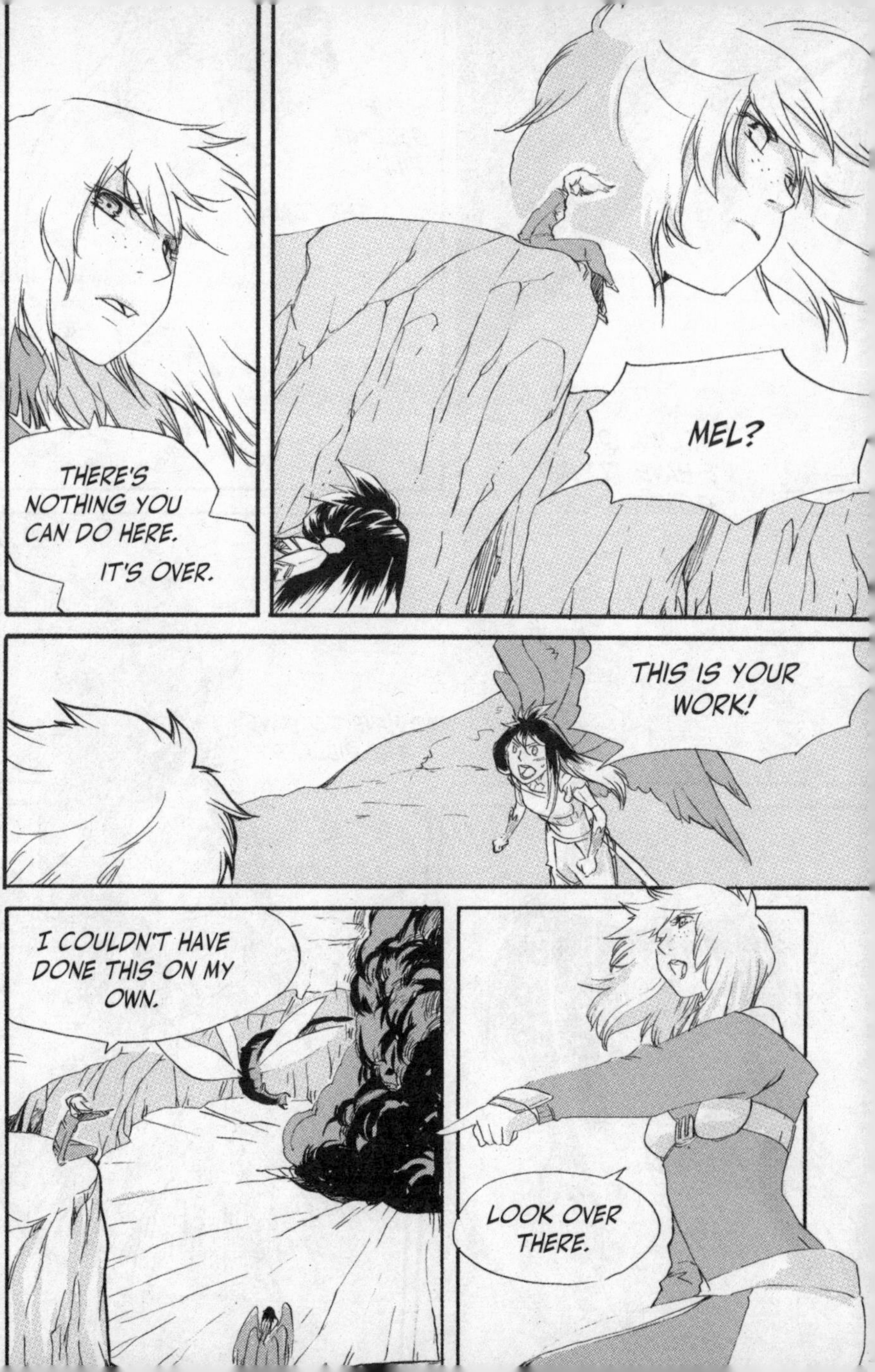
MEL?
THERE'S NOTHING YOU CAN DO HERE.
IT'S OVER.
THIS IS YOUR WORK!
LOOK OVER THERE.
I COULDN'T HAVE DONE THIS ON MY OWN.

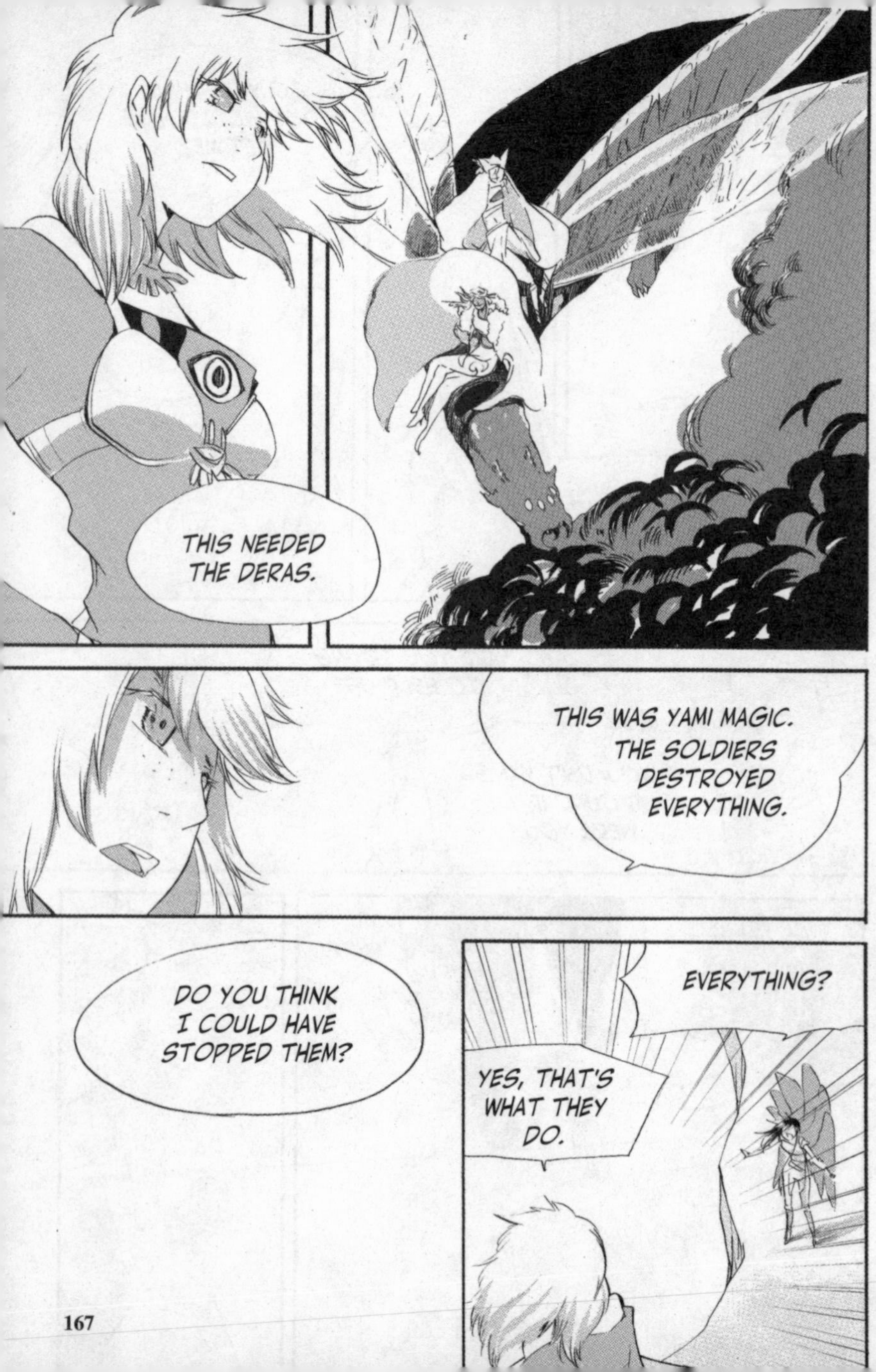
THIS NEEDED THE DERAS.
THIS WAS YAMI MAGIC. THE SOLDIERS DESTROYED EVERYTHING.
EVERYTHING?
YES, THAT'S WHAT THEY DO.
DO YOU THINK I COULD HAVE STOPPED THEM?

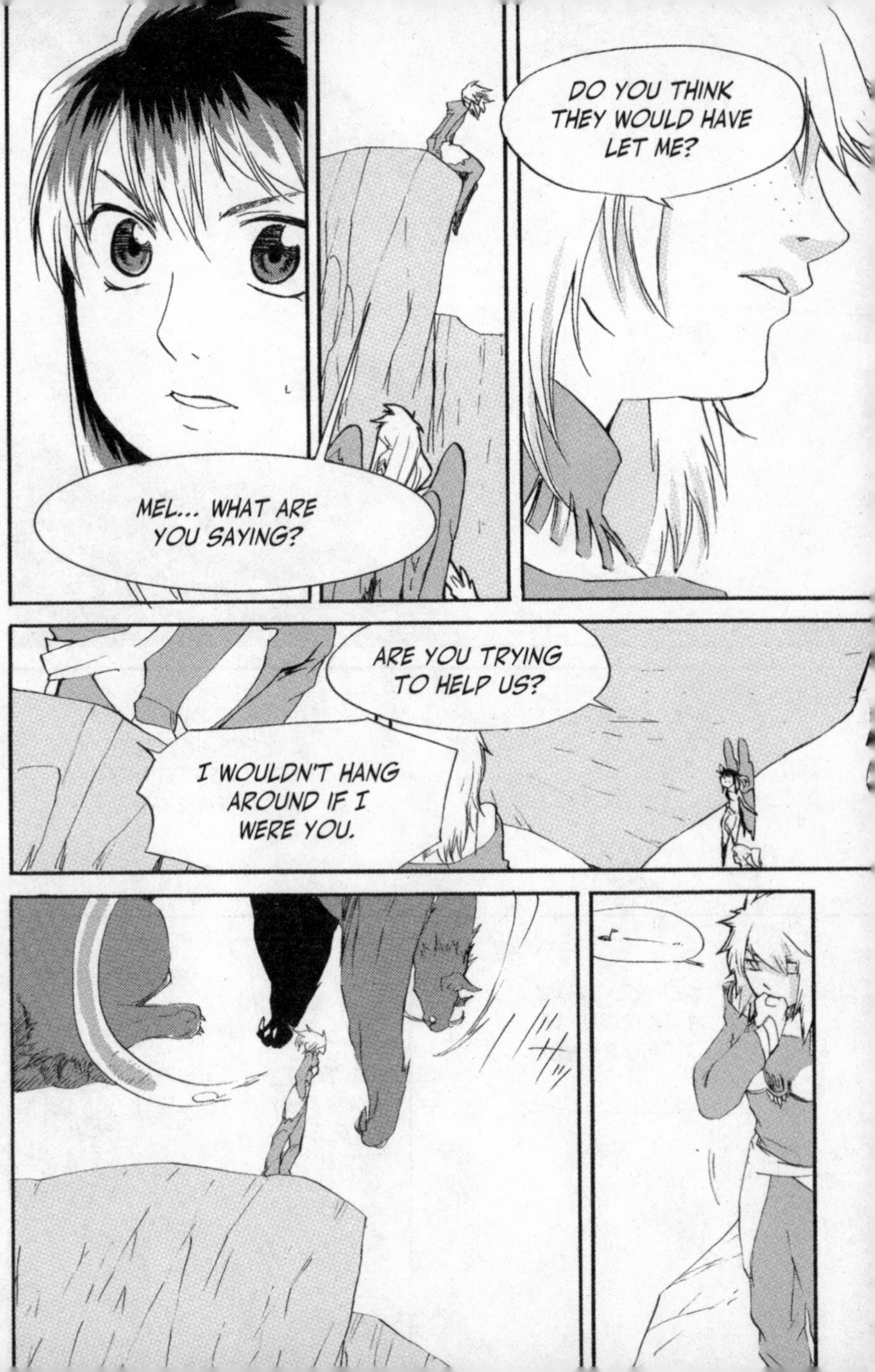
DO YOU THINK THEY WOULD HAVE LET ME?
MEL... WHAT ARE YOU SAYING?
ARE YOU TRYING TO HELP US?
I WOULDN'T HANG AROUND IF I WERE YOU.

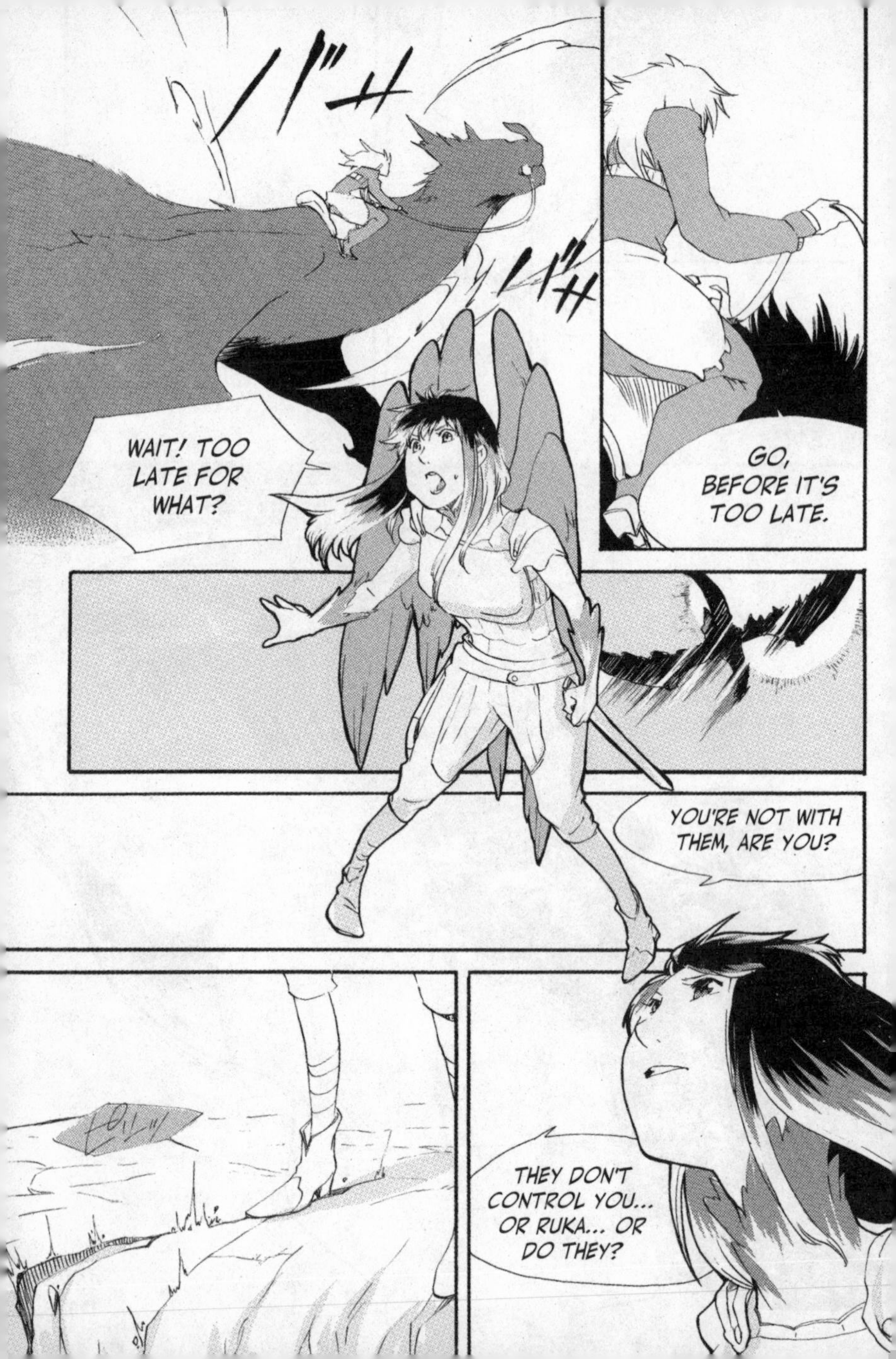
GO, BEFORE IT'S TOO LATE.
WAIT! TOO LATE FOR WHAT?
YOU'RE NOT WITH THEM, ARE YOU?
THEY DON'T CONTROL YOU... OR RUKA... OR DO THEY?

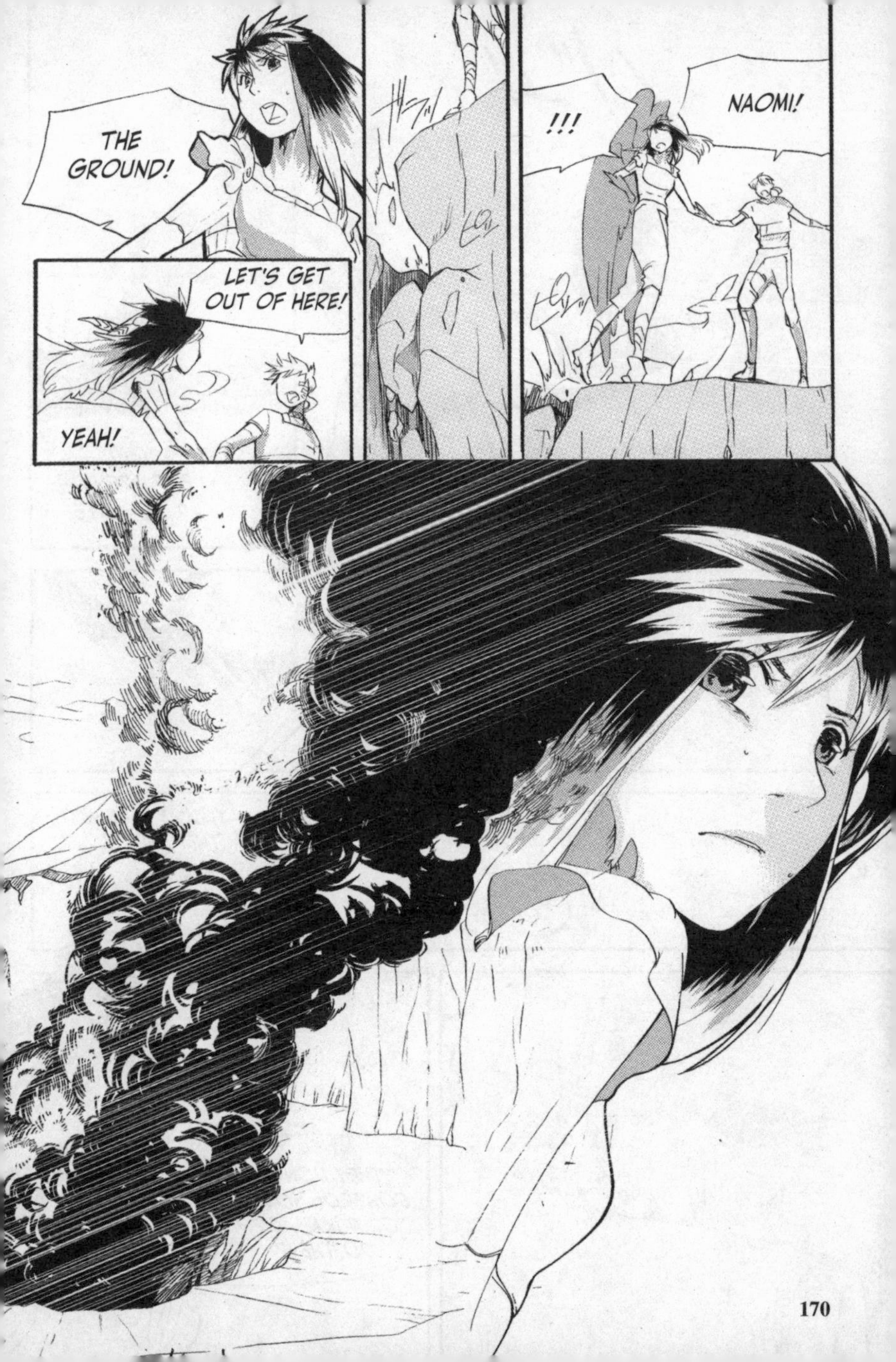
NAOMI!
!!!
THE GROUND!
LET'S GET OUT OF HERE!
YEAH!

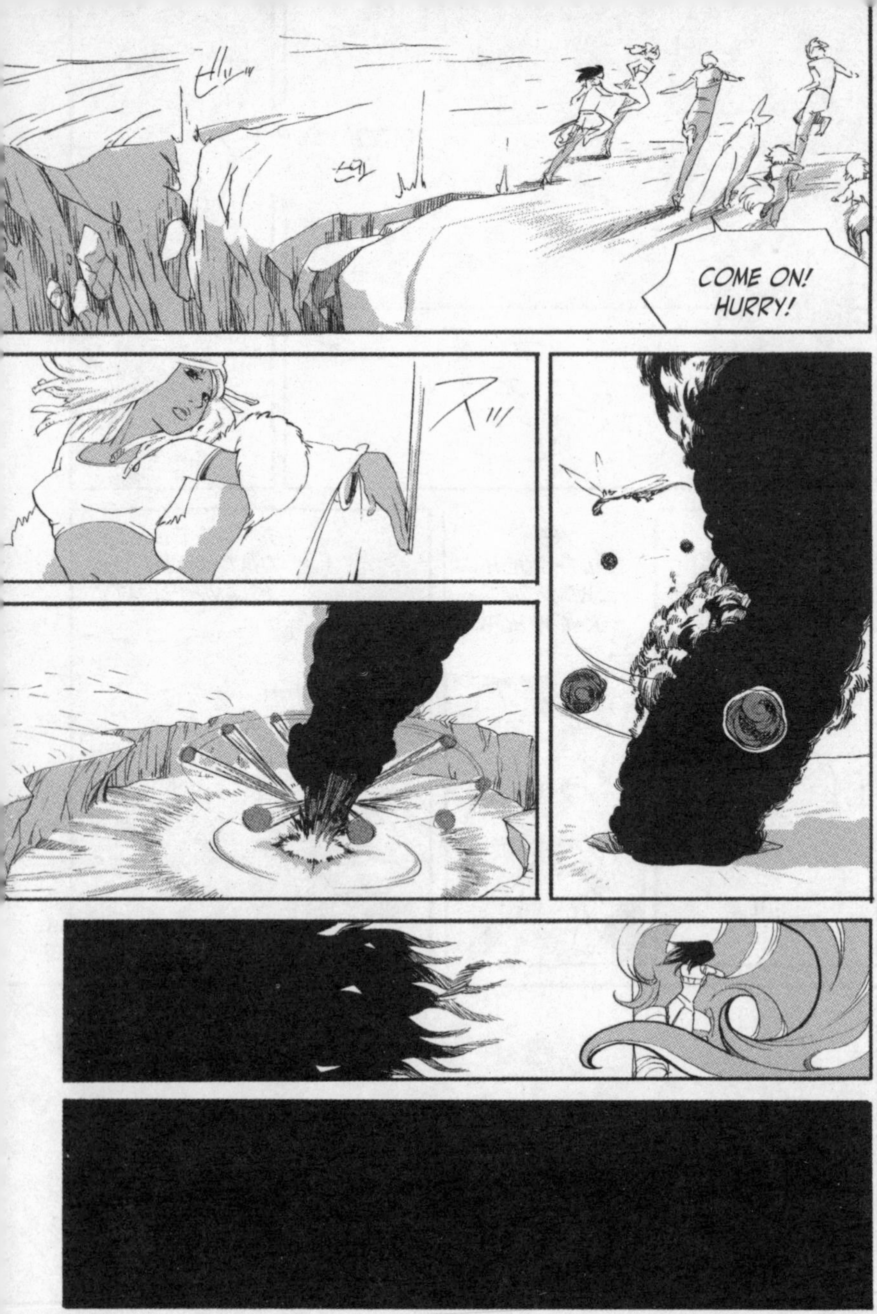
COME ON! HURRY!

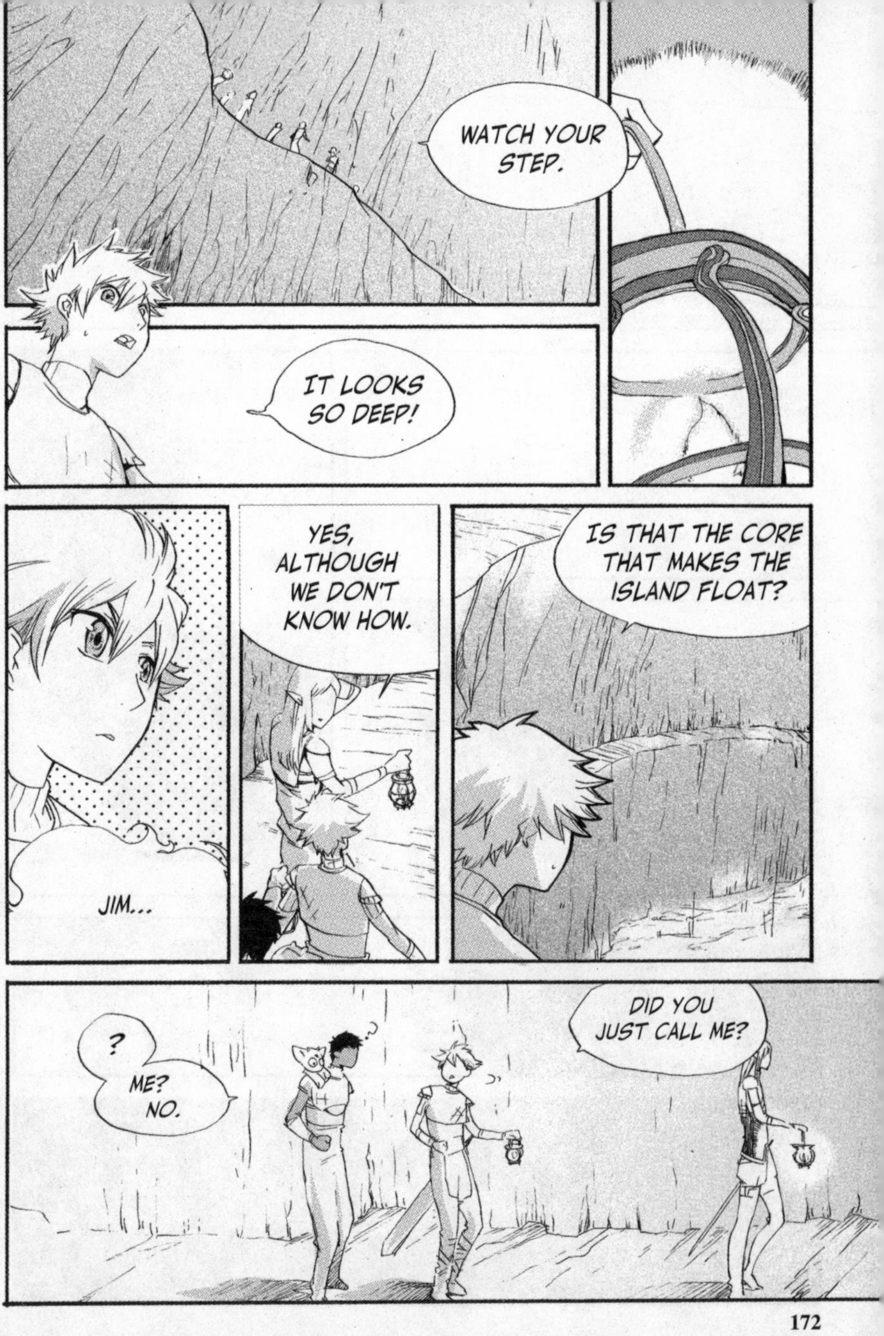
WATCH YOUR STEP.
IT LOOKS SO DEEP!
IS THAT THE CORE THAT MAKES THE ISLAND FLOAT?
YES, ALTHOUGH WE DON'T KNOW HOW.
JIM...
DID YOU JUST CALL ME?
? ME? NO.

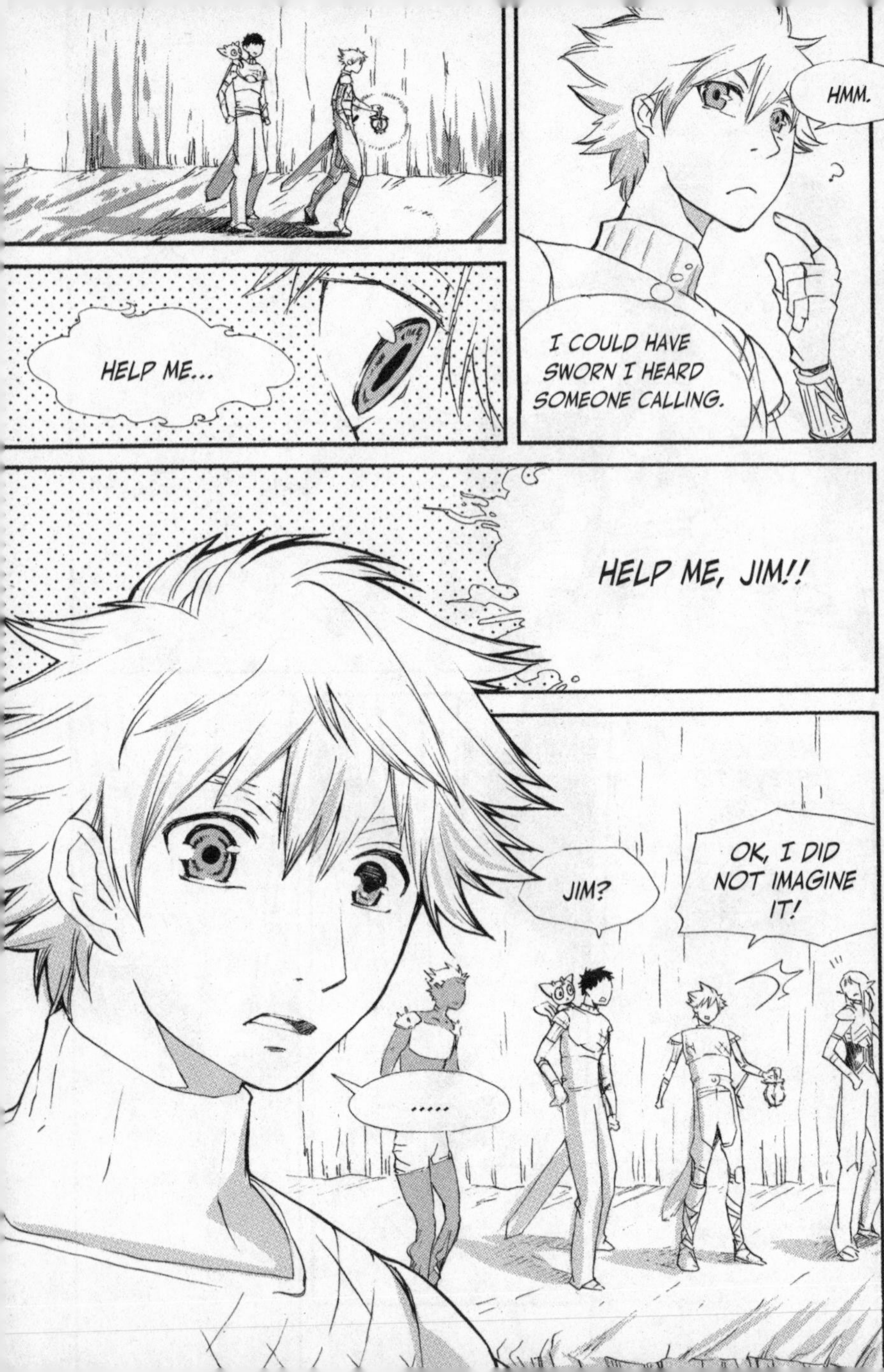
HMM.
I COULD HAVE SWORN I HEARD SOMEONE CALLING.
HELP ME...
HELP ME, JIM!!
OK, I DID NOT IMAGINE IT!
JIM?
......

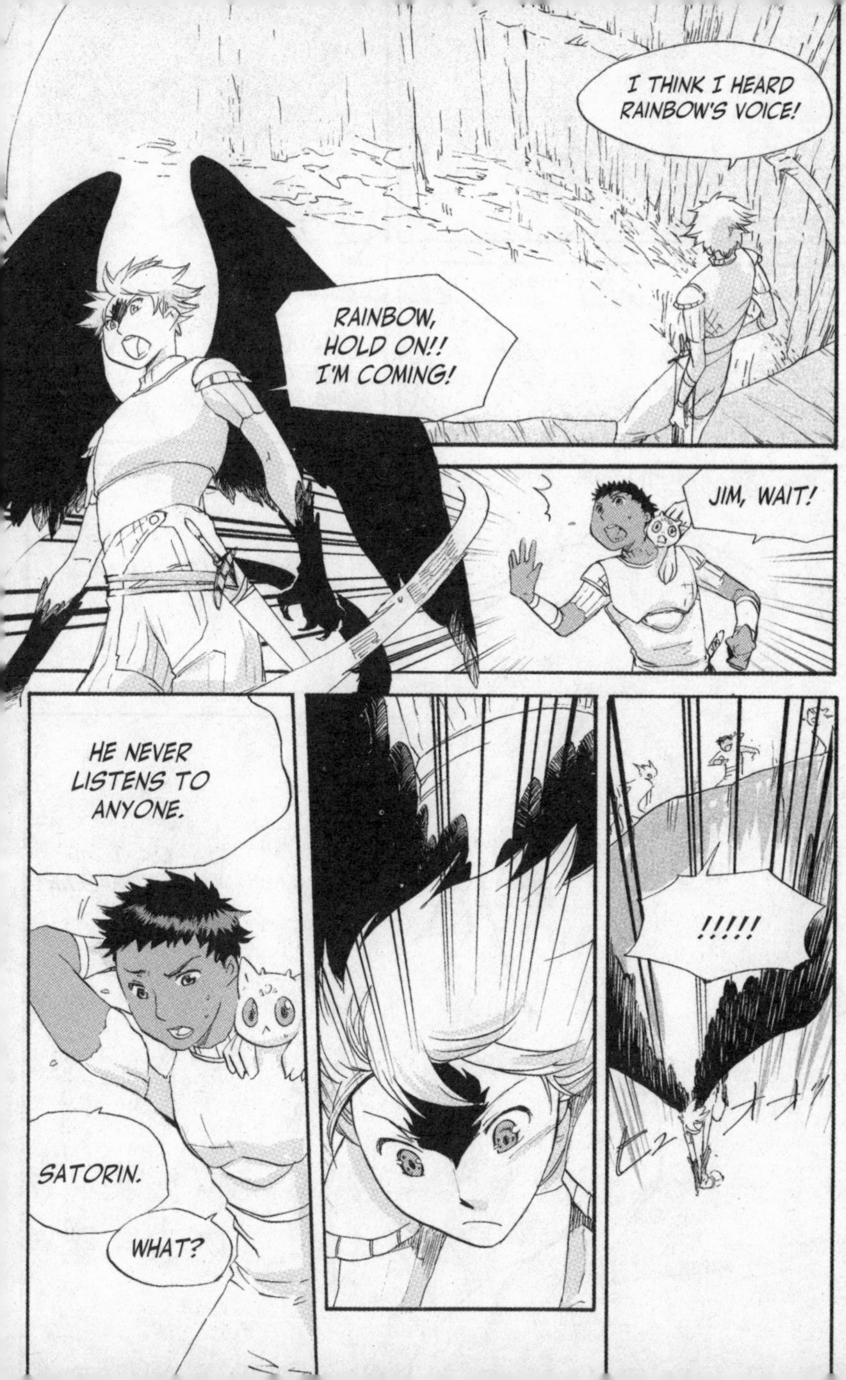
I THINK I HEARD RAINBOW'S VOICE!
JIM, WAIT!
RAINBOW, HOLD ON!! I'M COMING!
!!!!!
HE NEVER LISTENS TO ANYONE.
SATORIN.
WHAT?

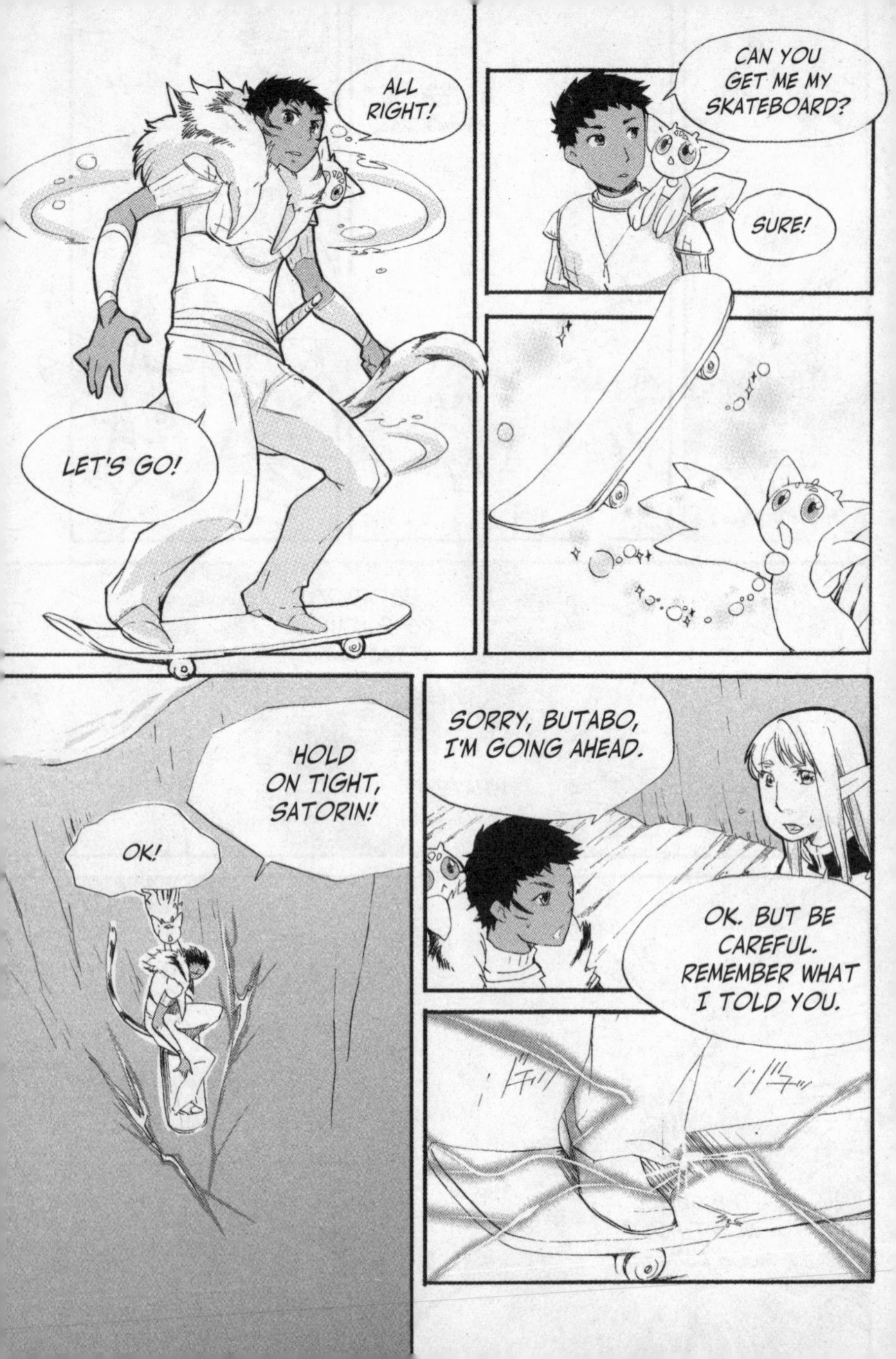
CAN YOU GET ME MY SKATEBOARD?
SURE!
ALL RIGHT!
LET'S GO!
SORRY, BUTABO, I'M GOING AHEAD.
OK. BUT BE CAREFUL. REMEMBER WHAT I TOLD YOU.
HOLD ON TIGHT, SATORIN!
OK!

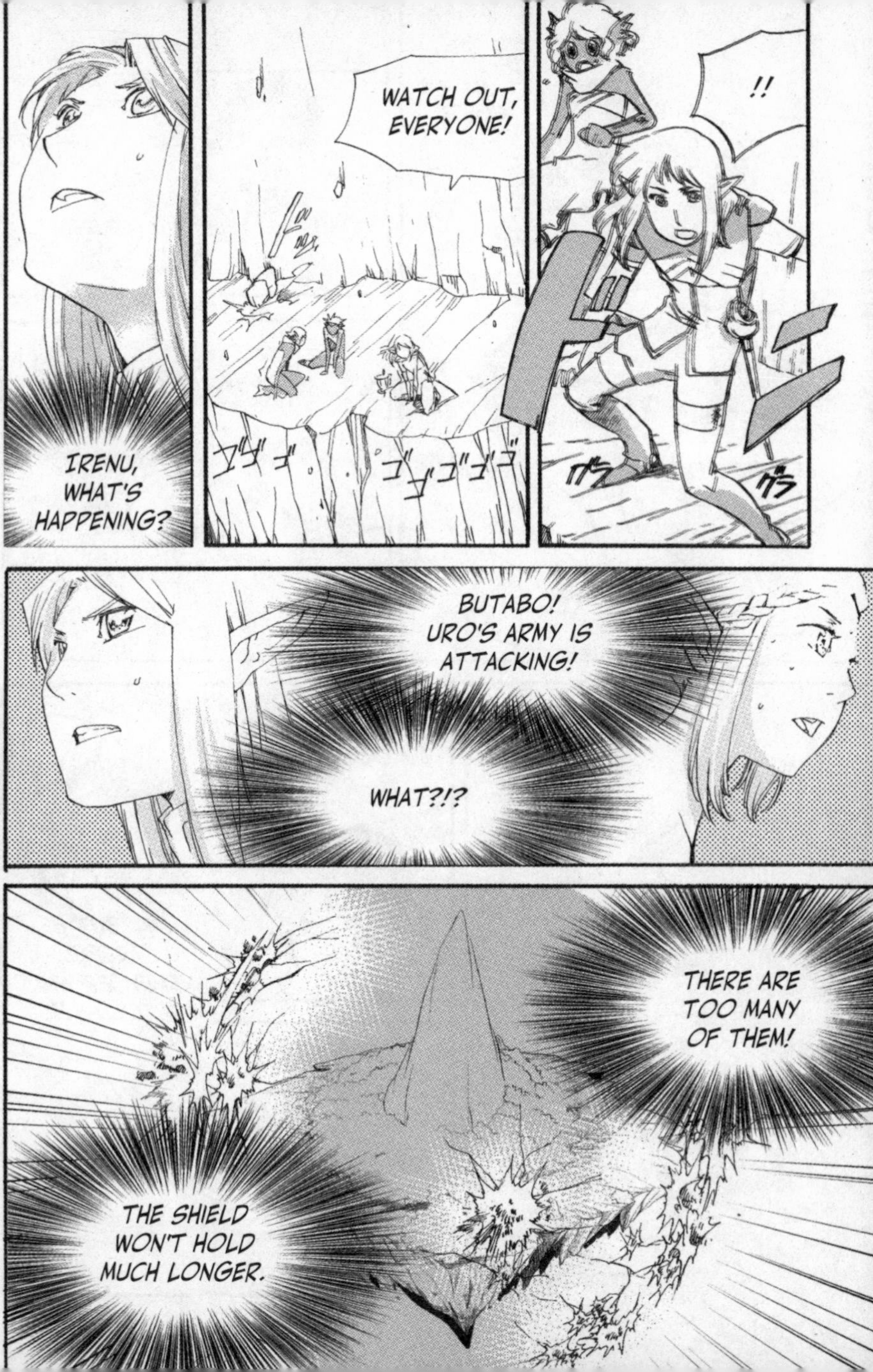
!!
WATCH OUT, EVERYONE!
IRENU, WHAT'S HAPPENING?
BUTABO! URO'S ARMY IS ATTACKING!
WHAT?!?
THERE ARE TOO MANY OF THEM!
THE SHIELD WON'T HOLD MUCH LONGER.

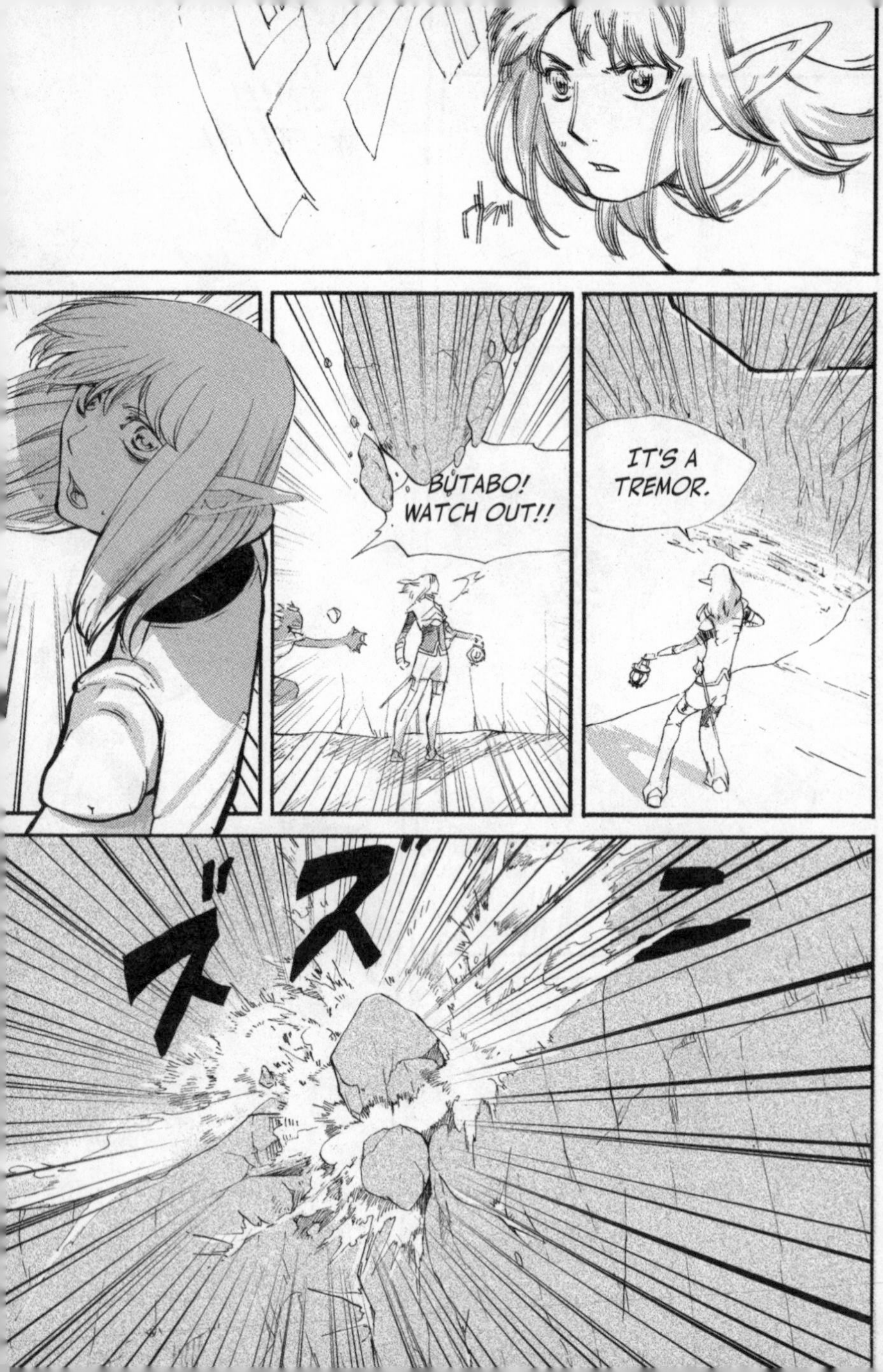
IT'S A TREMOR.
BUTABO! WATCH OUT!!
ズズー

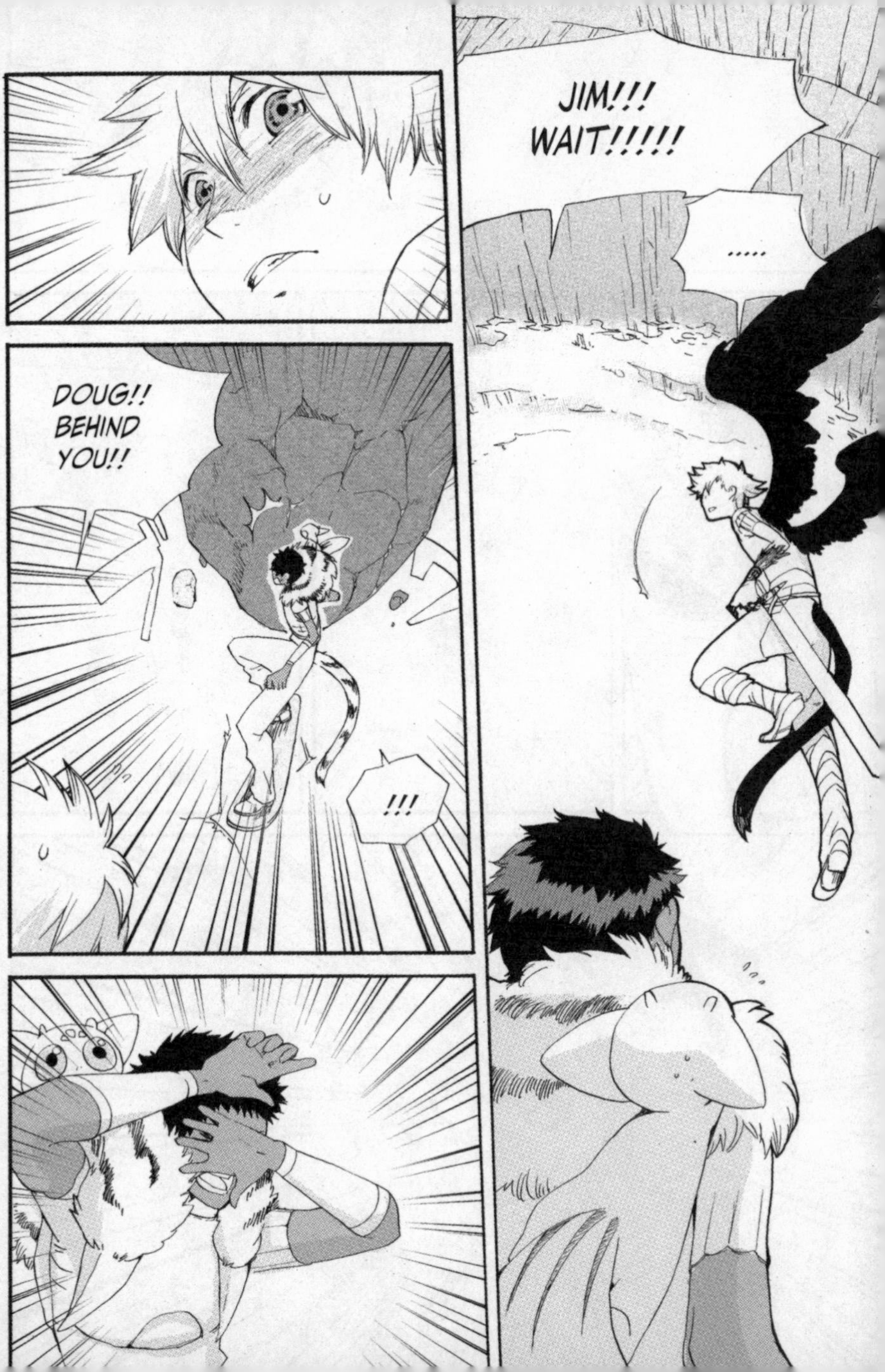
JIM!!!
WAIT!!!!!!
.....
DOUG!!
BEHIND
YOU!!
!!!

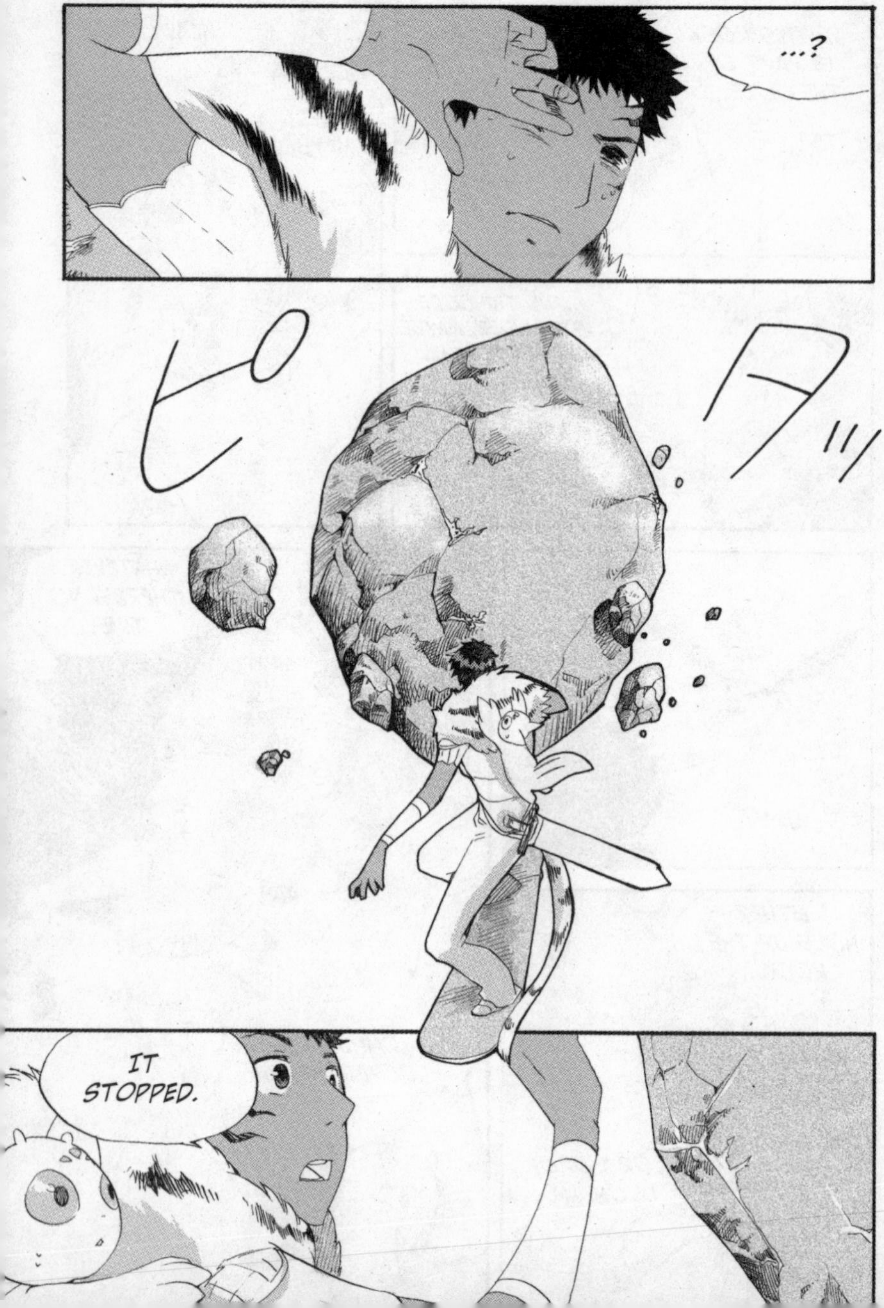
...?
ピタッ
IT STOPPED.

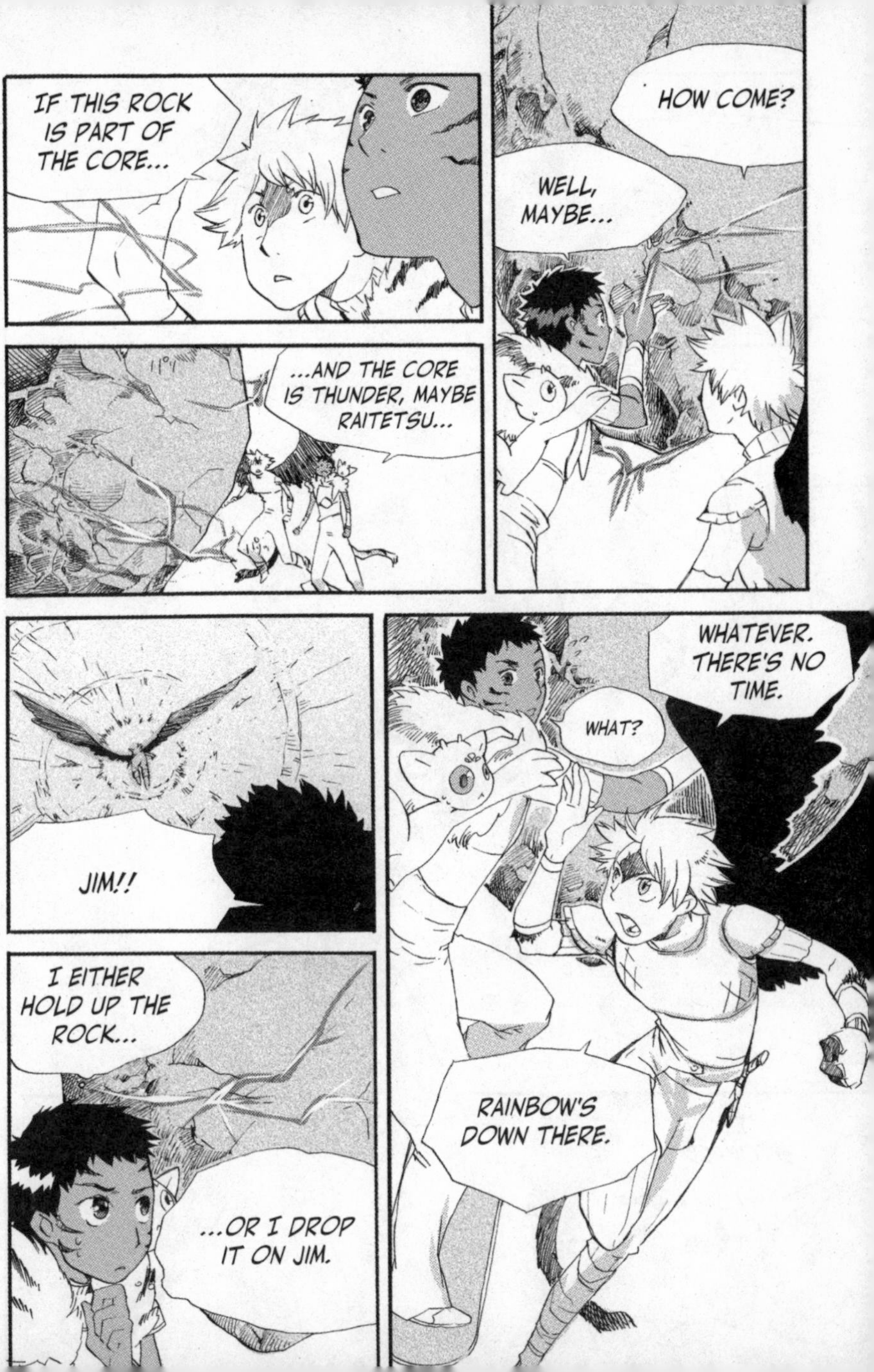
HOW COME?
WELL, MAYBE...
IF THIS ROCK IS PART OF THE CORE...
...AND THE CORE IS THUNDER, MAYBE RAITETSU...
WHATEVER. THERE'S NO TIME.
WHAT?
RAINBOW'S DOWN THERE.
JIM!!
I EITHER HOLD UP THE ROCK...
...OR I DROP IT ON JIM.

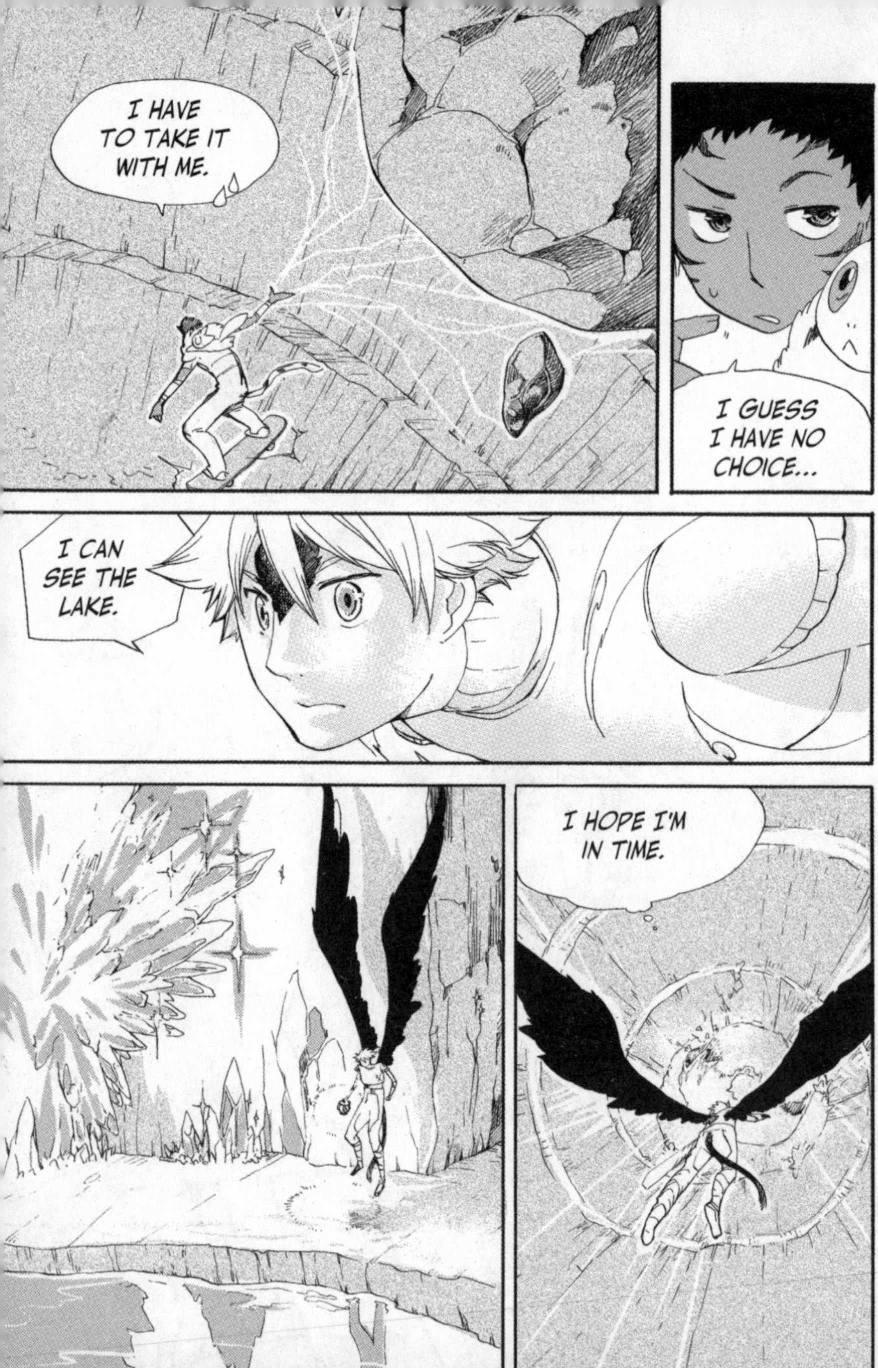
I GUESS I HAVE NO CHOICE...
I HAVE TO TAKE IT WITH ME.
I CAN SEE THE LAKE.
I HOPE I'M IN TIME.

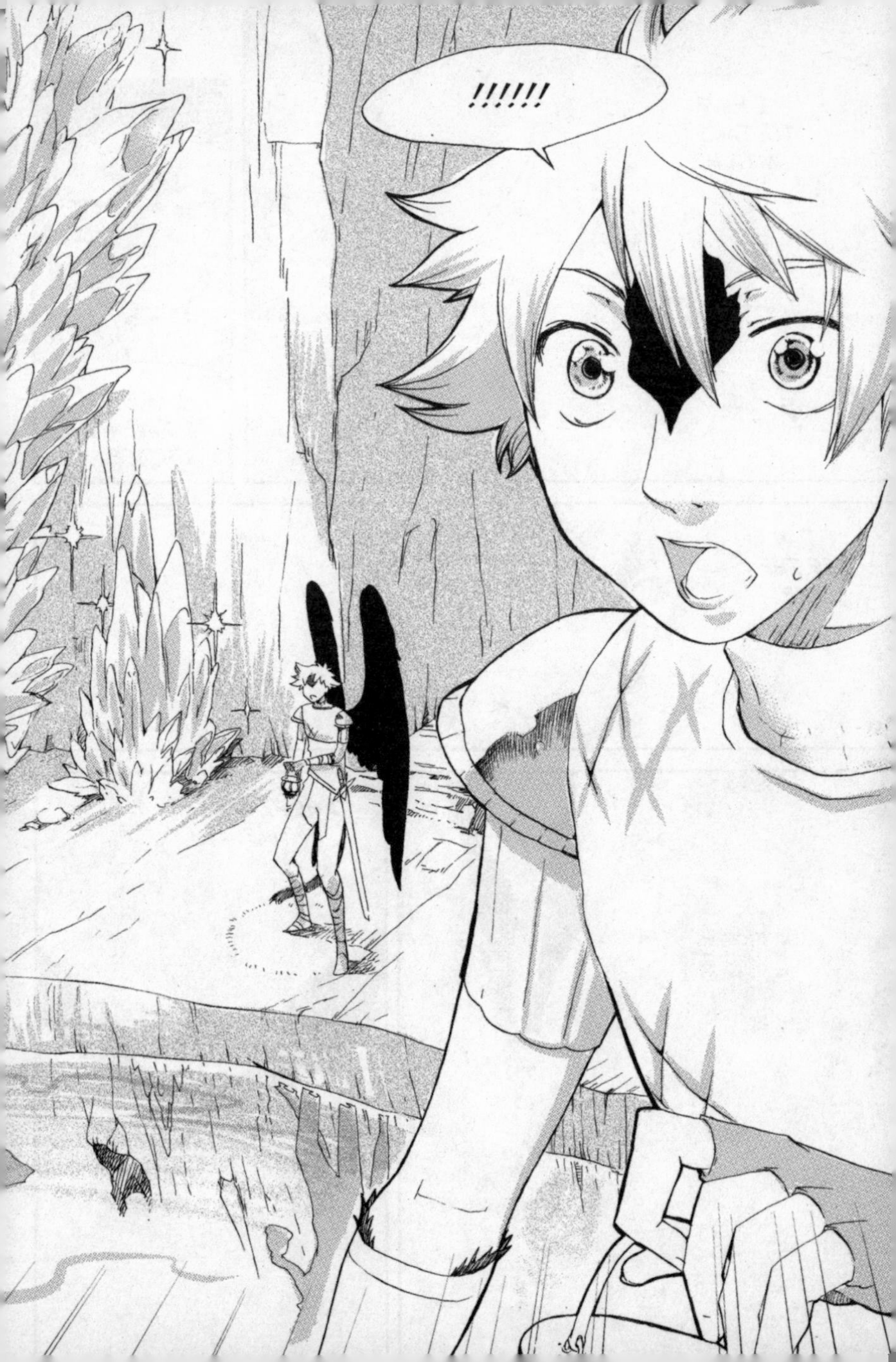
!!!!!!

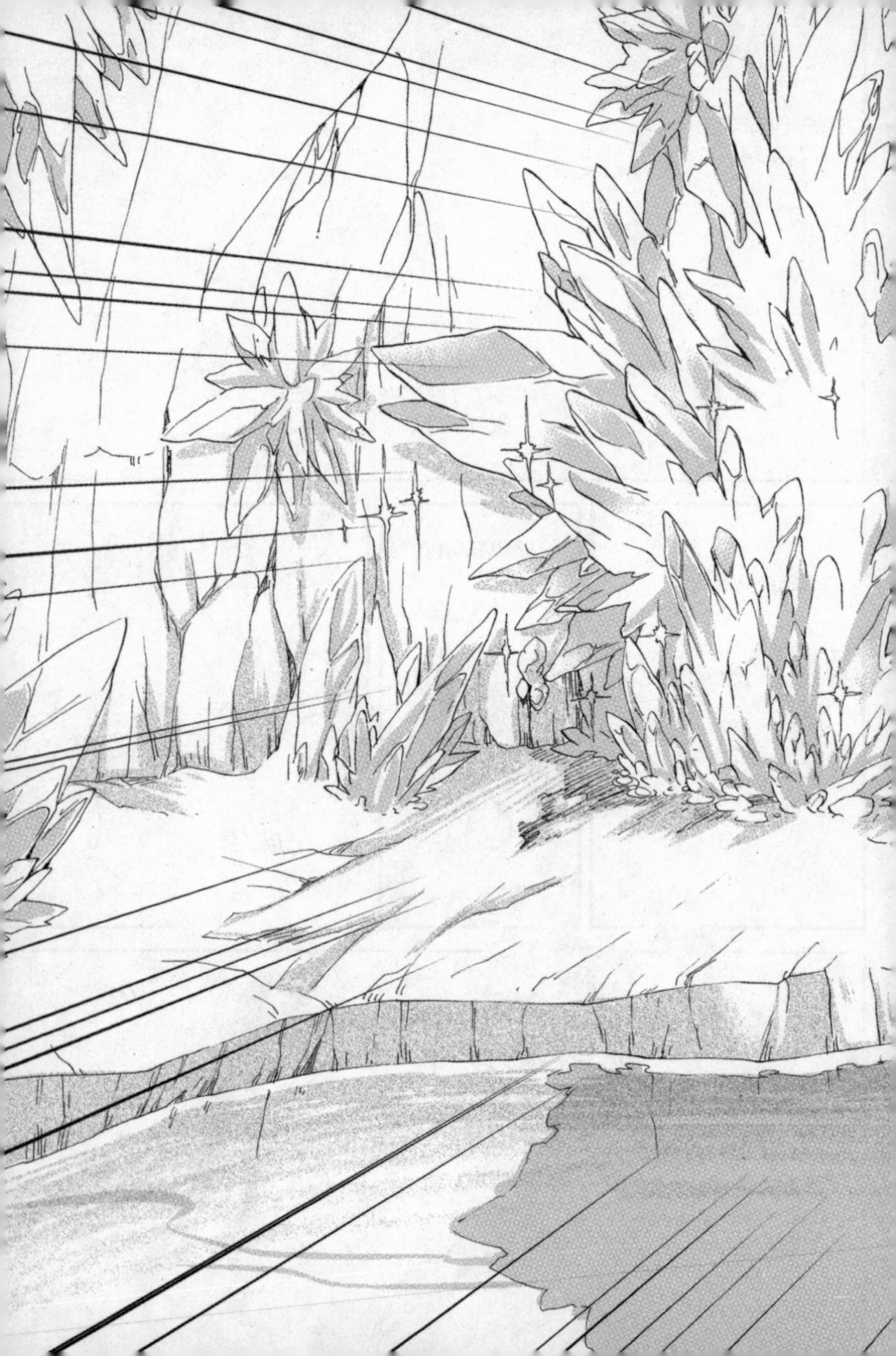

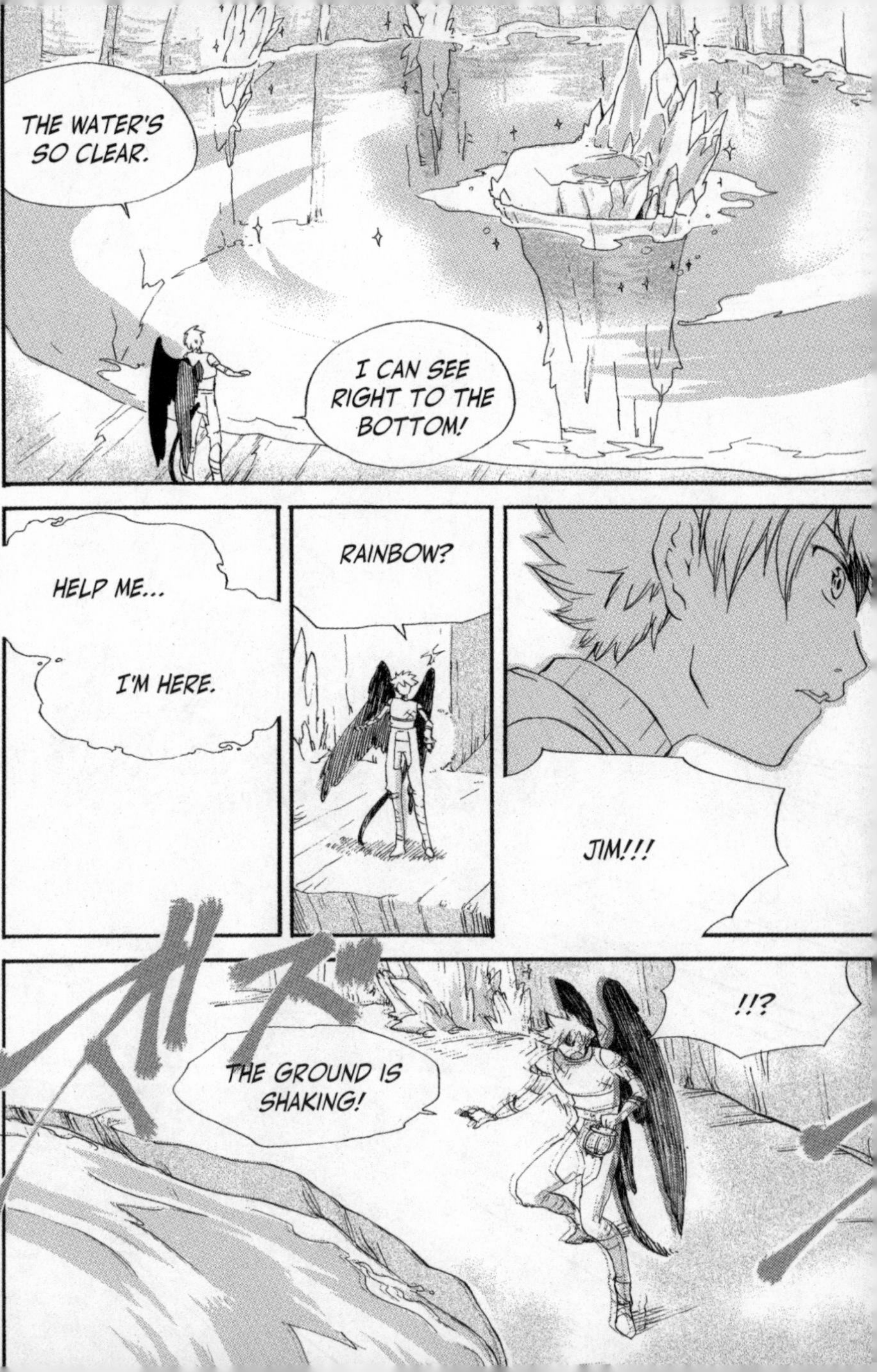
THE WATER'S SO CLEAR.
I CAN SEE RIGHT TO THE BOTTOM!
JIM!!!
RAINBOW?
HELP ME...
I'M HERE.
!!?
THE GROUND IS SHAKING!

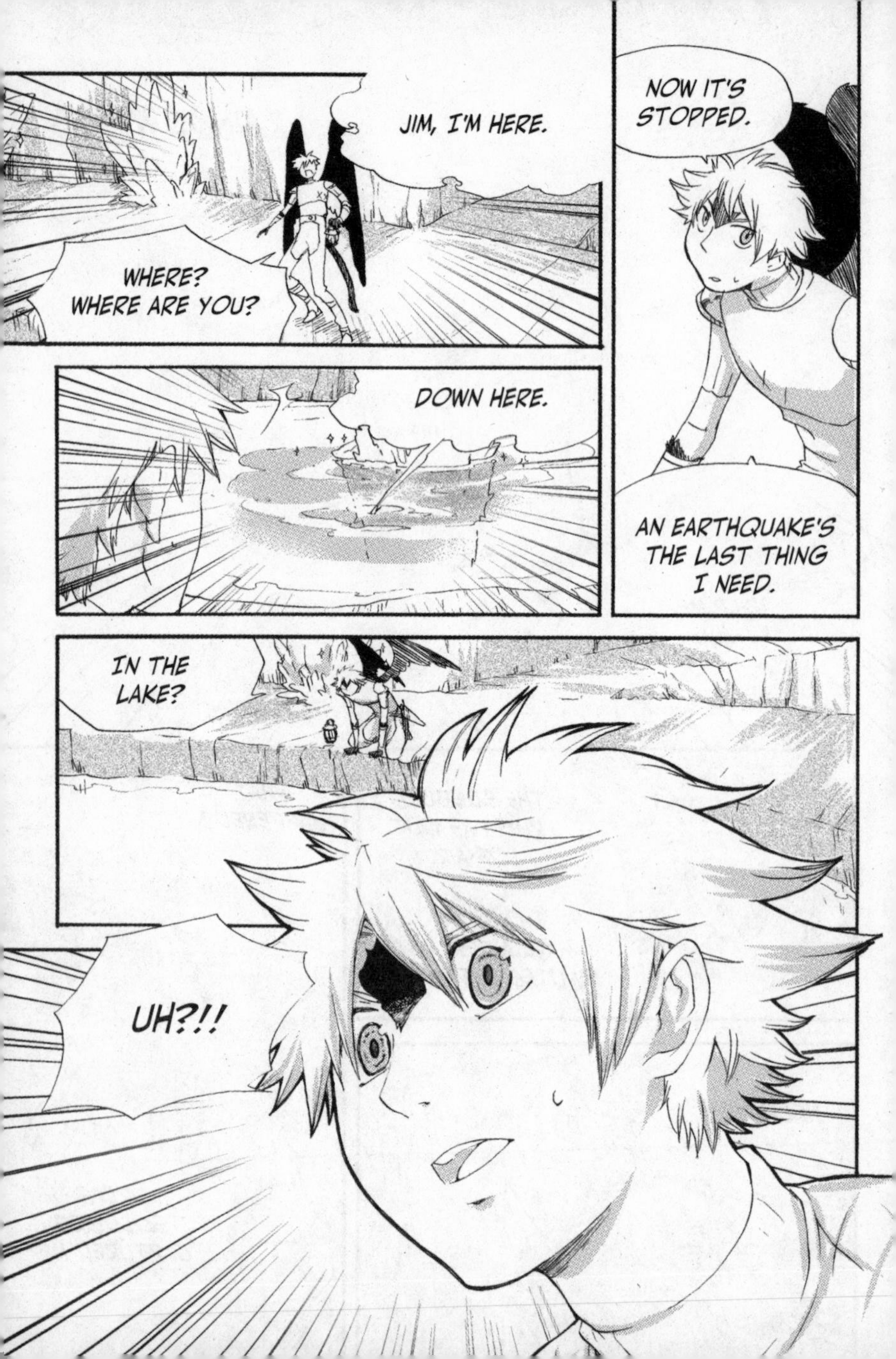
NOW IT'S STOPPED.
AN EARTHQUAKE'S THE LAST THING I NEED.
JIM, I'M HERE.
WHERE? WHERE ARE YOU?
DOWN HERE.
IN THE LAKE?
UH?!!

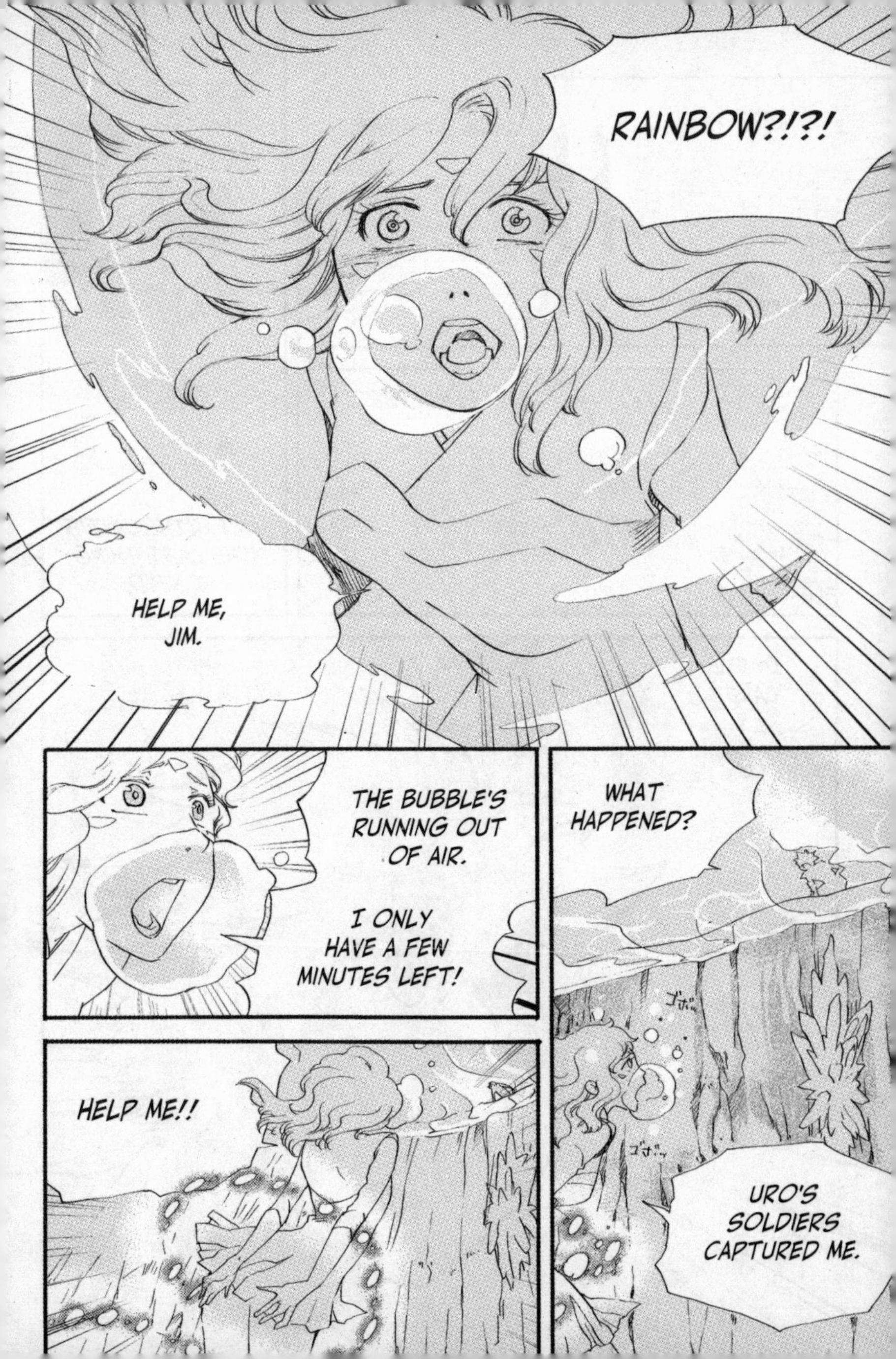
RAINBOW?!?!
HELP ME, JIM.
WHAT HAPPENED?
URO'S SOLDIERS CAPTURED ME.
THE BUBBLE'S RUNNING OUT OF AIR.
I ONLY HAVE A FEW MINUTES LEFT!
HELP ME!!

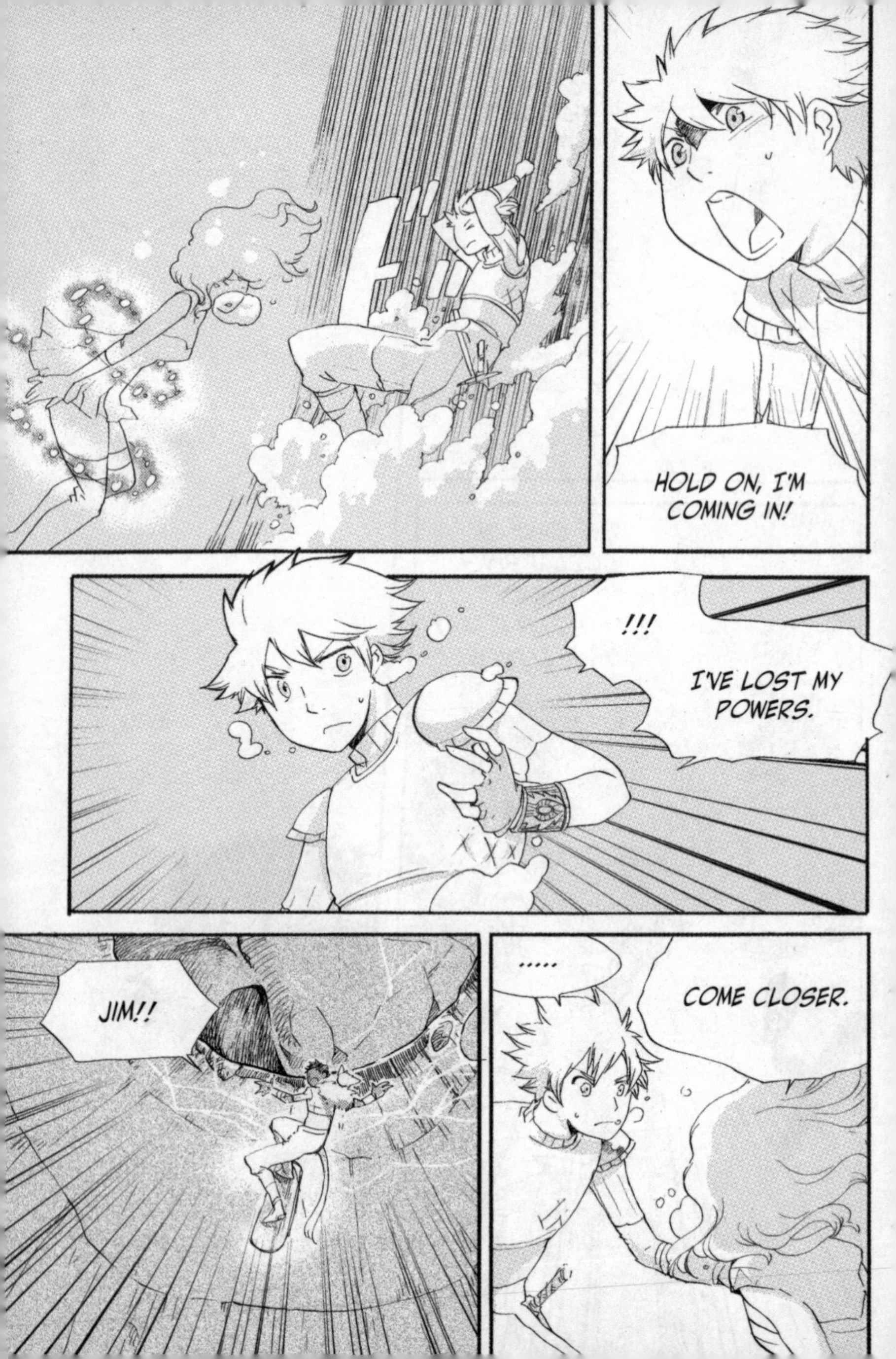
HOLD ON, I'M COMING IN!
!!!
I'VE LOST MY POWERS.
......
COME CLOSER.
JIM!!

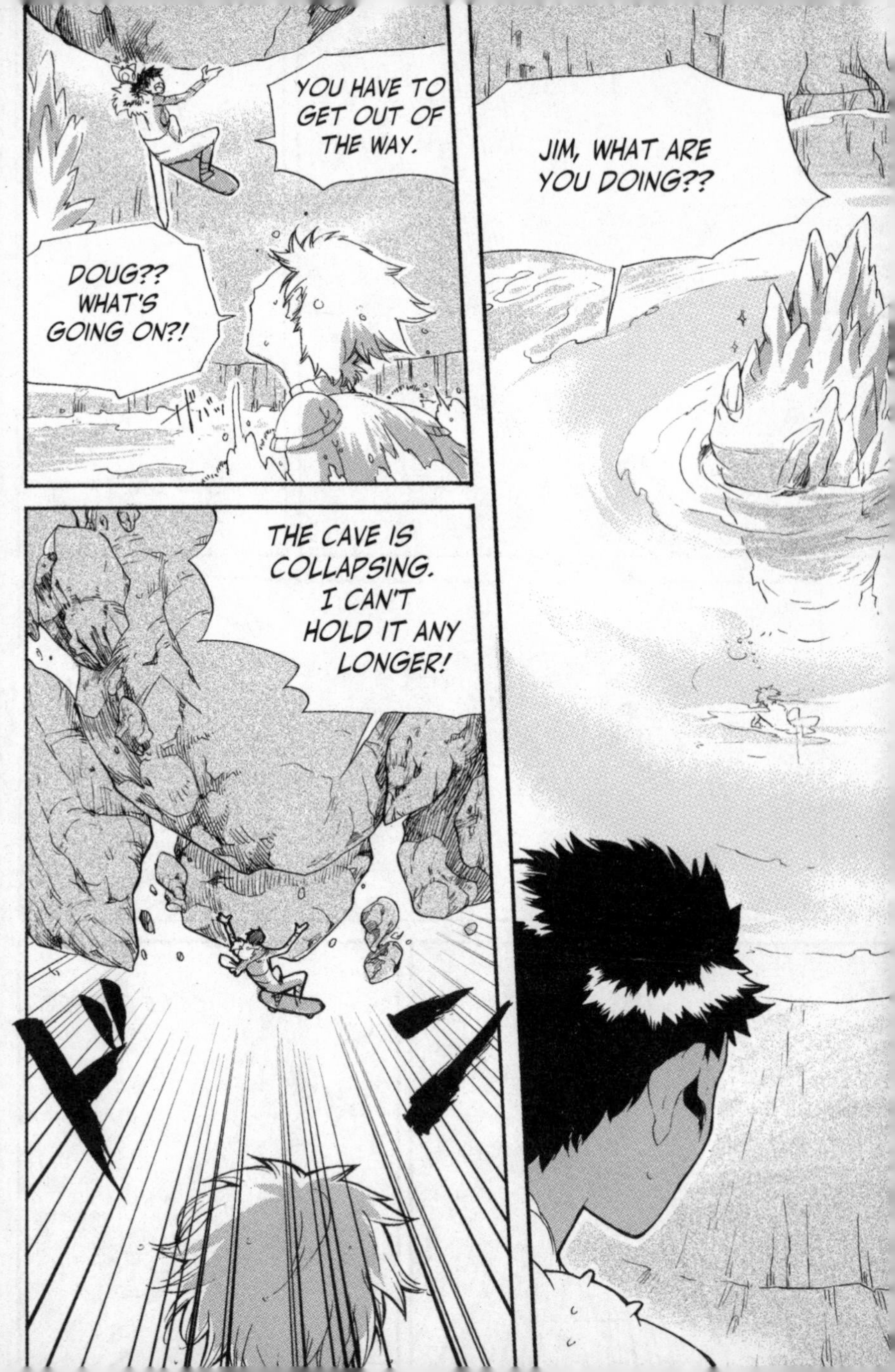
JIM, WHAT ARE YOU DOING??
YOU HAVE TO GET OUT OF THE WAY.
DOUG?? WHAT'S GOING ON?!
THE CAVE IS COLLAPSING. I CAN'T HOLD IT ANY LONGER!

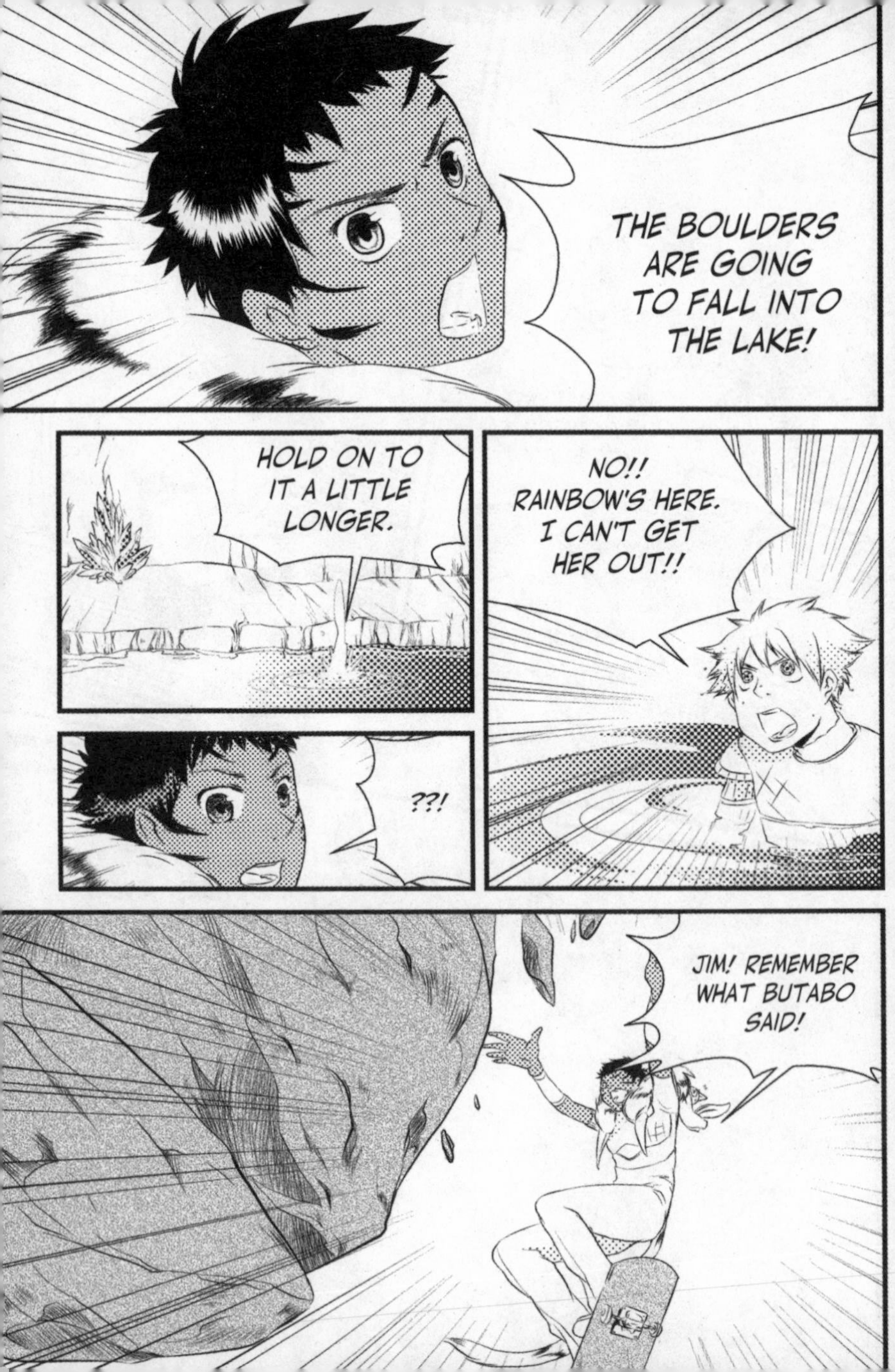
THE BOULDERS ARE GOING TO FALL INTO THE LAKE!
NO!! RAINBOW'S HERE. I CAN'T GET HER OUT!!
HOLD ON TO IT A LITTLE LONGER.
??!
JIM! REMEMBER WHAT BUTABO SAID!

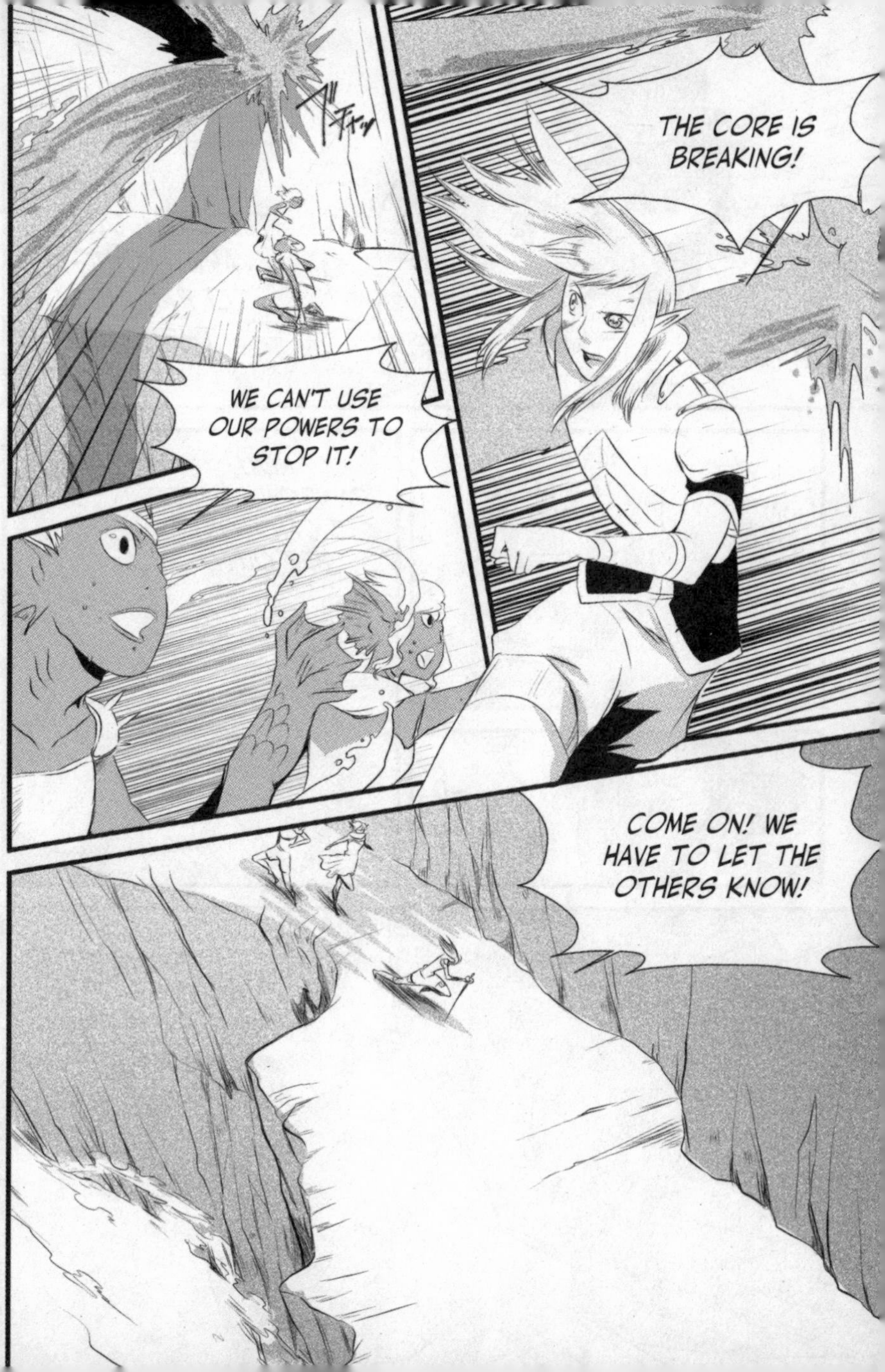
THE CORE IS BREAKING!
WE CAN'T USE OUR POWERS TO STOP IT!
COME ON! WE HAVE TO LET THE OTHERS KNOW!

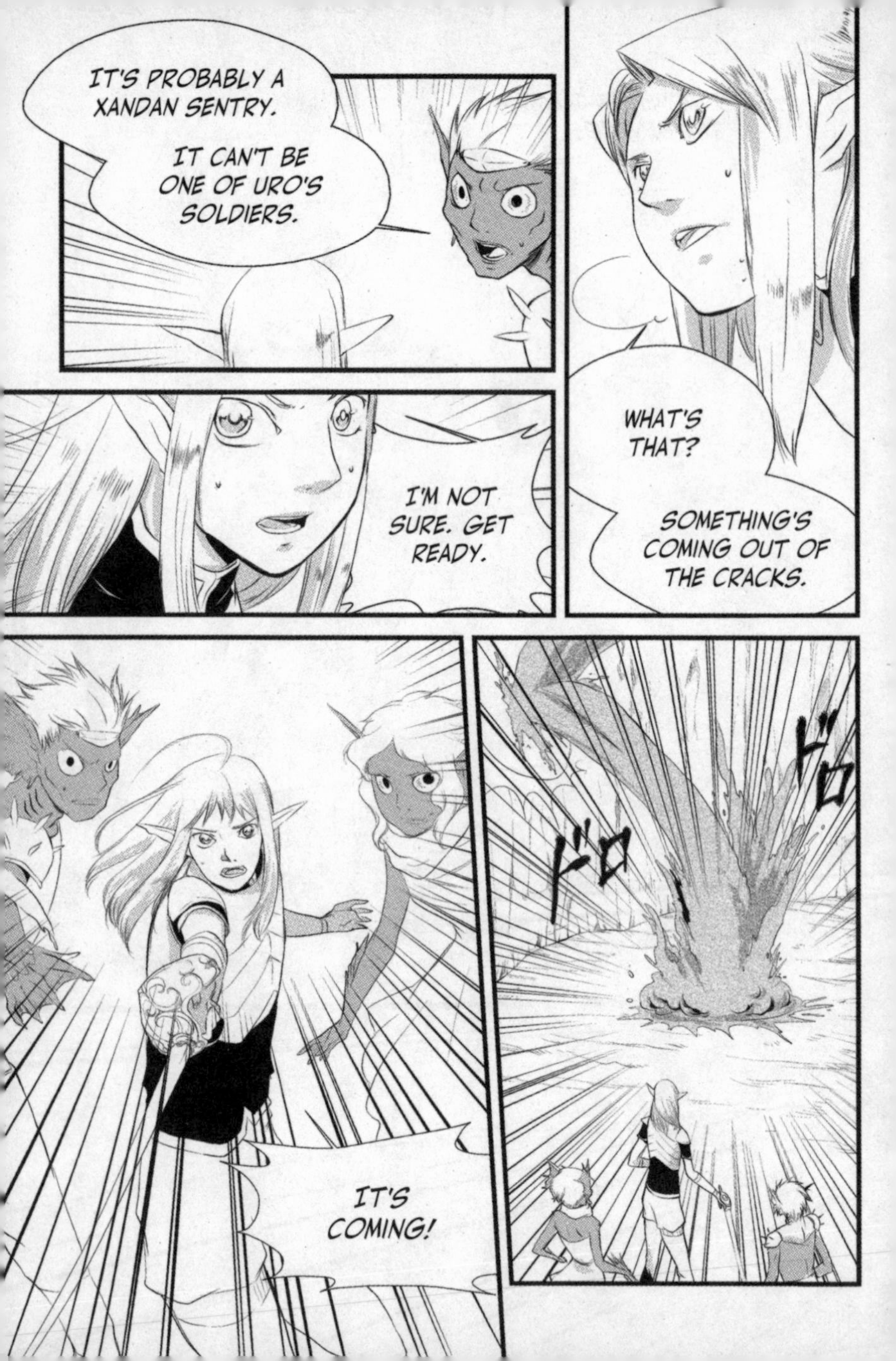
WHAT'S THAT?
SOMETHING'S COMING OUT OF THE CRACKS.
IT'S PROBABLY A XANDAN SENTRY.
IT CAN'T BE ONE OF URO'S SOLDIERS.
I'M NOT SURE. GET READY.
ドロ
ドロ
IT'S COMING!

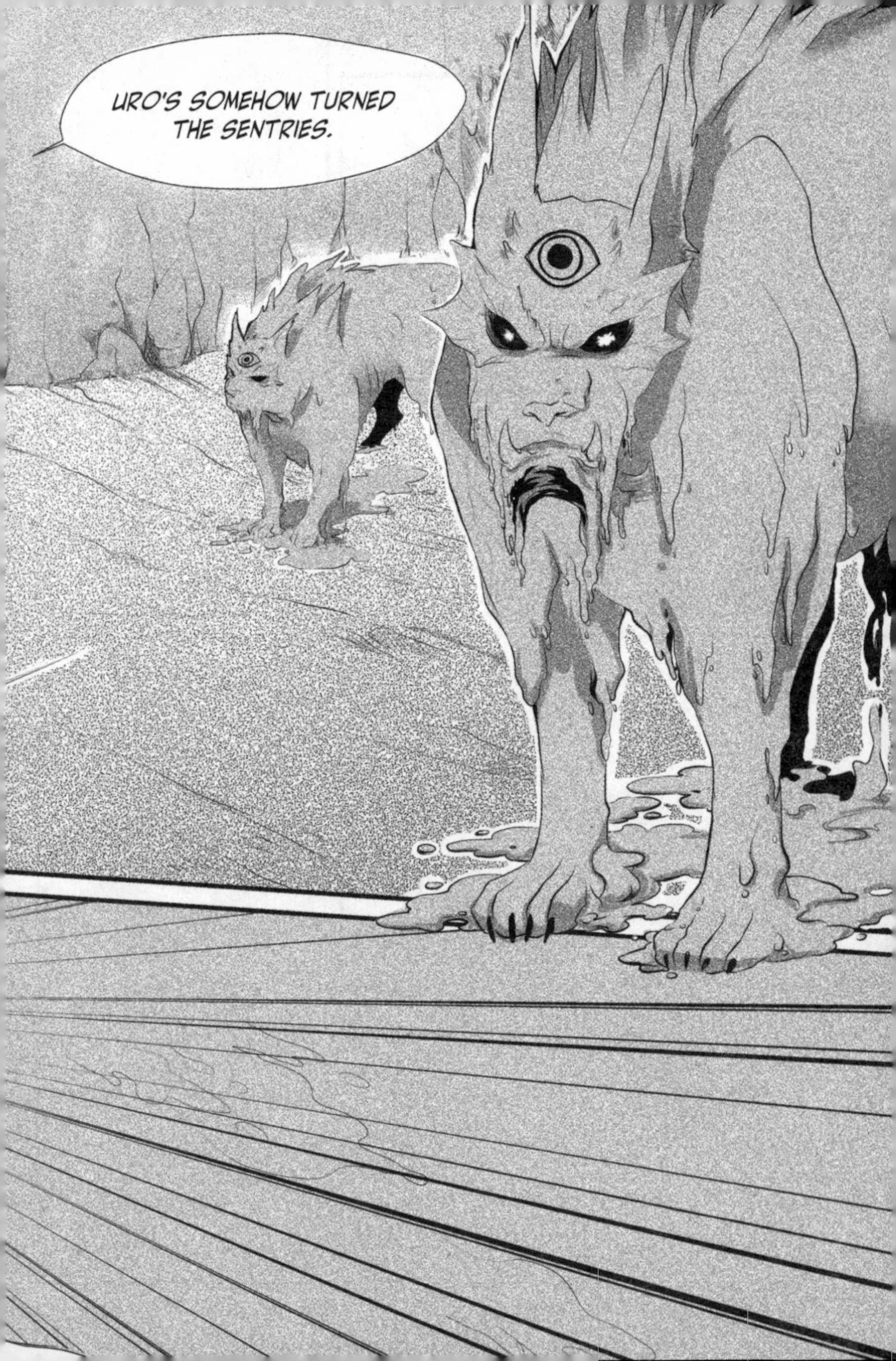
URO'S SOMEHOW TURNED THE SENTRIES.

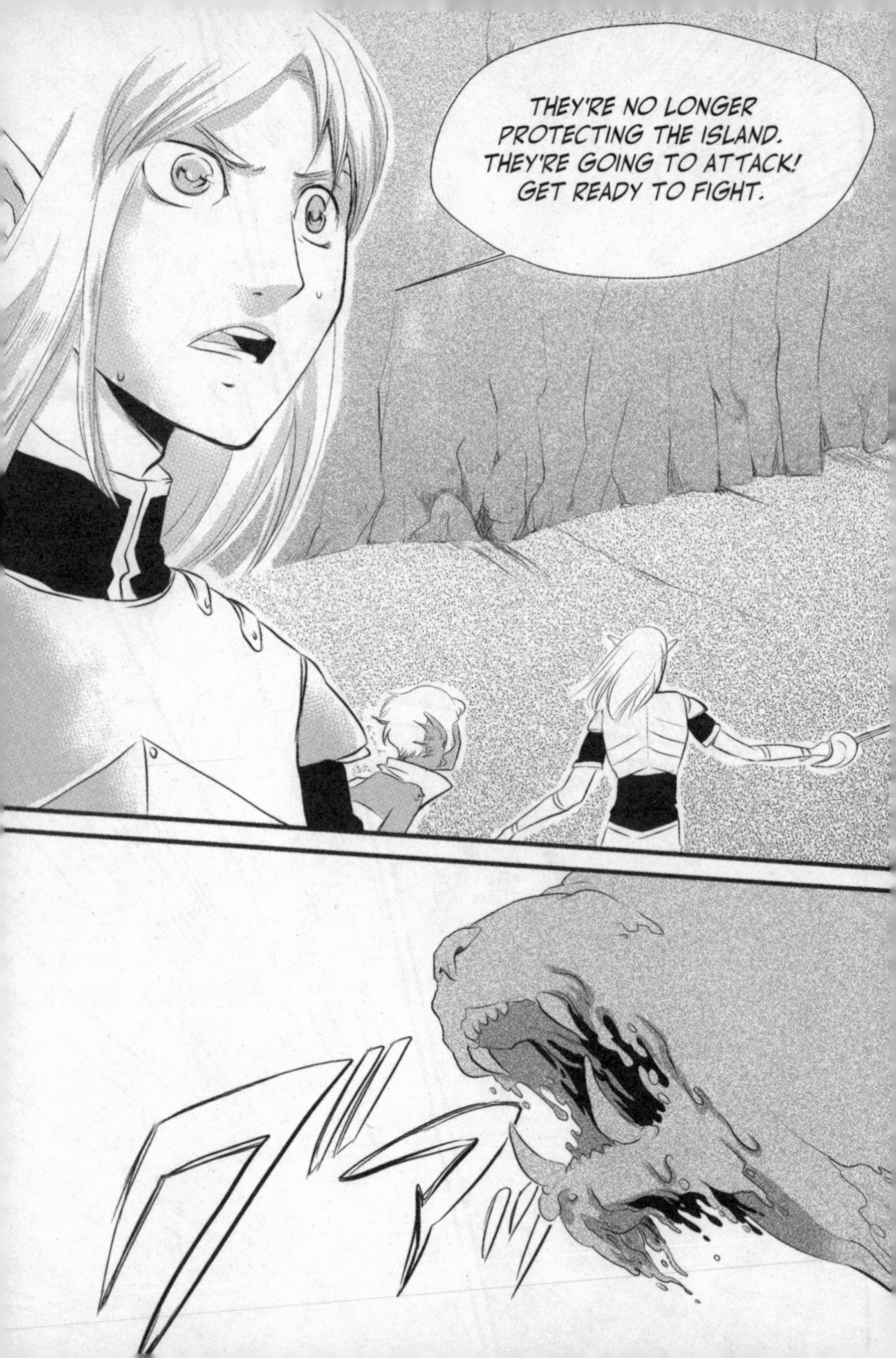
THEY'RE NO LONGER PROTECTING THE ISLAND. THEY'RE GOING TO ATTACK! GET READY TO FIGHT.

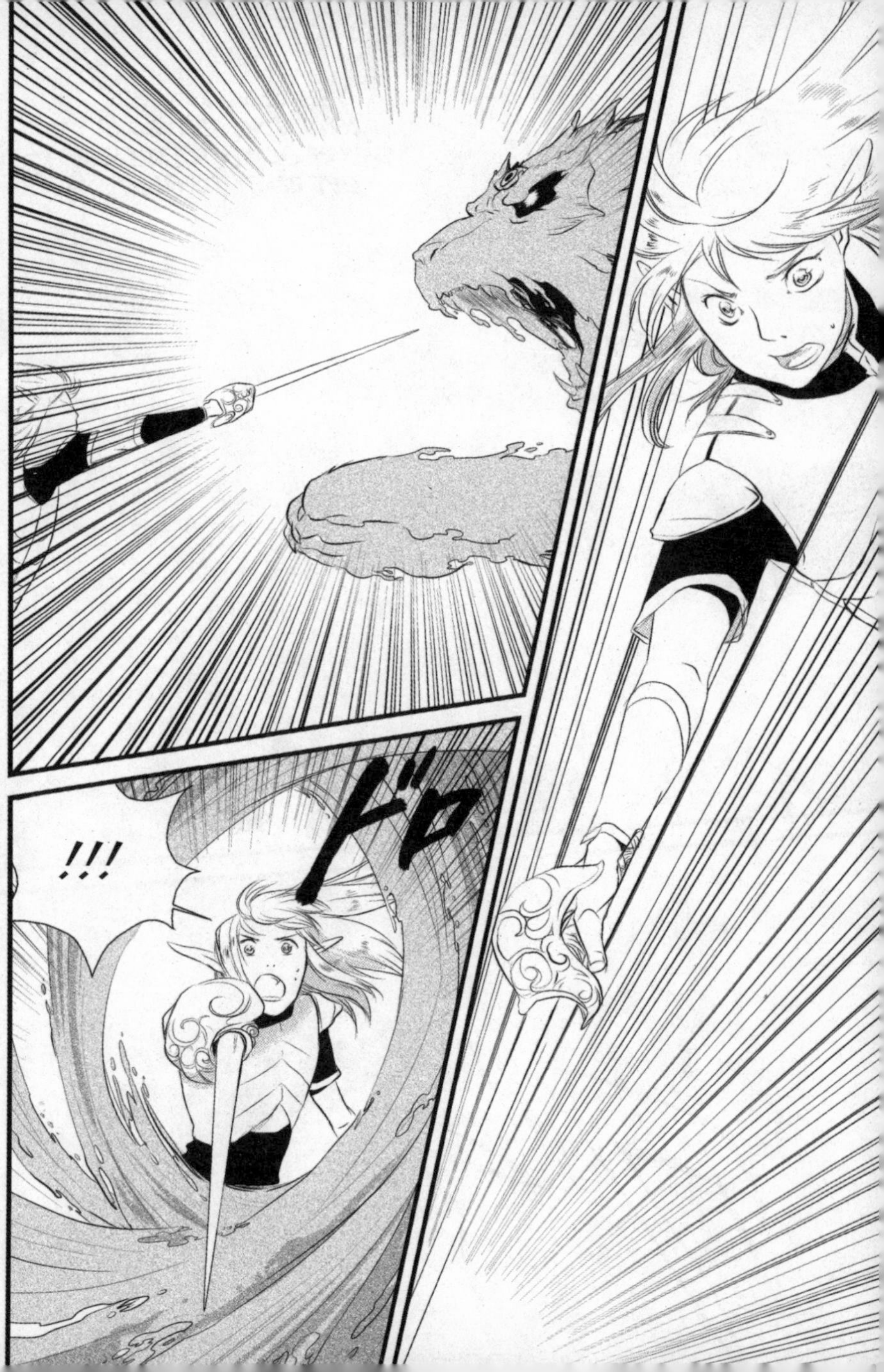
ドロ
!!!

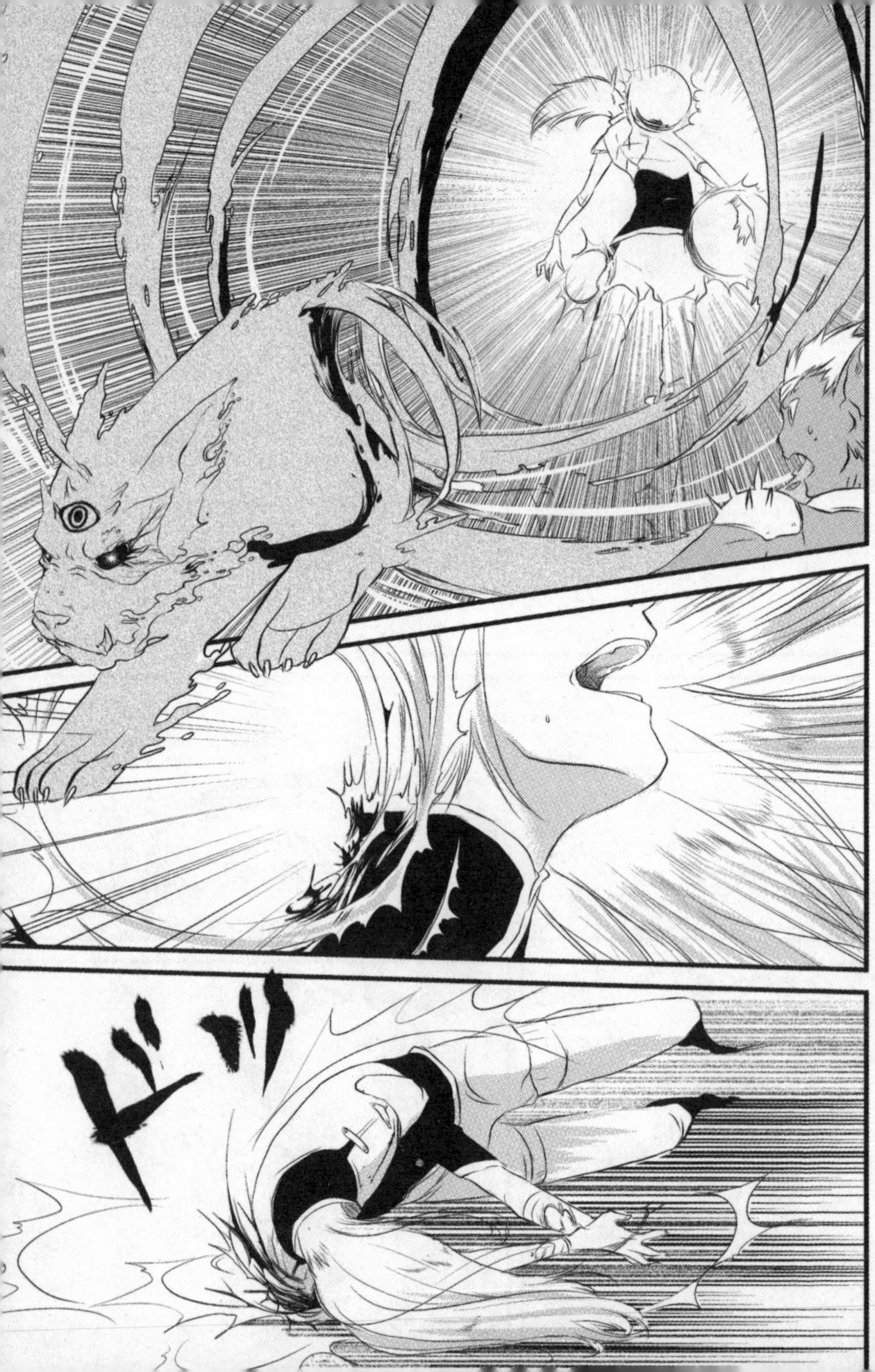
ドッ

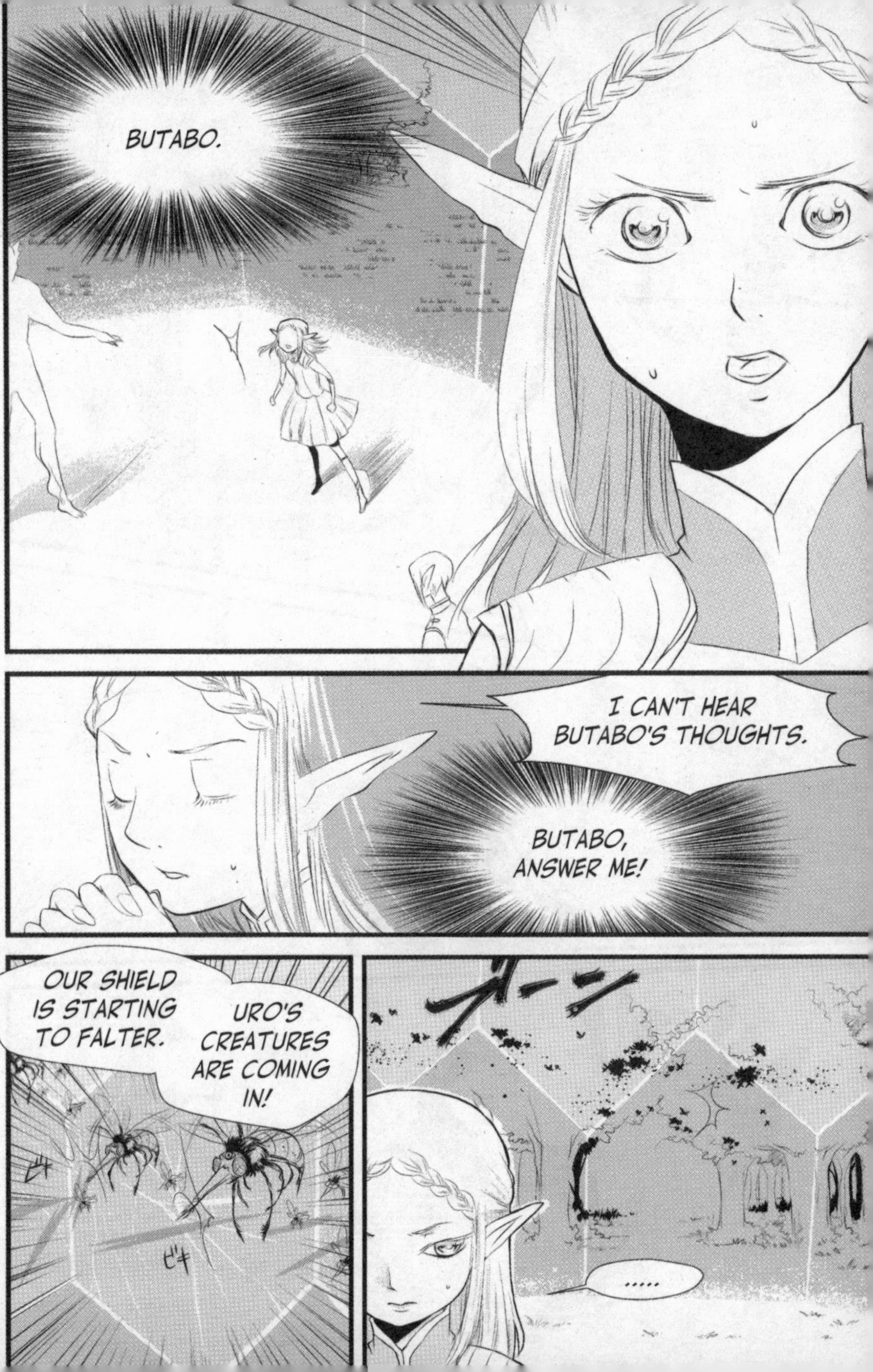
BUTABO.
I CAN'T HEAR BUTABO'S THOUGHTS.
BUTABO, ANSWER ME!
オーン
......
OUR SHIELD IS STARTING TO FALTER.
URO'S CREATURES ARE COMING IN!
ビキ
ビキ

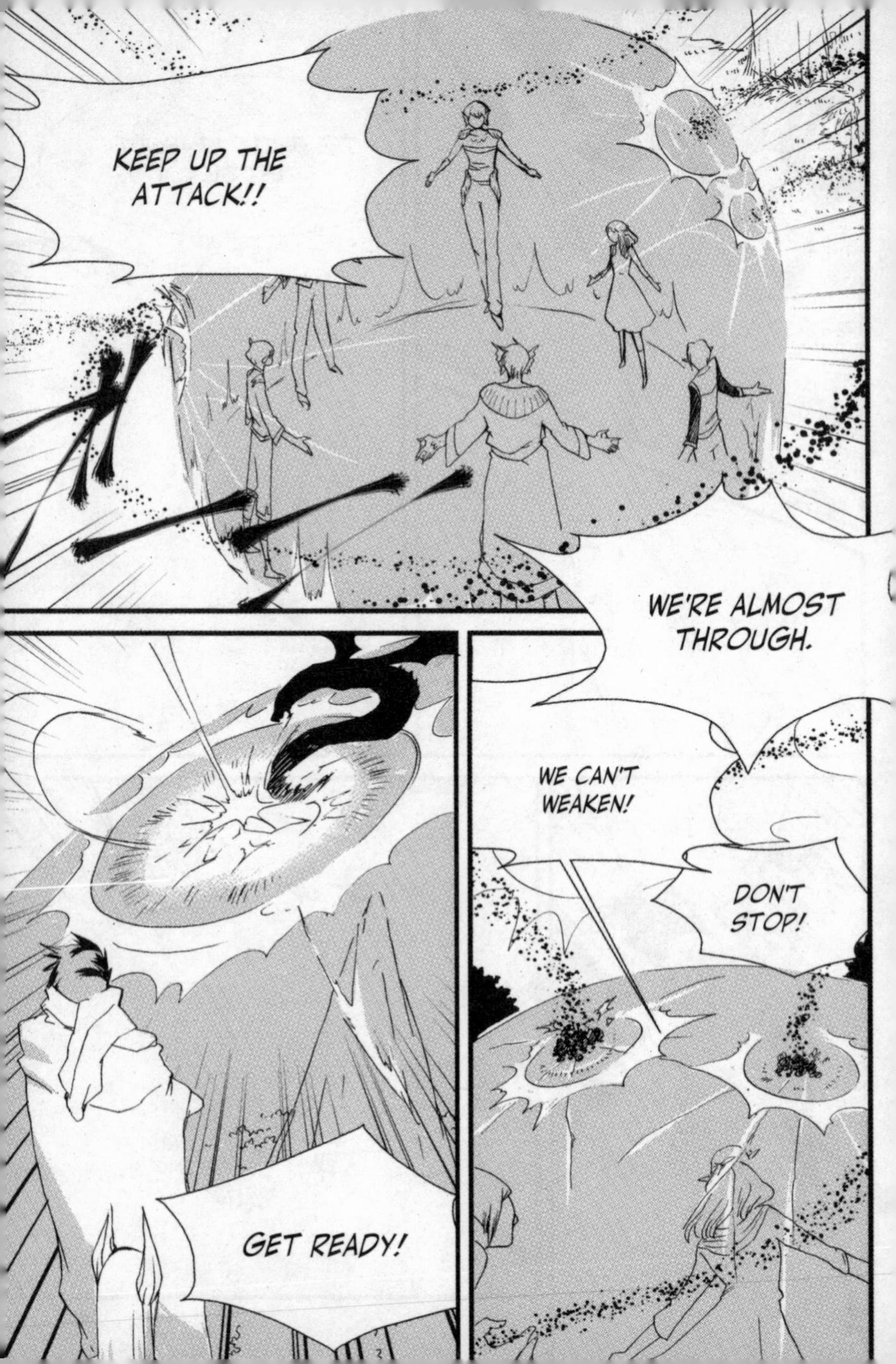
KEEP UP THE ATTACK!!
WE'RE ALMOST THROUGH.
WE CAN'T WEAKEN!
DON'T STOP!
GET READY!

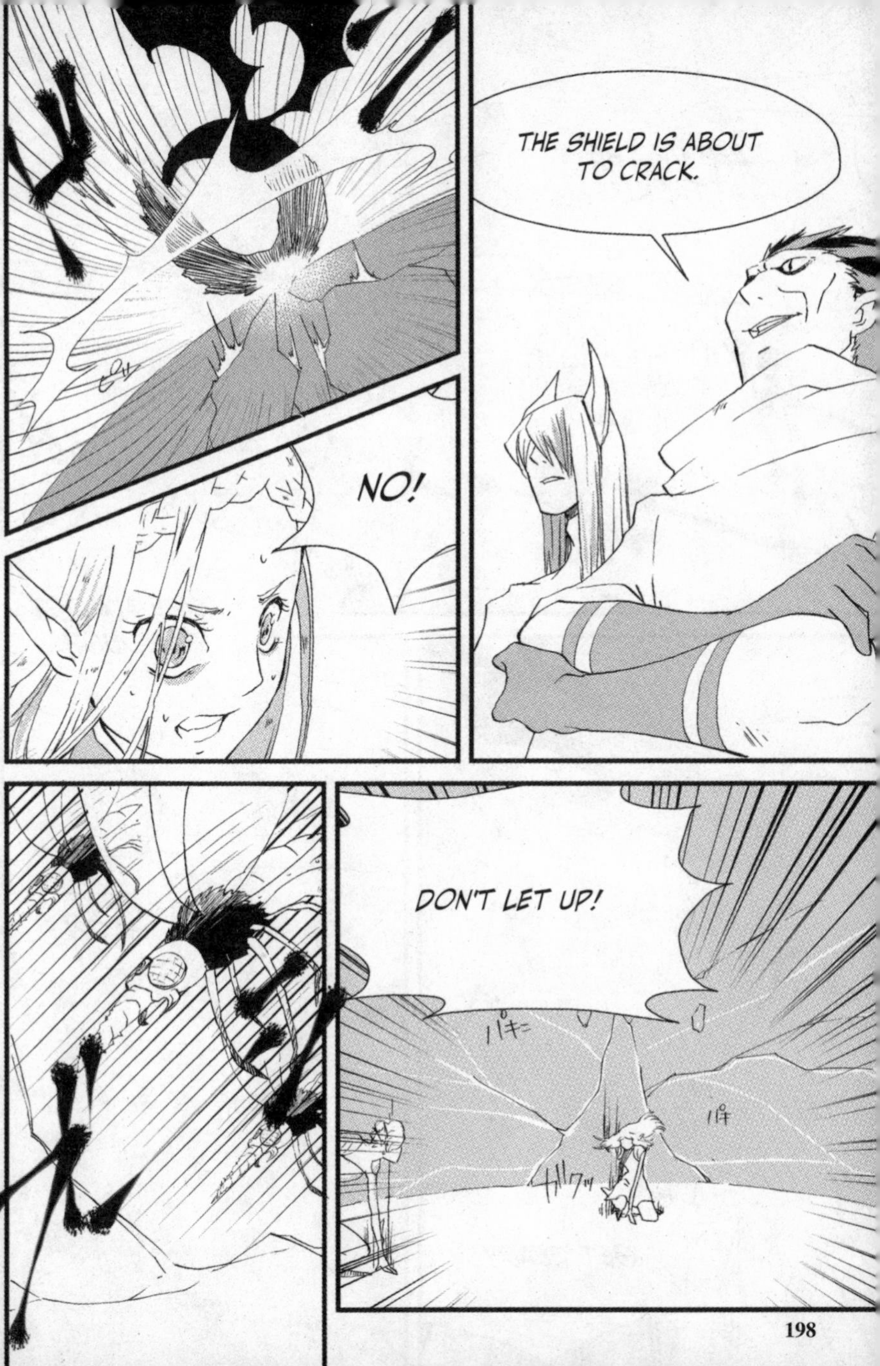
THE SHIELD IS ABOUT TO CRACK.
NO!
DON'T LET UP!

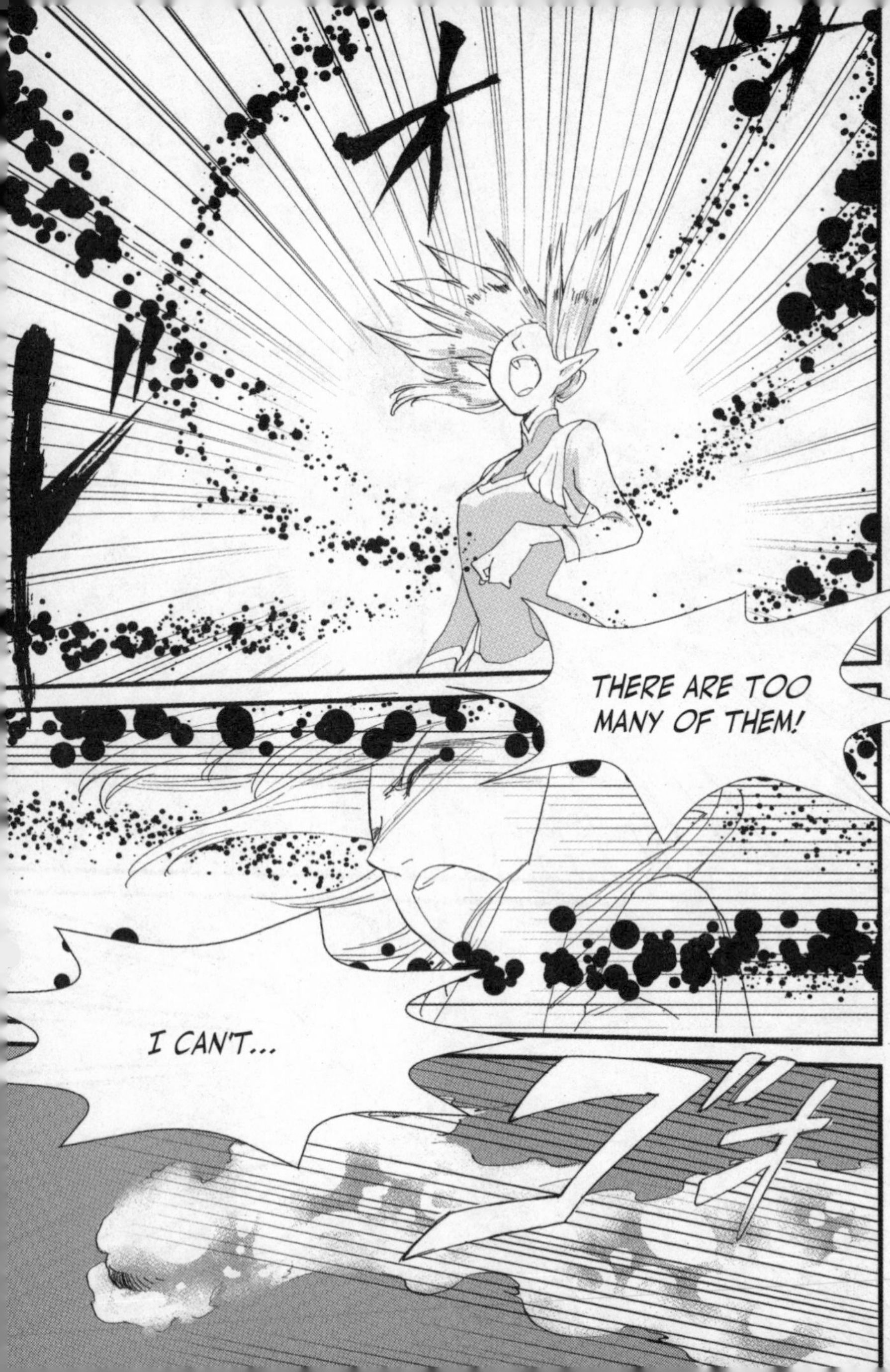
THERE ARE TOO MANY OF THEM!
I CAN'T...

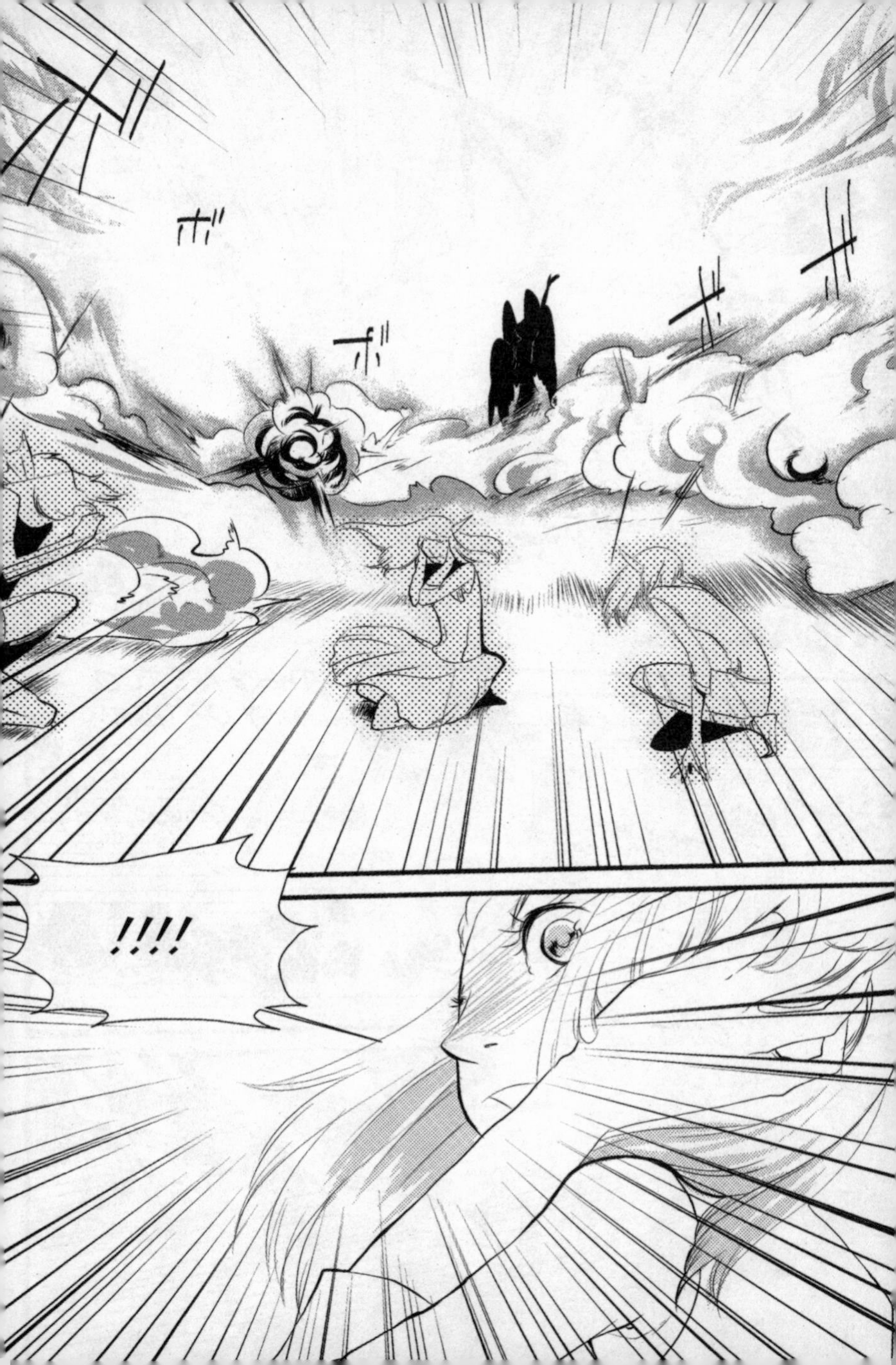
!!!!

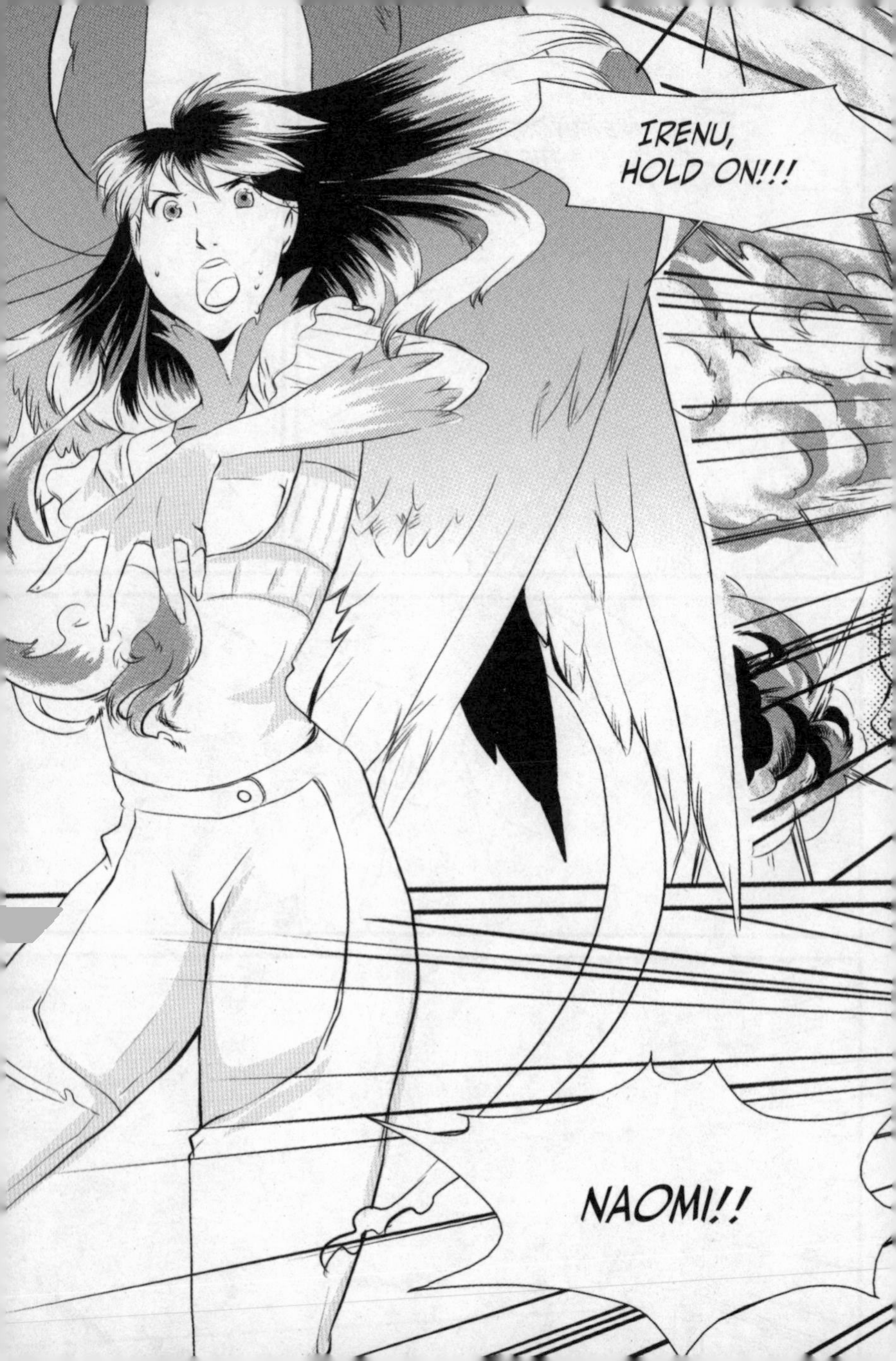
IRENU, HOLD ON!!!
NAOMI!!

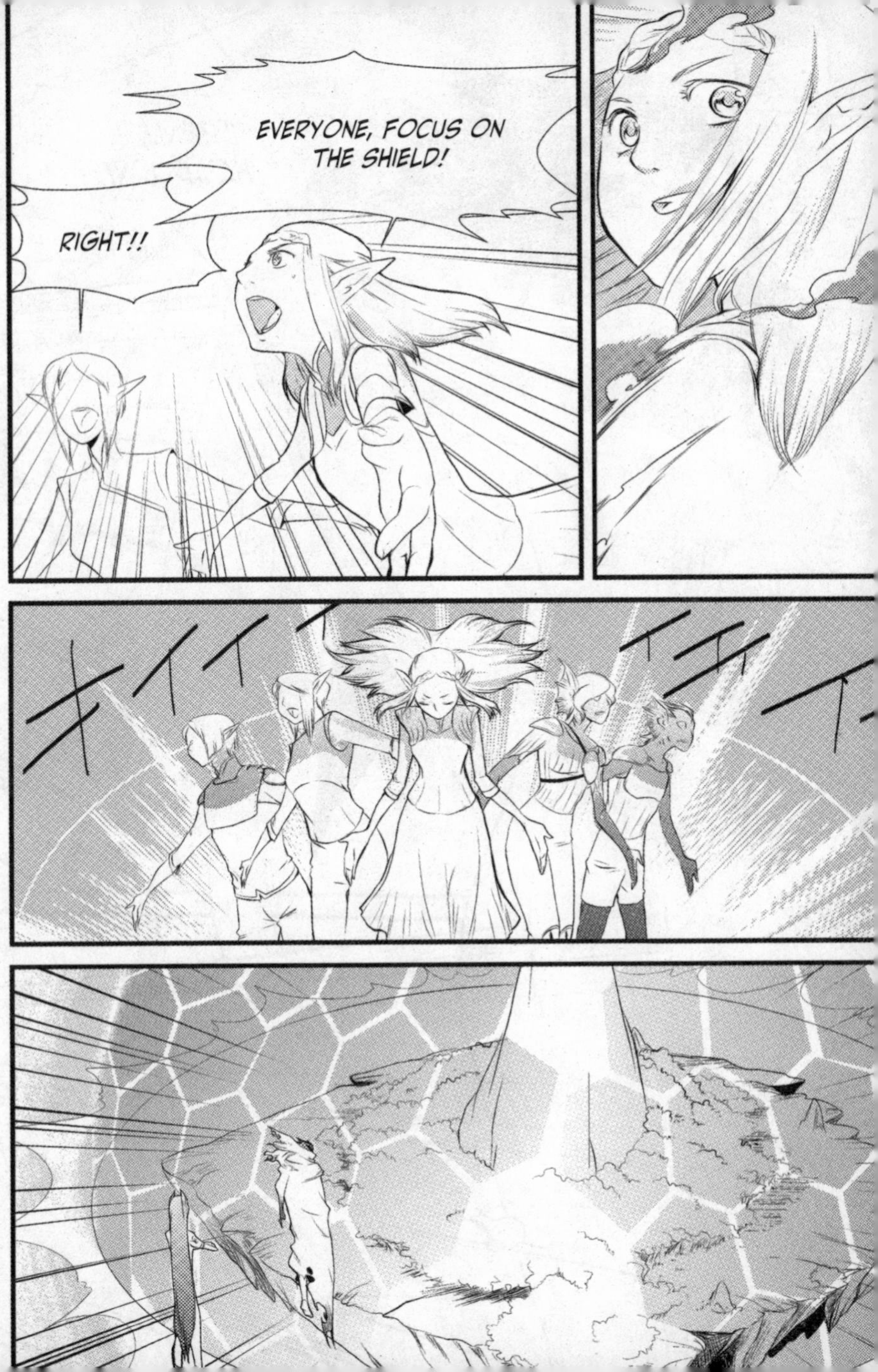
EVERYONE, FOCUS ON THE SHIELD!
RIGHT!!

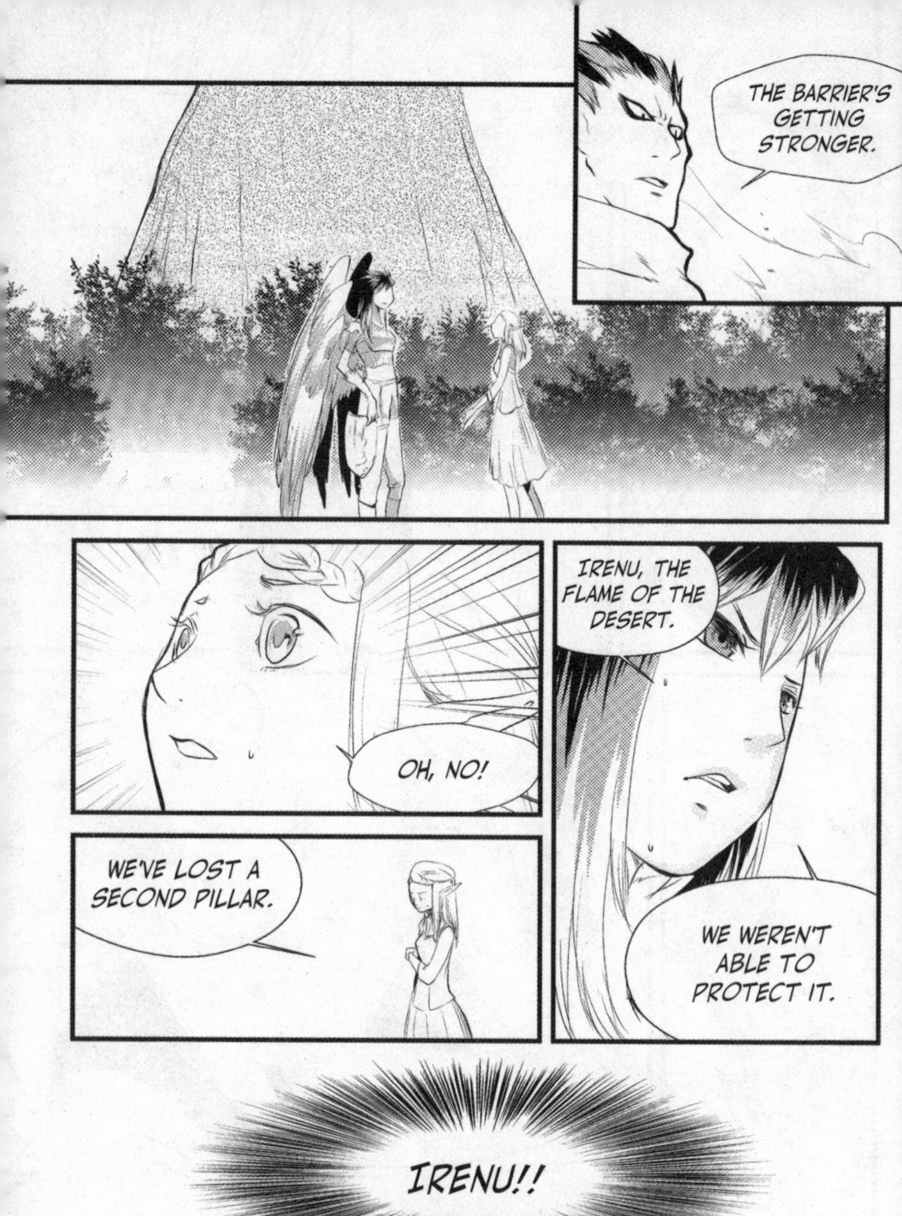
THE BARRIER'S GETTING STRONGER.
IRENU, THE FLAME OF THE DESERT.
WE WEREN'T ABLE TO PROTECT IT.
OH, NO!
WE'VE LOST A SECOND PILLAR.
IRENU!!

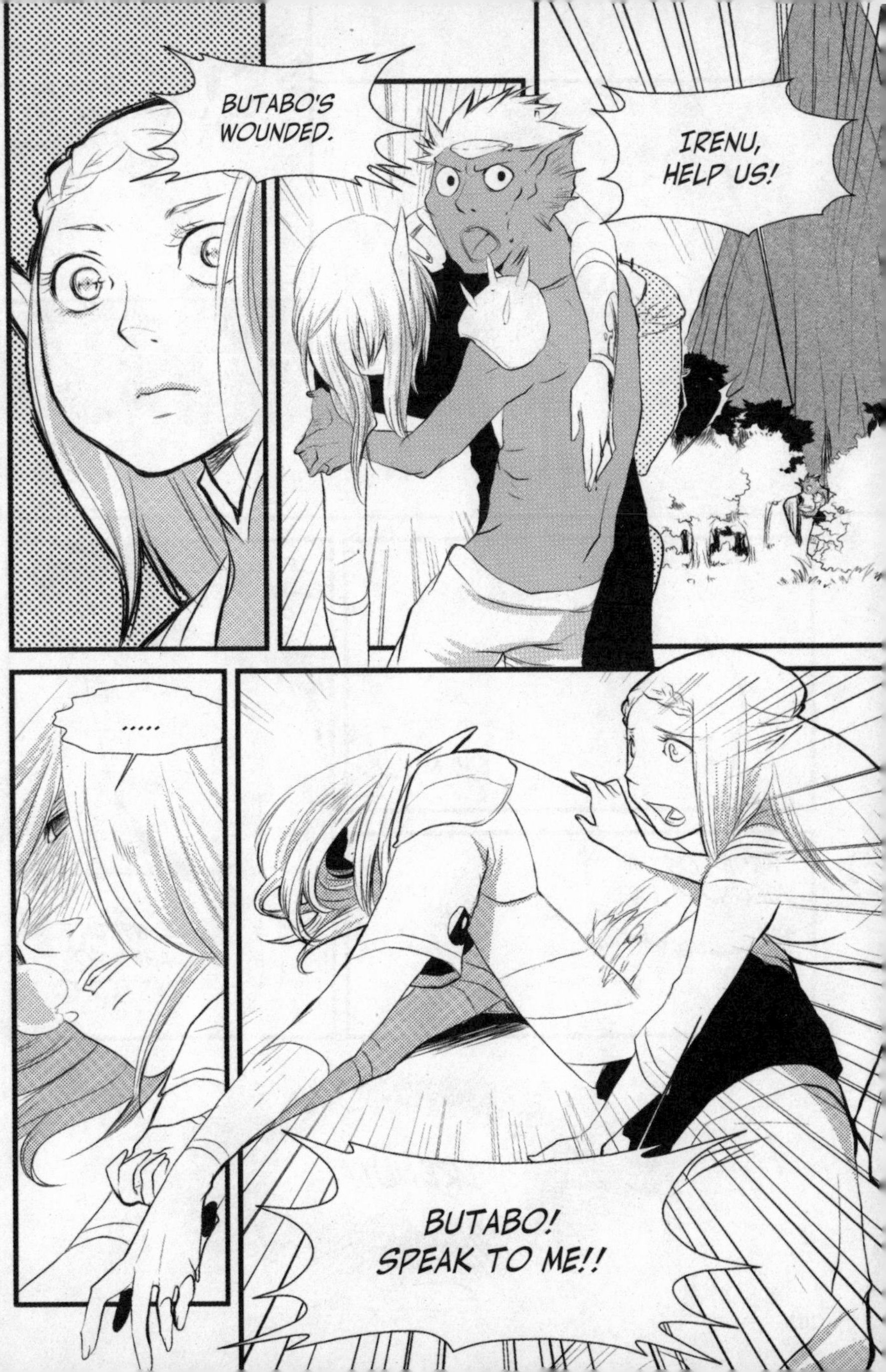

IRENU, HELP US!
BUTABO'S WOUNDED.
BUTABO! SPEAK TO ME!!
.....

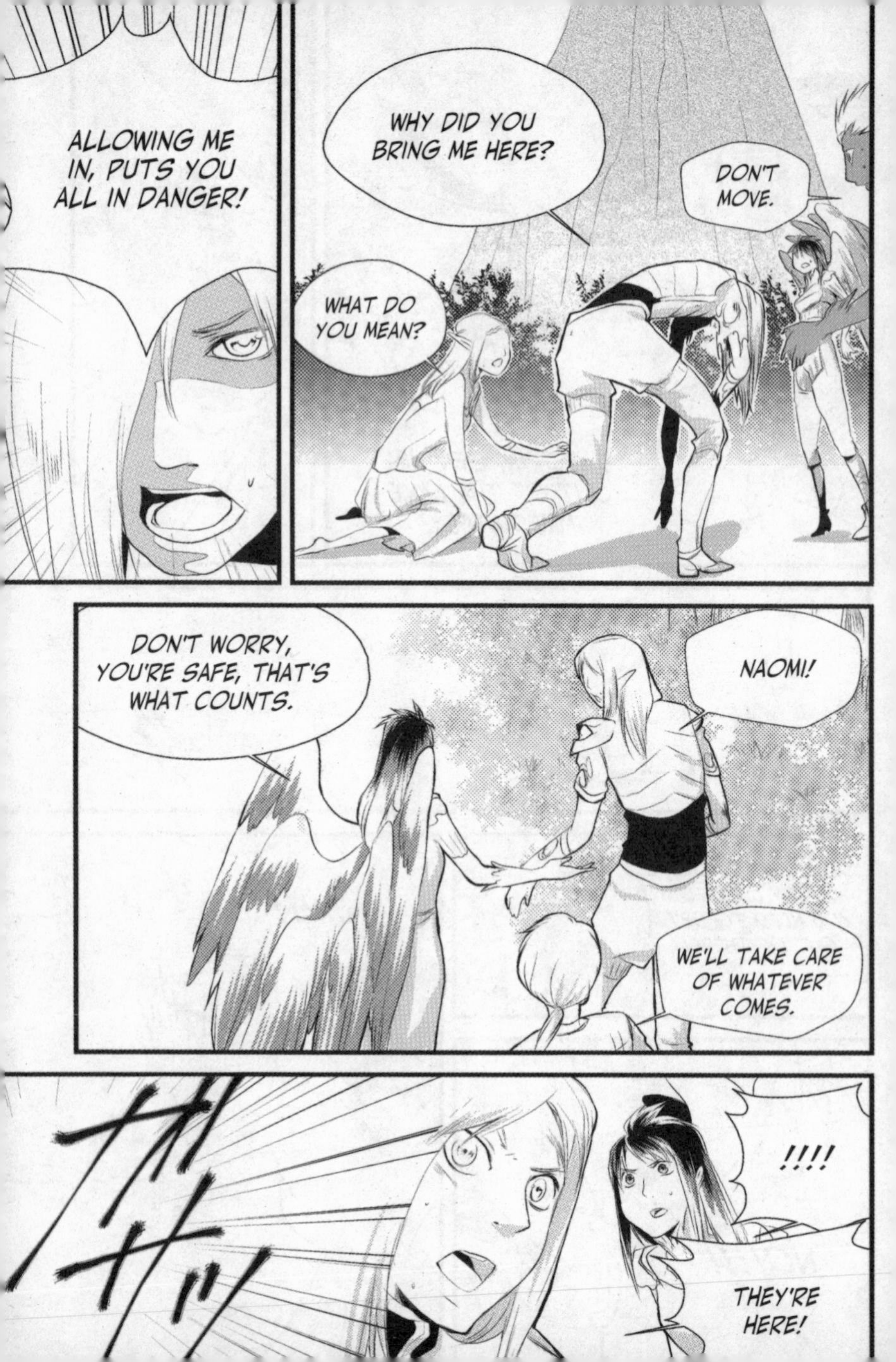
DON'T MOVE.
WHY DID YOU BRING ME HERE?
WHAT DO YOU MEAN?
ALLOWING ME IN, PUTS YOU ALL IN DANGER!
NAOMI!
DON'T WORRY, YOU'RE SAFE, THAT'S WHAT COUNTS.
WE'LL TAKE CARE OF WHATEVER COMES.
!!!!
THEY'RE HERE!

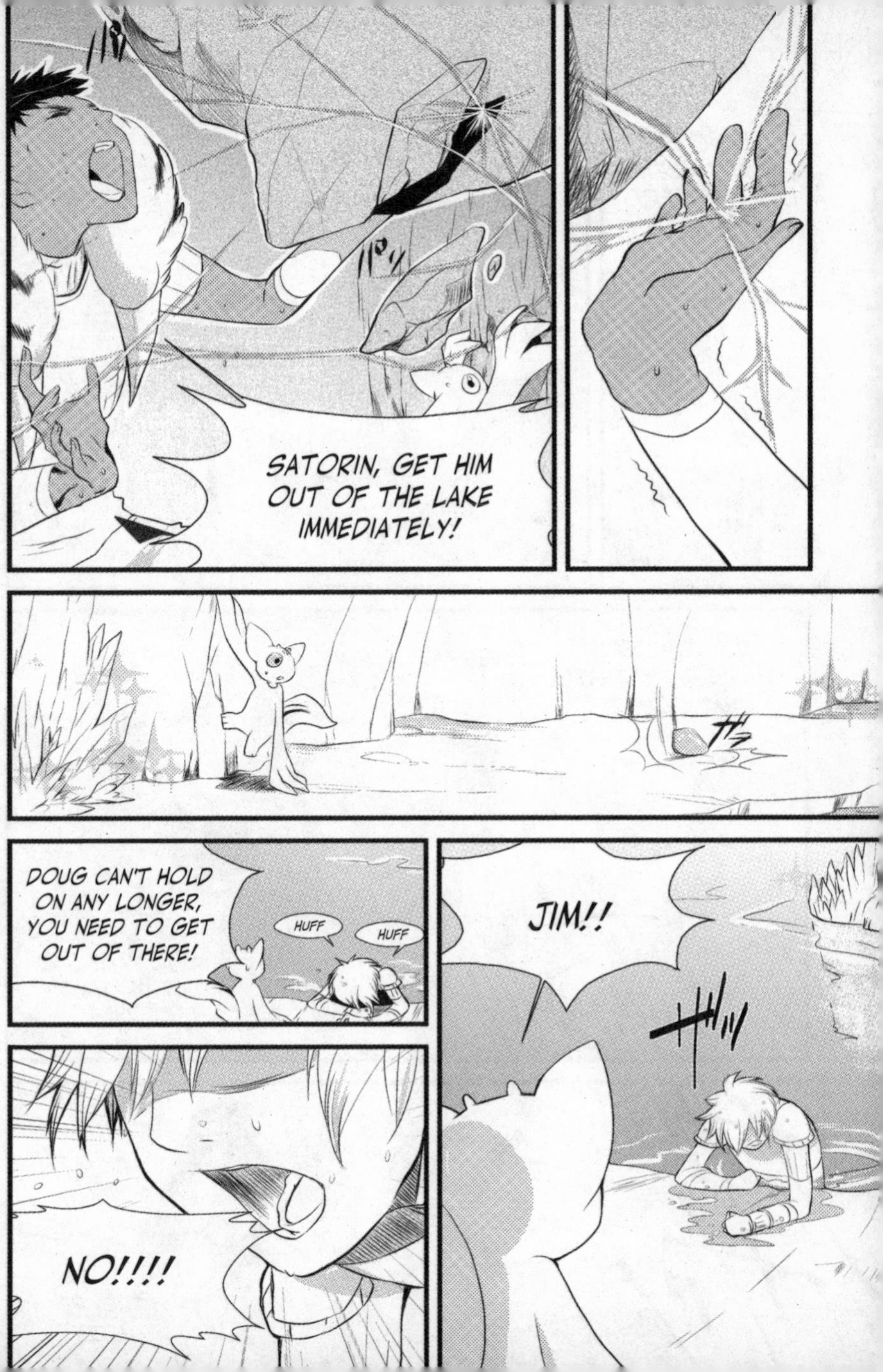
SATORIN, GET HIM OUT OF THE LAKE IMMEDIATELY!
JIM!!
DOUG CAN'T HOLD ON ANY LONGER, YOU NEED TO GET OUT OF THERE!
HUFF
HUFF
NO!!!!

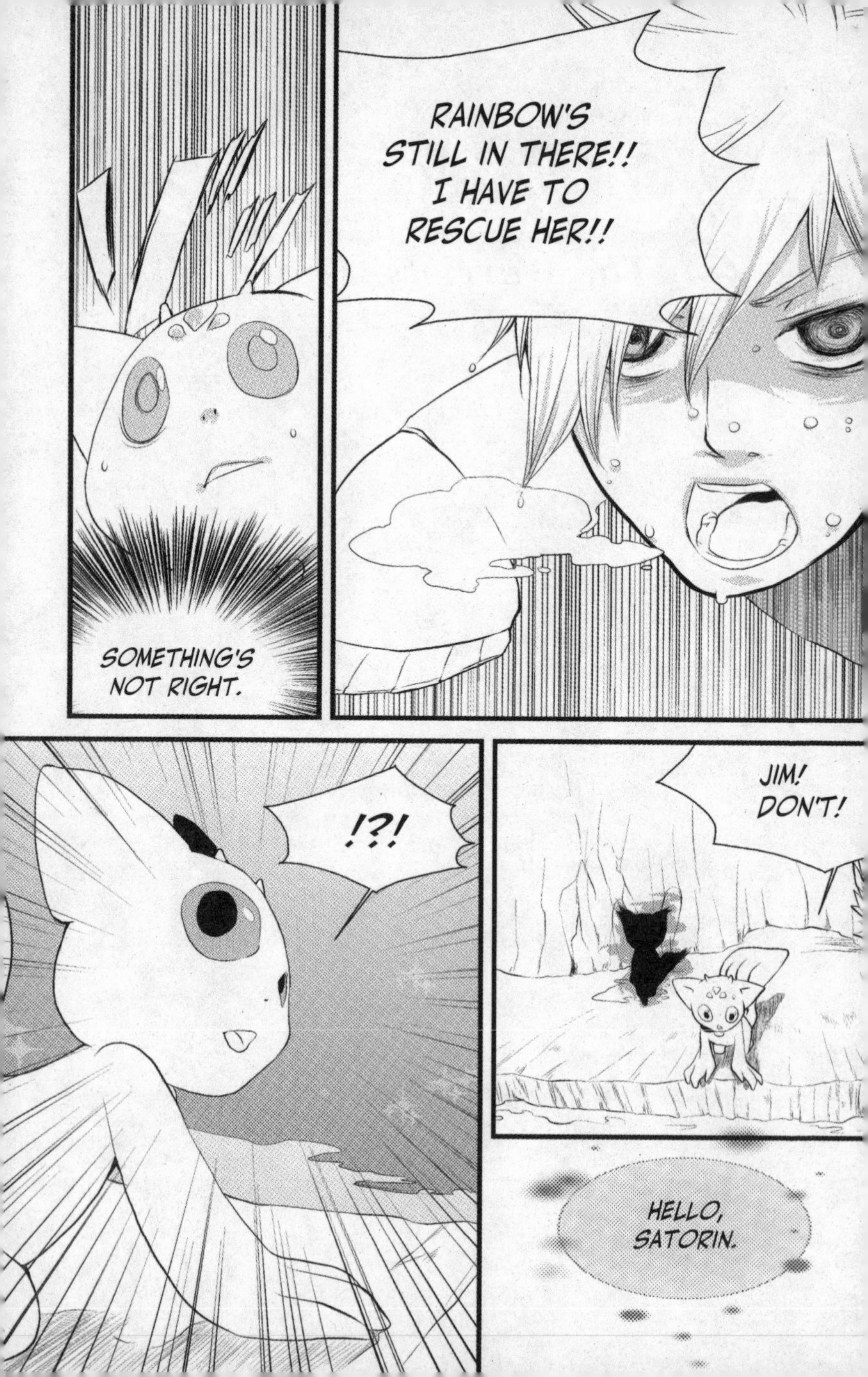
RAINBOW'S STILL IN THERE!! I HAVE TO RESCUE HER!!
SOMETHING'S NOT RIGHT.
JIM! DON'T!
HELLO, SATORIN.
!?!

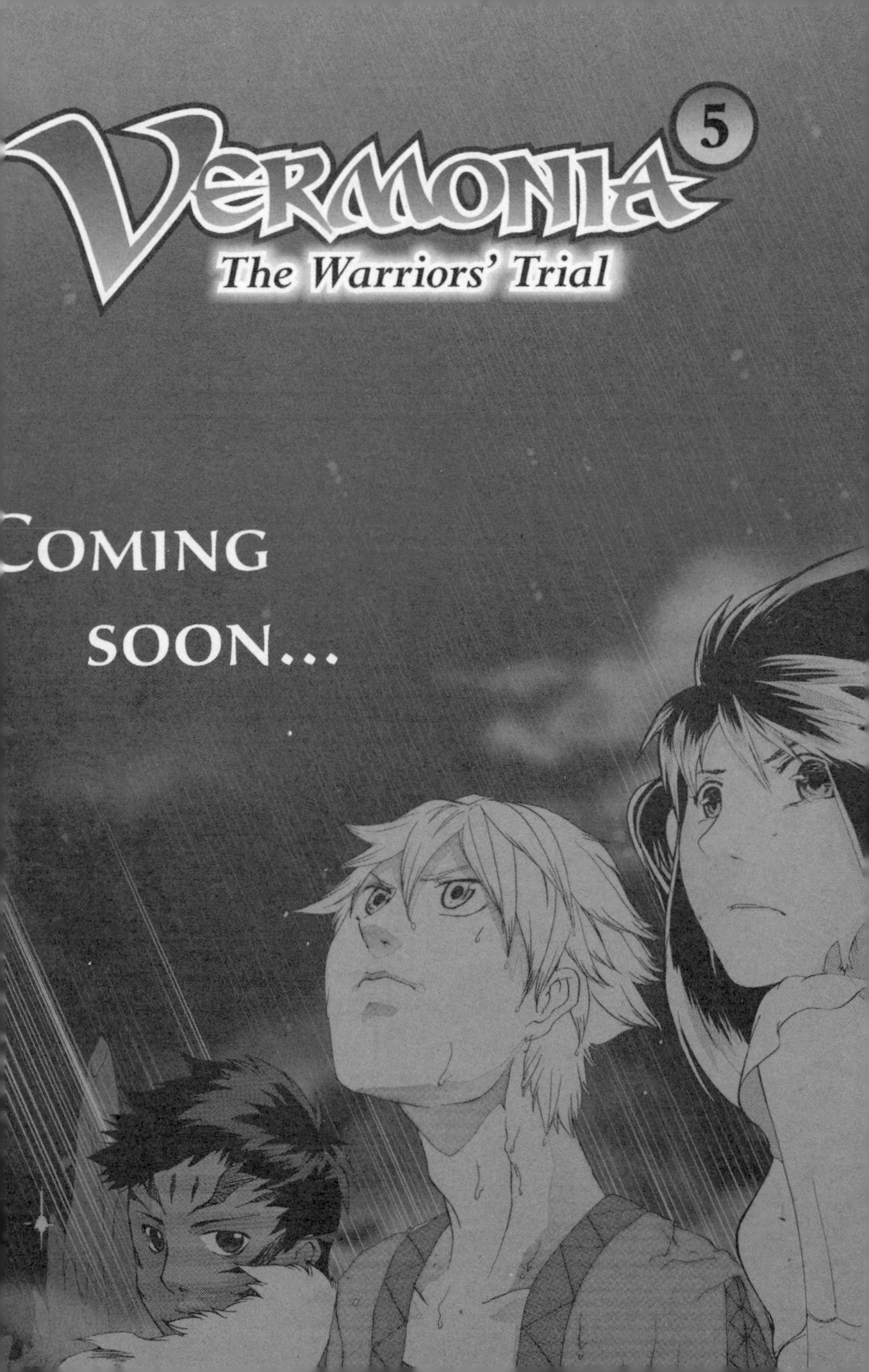
Vermonia
5
The Warriors' Trial
Coming
soon...

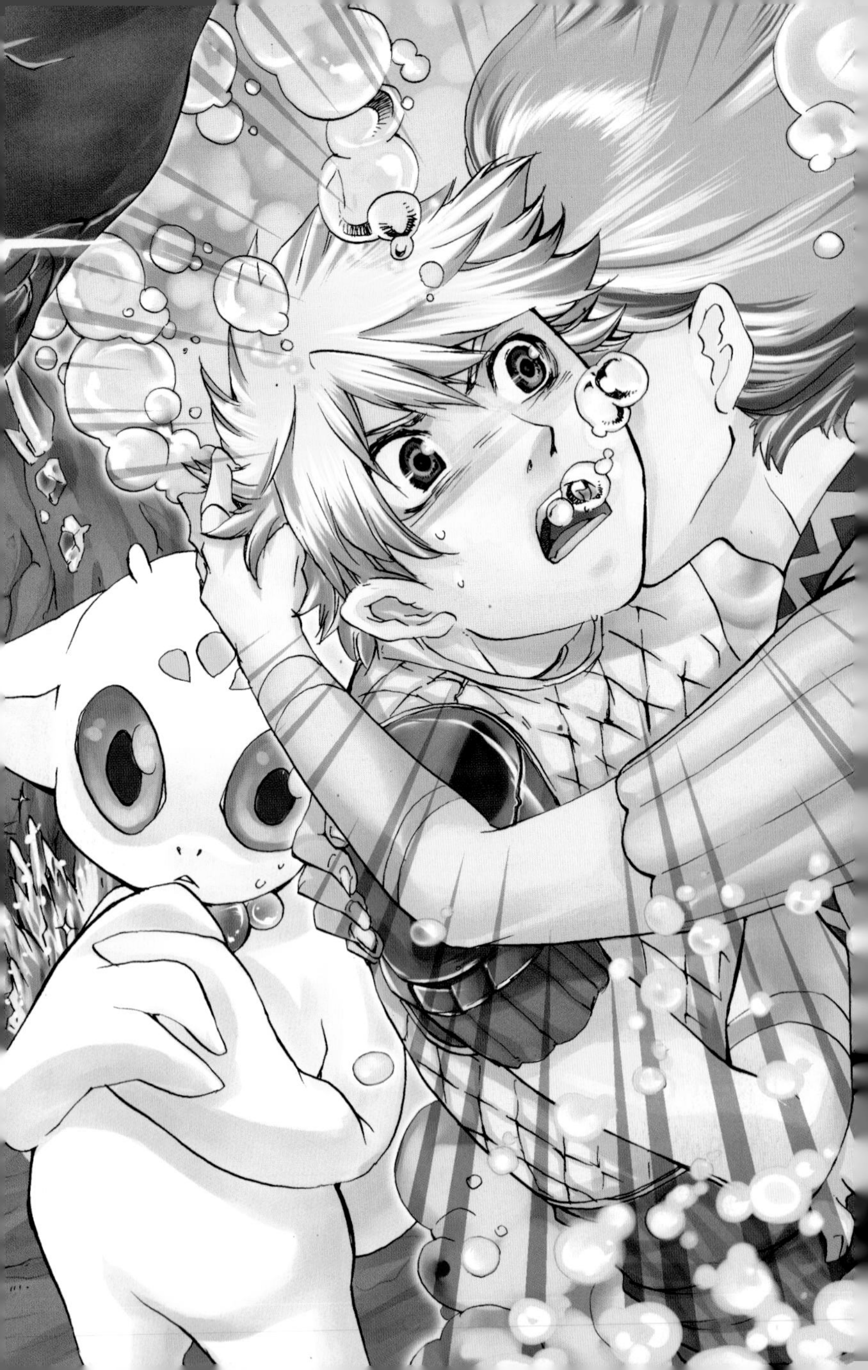

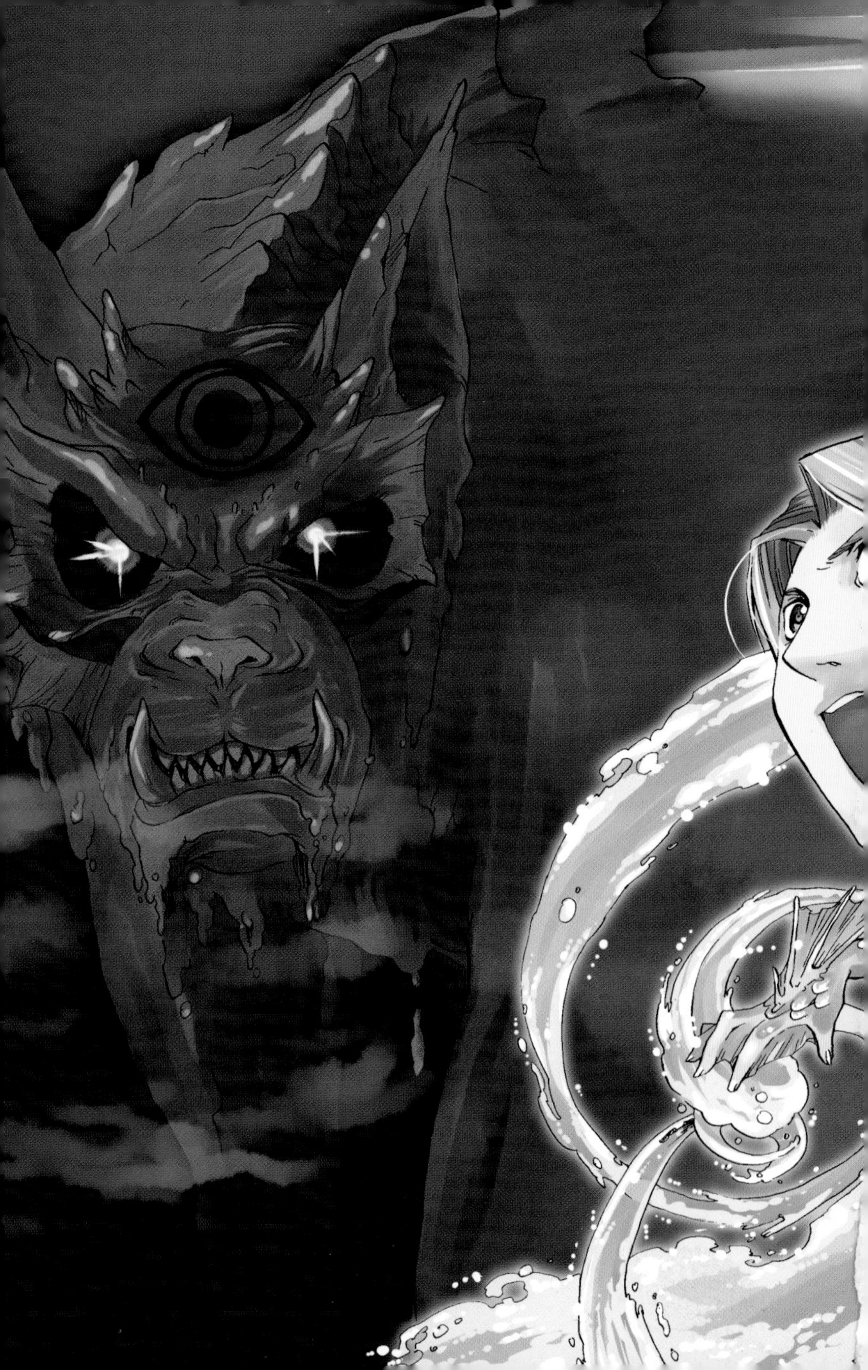

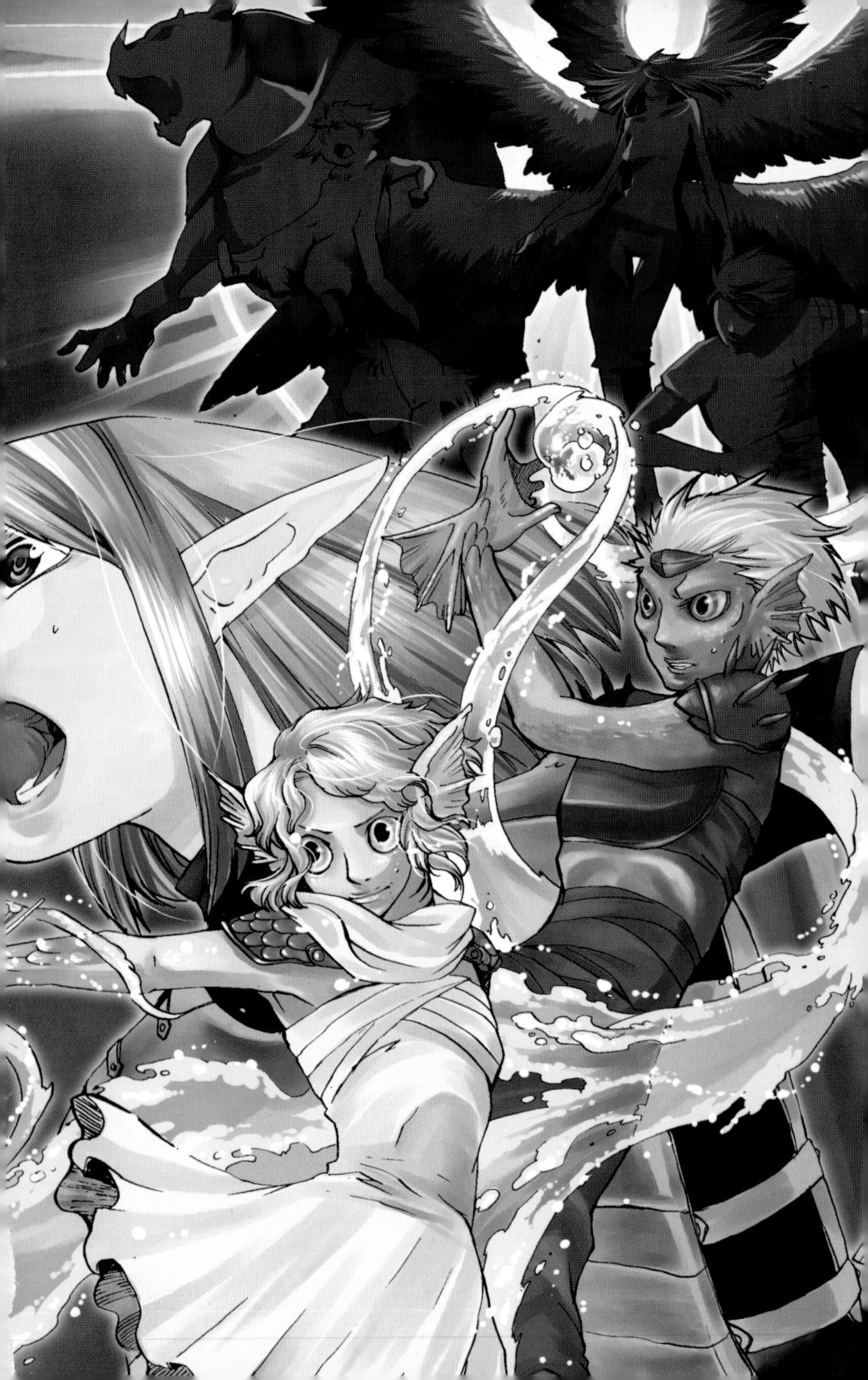

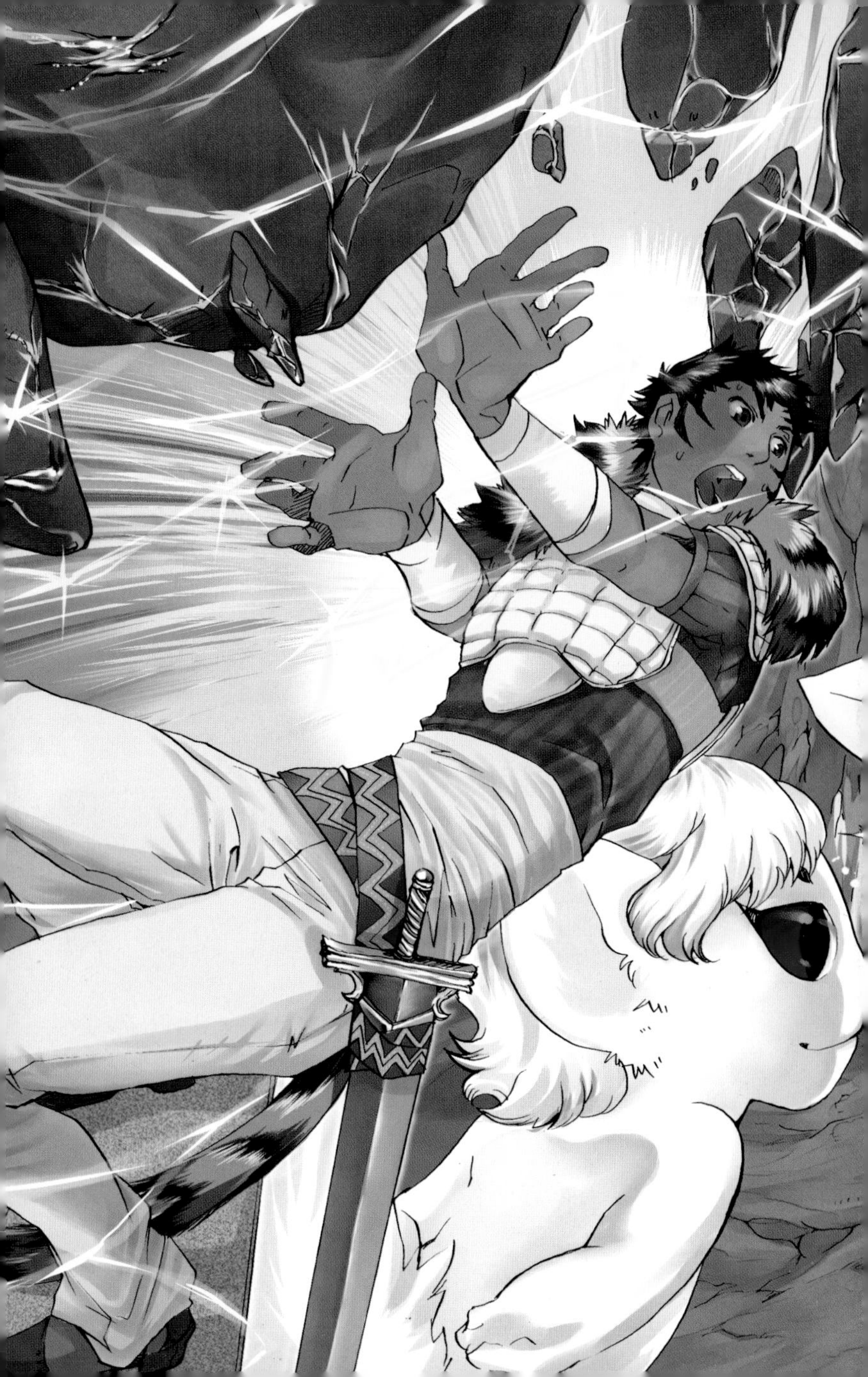

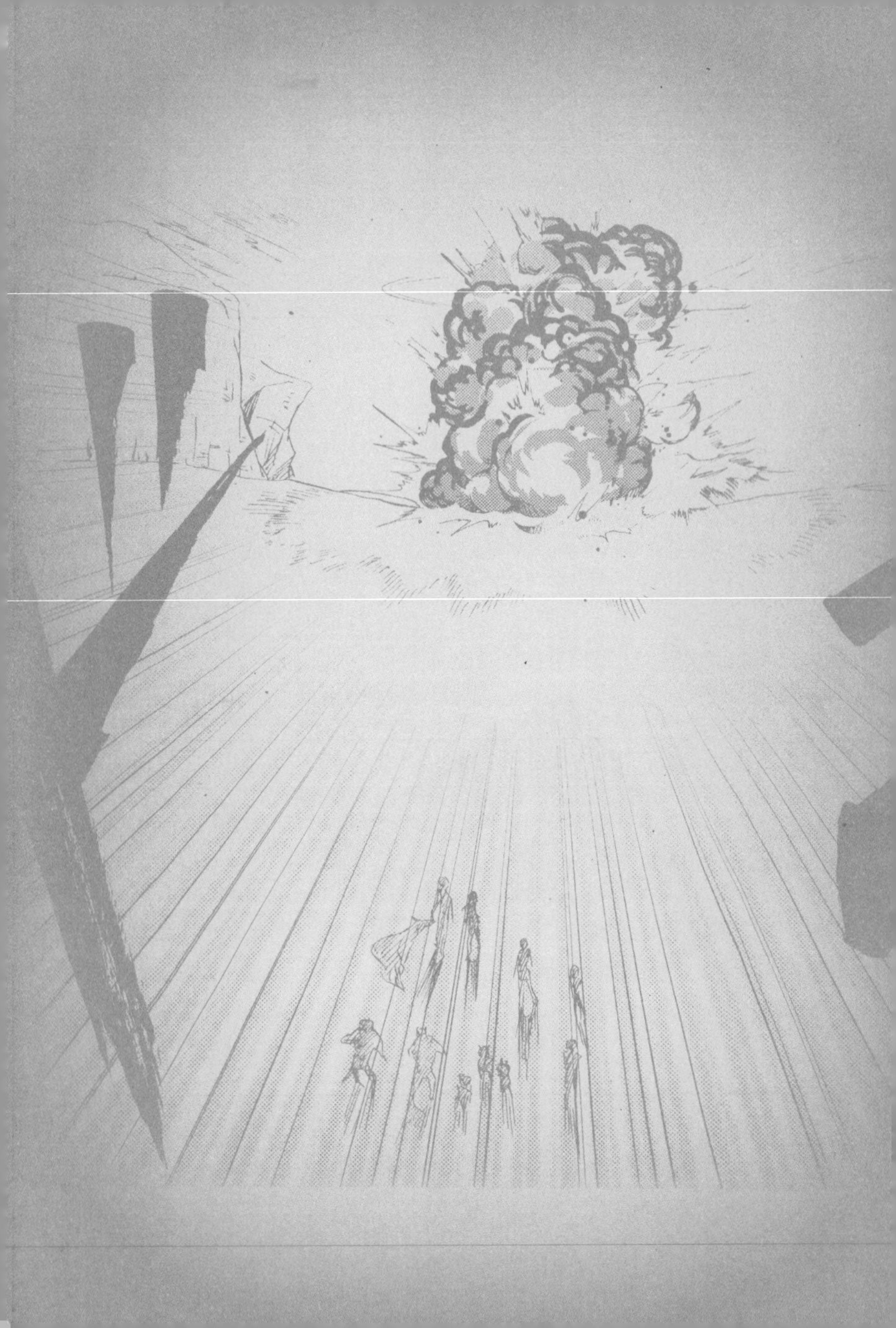